PRAISE FOR NICOLE BYRD'S NOVELS . . .

Lady in Waiting

"Byrd's unpretentious writing style and sense of humor render this a delicious read." —*Publishers Weekly*

"Byrd sifts a measure of intrigue and danger into her latest historical confection, which should prove to be irresistible to readers with a taste for deliciously witty, delightfully clever romances." —*Booklist*

Dear Impostor

"Madcap fun with a touch of romantic intrigue . . . A stylish Regency-era romp . . . satisfying to the last word." —*New York Times* bestselling author Cathy Maxwell

"A charming tale of an irresistible rogue who meets his match. Great characters, a plot that keeps the pages turning, and a smile-inducing ending make this a must-read. Delightful, charming, and refreshingly different . . . don't miss *Dear Impostor.*" —Patricia Potter

"*Dear Impostor* is the real thing—a story filled with passion, adventure and the heart-stirring emotion that is the essence of romance." —Susan Wiggs, author of *The Firebrand*

continued . . .

"One of the most entertaining romances I've read in a long while. The story line is inventive, the characters are dynamic, and the pacing is lively . . . *Dear Impostor* is the rare romance that . . . never hits a false note . . . Readers who . . . are looking for a well-paced story that sparkles with originality are advised to run, not walk, to their bookstore and seek out *Dear Impostor*. I highly recommend it."

—*The Romance Reader*

"A terrific story with heartwarming, realistic characters . . . Do not miss *Dear Impostor* . . . The tale is beautifully written and enticingly romantic and is a Perfect Ten for me."

—*Romance Reviews Today*

"This expanded, high-action Regency has wonderful underlying touches of comedy and makes for rewarding reading."

—*Romantic Times*, 4 stars

Robert's Lady

"*Robert's Lady* is a most excellent debut."

—*The Romance Journal*

"A moving tale of love lost and love found."

—*Romantic Times*

"Nicole Byrd has created a masterpiece . . . with the perfect blend of mystery, suspense and romance. This is one romance story you hate to see end."

—*Romance Communications Reviews*

"Highly recommended . . . more than a fabulous Regency romance. Rising star Nicole Byrd shows much talent and scope."

—*Under the Covers*

"Vivid . . . fully developed characters and a story set at a fast clip."

—*The Romance Reader*

"A very strong debut . . . I'll be looking for Ms. Byrd's future releases."

—*All About Romance*

Widow in Scarlet

Nicole Byrd

BERKLEY SENSATION, NEW YORK

WIDOW IN SCARLET

A Berkley Sensation Book / published by arrangement with
the authors

PRINTING HISTORY
Berkley Sensation edition / September 2003

ISBN: 0-425-19209-1

A BERKLEY SENSATION ™ BOOK
Berkley Sensation Books are published by
The Berkley Publishing Group,
a division of Penguin Group (USA) Inc.,
375 Hudson Street, New York, New York 10014.
BERKLEY SENSATION and the "B" design
are trademarks belonging to Penguin Group (USA) Inc.

PRINTED IN THE UNITED STATES OF AMERICA

10 9 8 7 6 5 4 3 2 1

For my husband, Chuck.
Without your love, I would not be writing romance.
CZ

Prologue

The narrow street was quiet—deceptively so.
Nicholas Ramsey, Viscount Richmond, stood at the dust-streaked window and gazed down at the first tendrils of mist swirling around the lampposts. A shabby chaise rolled along, pulled at a decorous trot by two ragged-looking steeds, their hoofbeats echoing hollowly, and the shops that edged the lane sat silent and dark. But somewhere below in the tangled maze of streets, a messenger was wending his way toward a prince, with news of a fabulous treasure safely delivered. If all went well, Nicholas could be the toast of the Ton tomorrow. And if not—if not—

Knowing just how much was at stake, Nicholas felt his shoulders knot with tension. He tried to draw a deep breath.

"Nicholas, my pet," a woman called, her voice drowsy from extended lovemaking. "Come back to bed."

Why would she not sleep? As she stirred, he could detect the heavy scent of her camellia perfume. Too sweet and too cloying, it already clung to his skin and to his linen shirt. He wished for his bath to wash it away, wished for his own bed, longed to be away from this seedy room in an inn he would not normally have allowed his worst steed to visit. But he could not leave, not yet.

"In a moment, my dear," he answered, his tone courteous as always. For an instant he could not remember her Christian name. Mary, was it? No, Marion. She was pretty, of course, in a vapid sort of way, and not terribly bright; he approved of the first and was bored by the second. Ignored too often by her indifferent husband, she had flirted and smiled and sought him out, delighted to fall into an easy dalliance.

Tomorrow there would be a different woman, and he would have nearly forgotten Marion, but she would remember him, fondly, he hoped. He tried to leave his women with good memories, and there were not really as many of them as the Ton whispered, but he did not mind the rumors. Sometimes they served a purpose, as they did now, when his tryst hid a deeper design.

He gazed again into the empty street. They had taken every precaution. It had to go smoothly—

The irony was that anyone in the Ton would have described Nicholas, reasonably enough, as a selfish, jaded rake with few morals left and scant concern to spare for others. No one would have connected him with secret missions of state. But the prince regent had asked, and it was hard to say no to a prince, even one like Prinny, who was even more dissolute than Nicholas himself. Still, he was risking a great deal on the events of the last weeks—

"Darling!" This time Marion raised her voice, and she sounded impatient. Nicholas bit back a curse. Why could she not fall back asleep?

"I thought you'd drifted into slumber, my dear," he lied. He heard the rustle of fabric as she wrapped herself loosely in a sheet. Her bare feet padded silently across the plank floor, but her overly strong perfume warned him of her approach, so he did not jump when her hands touched his shoulders, then slipped up to caress his neck.

"I swore I wouldn't waste time sleeping when I finally

had you in my bed, Nicholas." Tracing irritating patterns across his back with a sharp nail, she leaned closer, her warm breath feathering his ear. "I couldn't be farther from sleep. I feel . . . invigorated."

Was that—? He peered intently into the foggy night. But no, it was a prostitute, settling herself into a doorway to call to the next man who passed her.

"Nicholas, look at me!"

Reluctantly, he turned and forced a smile, then lowered his face to press a kiss to her plump shoulder. He hadn't missed the vexation in her narrowed hazel eyes, nor the pout on her thin lips.

"Then, by all means, Marion," he said, "allow me to exhaust you."

She giggled, her gaze dropping toward the street as Nicholas's skillful lovemaking continued. So she was the one to observe the figure all but obscured by the deepening gloom. The man in the black coat strode quickly along the walkway, waving away the whore's salutation. If he seemed to avoid the faint circles of hazy light shed by the streetlamps, it was not difficult in the fog now drifting in thick opaque patches.

Absently, Marion noted that the man on the pavement glanced often over his shoulder, and his steps were hurried and erratic in their rhythm. Then the stranger looked up just as the mist parted, and she caught a glimpse of his face, pale beneath the brim of his dark hat.

For a moment Marion's attention wavered, distracted from the pleasure of Nicholas's talented fingers. The man below paused to wipe his face with a handkerchief; he seemed to perspire, despite the cool damp air and billowing fog that cloaked familiar buildings and turned the street into a tunnel of darkness. And he peered hard into the soupy air, as if to detect another pedestrian, especially one who walked behind him.

But the walkway was untenanted now, and the street seemed empty, too. The man drew a longer breath and straightened his shoulders, which had been hunched as if in apprehension. He walked on, and she caught a glimpse of something else—

Nicholas's touch slipped lower, his hands sliding easily over her well-shaped hips before cupping her intimately in his warm palm. The sheet that had covered her fell away and puddled at their feet.

Smiling, she drew her attention from the street, from all but the rhythmic pleasure of Nicholas's touch. If from the corner of her eye she glimpsed another apparition, she paid it no further mind as she was lifted abruptly into the air. With an anticipatory sigh, she wrapped her legs around her lover's firmly muscled waist and allowed him to carry her back to bed.

The man below hastened on and disappeared into the darkness. And now there was no one at all to note the unmarked black chaise that waited, a block behind him, or the black horses which drew it, their hooves muffled, as the vehicle followed him at a slow, inexorable pace.

One

*"Suffering in silence is the mark,
not of a saint, but of a fool."*

—Margery, Countess of Sealey

London: 1816

"*What you need, Lucy darling,*" declared the countess of Sealey, sipping her tea, "is a lover."

Lucy Contrain bobbled her teacup, nearly spilling the last few drops of liquid. She glanced at the lap of her dark gown for damp spots and found none. Relieved, she looked back up at the countess, not sure she had heard correctly.

The countess trilled her distinctively high-pitched laugh and took the dangling bit of ivory-colored Wedgwood from Lucy's slackened hold. "Careful. Don't stain your gown." Then, eying the somber, conservatively cut frock, she handed the cup back. "On second thought, spill it all. I'll pour the whole pot on you if it will get you to the modiste and into brighter colors."

The countess raised her gaze from the offending garment and focused on Lucy's face. "Close your mouth, dear," she added, not unkindly.

Lucy shut her mouth with what she knew was an audible snap of her teeth. Good Lord, she'd been gaping like an idiot. But a lady did *not* speak of taking lovers in the same manner in which she'd speak of taking a walk.

"I'm barely out of mourning, Lady Sealey."

"Out is the significant word, Lucy. And of course, not just any lover, mind." The countess seemed to ponder the question. "You need someone who will cheer you."

Insanity, Lucy thought. She took a deep breath, but before she could speak, the countess turned to another woman seated nearby.

"Who do you think, Angela?"

"Mr. Bertram," the short woman suggested. "He has lovely manners."

"He's also a pinchpenny and going dreadfully bald," Lady Sealey objected. "We must find someone better for Lucy. Roberta?"

The woman addressed had flaming red hair and a curvaceous figure beneath her expensive gown; she smiled as if at some delightful memory. "The viscount Richmond, unquestionably. He has a way with widows."

"He has a way with women," the countess corrected, her lips curving with an almost roguish grin. "Widows, single, married, none can resist him."

Several of the other women sighed, whether with pleasure or regret, Lucy could not tell, but one whispered to another behind her fan, her expression disapproving. Lucy heard only a few scraps of words: "an outrageous man," and something about scandalous behavior. . . . Good heavens, she was being pushed upon some elderly satyr who had ravished every available lady in the Ton? And the countess had seemed like such a nice woman, somewhat advanced in her views perhaps, but kind—it only proved how wrong first impressions could be.

"I—I really couldn't," Lucy said.

The countess lowered her voice. "You've been in strict mourning for over a year, my dear, and for a man hardly worthy of a sennight."

Lucy looked up and caught the unexpected shrewdness in the countess's hazel eyes. Lady Sealey was rumored to have had her share of lovers in her time, perhaps more than her share; even with silver in her hair, she was still handsome. But—

"I don't think you could know that," Lucy said, her voice quiet but steady.

"Of course I cannot," the older woman answered. "I surmise, that is all. If you loved him desperately, despite the fact that he left his affairs in great disorder, his reputation smudged by unsavory rumors, and his wife unprovided for, I would never suggest such a thing."

She paused for several long moments, and Lucy found that she had no words to fill the gap. She wished, for an instant, that she had not shared so much of her private life with this new confidant.

The fact was, she had not loved Stanley with any great passion. They had come together out of mutual expedience, and for a while the marriage had seemed to work well enough. He had treated her kindly, with an almost reverent respect that was a welcome change from the leers which other men had thrown her way when she had been single and poor and unprotected. He had provided her with a home, and she had tried her best to love him, even though . . . she pushed those thoughts away. But now, a year after his sudden death, she had found she was, if possible, in an even worse way than she had been as a penniless young lady with a widowed and ailing mother.

Now, she was not only penniless once more, but deeply in debt, and alone.

Absently, Lucy rubbed the thin fabric of her black gown. It had once been a soft blue, but she had dyed it after her husband's death, when it had been necessary to go into mourning and she had discovered that her modiste would no longer grant her credit.

She could not replace her mourning gowns; blue could be turned into black, if one were careful and the fabric didn't fray too much from the stress of the dying process, but black could not be covered by lighter colors. She was stuck with her black gowns, just as she was stuck with Stanley's crippling debts. And when her last penny was gone—

Lucy took a deep breath. She would not fall into a melancholy, nor would she panic. One day at a time, she told herself, as she had often done through the last difficult months. Sometimes, even one hour at a time—one could deal with a difficult hour, but not the realization that the rest of one's life stretched ahead just as bleak and desolate as today. She would be hounded by creditors, pushed further and further into the fringes of polite society, and no one would even notice her absence. . . .

It was enough to shake even Lucy's resolve, and Lord knew, that had been tested enough. She blinked hard. Fortunately, the countess had looked away. The older woman motioned toward one of the gold-rimmed plates on the tea table before them.

"You need to treat yourself more, Lucy dear. Try a scone, my cook has a delightful way with them."

Lucy accepted the pastry and took one bite; the scone was so light and flaky and good, it was all she could do not to shove the whole thing into her mouth. She had eaten nothing since a bowl of porridge early that morning. Lucy forced herself to chew slowly. As the conversation drifted into other channels, scandalous gossip and the latest style in bonnets, she could quietly eat another, and then accept a cucumber sandwich from the footman who bent over her to offer the silver tray.

It was heaven. Just for a moment she could relax and forget the harrowing circumstances which troubled her sleep and woke her too often, waiting for more calamity to fall about her like shards of glass raining upon her head from a fragile ceiling crashing down. The protection she had thought she would gain from her marriage had been an illusion, as false as the love she had hoped might grow from a pleasant acquaintanceship. And the guilt that stabbed her when she thought of Stanley's death—

No, she would not dwell on it, not just now. Surely she deserved a small escape from her troubles.

"Have you seen the newest mode in half boots?" a lady on her left asked. "There's a shop on Bond Street . . ."

"And then he said, 'If only you were ten years younger,

my dear.' Can you imagine the nerve of him!" another feminine voice said from her other side.

"She *says* she's engaged to a marquess, but—you know—no one has heard of him or his title, and I think—"

"A sponge soaked in red wine, yes. I'm told this is the French way of avoiding unwanted increasing . . ." This voice dropped to a whisper.

The first lady with the interest in boots went on, "The nicest kid leather, and in just the right shade for my new walking costume. I was so wearied of the black!"

The voices rose and fell all around her. Lucy nodded and smiled and tried to look interested, and she waited. In another hour, the other ladies began to depart, but Lucy hung back. What she wanted to ask the countess had to be done in privacy. There was enough gossip about her husband's debts; she did not wish to add fuel to the flames.

So when the room was almost empty Lucy rose to make her farewells, too, but after she had thanked the countess for inviting her, she hesitated.

"Yes, my dear?" The countess lifted one carefully plucked brow, and her smile seemed genuinely kind.

"I'm told that your acquaintance is wide, my lady, and I thought—I thought—"

"I might introduce you to some nice young men?" The countess suggested.

Lucy grimaced. "No, no, that is—I only thought—if you should hear of some respectable lady who is in need of a companion—"

She paused, and the other woman's eyes narrowed.

"As bad as that?"

Lucy forced herself to look the countess in the eyes when what she really wanted to do was study the patterned carpet beneath her feet.

The countess reached to pat her hand. "I will keep my ears open, Lucy, dear. In the meantime, do you need—"

Flushing, Lucy shook her head. She could not bring herself to accept charity from a comparative stranger. As desperate as her circumstances were, she had not yet steeled herself to abandon all of her pride.

"Very well. Do not forget my suggestion, dear," the older lady added. "A lover would lift your spirits nicely, you know. And lovers are much more convenient—less troublesome than a husband, and easier to be rid of if your fondness fades."

Lucy was surprised into a laugh. "I do not think to marry again," she said, with complete truth.

The countess nodded. "Then a lover is just what you need," she repeated, her tone serious.

Lucy made some answer, curtsied, and said her good-byes. In the hall, she paused to accept her shabby cloak from a maid. The countess's liveried footman opened the outside door. His gaze was impassive; he might disdain her less-than-fashionable appearance, but being as well-trained as all of the countess's servants, his feelings would never be permitted to show in his expression.

Some of the Ton were not so circumspect. Lucy had seen the scorn on their faces, the cynical pity that colored their voices or made their condolences ring less than true. The fact was, it was easy for Lucy to put aside all thought of remarriage. Who would wed a lady who had few assets and too many debts, whose social standing was only moderate, who had no wealthy friends or family to lend her aid and credence?

Self-pity hovered at the edges of her mind, but Lucy pushed it back. No, she would not succumb to dismal thoughts. Something would happen; perhaps the countess would think of a sweet-natured invalid in need of a lady to share her quiet life. Lucy would become a nursemaid, of sorts, and end her days in some quiet watering place, old before her time.

Oh, there was that dratted melancholy again. Lucy walked more briskly; the air was chill and her cloak was thin, and the rapid pace served to both warm and distract her. When at last she reached the modest home she had shared with her husband, she was startled to see a sheet of paper tacked to the door.

What now?

Lucy pulled it off and glanced at the formal wording as she fumbled to unlock the door.

Dear God, they were taking her home! Unless—no, she had thirty days to discharge the debt of—of a thousand pounds!

She felt her heart hammer inside her until her whole body seemed to shake. Her mind felt frozen with shock, and the words ran round and round inside her head like manic mice. A thousand pounds! A thousand pounds!

Who was this Thomas Brooks who claimed he was owed such a monstrous sum? He was not one of the many tradesmen who continued to pound on her door day and night to demand payment of their outstanding bills.

And how could she pay such a staggering amount, when she could not even marshal the resources to pay off the coal merchant or her late husband's tailor? But her home—she had lost a beloved home once before, when she was still very young. This house was small and unfashionably situated, but it was her refuge, her security . . . the core that had sustained her as the rest of her life shattered around her.

Inside, Lucy leaned against the door, her knees weak. This was the end. She had no choice left—darkness seemed to close around her, and she drew deep, shuddering breaths.

At last, when the fog of misery receded a little, she straightened, pushing the offensive paper into her reticule—she did not wish, could not bear, to speak of it yet—and walked toward the kitchen.

"I am home, Violet." Her voice sounded shaky.

The narrow hall seemed to echo with her words; its emptiness was apparent at once. The handsome pier glass that had once occupied the central space on the wall was long gone, sold to provide a little money to pay the household expenses. The most valuable furniture had been claimed by her creditors, and much of the rest sold, also, as necessity dictated. Now little remained. The drawing room was bare, even the carpet gone. Lucy made her way to the kitchen, instead, where a thin slip of a girl in a shabby brown uniform sat on a three-legged stool before the very small fire.

The maid jumped to her feet. "Oh, ma'am, I didn't hear you come in."

"It's all right." Lucy pulled another stool up to the hearth and motioned to Violet, her only remaining servant, to sit. When Lucy had told the rest of her small staff she could no longer afford to pay them, she had accepted their tearful farewells and sent them off with glowing recommendations and her last few shillings. Violet alone had refused to leave her mistress, wages not withstanding.

Now the two of them shared the house until it seemed it, too, would be taken from them.

"I brought you a scone." Lucy pulled a handkerchief out of her reticule and, unwrapping the dainty bit of clean linen, took out the pastry she had slipped into her bag.

Violet took it eagerly, then hesitated. "Don't you want 'alf, ma'am?"

"Oh, no, I had my fill at the tea," Lucy told her. "Eat it. We have only vegetable soup for our supper."

And it would be thin and watery. Lucy was only too aware of how bare the kitchen larder was. A few potatoes were left in the bin, a few onions strung on a rope above the empty shelves. And then—

Lucy shivered and held out her cold hands to the small circle of flame. They were almost out of coal, too. Could she bring herself to apply to her cousin Wilhelmina?

Perhaps the countess would think of a possible employer for Lucy—

A loud bang pulled her out of her gloom.

Violet shrieked and put one hand to her mouth. "What was that?"

Lucy had already jumped to her feet. Grabbing a broom leaning against the wall, she ran toward the front of the house. The front door was open—she had not locked it after she had come inside.

Cursing herself for such carelessness, Lucy glanced into the drawing room—still empty—then looked into the dining room. Two brawny men dressed in rough clothes were carrying out her mother's Queen Anne dining chairs.

Lucy shouted. "Put those down!"

The man closest to her frowned, but he showed no sign of obeying.

"Violet, summon help!" Lucy called. She lifted her broom and brought it down hard, again and again, upon the man's shoulders and balding head.

He snorted in outrage, but the broom was too light to do any real damage. The robber showed no inclination to drop the two chairs he held. However, burdened with the furniture, he could do little to stop her. She hit him again and again until the broom shaft splintered.

Was nothing in her life as solid as it should have been?

Lucy uttered the same words the coal merchant had used when she'd told him she couldn't settle his bill, then threw the wooden pieces at the thief. He shrugged off the lightweight projectiles.

Damnation!

The man trudged on toward the front door. At this rate she would never see her mother's cherry-wood dining suite again, and she had held it out to the last, despite her increasingly empty pockets.

Lucy looked about her for a more effective weapon. There—the ugly gold vase cousin Wilhelmina had sent her for a wedding present. That had not been held back out of sentiment; it was so ugly that even the secondhand dealers would offer her only pennies for it.

Lucy snatched it up and brought it down upon the bald man's head. There was a satisfying crack. The vase split into several large shards, and the man roared in pain, dropping the chairs.

At last the vase had come into its own. She pushed the man toward the hallway, and for a moment he was too dazed to fight back.

But the other man came to his mate's aid. Dropping the chairs he held, the second man, who was slightly shorter but just as broad as the first, wrapped his arms about Lucy's waist and dragged her off his partner.

"Let go of me!" Lucy shrieked. "And get out of my house."

The man who held her—his arms were hairy and corded with muscle, and he smelled strongly of sweat and cheap gin—grunted but did not reply. He forced her into the corner and shoved her roughly to the floor.

She hit the bare wood hard and for a moment could not get her breath. Blinking, she saw the two men retrieve the furniture they had been carrying. Each lifted two chairs and turned once more for the door. Desperate, Lucy pushed herself to a sitting position and looked around for anything with which to impede the theft. Then the sudden stillness of the two men alerted her to the newcomer's presence.

A third man stood in the doorway. Another ruffian? Was he here to assist them with her table, next?

Then she saw that this man was dressed like a gentleman, with a well-cut blue coat and spotless linen, and he frowned at the scene before him.

But he was a stranger, and from his stance, as much as his clothes, not the kind of man who usually strolled this narrow and unfashionable London street. Was this the man who had hired the petty crooks who now pilfered her last few pieces of furniture?

"You should be ashamed," Lucy snapped, her voice reedy as she fought for air, but her tone still defiant. "You might as well steal sugar drops from a baby!"

The man—he was tall and, except for the broadness of his shoulders, might have seemed too thin—looked down his nose at the two men, who stared back at him as if suddenly uneasy.

"You suffer from a misapprehension, madam," he said. Then, his gaze fixed on the first robber, he added in a voice of cool authority, "Why are you taking this woman's household goods?"

The bald man shifted his feet, his arms still full of chairs and a trickle of blood running down the side of his head from the impact of the vase. "She owes money, she does."

Lucy managed a deep breath, at last, and tried to regain her composure. "If it's the butcher, I just paid him ten pounds, and if it's the coal merchant—"

The bald man shook his head. "None of 'em," he said. "'Tis the bootmaker in Timmons Street, Covney and Son."

Lucy bit her lip. Another bill she had not even added to the already alarming total of her husband's debts?

To her surprise, the unknown gentleman demanded, "How much?"

They all stared at him.

"Over forty bob," the bald man answered, his tone suspicious.

The gentleman reached inside his jacket and pulled out a handful of money. "Put down the chairs," he ordered. "Take this to your employer and do not trouble the lady again. Is that clear?"

The two men gaped at him, but after a pause, they lowered the chairs, and the bald man accepted the money.

"Make sure all of it gets to your employer," the gentleman added, his tone stern. "Or I shall seek you out and take anything missing out of your unwashed hides." He took one step forward, and the bald man actually retreated a few paces.

"Yes, gov," he agreed. "We won't touch a farthing."

"See that you don't. Now leave us," the tall man ordered.

They edged around the stranger and in a moment Lucy heard the door slam behind them. She made a mental note to keep it barred hereafter, but just now . . . she stared up at him, deeply puzzled, then realized she was still sitting in a most unladylike posture on the bare floor.

Flushing, she pulled her skirts down to cover her ankles, which the gentleman eyed with obvious and unabashed appreciation, and was about to scramble up when he put out one hand.

She gazed at it for an instant, then accepted his support—his grip was strong—and allowed him to pull her to her feet.

"Who are you?" she demanded, with less tact than she might have done. Then she added belatedly, "That is, I thank you for your help, but—"

"My apologies for walking in unannounced," he said. "But the door was open, and I heard sounds of a scuffle. Nicholas Ramsey, Viscount Richmond, at your service. I don't believe we have met, but we have acquaintances in common."

Lucy's eyes widened. "Umm, yes," she said. "I have heard the countess of Sealey speak of you."

This was the famous ladies' man? But why—she glanced from his severe expression and strong chin to the steely dark eyes. He was comely enough, in a rather Spartan way, but as far as wooing the ladies—

Then he smiled.

Lucy blinked, and suddenly she no longer doubted the reports of the women at the countess's tea party.

His eyes gleamed with wicked humor, and his mouth, which had seemed so stern, now lifted in a sensual grin that made him appear almost boyish. She felt her thoughts go all atumble, like chaff in a wind storm, and she could not think at all. He was magnificent, and she could hear her own pulse beat faster. He said her name, and she had to shake her head before the words made sense.

"Ah, yes, Margery," he said. "Then perhaps you know—"

Lucy's thoughts flashed back to the sighs and raised brows of the other women. She felt her cheeks burn from her too vivid imagination.

"Know what, my lord?" Lucy asked cautiously.

"Mrs. Contrain," the notorious viscount said. "I need you most desperately."

Two

"*You* *must be mad,*" *Lucy* blurted.

He couldn't possibly mean it. She could not have heard him correctly. He didn't even know her. And she knew very well he hadn't been so suddenly entranced by her mediocre charms. No, no. "You need—"

"I need your help," he said. "Desperately."

She shook her head, still befuddled. "My help?"

She stared at this most unexpected visitor. His raiment was understated but obviously expensive, his blue coat well cut, his pantaloons sleek over muscular legs, his cravat simply but elegantly arranged, his linen immaculate. His boots—she knew from very recent experience—would have paid her coal bill for six months.

And it was more than simple affluence that produced his air of self-confidence. His dark eyes were bright with intelligence; his wide mouth, when he bothered to smile, altered his normally cynical expression into one of charm and beguilement. When he smiled, she would have sworn there was a heart beneath that smooth world-weary countenance. He gazed at her now with the easy assurance of one who is accustomed to getting his way.

What could such a man need from her?

Lucy glanced down at her shabby black gown, then around her at the almost-empty house, the room bare except for the chairs and tables. The difference between the two was patent. Perhaps she should have felt foolish, but she was not the one who had barged into a stranger's house. And after all, he had come to her aid.

"I thank you for your help with those—the men who tried to take my furniture," she said. "But truly, I cannot see how I may be of assistance."

Something leaped in his dark eyes, and again, he smiled.

Lucy blinked and told herself to breathe. Slowly.

He put out one hand, and before she could stop herself, she found that she had extended her own hand to meet his.

He lifted her fingers to his lips, kissing them with a whisper-soft touch that made her wonder how his wide, supple lips would feel against her mouth, her neck, her—

Her husband had never made her feel like this. Was it a sensation that could only be induced by a wicked dark-eyed rogue, who, she remembered the whispers at the tea party, was barely acceptable to the politest of Society? As a respectable woman, she should likely not even acknowledge to herself how strange, how—how aware this man made her feel.

Surely he did not expect her to compromise her virtue? He had no reason to suspect that she might be—that she was not—

Flustered, she realized he was speaking, and with enormous effort she pulled herself together. "Excuse me?"

"I said, I need to go through your husband's belongings."

Her confusion forgotten, Lucy pulled her hand back. The request was so odd, it was almost beyond rudeness.

"My husband is dead," she said, keeping her tone

steady with an effort. "Is this some kind of ghoulish prank?"

His gaze dropped to her black gown, and she realized what an inane statement she had made. He must know that she had been widowed.

"I don't meant to offend you," he said, his voice calm. "I would not ask if it were not truly important."

Somehow, she almost believed him. "But why?" she demanded.

"I believe he may have something of great value that had been entrusted to my care," he said.

How dare he come into her house, unsettle her in so many ways, and speak only in riddles? Lucy's bewilderment was rapidly turning to anger. "Are you accusing my husband of being a common thief?" she demanded, her tone hard.

"It is a long and complicated tale," the viscount said. "And much of it not fit for a lady's ears."

For the pampered and delicate ladies he knew, perhaps not. Lucy had learned much about the world since her husband's death, and if this man thought she was easily shocked, he should think again.

"If my ears are so delicate, then I assure you that the rest of me couldn't bear allowing a stranger to rifle my dead husband's things," she retorted, steeling herself against another brilliant smile. "However grateful I am for your assistance, I must ask you to take your monumental gall back out the door you came through."

He shook his head. "I have handled this poorly—" he began.

Lucy cut him off. "You have indeed," she snapped. "Please leave, at once."

Lord Richmond took the dismissal in good grace, but he met her gaze, his expression serious.

"Very well, if you wish it, I will go," he told her. "Bolt your doors and take care whom you allow into the house, Mrs. Contrain. I shall see you again."

Before she could demand an explanation for his concern over a total stranger, or protest the manner of these commands, because that was just how he'd pronounced them—as if they were royal edicts—he had bowed to her and left the room.

What could he mean? And why should he care? She sighed. As it always did when provoked, Lucy's temper cooled quickly, leaving her once again discouraged and weary. She glanced about her; the bare windows showed her that the sky outside was darkening. She had a sudden feeling of being exposed, exposed and unprotected, as if malevolent forces were spying upon her.

Nonsense. All she had to fear were the usual army of creditors, all wanting their payments. That was enough to worry herself with . . . then a new thought caused her to throw up her hands in dismay.

She owed the outrageous viscount money. How on earth would she repay him? She had little left to sell. She felt a moment of panic, then shook her head. It was like throwing a cup of water into the sea. Forty more shillings added to her debts made little difference. She took a few deep, soothing breaths and raised her head high. She would deal with one concern at a time.

She would most certainly bolt all the doors and check the window locks, too.

Just then, Violet hurried into the room. "The butcher's boy is right behind me, ma'am," she blurted, breathing hard from her run.

"It's all right, they have gone," Lucy said. "I will explain in a moment, but first—bar the kitchen door."

~⇌~

The next morning Lucy woke as the first faint streaks of light brushed the dark sky above the rooftop next door. She had slept little, waking often to fret over the intractable pit of debt that seemed certain to swallow up what was left of her home. A thousand pounds!

What would she do? Where could she go? She had no immediate family left alive, and to throw herself upon the mercy of Cousin Wilhelmina . . . It was a bitter prospect.

And when she did sleep, her dreams were troubled, and she would fight to wake herself, to avoid reliving the shock of hearing a stranger blurt out the news of her husband's death, a scene which replayed itself over and over inside her head, like actors stuck endlessly repeating a bad play. . . .

So it was no wonder she felt almost as exhausted as she had when she'd retired, her eyelids heavy and her stomach growling with emptiness. She had given most of the thin soup last night to Violet, but even so, they had both gone to bed unsatisfied.

Lucy sighed. She would not give up, but every day it grew harder to face the world with some semblance of determination.

And lying here indulging herself with doldrums did nothing at all to help. She sat up and pushed back the covers. Pulling a shawl about her nightgown, she washed her face and hands and dressed rapidly, regarding the usual dark-hued dress with loathing. She was sick of her black gowns, but unless she went naked, she had no choice about her costume. She had not had an extensive wardrobe to begin with, and she had been too numb after Stanley's death to consider that she should not dye all of her gowns.

Violet came into the room in time to button the back of Lucy's frock and brush her long, fair curls into some semblance of order. When she was presentable, Lucy pulled aside the thin cotton curtain she had kept over her bedroom windows for decency's sake—the heavier draperies had been sold months ago—and allowed the wan spring sunshine to pour unimpeded into her room. The light seemed as pale as her own hopes; storm clouds were approaching, and rain threatened.

"I got some gruel on the fire, ma'am," Violet said. "I'd best get down so h'it don't burn."

"It," Lucy corrected. They had been working on elocution lessons. "Yes, indeed," Lucy agreed, and the little maid hurried out. What would she do without her one loyal servant? Violet was seventeen, though her petite frame made her look younger. Lucy herself had not been much older when she had married Stanley.

Thinking of her husband reminded her of the viscount's strange request. Why would a stranger wish to examine her husband's belongings? Or was he a stranger at all? Had the viscount known her husband? She had met almost none of her husband's companions. There had been times when Stanley had gone off to dinners at his club, he'd said, and had not returned until late the next day, often in such a drunken state that he'd tumbled into bed fully clothed.

She had known that Stanley kept secrets from her, but he had refused to answer any questions about his activities. Husbands were like that, Lucy supposed from her limited experience, and wives had little recourse. Stanley was courteous to her, most of the time, but on occasion he had turned surly and withdrawn, and she'd found it useless to press him.

Was that the kind of man Lord Richmond was?

Somehow, she hoped not.

And she could not dwell on an arrogant and good-looking stranger whom she was almost certain never to see again. Just because his strong-jawed face and Roman nose, his charming smile and dark eyes lingered in her memory, it was folly to wish she could have met him under different circumstances. What could he want with a widow on the verge of financial ruin? Lucy made her way down the short staircase and turned toward the kitchen.

After they shared the gruel, she would help Violet with the sweeping, and then—

"A boy brought this, ma'am," Violet said, holding out a small sheet of paper.

Lucy unfolded the page. *I am in town at The Royal Arms, near Hyde Park. I shall expect you at eleven o'clock. Wilhelmina.*

Why had Wilhelmina come to town? Lucy tried to think. Her elderly relative cared nothing for the season.

Was it possible Wilhelmina had heard of Lucy's plight and had come to offer help?

Unlikely!

Lucy had been avoiding the thought of applying to her cousin for aid. But now that Wilhelmina was in London, the issue must be faced.

Lucy sighed. It would be a long walk. "I have to go out," she told Violet.

After their paltry breakfast the little maid fetched Lucy's shabby cloak and then took her own shawl from the pantry and tied it around her shoulders.

Lucy locked the front door carefully and double checked its security, and then they set out. The narrow Cheapside streets were crowded with drays and wagons making morning deliveries. An occasional hackney or carriage added to the congestion. A hot-pie vendor called out to them, and Lucy shook her head, although the smell of hot pork and pastry made her mouth water and her nearly empty stomach rumble. The thin bowl of gruel had done little to appease her hunger, but she had no coin to give him. She would have to find something else to sell, soon. Could she bear to part with her dining room suite?

Sighing, she paused to avoid a stout maid hurrying past with a shopping basket looped over her arm. It was a fair day despite the usual gray smoke from city chimneys which hung over the rooftops and shadowed the blue sky. Lucy thought wistfully of the peaceful country home she had known so briefly in her childhood.

"Mind the coal wagon, ma'am," Violet said.

Lucy stepped back as the wagon lumbered through the intersection, leaving a cloud of dark coal dust floating in the air. Coughing, she hurried on.

They were both dusty and tired by the time they reached the inn. Inside, Lucy tucked a stray lock of hair beneath her bonnet, then approached the barrel-girthed man who seemed to be the inn's host and asked for her cousin.

She was directed up two flights of stairs to one of the

smaller bedchambers. When Lucy knocked at the door, a familiar voice said, "Come in, then."

Her stomach clutched and Lucy took a long breath as she attempted to force her expression into one of pleasant anticipation, instead of the dread she really felt.

"Wait here," she told Violet. Lucy opened the door and stepped inside.

The room was narrow, and her cousin sat at the far end. Wilhelmina's feet were propped comfortably upon a footstool, and she had a shawl wrapped around her shoulders despite the warmth of the fire.

Lucy walked closer. "You look well, cousin."

The elderly woman motioned to a plain wood chair. "More than I can say for you, Lucinda. Black does not become you, though I suppose you have no choice about it."

Lucy tried not to show how grating were her cousin's comments. "What has brought you into town?" she asked politely.

"A newly-moneyed mill owner from the North Country offered me a handsome price to lease the house for the summer," the older woman told her. "Just as well, too, I've lost my housekeeper. Oh, pour yourself a cup of tea, if you like."

Lucy moved to the small table. There was only half a cup of tea left in the pot and the milk jug was empty, but she did not point out the lack. Her throat was dry after the long walk. With an inner sigh, she thought of Violet, but it couldn't be helped.

"I'm so sorry to hear about Mrs. Jasper," she said. "Was it a sudden illness?"

"A sudden offer of more pay," Wilhelmina snapped. "The squire's wife had the nerve to hire the woman from beneath my nose, after ten years of service, too!"

Good for Mrs. Jasper. Lucy tried to hide her smile.

"So I came to town for the summer. I shall hire a replacement before I return home in September," her cousin continued. "I thought of you. Stanley left you in a bad way, did he not?"

There was more curiosity than sympathy in her tone. Lucy lowered her eyes to conceal her anger.

"Stanley had some debts, yes," she said.

Wilhelmina shook her head. "I hope you don't expect me to pay off his obligations."

"Of course not." Lucy drank the last of the tea, which now tasted even more bitter. "I should not dream of it."

"Good," the other woman grunted. "However, since you seem to be in difficult circumstances, and I will soon need a housekeeper—you could likely wrap up your own household by the end of the summer—"

This was clumsy, even for Wilhelmina. "You wish to hire me as your housekeeper?" Lucy demanded.

"That would hardly be suitable, but we can help each other without such a formal arrangement," Wilhelmina said. "I recall that when you resided with me, you were quite prudent in your household management."

As if she'd had a choice. And no, her cousin would never hire her—that would mean an annual salary. Wilhelmina would use Lucy as an unpaid servant, dependant on her relative for every penny, forced to plead for any small sum necessary for her own personal needs.

"As my mother was," Lucy pointed out quietly.

Wilhelmina looked up, her arm raised and her stout figure straining against the too tight bosom of her dress. She set the teacup down with a clatter.

"I had a housekeeper when you and your mother resided with me. Although I believe Rowena did assist me occasionally."

Occasionally? Lucy thought of her meek, sweet-tempered mother, forced to accede to their only relative's every whim. It had been the proudest moment of Lucy's life when, after her marriage to Stanley, she had been able to remove her mother from their cousin's tyrannical control. She would always be grateful to Stanley for that—whatever his other failings may have been. For the last year of her life, Lucy's mother had resided with her daughter and new son-in-law, and while there had not been an abundance of funds, at least there had been peace and tranquility, and Lucy had been able to pamper her mother in small ways.

Lucy blinked hard. She would not give in to tears, not at the thought of how much she still missed her mother, nor over the bitterness of being forced to retract her private vow that she would never ever return to her cousin's house.

"I shall bring one maidservant with me," she said slowly.

"No indeed, I have no need for another mouth to feed or wage to pay," Wilhelmina interposed. "I have enough chambermaids, and you certainly have no need for a lady's maid. You know that I live quietly."

"Every lady of quality has a maid," Lucy argued. "But that's not the point. Violet stayed with me when I had no one—"

"But you shall need her no longer," Wilhelmina pointed out. "And I have no money to waste."

"I cannot turn Violet away," Lucy insisted. "It's always hard for a servant to find a new place—"

"There is no debate, Lucinda," Wilhelmina announced. "I will contact you when I am ready to return to Surrey. Pray do not bring any unnecessary baggage. I had to bring three trunks with me, and the coach will be crowded enough."

"No," Lucy said, her anger suddenly impossible to contain. She blinked hard but this time not against tears. A red fog momentarily obscured her vision.

"You have no need of an extensive wardrobe. You know I go into company very seldom. And you certainly will not—"

"No, I mean I am not going back with you. I will not work as your unpaid servant. My mother did it for years after my father's death, for my sake, and it was a miserable existence."

Lucy found she was on her feet, glaring at her cousin, who gaped at her in surprised affront. "Enduring your petty slights, month after month, year after year! I swore I would never return to your house; it was folly for me to expect that I might find a genuine welcome. I will never return. I would starve in the gutters first, so help me God!"

And while her cousin's large mouth worked like a fish out of water, and her face flushed with outrage, Lucy turned on her heel and stomped out of the room, banging the door behind her.

Violet looked startled. "Ma'am, are you all right?"

A clash—the sharp sound of china shattering against the other side of the closed door—made Lucy jump. She hoped the inn charged her parsimonious relative double for the damage.

"I'm fine," Lucy said. "Let us go home."

As Lucy and Violet walked the long way home, Lucy drew deep breaths that seemed to come from a place inside her that had never been released before. And she realized that for the first time since her mother's illness and death, and Stanley's accident, she felt truly whole. She would not follow her mother's path; she would not become her mother, always sweet natured but dreading any open conflict. Not even her mother would really wish her to return to their cousin and live such a dismal existence. . . .

Mind you, her mother would also not want her to starve. How she would survive, Lucy was not sure, but even as she shivered at the great void that yawned almost at her feet, she vowed she would keep fighting.

They made their way home slowly, stepping around piles of steaming manure left by the horses and mules, with no pennies to spare for the ragged street sweepers who usually cleared the intersections for ladies who traveled on foot. When they entered their own street, Lucy was startled to see a purple-liveried footman standing in front of her door.

Surely *he* had not come to reclaim her last bits of furnishings in lieu of cash. Lucy hurried up to the servant, who extended a note.

"Good morning, ma'am. Please deliver this to Mrs. Contrain."

Lucy didn't bother to explain that she was the mistress

of the house; apparently, she didn't look it. She thanked him, instead, and as he walked away, she and Violet entered, and she locked the door behind them. Who was writing to her? Duns were not usually delivered by well-accoutered footmen. She broke the wax seal and unfolded the heavy sheet. Scanning the words on the page, Lucy gasped.

"What is it, ma'am? Bad news?" Violet stood on tiptoe to unfasten her mistress's cloak.

"No," Lucy said, hearing the puzzlement in her own voice. "It's—it's an invitation to dinner this evening, from Mrs. Morris."

Violet looked relieved as she untied her shawl. "Oh, a friend of yours, ma'am?"

"No, that is—I believe I met her at the countess of Sealey's tea party yesterday. It's very kind of her to invite me," Lucy said aloud, then glanced down at her shabby dress and sighed. "But I really don't see how I can go; my wardrobe is sadly lacking."

"Oh, but, ma'am, it would be a real dinner," Violet pointed out, her tone wistful. "T'ink of all the lovely food."

Dare she go clad in virtual rags to a well-to-do dinner party, when she barely knew the hostess? As generous as this gesture was, Lucy thought not.

"I will have to write Mrs. Morris a note and tell her I am unable to attend," she said. "I have a little of the good paper left."

The writing desk had been sold long ago, but she still possessed a lap desk that had been her mother's. Going up to her room, Lucy sat on the small chair in the corner and prepared to write a polite note of regret. But just as Lucy dipped her pen into the inkwell, a knock resounded faintly from below.

Now what? Lucy put aside her paper and pen and went to glance out her window. Another footman stood at the front door.

Perhaps Mrs. Morris was withdrawing her too precipitous invitation, Lucy thought wildly, then shook her head.

No, that was ridiculous, and anyhow, this servant wore handsome crimson livery, not purple.

She heard Violet open the door, and the murmur of words exchanged. Then the door shut, and Lucy found her questions impossible to restrain. She went to the top of the narrow stairs just as Violet started up, a large box in her arms.

"A parcel for you, ma'am," the maid said, her eyes bright with curiosity.

Lucy returned to her bedchamber, and Violet set the box on the neatly made bed. Lucy pulled off the string and lifted the top, then both women gasped.

"Ooh!" Violet made a soft noise. " 'Ow beautiful, ma'am."

Lucy put out one hand to touch the soft lustrous silk that spilled from the box. "Oh, my," she said faintly. "But who—?"

She lifted a shimmering blue gown. Below lay an even more formal garment, an elegant dinner dress of pale pink, trimmed with white lace, and below that, a morning gown of striped ivory and pale green, and another dinner gown of a shimmering maize tint.

Speechless with surprise, Lucy couldn't help admiring the lovely lines of the dresses. But who would send these to her? Was this a mistake, a delivery gone awry?

At last she saw the note that had fallen to the side when she lifted the first dress. Lucy took up the single sheet and read aloud, "My dear, these dresses have, sadly, become too small for me to wear. Too many years and too many bonbons have widened my figure, I fear. I thought you might do me the pleasure of making use of them." The missive was signed, "Margery Sealey."

"Ooh, ma'am," Violet cooed again. "Just like Christmas."

Better, Lucy thought. Their last Christmas had been bare and sad. And the countess delivered much better parcels than Father Christmas had ever left during Lucy's genteel but poverty-stricken childhood.

It was amazingly kind of the countess to come to her

aid. Had the dinner invitation been a suggestion from the countess, as well? Lucy felt tears prick behind her eyelids and blinked hard to hold them back. She had braced herself against hardship and privation for so long that an unexpected kindness shattered her composure much more quickly than a harsh word or creditor's threat.

"Try it on, ma'am," Violet urged.

Lucy picked up the pink dinner dress, delighting in the fluid flow of the garment and the soft touch of the silk in her hands. It was of fine quality, and the lace trim was obviously expensive; flounces at the hem were trimmed with silk roses. She held it up to her body, and Violet smoothed out the fabric, measuring its shape with an experienced eye.

"Just a nip 'ere and a few stitches there, and it will fit you just right, ma'am."

"I believe you're right, Violet," Lucy said. She felt a sudden thrill of excitement that such a treat should come her way. To have something other than her drab black gowns to wear, after so long, and even more, to have somewhere to wear it!

"I think I shall go to dinner after all," she said.

The rest of the day passed in a whirlwind of happy activity. She and Violet stitched and snipped and altered the gowns to fit Lucy's slimmer shape. Lucy found evening slippers in the back of her wardrobe, a bit thin at the soles, but no one would see that, and she had her mother's modest pearl eardrops and her grandmother's delicate gold pendant to hang about her neck; the only jewelry that remained. Her one cloak was black and shabby, but it would be put off at the door, and with luck few people except the servants would see it.

She was going to a party. Lucy felt as giddy as a green girl, and she had not had that feeling for much too long. During her marriage and after her husband's death, she had always had to be responsible and sober and—and she was going to a party. After the long period of mourning, even a simple dinner party seemed like the height of gaiety.

When the alterations on the dress were completed to both their satisfactions, Lucy helped Violet bring up hot water—the usual formalities between mistress and servant had been blurred amid the travails of Lucy's straitened lifestyle—and Lucy bathed and dressed. Although her linen shift was thin with long wear, the feel of the elegant silk gown against her skin was like a caress.

When her fair hair was carefully arranged, Lucy gazed at herself for a moment in the only looking glass she still owned, a small square on her bedroom wall.

"You look beautiful, ma'am," Violet avowed. "I 'ope you have a smashing good time."

"Thank you, Violet," Lucy said. And despite the fact that she would know few people there except her hostess, whom she had just met, she somehow thought she might. The evening seemed ripe with possibilities.

She would have a long walk ahead of her, since she had no coin to spare to hire a hackney, and, of course, she had no carriage of her own. But Violet seemed more than willing to lend her company again. The maid had already donned her shawl when a rap sounded at the front door.

"Now what?" Lucy murmured. She nodded to Violet, who slipped off her outer garment and hurried to answer. Lucy waited in the dining room, anxious about some last-minute impediment and pacing up and down in case this treat had indeed been too good to be true. When Violet returned, the servant's explanation was even more unexpected.

"The countess of Sealey awaits you in her carriage, ma'am." Violet grinned broadly.

"What?" Lucy paused, unable to believe her ears.

"She said she is going to the same party, she would enjoy your company, and it was on her way."

The first statements might have some truth to them, Lucy would hope, but the last—the countess traveling through this unfashionable part of Cheapside? No, never. Lucy's first impression had been correct, after all; the woman was an angel.

"Go on, ma'am," Violet whispered. "The groom is waiting to hand you up."

So, remembering to whisper to Violet to bar the door, Lucy made her way out of her house and allowed the manservant to help her into the elegant carriage.

"Lucy, dear, you look charming," Lady Sealey said. "I'm so happy you decided to come."

Lucy knew that her cheeks had reddened. "My lady, you've been so kind," she began. "I don't know how to thank you—"

But the older woman waved her words away. "Expressions of gratitude are such a bore, don't you agree?" She smiled to take the rebuke out of her words. "Let us talk about something more diverting. I just heard the most delicious piece of gossip about the duke of Argyll's newest lover. They say she is only eighteen, and he old enough to be her grandsire."

Perhaps *angel* was not precisely the best term for her benefactress. But Lucy still felt a glow of gratitude that eased her own nervousness as she prepared for her first formal dinner in what seemed like much more than a year. In her family's impoverished circumstances, Lucy had had little chance for a social life before she was married, and afterward, she had lived a strange solitary life, chatting now and then with the neighbors she met in local shops, but rarely going out. Invitations had been few, and her acquaintance with polite society not extensive.

It had been the vicar's wife, popping in a few months after Stanley's death and finding Lucy sobbing all alone, who had insisted she call upon Lady Sealy and who had provided a note of introduction. But even the Countess's teas had not prepared her for this.

So when they pulled up in front of an impressive mansion, Lucy's eyes widened. The tall windows glowed with golden light, and carriages crowded the street in front. Her suspicions had been correct; this would be nothing like the modest events she had, on rare occasions, attended before her marriage. Tonight she was on her own, and she was stepping into a whole new world.

Lucy glanced at the countess, who smiled in encouragement. Not alone, exactly. And in her lovely remade dress, Lucy felt newly confident, almost enchanted. Perhaps the fairy tales that she had heard at her mother's knee were not as far-fetched as the older Lucy would have said.

Not that she was likely to meet a Prince Charming, but just to chat and dine and hear the music that floated down the wide stairs she could glimpse through the open doors. . . . Lucy found that her heart was beating fast.

The countess had been handed down; now it was Lucy's turn to step out of the carriage, accept the groom's arm to steady her, then follow the countess up to the door. The older woman swept through into the anteroom, and while the servants all ministered to her needs, a footman taking her lovely fir-trimmed cloak, a maidservant adjusting the folds of her satin skirts, the butler bowing and offering his arm up the stairs, Lucy had a moment to collect her thoughts.

She felt out of her element, a little frightened but also almost dizzy with excitement and anticipation. The hall sconces flickered and glowed, the paper on the walls was of the latest style, and a table against the wall held a bouquet of hothouse flowers. Savory scents drifted from the back part of the house, where cooks labored over the dinner repast . . . a real dinner . . . Lucy's mouth watered, and she swallowed hard. First, she had to face the guests and avoid disgracing herself in polite conversation; she could enjoy the meal later.

While the countess climbed the stairwell, a footman found time to take Lucy's cloak. With her shabby outer garment removed, Lucy felt a new surge of confidence. Enjoying the light rustle of her well-made skirts, with shoulders back and head high, she followed slowly, content to take her time as she approached the drawing room, which held the other guests.

As she approached the doorway, however, her self-assurance faltered. Lucy felt her knees go suddenly weak. She had spent so little time in Society, what if she could not think of anything to say? What if she forgot the names of the people she would meet tonight? What—

Now she stood in the wide archway, and the footman was announcing her name. For a moment, she could not seem to focus, then she gazed at the strangers who crowded the room. A great number of people, surely, for a simple dinner party.

The woman standing near the doorway turned toward her, and Lucy recognized a woman hardly older than herself whom she had chatted with at Lady Sealey's tea party.

"Mrs. Contrain—may I call you Lucy? You must call me Gina. I'm so glad you could come."

"Of course, I—it's kind of you to invite me," Lucy stammered, dipping a curtsy.

"Not at all." Mrs. Morris's smile seemed genuine as she returned the gesture. "You have been shut away long enough. I remember when the dear countess had to urge me to come out of seclusion and rejoin the human condition, as she put it. It's such a blow to lose one's dear husband, and the pain takes a long time to ease. But life must go on, and I'm delighted you had the courage to join us tonight."

Lucy bit her lip for a moment, then managed to return the smile. "It's so good of you to consider my plight."

"If we widows do not look out for each other, our situation would be even sadder," Mrs. Morris declared. "I want to introduce you to some of my friends; I understand your acquaintanceship in London is limited."

Lucy nodded. That was true enough, though she hoped she did not have to explain why. She had never fathomed the reasons why Stanley had not wished to take her out; he did most of his socializing in male company, he'd said; it wouldn't be proper, he'd said . . .

But many couples went out together. She had often felt lonely, sitting home alone with her sewing and her books.

"I have several friends here I'm sure you will be pleased to know—" Mrs. Morris began, but the footman at the door was announcing more guests.

Her hostess turned to offer greetings, and Lucy moved perforce further into the big room. Her stomach felt quivery with nervousness, and she took a deep breath to steady herself.

A footman bearing a silver tray approached to offer her wine. Lucy accepted a glass and sipped the sherry; it gave her another moment to consider the assembled company. There were not as many as her first dazzled glance had suggested, around a dozen, she thought. The countess was seated on the far side of the room with several guests around her, chatting and laughing. Lady Sealey's vivaciousness and easy wit always attracted people to her. Lucy considered joining the group, but decided that would be cowardly.

She looked around. Two women stood nearby chatting, and one, a curvaceous brunette with merry brown eyes and an easy smile, glanced her way. Lucy was emboldened to move forward, and the other lady turned to another guest.

"Mrs. Morris promised to introduce us properly to her new acquaintance, but she is still greeting latecomers," the woman said. "I am Julia Blythe. My husband lingers as usual in the corner of the room with the other men, discussing his newest hunters and their paces."

Lucy laughed, but she still felt a flicker of nervousness as she dipped a curtsy. "Good evening. I am Mrs. Contrain."

"Delighted," the first woman said, returning the curtsy. "Perhaps you are an accomplished horsewoman, Mrs. Contrain?"

"Oh no, I fear I know little about horses," Lucy confessed.

"Good." Julia's musical laugh rang out. "Then you will not show up my own ignorance. I think I fell off my pony too often when I was small, and it has made me nervous around the great beasts ever since."

"I have little practice on horseback, so I understand your feelings," Lucy said, then paused as a new couple appeared at her elbow, the guests who had come in behind her. The woman was handsome, with auburn hair, the man stout and complacent.

"Mrs. Blythe, how nice to see you again," the woman said. "And your friend."

Julia Blythe made introductions. "Mrs. Contrain, Mr. and Mrs. William Tennett. Have you just come back into town?"

"Contrain?" The woman stared at Lucy, her expression hard to read. "Not Mrs. Stanley Contrain?"

"Yes," Lucy agreed. "Did you know my husband?"

For a moment the silence stretched, then Mrs. Tennett shook her head, and her expression eased. "No, no, I fear I have mistook the name. It was Coltrain I believe, a man I met last week at a very tedious gathering—"

"That would not have been my husband," Lucy told her.

"And that is what rusticating too long can do to one." Mrs. Tennett plied her fan. "Really, the tedium of country living cannot be overstated. No one to dine with but a few dozen families, and too many of them have never been out of their own shire, so provincial in their tastes. Our housekeeper cannot obtain a decent lobster or sea turtle, and the local dressmakers, so far behind the latest fashions—"

"Ah, I see some wine," her husband interrupted. He bowed to the ladies and set off in pursuit of the servant with the silver tray.

Mrs. Tennett barely paused. "I adore the flounce on your gown, Julia. I cannot wait to have some new gowns made up; the season will be in full swing before we know it. And your dress is lovely, too, my dear." She turned to Lucy. "It reminds me of one the dear countess wore last season."

Lucy blinked. She felt as if someone had splashed icy water into her face. Gathering her wits, she said smoothly, "Yes, the countess was kind enough to introduce me to her modiste, whose styles I much admired."

"Of course," Mrs. Tennett said. "I should try her myself, if William would not grumble so much about the extent of my dressmaking bills. 'Marion,' he says to me, 'the prince himself doesn't spend as much money on clothing as you.' " She giggled. "Of course, he doesn't. The prince may be of royal blood, but he is just a man, is that not so? Now, Mrs.—ah—Contrain, what is that wonderful modiste's name again?"

Caught in her own—she had thought—rather cunning falsehood, Lucy hesitated, but it was Julia Blythe who came to her rescue.

"Everyone knows Madam de Quincy," the brunette said, adding, "She has so many devotees among the Ton that I fear she has a waiting list for clients, Mrs. Tennett, but you could certainly send her a note and tell her of your interest."

"Ah well, I don't have your figure, Julia, or Mrs. Morris's elegant posture." Marion Tennett sighed. "Perhaps I shall remain with my own modiste; she does at least know how to minister to my own short stature."

The woman chatted on, and Lucy could relax again. If there were no more unexpected sartorial pitfalls, she thought this could still be a delightful evening. Looking across the room, she saw her hostess confer briefly with one of the footmen.

"Has dinner been delayed?" the artless Marion remarked, apparently following Lucy's gaze. "I wonder if we are waiting for some important latecomer?"

Without waiting for an answer, Marion Tennett plunged back into her detailed plans to correct the shortcomings in her wardrobe. Lucy allowed her mind to wander. The large drawing room with its peach-colored wall coverings and crystal chandeliers sparkling with light, the hum of conversation, punctuated with laughter—it was like waking from a long night of drab and lonely exile. One part of her mind knew that this evening was only a happy accident. She could not dine out forever on a few donated dresses; her poverty and her debt-laden reality still waited outside this pleasant interlude. But she could enjoy tonight, and she saw no reason not to savor the moment.

Then Mrs. Tennett's ceaseless chatter paused, and from

the expressions of the other women, Lucy knew that someone approached. She had already felt his masculine energy, sensing his presence even though she had not yet turned her head.

"Good evening, ladies," the deep voice said.

Lucy felt a prickle of excitement run through her, and she tried to keep her expression composed. She turned slowly to meet those dark eyes with the wicked twinkle, which seemed to speak to her as if she were the only woman in the room.

Nicholas Ramsey, Viscount Richmond stood before her.

Three

"Allow yourself a little pleasure every day."
—MARGERY, COUNTESS OF SEALEY

*T*he viscount looked formidably elegant; his black evening jacket and showy white linen set off his olive-toned skin, deep brown eyes and dark hair. He wore a slightly cynical expression, but if one could read his eyes, Lucy thought, one would know there was more to the man than his facade of indifferent boredom, much more.

Then she pulled herself up abruptly—just how many of the women in the room would feel that the glint in this arrogant gentleman's eyes was meant just for her? Surely, all the women in their informal trio. She saw that Mrs. Blythe appeared amused but a little flushed, and Mrs. Tennett—Mrs. Tennett looked downright coy.

The viscount bowed smoothly to them all. "The most beautiful guests all in one place," he said, his lips curving. "How fortunate for me."

Mrs. Tennett tittered and thrust her hand forward. "How good of you to notice," she told him, her tone arch. "Really, it has been too long, my lord, since we have joined company. We are all so happy, myself especially, to see that you have graced Mrs. Morris's little gathering."

"How could I resist such enticing temptations?" Richmond answered. The woman giggled again and released his hand with apparent reluctance. "Ah, I believe we are summoned in to dinner."

The butler had made the announcement, and couples were pairing off in the usual stately fashion.

"You should not be so late, wicked man," Mrs. Tennett told him, flicking her fan in his direction. "You are the one who has delayed our repast." Then her husband approached to take her into the dining room, and with obvious reluctance she turned away.

Julia Blythe smiled and drifted off to be reclaimed by her spouse, and Lucy felt, for a moment, intensely alone. This was how it was to be, from now on; she must make her entrance unaccompanied. For an instant, she longed to be back in her own bare house, hiding out in the kitchen and sharing cooking tips with her maid for dinners they could not afford to prepare. Then she gave herself a mental shake. She would not cower. If she had to confront a solitary life, she would do so with all the courage she could muster.

She set her half-empty wineglass on a nearby side table and turned toward the double doors. Then she saw that Richmond still stood beside her and now offered his arm.

"May I escort you in to dinner?"

The simple question resounded with undertones. How did he do that, make her pulse jump when he tucked her hand into the crook of his arm, where it seemed to fit so easily? She felt the hard muscle of his arm beneath the smooth superfine and tried to suppress the sensations that, with no apparent effort, this acknowledged rake induced.

"You should take in the countess, surely." Lucy tried to withdraw her hand, but he put his own hand over it, holding it lightly.

"No indeed, she has been claimed by Lord Whitman, one of her old and dear friends." His deep voice carried the hint of both fondness and amusement. Lucy looked across the room to see the elderly man who had taken the countess's arm, his expression besotted, as he escorted her toward the dining room.

"Then another lady of rank—" Lucy tried to argue, but Lord Richmond shook his head.

"No one has greater claims to my attention than you do, Mrs. Contrain."

It was nonsense, she knew it was nonsense, but she could feel the aura of male strength that emanated from him, as impossible to ignore as if she were a falling leaf sucked into a whirlwind. Worse, one part of her wanted to plunge deeper into the wicked charm of his dark eyes.

She bit her lip, recalling his careless arrogance, his unfathomable questions, his unconscionable desire to pry into her dead husband's effects. She would not forget her very justified anger. And besides, he was a rake and not to be trusted. She knew this; the gossip at the tea party. . . . He must say this to all the ladies.

"Not all," the viscount murmured, and she blinked again. Surely she had not uttered her thought aloud?

"You are thinking that I say this to all the women," he explained helpfully.

Lucy tried to hide her chagrin. It was true, her thoughts were often revealed by her expression; she must learn to be less transparent.

"Was I?" she parried. "Surely *I* would not be so rude." If she put subtle emphasis on the pronoun, he ignored her reminder of his earlier improper behavior.

"Oh no," he argued. "Not rude, only cautious, I think. And just so that you know, I do not offer outrageous compliments to all the women in the room, only those whom I wish to know more intimately."

Worse and worse. And before she could react to the impropriety hinted at in that remark, they were in the dining room, and he had released her hand. The table arrangement forced them to part; she was not, of course, so lucky as to draw the viscount as her dinner companion.

She pushed back her pang of regret that he was seated further along the table. It was just as well; he was a rascal and surely up to no good. She should be thankful to be spared his company.

But somehow, after Lord Richmond, no one could seem as scintillating. It hardly mattered that she had drawn an elderly man with little conversation seated on her right, and on her left a young stripling whose ruddy face could hardly be seen between his high shirt collars. He seemed more interested in directing all his chatter toward Julia Blythe on his other side.

But the footman was offering Lucy a tureen of delicious turtle soup, and after that came stuffed flounder, and then lightly sauteed mushrooms and beef tips, roasted chicken flavored with rosemary, and tender leg of lamb, not to mention an endless array of side dishes.

Lucy savored every bite, the delicate herbs and spices lingering on her tongue—she had never appreciated good food so much until her means had become so limited, not that she had ever had a cook as skilled at this—as she listened to the conversation around the table.

She seemed to pick out Lord Richmond's deep tones without conscious effort; they were often accompanied by the merry laughter of the women in his vicinity, and even the men appeared to regard him with respect.

"You finessed that last race, Richmond," a man was saying. "I was certain my roan could outpace your gray, but I think you put a hex on my poor beast. He threw a shoe in the last furlong and your steed ran away with no competition at all."

"Just bad luck, MacKay," the viscount assured the other man. He grinned. "If I had such magical powers, I would save them for more worthy pursuits."

The men laughed, and the women blushed and giggled. No one seemed to have any doubt as to the arena in which the viscount was most interested.

Lucy listened despite herself, even as she relished the excellent food as a succession of courses was offered to the dinner guests. At last, when she had managed a few bites of sherry trifle and just a taste of the spice cake trimmed with real flowers, she felt she must wave away the tray of cheeses. No, she changed her mind hastily and accepted a large piece of hard cheese. Under cover of one of the viscount's stories, which as usual induced a gale of laughter around the table, she slipped it into her reticule, adding it to the store she had already collected. There was still Violet at home to consider.

When the ladies withdrew, Lucy felt as full as a stuffed hen, a feeling as pleasing as it was unaccustomed. What a change this dinner was from the thin vegetable soup she had had the night before.

"Share the jest," Mrs. Blythe suggested as Lucy walked into the drawing room, still smiling. "You seem to have a merry thought."

"Just thinking about the skill of our hostess's cook," Lucy admitted. "The dinner was such a delight."

Mrs. Morris looked gratified. "I'm so glad you enjoyed it, my dear."

"Yes indeed," Marion Tennett agreed. "I should love to have the recipe for that mushroom and beef dish. Do you think it included sage or thyme?"

Their hostess laughed. "I can only guess. My cook is such a tartar, she doesn't allow me to share the secrets of her finest dishes."

"Oh, my own chef is just the same," Julia Blythe agreed.

The conversation became general, and all the ladies discussed recipes and the challenge of finding a really good cook. Soon the drawing-room doors opened again, and the men rejoined them.

The women all seemed to glance toward Lord Richmond, but Lucy made certain that she did not stare; she would not suggest an interest she did not—really, she did not—feel, and in any case, she would never be as obvious as Mrs. Tennett, who eyed him like a hungry cat who has a songbird almost within reach.

Instead, Lucy looked about her at the other guests. She was pleased to see that one of the men sought out their hostess, and Mrs. Morris's blush when the stout gentleman with the good-natured smile came to sit beside her showed that she apparently returned his favor. How lovely that at least one widow was finding a new interest in her life, Lucy thought, trying not to feel wistful.

Then, as if her thought had drawn him, she found that the viscount had slipped past the eager Marion with a skill born of long practice and now seated himself at Lucy's right hand.

"What makes your eyes twinkle, Mrs. Contrain?" he asked, his tone low and intimate. "Perhaps I might share the jest?"

"Everyone seems to think I am withholding banter," she countered, even as her pulse jumped at his nearness. Really, it was scandalous how the man affected her thinking; all her powers of reason seemed to evaporate when he came near. "I am a most serious person, with few witticisms to share."

He smiled. "If you say so, madam. But I suspect there are depths of merriment that you could plumb, if you chose."

"A merry widow?" She frowned, wondering if he was making sport of her. "That seems a contradiction in terms, does it not?"

"I mean no disrespect," he countered, arching those dark brows. "But even a widow may know gladness and mirth. In truth, a widow with a happy marriage in her past should be one of the wisest and most serene women in the world."

Lucy found that his comment—unexpectedly—stung her to her core. With more emphasis than she had intended, she snapped, "When she has lost everything she holds precious?"

"But she has known love and genuine devotion," the viscount said, his tone quiet and almost tender. "That in itself puts her ahead of most of the mass of people on this benighted planet, my dear." His own expression had sobered.

For an instant, she looked into his dark eyes and sensed that this man knew, more than most, what it was to be truly alone. The understanding hung between them as if they shared some unique and private secret that no one else could guess. She felt as if she had not really seen him before, not guessed at the pain or the privation he might be hiding. Then he glanced aside and his expression was again veiled.

"Perhaps we should discuss jewelry?" he suggested. "With your eyes, you should wear sapphires, my dear, or rubies—every woman looks well in rubies."

Lucy felt totally asea at the sudden change of topic. She hesitated, and into the silence Marion Tennett's shrill laughter rang out.

"What, are you trying to keep the wicked viscount all to yourself, Mrs. Contrain? For shame. Even a child knows one cannot hoard all the best sweetmeats in the box."

The moment was gone. Lucy flushed, and Lord Richmond turned his head to regard the intruder with a frosty expression.

"I take exception at being regarded as only a piece of confectionary," he said. "I am not available to the most eager hand." Some emotion vibrated between the two of them, and Lucy sensed there was more behind the light words than she could guess.

Marion Tennett flushed. Turning away from the viscount, she contemplated Lucy with a slightly strained smile, though her eyes were hard.

"I have been straining my poor memory, my dear, and I believe I did know your husband. A charming man he was, so kind to the ladies. You were a fortunate woman."

Lucy gazed back at the other woman, trying to conceal her puzzlement. Stanley had often told her how he frequented male-only gatherings when he went out alone, and he had never mentioned this woman. Was Mrs. Tennett lying, or—she did not seem the brightest of women—was she simply mistaken?

"Are you sure you are thinking of the right man?" Lucy asked. It had been over a year since Stanley's death; perhaps Mrs. Tennett was picturing another gentleman.

Marion Tennett's smile soured. Her always-shrill tones

seemed to pierce the other conversations in the room.

"Oh no, I'm quite certain. In fact, when I heard that he had ... um ... died, I remarked to myself that I had seen him on his last evening of life."

Lucy blinked. "You could not have," she contradicted.

Mrs. Tennett lifted her chin, and her voice grew even louder. "I assure you I did, my dear. Perhaps you did not know your husband as well as you thought."

A woman nearby gasped, and the other guests in the room suddenly fell silent.

Lucy steeled herself not to reveal any emotion. What a hateful comment to make over such a slight grievance, and likely quite inaccurate. It was obvious that Marion Tennett wanted the viscount's attention for herself, but to attack a just-met acquaintance for such a trivial offense ... With effort, Lucy kept her expression even, but while she fought for control, she could not seem to frame a suitable response.

The viscount did it for her. "Every man is a mystery to all but his Maker," Lord Richmond said, his tone as hard as Mrs. Tennett's narrowed eyes. "How can we hope to know another human's inner self?"

"Oh, my dear," Julia Blythe spoke quickly, as if trying to smooth the situation. "Believe me, no wife knows her husband's every thought, no more than his every movement. What a bore life would be, if that were so."

"Nor do husbands know their wives' every impulse," the countess put in from across the room. "And a good thing it is for marital harmony, too!"

This produced laughter, and the tension in the room eased. Lucy drew a deep breath and glanced at Marion Tennett, who tapped her fingers irritably against her voluptuous hips.

Lord Richmond flashed Lucy a quick glance, then leaned closer to Mrs. Tennett and spoke quietly into her ear. The woman flushed, then nodded.

Lucy felt a stab of disappointment, but she scolded herself. Despite an instant of apparent accord, she had no interest in monopolizing the attention of the most desir-

able man in the room. Let Marion Tennett have the ne-
farious viscount to herself; she obviously would go to any
ends to obtain his notice.

Sure enough, Lord Richmond moved away to chat with
Mrs. Tennett for a short time, but then went on to spend
several minutes talking to a trio of men. She heard laughter and snippets of more horse tales, anecdotes of the
hunting field, but she was careful not to look his way.

Lucy turned toward Julia and refused to show any in-
dication of the strange lack she felt over Lord Richmond's
absence. There was no point in developing an appetite for
rich pastry when one has no money even for bread, she
told herself, smiling with great determination at Julia's
story of her plans for a new gown for the countess's next
soiree.

Yet the unaccountable hunger inside her still ached, a
deep longing that he seemed to elicit on so many levels.
Even with her gaze turned away from him, Lucy could
sense his presence, pick his voice out from the other male
bass and alto tones that rose and fell in conversation. She
was being a fool, she thought, and tried harder to block
out any awareness of his presence.

But when, shortly, the viscount strolled back across the
room and declared, "Have you seen Mrs. Morris's prized
vases? They are quite remarkable," Lucy felt somehow no
surprise at all.

It seemed natural to put her hand lightly upon the crook
of his arm when he offered it, though the spark of energy
that leaped between them almost made her gasp, and to
follow him across to the cabinet where the antique pieces
were displayed. Lucy bent closer to the glass and pretended to examine the china.

When he spoke, his subject matter was totally unexpected. "Is it true that your husband did not go out the
night he died?" the viscount said abruptly, with no prelude
at all to his indelicate question.

Lucy stared at him. "He went only to his club to spend
a quiet evening playing whist, or so I was told."

"If that is true—but what is Marion up to?" Lord Richmond frowned. "Perhaps just making mischief."

Lucy told herself she should walk off right now, sever any connection to this enigmatic man. She had always been such a sensible girl; her mother had often said so. Why did he seem to slip beneath her defenses, disarm her rational decisions? Why did she not turn away?

"I have no idea, but perhaps you should return to her side," Lucy murmured.

He raised those heavy brows. "You tire of my company so quickly?"

"No, but Mrs. Tennett seems somewhat unpredictable," Lucy explained, staring at the elaborate pattern of the vase in front of them. The beauty of it made even more obvious the contrast between this urn and Cousin Wilhelmina's deplorable taste, and the gift vase's ultimate use. Funny, she'd never thought she'd be grateful for the hideous thing. "Perhaps you should rejoin her before she becomes agitated once more."

"No need," he said. "I have told Mrs. Tennett I will visit her later, but only if she refrains from making any more scenes."

His easy assurance that the woman would obey his hardly proper suggestion was galling. Yet, as Lucy stole a covert glance toward the side of the room, she saw that Mrs. Tennett had indeed lowered her voice and turned her attention to the other guests.

"I am happy to hear it," Lucy answered, aware that her voice sounded stiff. Did he think he could manipulate any woman he chose? "But if she is so desirous of your company—"

"Ming, I believe," Richmond interrupted, his tone carrying, as if he intended the comment for those others in their company who might be watching. He lifted one hand as if to point out a feature of the vase, and brushed her own hand in the process.

Lucy felt the slight touch resonate with the sensual power Lord Richmond carried within him, the force that her own inner being seemed to respond to so readily. Why did he awake these feelings, and with such embarrassing ease? She had ample proof that he was a rake of the most disreputable kind, and she should not allow herself to be affected by his touch, his glance, even his words. His words . . . it was hard to concentrate on his words, but in a moment she realized he was speaking again, and not about the china.

"Why would I want to seek out that sharp-tongued termagant when I have beside me the most enchanting woman in the room?"

Her own eyes narrowed, Lucy glanced up at him. "Are you making sport of me?"

"Do you value your own charms so little?"

She met his stare, and for an instant they gazed at each other, their faces only a few inches apart. His eyes were as deep as midnight pools. The other guests could have disappeared up the chimney in a cloud of smoke, for all the awareness she had of them.

Lucy felt dizzy, as if she could hardly breathe.

"What kind of fool was your husband, that he did not prize you for your delectable warmth?" the viscount whispered.

Lucy took a deep breath. "You cannot—you must not—"

"No, I mustn't," he agreed. His eyes were once again hooded by heavy lids, and the cynical tone was back. "But we have much more to discuss, my dear Mrs. Contrain. Will you be at home tomorrow afternoon?"

"Yes, I mean, you don't propose to call?" The suggestion filled her with both pleasure and alarm. She tried to pull herself together.

"I do, indeed," he agreed, his voice still low. "I still have questions I must ask you about your husband."

"Oh." Lucy had been about to protest, but his matter-of-fact answer pulled her up short. "If you're going to make outrageous demands once more, I don't see—"

"You will," he said. "I think I shall have to tell you the truth."

"That would be a good place to start," she retorted,

glaring at him. She had found a measure of rational thought again, and she tried to cling to it.

"And besides—" The viscount took her hand and cradled it within his own. They were still turned away from the rest of the room, and she thought—she hoped—that no one else could see his quiet movement, though the feel of his strong fingers sent shivers of delight up and down her spine.

"I cannot make love to you properly with a dozen people looking on." He lifted her hand as he spoke and kissed her fingers with a feather-soft touch that made her long for more.

Lucy's breath caught sharply in her suddenly dry throat. Through sheer force of will, she kept her own voice level.

"Then I shall invite a hundred, my lord, to ensure that you don't!"

Four

The next morning Nicholas made his way to the small backstreet in Cheapside where the Contrain house was situated. It was a tiny house and seemed poorly maintained; the paint on the door frame was peeling, and the windows had a vacant look. Had the late Stanley Contrain taken such poor care of all of his possessions?

He would not be at all surprised.

Nicholas frowned as he considered the events of the preceding evening. Mrs. Contrain had reacted to his mild flirtation with such surprise that he had some idea of just how unloved and unappreciated she had been during her brief marriage. For some reason, that stirred anger inside him. She was a most engaging woman, radiating warmth and an unassuming honesty that was, in his experience, rare enough. She'd probably been unfailingly loyal to that bastard she had married. Nicholas muttered a curse beneath his breath, then shook his head.

Mrs. Contrain's past was not his concern. He had to think about his own problems, the friend he had lost, the suspicions Nicholas himself was still tainted by, the commission the prince had laid upon him, most of all, the pressing need to find the missing gem. Nicholas had been searching for over a year for some clue, and now that he had come across clear evidence pointing to Contrain's possible link to the robbery, this opportunity must be seized. If it distressed the man's widow, he could not allow that to sway him. He took a deep breath and approached the faded blue door, rapping smartly.

There was no answer—was she going to pretend that no one was home? After a moment, he heard a faint sound of movement, then the door opened slightly.

A slip of a maidservant peered up at him through the crack, her narrow face twisted into a forbidding frown. One brown curl had escaped from her neat, if threadbare, cap, and she regarded him with disapproval.

"Lord Richmond to see Mrs. Contrain," Nicholas announced, hoping to overawe her enough to be granted admittance. But he found it a useless effort.

"The mistress is not at 'ome," the servant announced with all the grave dignity of one belonging to a much more prosperous household.

He could easily have thrust open the door, but it was not his habit to bully underlings, especially girls as young and slight as this. And anyhow, what would Mrs. Contrain think of such dastardly tactics? No, he had to have permission to enter, and he would get it, sooner or later.

"I really need to speak with her," Nicholas said, his tone gentle. "If you could suggest to her—"

"She h'aint at 'ome!" the girl repeated, looked annoyed that he should question her pronouncement. "She didn't want to see you—I mean, I weren't supposed to say that—she 'ad—um—h'an urgent h'appointment.'

With effort, Nicholas kept his expression sober. "Yes, I understand. When Mrs. Contrain returns, please tell her that I must see her. I need to speak to her, really desperately, and—" he paused for emphasis "—I shall return again and again until she grants me an audience."

The maid's confusion faded, and she looked perturbed again, though she struggled to master her errant *h*'s. "I don't see what is so important about a few piles of the master's old clothes."

Then Contrain's personal belongings hadn't all been thrown out or sold, Nicholas thought, his pulse leaping. Perhaps there was a chance he could find some clue. It was a desperate hope, but after so many months of fruitless pursuits and cold trails, he would grab any chance he could.

"I'll be back," he repeated.

She shut the door with unnecessary firmness, and this time he allowed his grin to show.

Nicholas glanced up at his driver, who had brought him to this unfashionable district. "Mason, take the carriage home."

"Milord?" The coachman looked startled. "Surely you're not going to walk home?"

"No, I have business here. I will take a hackney when I am done."

The servant looked perplexed, but, very wisely, he kept his thoughts to himself. "Yes, milord."

The coachman flicked the reins, and the elegant midnight-blue carriage moved away at a sedate trot. Nicholas headed back up the narrow street, avoiding a cart full of onions and the swaybacked old gelding who pulled it. He would wait a while and see if Mrs. Contrain returned; he was impatient to confront her. Perhaps he was simply impatient to see her again.

This would not do, he reminded himself. Business first. He could not risk losing the track of the missing ruby just because he kept remembering the way Lucy Contrain's fair hair framed her delicate face, or how much he wanted to run his hands down the graceful curve of her hips . . .

At the top of the street, he found a rundown ale house, and he entered, stooping a little to avoid hitting the top of the low doorway. Inside, the smoky air stank of stale ale, unwashed clothing, and a fire which did not draw properly. Most of the half dozen men seated inside looked from their dress to be tradesmen, with a sprinkling of common laborers lounging at a table at the corner. The chatter paused when he entered as the customers eyed this newcomer, then the talk resumed as he made his way to the bar.

"Do you have any burgundy?"

The man behind the counter grunted and shook his head.

"Never mind. A half pint of ale, please." Nicholas didn't want to insult his palate more than necessary.

However, when the mug was put before him, he found the brew better than expected. He took the drink to a table near the small, grimy window so he could look out upon the street.

For over half an hour the street was quiet, with only an occasional peddler or tradesman's cart passing, and sometimes a shabby carriage. A man with a peddler's knapsack slung over his shoulder dawdled along the street, occasionally calling to a passerby. Nicholas watched and sipped his ale absently, his thoughts elsewhere. From the timbre of the little maidservant's voice, he believed that Mrs. Contrain was truly not at home. However, she could not stay away forever.

A coal cart rumbled by. His gaze sharpened as he saw a feminine figure walking along the side of the street, a shopping basket over her arm, and a plainly dressed servant a few steps behind. No, even from here he could tell that the woman was too broad in the hips and her bonnet too flashy; that could never be Mrs. Contrain. Lucy Contrain had a figure most pleasingly proportioned, and her fair locks suited the rosy-hued complexion of her oval face. His reflections turned to an image of Lucy just rising from her bed, hair still tousled, eyes blinking at the early light. God, if only they had met under different circumstances—

Then, as if his fancy had conjured her up, he spied her slim figure hurrying, all alone, along the street, skirting a pile of fresh horse droppings and glancing up and down the narrow lane. Just behind her trudged a man with a peddler's deep knapsack. Nicholas's gaze passed over the second figure without pausing, then he narrowed his eyes and looked more closely. Wasn't this the same man Nicholas had seen earlier? He noted for the first time that the peddler's knapsack sagged limply, as if it were empty. Now the man quickened his pace, coming ever closer to Lucy. With a sense of strong disquiet, Nicholas threw a coin onto the table and jumped to his feet, hurrying outside.

"Mrs. Contrain, take care!" he called, taking long strides to intercept her.

But as Lucy Contrain glanced up, her expression startled, the man behind her closed the gap between them. He grabbed her hand, and she shrieked in surprise and pulled it away.

But he reached to clutch her shoulders The peddler shook her slight frame like a rag doll and leaned close to her face. Lucy's eyes were wide, but she lashed out, kicking his shin and making her assailant swear loudly.

Then Nicholas reached them. He took strong hold of her attacker, breaking his grip on Lucy, and shoved the man into the brick wall that lined the road. Instead of fighting back, the man cowered, and Nicholas reluctantly lowered his fists.

"What do you think you are doing?" Nicholas snapped. "Laying hands on a lady!"

"No offense, gov, no offense," the man whined. "Just hoping for a few pennies, ma'am. I'm a poor man down on his luck."

"If I see you anywhere near this lady again, or on this street, you'll be down on your knees," Nicholas promised, his tone steely.

The man muttered, "Didn't mean no harm, gov."

"Are you all right?" Nicholas turned to Mrs. Contrain. She nodded, though her face looked pale.

"Yes, but—"

While Nicholas's attention was diverted, the would-be mendicant took to his heels. Nicholas swore beneath his breath. He wanted to pursue the stranger, but Mrs. Contrain looked very distressed. He could not leave her alone on the street.

"We should get you home; you need a sip of brandy."

Lucy Contrain swallowed a humorless laugh. The man expected to find brandy in her almost-stripped-bare home? "No, really, I'm quite all right," she said, and tried to believe it. But the shock of the stranger's assault, his hands gripping her arms with surprising strength, his nails pinching her flesh—she shivered again. "And besides—" She hesitated, not sure why she felt she could confide in Lord Richmond, who was barely more than a stranger himself.

Dear God, she was so tired of being alone, of having no one with whom to share her problems, no one to offer advice. Treacherous tears suddenly flooded her eyes. Chagrined, Lucy put up one hand to brush away the useless drops, and with her hand lifted, she gazed in dismay at the delicate kid glove. One finger was exposed; the man had ripped the thin, much-worn leather.

"Oh," she said. "He tore my glove."

It was, somehow, the last straw. Tears came in earnest, and she put up one hand to shield her face.

She expected Lord Richmond to withdraw, perhaps avert his face and pretend not to notice her disgraceful weakness. Stanley had never reacted well to her rare bouts of tears, usually stalking away in disgust. She supposed that men did not care to see a woman weep; the frailty of it seemed to repulse them.

But instead of drawing away, Richmond put one arm around her shoulders. She felt the strong line of his arm, and its strength was impossible to resist. Lucy leaned her head against his chest and wept.

Nicholas looked down at the top of her black bonnet, which trembled from the force of her unabashed sobs. One part of his mind reflected ruefully on the damage being inflicted on Weston's latest masterpiece as she dampened his lapel; another part knew he was simply distracting himself from the rage he felt that such a woman could be driven to despair. Damn her worthless husband, damn everyone and everything that caused her distress. And why did he care? How had she slipped, so quickly, through the hard-won shell of detachment and cynicism that had served him so well for so long? Nicholas wasn't sure he should pursue the answer.

But even though the street was quiet, they were attracting stares. A boy carrying a load of firewood gaped, and a stout matron in a shabby gown paused to regard them.

"Perhaps we should go into your house," he suggested quietly.

She drew a deep shuddering breath. "It was my last pair of gloves," she said, as if in explanation. Hiccuping, she reached into her reticule and took out a small handkerchief to dry her cheeks.

The wispy bit of black-edged lace seemed hardly up to the job. He drew a handkerchief from his own pocket and offered it to her. Lucy accepted the clean square of fine linen with a brief word of thanks. She wiped her face and blew her nose with an uninhibited vigor which made the sides of his mouth lift. She offered it back to him, but he shook his head, hiding his grin. "No, no, please keep it."

Then he took her arm, and they soon reached her own door. This time, the little maid opened it quickly.

"Oh, ma'am, what's amiss?" The girl sounded agitated as she took in Lucy's pale cheeks and reddened eyes. "Did 'e 'urt you?" She glared up at Nicholas as if she would launch her petite frame at him, like a kitten attacking a wolfhound.

"Oh, no," Lucy Contrain answered, and Nicholas spoke at the same time.

"Mrs. Contrain had an unfortunate encounter with a ruffian in the street. She is naturally unsettled. Do you have any brandy in the house?"

The maidservant blinked. "No, sir. Uh, milord. The wine merchant said h'it'd be a cold day in 'ell before 'e extended the Contrains any more credit—"

"Violet!" Lucy Contrain said, her tone more entreaty than reprimand.

"Oh, sorry, ma'am." The maid blinked, looking contrite. "I mean, we don't 'ave no brandy, milord."

"Have," Lucy corrected.

Nicholas thought about where to find a restorative for Mrs. Contrain. He already knew that the alehouse on her own street stocked no wine. But—

"You'll need to go to the wine merchant's on the corner of Hayes Street," he said, taking a couple of guineas from his pocket and handing her the coins. Violet blinked at such largess.

"Take a hackney, it will be quicker," he added.

She gaped at him.

"Do you know how to hail a cab?" he asked patiently.

Violet drew her petite frame up and answered, her dignity back in place. "Oh, course, milord. I do h'it—it—all the time."

That was a patent falsehood, but he managed not to smile. "Good," he said. "Be as quick as you can."

In the meantime, Mrs. Contrain needed to get off her feet; he cursed himself for allowing her to stand in the hallway when she still looked wobbly as an overheated candle. Where were his wits?

"Would you like to lie down?" he asked her.

Violet paused with her hand on the front door, and both women glared at him. "Alone, of course," Nicholas added in exasperation. "I do not want you to pass out at my feet."

"It's all right, Violet," Lucy murmured to her maid, and to him she said, "I'll just sit down for a moment. I do feel a little shaky."

Violet nodded and continued out the door. Nicholas offered his arm again; Lucy was regaining her color, but she still did not look well. He wondered if she were eating enough; damn Contrain for his thriftless ways. How could he leave his wife in such dire straits?

"Would you like to go into the drawing room?"

Lucy laughed, but the sound was hollow. "No, I think not. Perhaps we can sit in the dining room for a moment."

She could hardly take a viscount into the kitchen, and unless they went up to her bedroom, which was totally unsuitable, there was no other room which offered more to sit on than the bare floor. She led the way to the dining room and sank onto one of the cherry dining chairs. It was most inconvenient being penniless.

Yet the thought did not bring with it the usual rush of desperation. Somehow, Lord Richmond's very presence made her feel less precarious. And on that thought she frowned, remembered the strange assault in the street.

"That man—" she began. "Beggars do not usually lay hands on their proposed benefactors. It is not the sort of action which engenders feelings of charity."

"No," he agreed, turning another chair so that he could sit facing her, giving her his complete attention. It made her feel a little self-conscious, having him gaze at her so seriously, as if what she said were important, but she continued.

"And he spoke very well for a beggar, did you notice?"

Nicholas blinked. Why had he not remarked on that? Lucy Contrain was a serious detraction; he must keep his wits about him. "I believe you are correct," he said slowly, thinking what this could mean.

"And his nails—when he gripped my arm, I stared at his hand. His nails were clean and evenly cut."

"Unusually precise habits for a poor workman down on his luck," Nicholas agreed, his tone grim.

"It seems very strange," she suggested, and paused, obviously waiting for his response.

He knew he could no longer put off declaring her his real mission. "I have a story to tell you, Mrs. Contrain," Nicholas said. "About a gem called the Scarlet Widow."

Lucy blinked. A jewel? What did all this have to do with—

The viscount held up one hand as if to forestall her question. "It gained the nickname because so many have been killed in the struggle to possess it. The official name is the Royal Ruby of Mandalay."

He had mentioned rubies, she remembered, at the dinner party. "Why are you telling me this?"

He motioned again for patience. "The ruby had been sold to the British Crown; it was meant to take its place in the crown jewels. The prince regent had a mind to use it to ornament his coronation robes when the time—ah—at last comes for him to ascend to the throne."

When the poor old mad king dies, Lucy clarified to herself, though she did not speak the thought aloud. Everyone knew just why the heir to the throne had been made regent.

"The prince knows that my family has had business interests in India and the East for years. Because of that, I was asked to oversee the transfer of this priceless gem. It was to be done in complete secrecy because there have been so many attempts to steal it."

Lucy's eyes widened. What an extraordinary tale. "And?"

"My business agent, Victor Montat, whom I trusted completely, was to bring the jewel from India. He had two armed guards with him at all times. All went well until their ship was damaged in a storm and forced to dock at Gibraltar. After repairs and several days' delay, the ship limped into Plymouth. When Victor and his guards came ashore, it was too late to set off for London, so they took lodgings for the night. During the early hours of the morning, the two guards were drugged, and Victor was stabbed. The ruby vanished."

Lucy gasped.

Nicholas stared out the bare windowpanes without seeing the tiny garden beyond. "Victor was my employee, and he met his death serving me. More than that, he was my friend. I will not rest until I find the hand that held that blade."

The grim determination in the viscount's deep voice made Lucy shiver. She felt almost sorry for the murderous thief when this tall man with his stern cold eyes found his prey. Almost. Still—

"You have my deepest sympathy for the loss of your friend," she said. "But if you'll pardon me for saying so, I don't see what this has to do with me."

He turned, and his dark eyes focused on her face. Lucy braced herself. Again, she sensed deep emotion barely suppressed.

"Because, Mrs. Contrain, I regret to inform you that I believe your husband was involved in the theft."

Lucy's lips parted, but she found no words. The silence hung between them, brittle as the first ice lidding a shallow pond.

"You think *Stanley* stole your ruby?" It was such a ridiculous idea that she almost laughed, but the sight of the viscount's severe expression made her slightly hysterical giggle fade before it could be uttered. Lucy glanced at the stripped-down room, the bare house that surrounded them. "Does it *look* as if I possess a priceless gem?"

He shrugged. "Perhaps you have it and are not aware," he told her quietly. "I am not suggesting that you yourself were privy to the theft."

Nicholas saw her blue eyes flash with anger. But then a second emotion sobered her. Biting her lip, she looked away from his intent gaze. The adorable Mrs. Contrain was no actress, that was certain. Her emotions flashed across her expressive face with an openness he would have admired, if the circumstances had been less compelling. For now he was simply thankful that she seemed ill suited to artifice. He preferred to believe her completely innocent of any involvement in her husband's larceny.

Lucy cleared her throat. "When did this theft take place? Why was it not reported in the papers?"

"The prince regent fears a great scandal; he has paid an enormous sum for the jewel, and to be missing both thousands of pounds and the ruby itself leaves him open for attack from his many detractors. He has enough of that already. In fact, I must ask you not to repeat this story to anyone."

She nodded as Nicholas continued. "The jewel disappeared on the night my agent was murdered, over a year ago. It was the last Sunday in February."

Lucy shook her head. "Stanley did not go to the west country last year."

"Are you certain? You are sure he was home with you that night?"

Lucy looked down at the slight film of dust on the

cherry table. She wiped it absently. How could she admit how often Stanley was gone from home, and how little she really knew of her husband's habits?

The viscount waited. His expression revealed little, but she sensed the impatience that raged behind his controlled demeanor.

"I believe," she said at last, "he went into Kent to visit friends that weekend."

He leaped on her admission. "And you did not accompany him?"

"No, I think—I think I had a slight cold." In fact, she had not been asked. She had quarreled with Stanley about it, she remembered, her heart sinking. Later, she had rebuked herself for the cross words uttered so shortly before his accident. . . .

Then another thought distracted her from the old guilt. Was it possible Stanley had had a different destination? Feeling a chill rush over her, she looked up at the viscount.

He watched her, his dark eyes hard to read. "A servant at the inn in Plymouth described a man resembling your husband. He was with two other men, and all three left very suddenly. A handkerchief was left behind, with the initials *SC* embroidered upon it."

"It could have been another man with the same initials," she argued.

The viscount shook his head. "I traveled to Plymouth and spoke myself to the innkeeper and his staff. The description fits your husband."

"But it has been over a year—how can you trust their memories to be so exact?" she shot back.

Lord Richmond hesitated, and Lucy felt a moment of relief. Yes, he had worried about that, too, she could tell.

"But it is enough to merit further investigation," he pointed out. "Surely you would wish to see your husband's name cleared of this charge? At least, if you really believe him to be innocent."

"Of course I do," Lucy protested, trying to sound as if no troubling doubts lingered in the back of her mind.

"Then you will not mind me looking through his effects?"

"For a gem fit to take its place in the Crown Jewels?" The idea was so absurd that Lucy did laugh this time, as much from nervous tension as real humor. "By all means," she said, jumping to her feet. She led the way to the narrow staircase, and up to the next floor.

At the door to her bedchamber, she paused. "I must warn you I have already sold some of my husband's best coats. I did check the pockets, but I hope I didn't overlook anything. How large is this ruby?"

"The size of a hen's egg," he told her.

Lucy blinked. "That, I would have noticed." She led the way to the chest in the corner where the last of Stanley's clothes were carefully folded. She had not, so far, been able to bring herself to market all of her husband's things.

When she opened the chest, the smell of mint, the dried leaves put in to repel moths, wafted from the layers of clothing, along with—still—the faintest hint of Stanley's own odor, part smoke from the gaming dens he had once visited, part the too-sweet scent he sometimes wore. Lucy drew a deep breath, then stepped back so that the viscount could kneel and lift out the clothes she had put so carefully away.

She felt disloyal watching a stranger check Stanley's discarded clothing, patting the shirts and running his hands over the trousers' seams. Surely Lord Richmond did not really expect to find a jewel worth a king's ransom here, in her tiny bedroom?

Lord Richmond worked his way slowly and methodically through the pile of clothing, laying each item out on the bare floor as he dug deeper into the chest. Nothing more illuminating than an old playbill emerged from the pockets, and Lucy had begun to relax when the viscount paused, about to put aside one of the jackets. He had already checked the pockets and found them empty. But something crinkled as he refolded the worn superfine of the coat.

He paused, and Lucy held her breath. She, too, had heard the tiny whisper of sound. "What is it?"

The viscount turned the coat inside out and ran his hand along the crease in the fabric. He examined the right side again; it seemed as if something had slipped through a hole in the pocket and lodged deep in the lining.

"Do you have a pair of scissors?" He glanced up, his face impassive. Only his dark eyes glinted with suppressed excitement.

Lucy rose and went to her clothespress, coming back with her small sewing basket. She took out a slim pair of scissors and offered them to the viscount. He took them and, with a careful economy, loosened the threads that closed the seam.

In a moment, he had made an opening wide enough to drag out a small folded piece of paper. Lucy sighed. It was only a faded receipt.

Lord Richmond raised his head, and his expression puzzled her. He smoothed the note and held it out so she could look more closely.

"An accounting from the White Stag Inn," he said succinctly. "The inn in Plymouth where the murder occurred."

Lucy felt her heart sink. Why did Stanley have such a paper in his pocket? Had he visited Plymouth, after all?

"Perhaps someone gave it to him," she argued, a bit wildly.

"Perhaps, but it seems more likely that it came from the inn, and that he was there," Lord Richmond told her.

Lucy swallowed, but she refused to concede defeat. "That is hardly sufficient evidence to condemn my husband as a thief!"

"You are right," her inquisitor agreed. He had finished his examination of the clothing. He transferred the stack back into the chest, setting the garments in neatly and shutting the lid. "But it is enough to encourage me to keep looking."

"What will you do now?"

"I think I will attempt to trace your husband's steps in

the last weeks of his life." For a moment, the viscount's face looked stern again, and he seemed lost in thought.

"You are determined to implicate Stanley in this foul crime?" Lucy frowned. Despite herself, she took a step closer.

The sharpness of her tone seemed to reach him. Nicholas Ramsey gave her his full attention. "Yes, until I am certain that I am mistaken, I fear I must. But you need not worry for yourself."

He reached out and put his large capable hand around both her own, which at the moment were clenched tightly together as if in supplication.

Lucy knew she should step away at once, but his grip felt so comforting in its implied strength that she allowed the contact to linger.

She waited for him to speak, but he gazed at her in silence, his expression hard to decipher. They stood so close she could detect the vein in his temple as it throbbed, and smell the deep masculine scent of his clothing. Some long dormant emotion stirred inside her, and she drew a deep breath.

She had forgotten, in the shock of his accusation of her husband, how improper it was that they should stand here together in her bedchamber. She was conscious of the neatly made bed only a foot from where they stood; the tiny room felt almost intimate. What was the notorious viscount thinking of her boldness, to bring him here?

His dark eyes were cloaked in a reserve impossible to penetrate. But she was certain that his breaths, too, came more quickly. A flicker of awareness seemed to jump between them. She felt her pulse quicken.

He lifted his hand as if to touch her cheek—

"Ma'am!" Violet exclaimed from the doorway. "Did 'e—what is—I mean," she finished weakly, "H'ere's the brandy, my lord."

Nicholas dropped his hand, and Lucy knew her face had flushed. "Thank you, Violet. Get out some goblets, please. We shall be down in a moment."

The maid curtsied, though her expression was perplexed. She turned on her heel and was soon out of sight. Lucy could hear her footsteps on the staircase.

Stepping back, Lucy tried to marshal her scattered thoughts. What had she said, last?

Lord Richmond spoke first.

"You must realize, Mrs. Contrain, this is a matter of the highest importance to the Crown. The prince regent has offered a reward of five thousand pounds for the ruby's safe return."

Lucy felt as if the breath was caught in her throat. She coughed, and then repeated, her voice hoarse, "Five thousand pounds?"

He nodded. "Yes, and his everlasting gratitude, if I remember his words correctly."

Lucy shut her eyes for an instant, thinking of the bare larder below stairs, of the home soon to be sold out from under her, lost to her forever. Her first and only home since her forfeited birthplace . . .

"I will help you!" she blurted.

Five

*T*he viscount raised his brows.

Her words came out in a rush. "Mind you, I am not saying my husband is guilty, or even involved in the crime. But if we can prove that he is not, it would help point you in the right direction and aid you in finding the real villain, don't you think? And perhaps, ah, merit a portion of the reward?" She held her breath.

His dark eyes glinted. "Yes, indeed," he agreed. "I would be most happy to have your assistance, and more than happy to see you receive compensation for your efforts. Perhaps first, you might tell me more about your husband's habits?"

Lucy wavered, assaulted by renewed feelings of disloyalty and guilt. Was it right to do this, even to keep her home? No, she was certain Stanley was not a thief. Whatever his faults had been, she had seen no suggestion of such a thing. She gathered her resolve.

"Actually," she said, "my husband said little about his engagements."

Lord Richmond's disappointment was almost palpable. "But you were his wife, surely—"

He hesitated, and Lucy knew that her cheeks were hot. Perhaps not all husbands, after all, were as reticent, or as reluctant to take their wives into company, as Stanley had been.

"However—" she said into the silence, and then it was her turn to pause. Her conscience pricked her about the admission that she was about to make. But glancing up, she saw that Lord Richmond's eyes had narrowed, and his attention was riveted upon her. How alarming he would be as an enemy, gazing at one just so, with his Roman nose and sharp, intelligent eyes. Alarming and intensely male—she felt her cheeks flush as he stepped closer.

"However?" he asked, his tone controlled.

"He had an appointment book—" she blurted.

"Ah . . ." The viscount drew a deep breath. "And you kept it, after his death?"

She glanced away from his keen gaze. "Of course."

"Perhaps we could look through its pages?" he asked quickly. When she hesitated, he added, "In order to establish his innocence or guilt?"

Lucy made up her mind. She could believe in Stanley or not, and if she believed in his integrity, this could not harm her late husband's name.

"Very well," she agreed. She went to the shelf in the corner of her bedroom and withdrew a small, slender book. She held it for a moment, then forced herself to open the cover.

Lord Richmond had crossed the room in three long paces. He looked over her shoulder as she turned to the back of the book.

"Perhaps we should look at the last month of his life," Lord Richmond suggested.

Lucy turned the pages. Most of the notations were short, and sometimes downright cryptic. On Tuesday and Thursdays, the letter *E* showed up weekly.

The viscount glanced at her. "Do you what or whom the *E* signifies?"

Lucky shook her head. "I have no idea. Perhaps a regular card game?"

"Your husband enjoyed gaming?" His tone was mild.

Lucy tried not to sound defensive. "Like most gentlemen, yes."

"Did he lose large sums?"

If only she knew—not that she could have prevented his gambling away his money if she had known! But she wondered now about the mysterious Thomas Brooks, who had laid claim to her home. "I don't know," Lucy answered slowly. "There were times when his mood seemed low, after a long night of cards, but other times he would brim with optimism, so I thought he must be holding his own, at least."

Raising her gaze to the viscount's face, she caught a look of skepticism before he smoothed his expression into one of polite agreement.

"I have heard him mention Watiers," she told him. She looked back down at the journal and turned another page. She blinked in surprise, and her expression must have caught Lord Richmond's attention. He bent closer.

"What is it?" she couldn't resist asking. "Do you know the name?"

He pointed to a notation, *Rockhaven, 2:00*; it was a Friday notation in her husband's appointment book.

"Ah, the duchess of Rockhaven? I did not realize your husband traveled in such exalted circles."

"Neither did I!" Lucy thought of Stanley's best evening coat, with its side seam neatly mended and the spot of wine on the sleeve that neither she nor Violet had been able to remove. Stanley rubbing elbows—stained elbows—with a duchess?

"He never mentioned attending her salon?"

"No!" Lucy couldn't help feeling annoyed. If Stanley were here, she would tell him just what she thought of his furtive ways. With a sigh, she remembered that was impossible. But why had he kept so many secrets from her? Then the last comment finally penetrated her swirling emotions.

"Salon? How do you know it's a salon?"

"The duchess always holds her salon on Friday afternoon during the Season," Lord Richmond explained.

And no doubt, he himself *did* move easily in those circles. Lucy looked over his expensive linen and well-cut coat, absorbing his air of easy confidence and the strong aura of vibrant masculinity that glimmered within his dark eyes—eyes the color of freshly spaded loam in a farmer's field. She suppressed a shiver of automatic response. This man would have entry wherever he chose. She could not imagine any woman—titled or not—refusing the pleasure of his company.

"I think we should start there," he announced while she was still absorbed in her musings.

"Where?" She pulled her attention back to his words. What did he mean, we?

"I will escort you to the duchess's salon this afternoon." He nodded toward the doorway, and she led him automatically toward the stairs.

"Me, call on a duchess?" Lucy felt a chill of alarm run through her. "No, no, I can't—I've never—"

"You wished to aid me in my investigation, did you not?"

"Yes, but—"

"I will pick you up at three o'clock," he announced when they reached the bottom of the staircase. "You may find out something about Stanley's habits, his friends. It will be easier for you to ask questions about him than it would be for me. You have a right, after all, to chat about your late spouse."

"I'm going to visit a duchess?" Her voice sounded thin.

The viscount glanced at her. "Right now, you should have some of that brandy."

Violet had put out goblets in the dining room. He poured Lucy a healthy portion of the brandy, then handed her the glass.

"To your health, ma'am."

Lucy stared into the amber depths of the liquor. *To her sanity,* more likely, if any more shocking revelations about Stanley's unknown activities were revealed. What had he been doing, frequenting a duchess's salon? It was not as if he had had any interest that Lucy had detected in arts or music or polite conversation. And why hadn't he told his wife? Hurt and anger both roiled inside her. Sighing, she tried to push away her feelings. She had enough current troubles without delving into the still painful slights of her marriage.

"I will see you in a few hours, Mrs. Contrain." The viscount bowed as she automatically extended her hand.

"But—" The warm touch of his hand, felt even briefly, disrupted her train of thought, and Lucy found herself uncharacteristically speechless as he strode away. In a moment, she heard the front door close. Violet hurried after him. Lucy heard the small thump as the servant barred the door, then she slipped back into the room.

"Are you all right, ma'am? 'E didn't—that is—'e wasn't un—improper while you was alone?"

"No, no, he was always a gentleman," Lucy answered, trying not to color. She looked away from Violet's curious stare, thinking hard. She was going to visit a duchess. Good lord, what would she wear?

"Violet, come upstairs, please." Lucy pushed away the half-empty glass. "We have work to do."

In her bedroom they went through the glorious contents of the countess's gift box. What did one wear to chat with a duchess? Lucy had no idea. It was an afternoon event, however, so she put aside the dinner gown and settled on an elegant dress of shining Caledon silk. After they had tightened the high waist and let out the bosom just a bit, the dress fit very well.

Violet took away her mistress's best half boots to be polished and buffed in an attempt to make them look respectable enough for such exalted company, and asked leave to go on an unexplained errand.

Lucy nodded absently. Left alone, she smoothed the folds of the silk skirt, delighting in its soft sleekness, then suddenly remembered her damaged glove. Oh dear, and gloves were so visible, too. She had no funds and no credit with which to purchase a new pair. And a lady could certainly not appear in company with her hands bare.

Sighing, she went back to her sewing basket and sat down to mend, as best she could, the ripped, worn leather finger.

In another half hour, Lucy put down her needle. The glove would not pass a close inspection, but it would have to do. She would try to keep her hands out of sight until she removed the gloves to partake of the tea the countess would likely serve. Lucy had a sudden picture of herself with hands tucked behind her like a timid child. She laughed ruefully. As if she were not nervous enough about the salon! She was about to rise from her bed when she heard a sudden loud, deep baying noise from below.

Oh, no, more invaders?

Lucy jumped up and headed for the stairs. She flew down the bare wooden treads and was more than astonished to meet a large and alarming creature that looked at first glance like a wild bear.

Dear God, had a circus lost its performing beast? Lucy gasped and put out her arms to defend herself from the animal's teeth, which she could see all too clearly as it loped forward, jaw open, drool swinging from its enormous muzzle. It appeared ready to launch itself upon her.

"Down, Lucifer!" Violet shrieked from behind the beast. "To h'earth."

To Lucy's shock, the creature heeded the admonition. It sat down on its haunch, and a large red tongue emerged from the doglike muzzle.

"What is it, Violet?" Lucy demanded, when she could get her voice to work again.

"I borrowed 'im from the butcher's boy, ma'am, to protect the 'ouse," Violet explained, sounding most pleased with herself. " 'E's called a Newfoundland; the butcher got 'im from 'is brother, who's a cook on a fishing boat. Nice dog,'e said, but grew too big for the ship. The butcher keeps 'im behind the shop to scare away thieves."

"He must be most successful," Lucy murmured. "This is a dog?"

The animal's broad body was covered with a black, shaggy, slightly matted coat of coarse hair, and the head was as large as a coal scuttle. When he stood, as he suddenly did, he met Violet at eye level. And he still looked very bearlike.

"Are you sure you can control him?" Lucy asked, trying not to sound as doubtful as she felt as she glanced from her diminutive servant to the enormous dog. "I am sure he will be most, um, protective, but if he devours us first, the protection will be of little use."

Violet nodded earnestly. "Oh, yes, ma'am; the butcher's boy told me all 'is commands, and he's going to bring me meat scraps to feed 'im. Besides, as long as 'e—I mean he—knows who you are, you're perfectly safe."

Lucy devoutly hoped so. She drew a deep breath, then regretted it. Lucifer, as befitted his name, seemed quite unacquainted with soap and water.

"Why don't you take him through the kitchen and let him sit on the back stoop, then we will have some soup."

"Yes, ma'am," Violet agreed. "H'up, Lucifer." She led the big dog away.

When the maid returned, she and Lucy ate a meager bowl of soup, while Lucy wondered again just why Stanley had withheld so much from her. Shouldn't a husband and wife have a more open understanding? Had she been too compliant with Stanley, and would it have improved their union if she had demanded more candor on his part, or would it only have increased the discord and distance between them?

If she had had more chance to see a marriage in action, perhaps she would have believed that she deserved more. Her own mother had been widowed young, and Cousin Wilhelmina had never married. And, truth be told, Lucy had been so grateful for Stanley's offer—how many men would marry a penniless young woman?—that she had not pushed him to explain his frequent absences. Stanley had said that men often dined out alone, frequented their clubs in male company, gambled or drank with male cronies, and she had believed him. But now, the doubts that had been pushed to the back of her mind gathered force and would no longer be ignored. . . .

Too late now to think what she should have done. Lucy shook her head, then paused with the spoon halfway to her mouth. Was that a rap on the door? Outside, the dog growled.

Lucy dropped the spoon into her almost empty bowl and jumped to her feet. Violet looked anxious.

"Let me go, ma'am," she offered. "I'll take Lucifer with me."

"No, let me take a look first."

Picking up a stout walking stick her mother had used when her joints had pained her, Lucy hurried to the front of the house. Half expecting more invaders, she went first to the parlor window to peer out. A young lad stood on her doorstep. He did not seem large enough to present a threat, so she motioned to Violet, who stood in the hall, to open the door.

Lucy strained to hear the murmur of voices, but she could not make out all the words. When Violet shut the door again, Lucy hurried to join her.

"What did he want?"

Then she saw that her maid held a small, neatly wrapped parcel. Now what? Surely not another bequest from the countess.

Violet's eyes sparked with anticipation. " 'E said 'is master was ordered to get these to you with utmost dispatch."

Lucy tore open the brown paper. When she saw the contents of the parcel, her mouth gaped.

Gloves—delicate, exquisitely crafted gloves of the finest kid, in a myriad of colors and lengths: white, tan, gray, lavender, whatever a costume could demand. At least a dozen pairs were wrapped neatly inside the package.

"There's a card, ma'am," Violet pointed out, beaming with vicarious pleasure.

Lucy grabbed it. *"To replace the glove that was damaged,"* the message said succinctly. *"Your servant, Richmond."*

Lucy felt her eyes prickle with tears, and she blinked hard. He had remembered. She picked up one glove, savoring the buttery softness of the fine leather, and slipped it on; it fit very well, considering that the glove maker had not had an opportunity to measure her hand. Had the viscount observed the size and shape of her hands so closely? No, surely not; it must be just a happy accident. Of course, she should not accept gifts from a stranger, much less from a gentleman whose reputation was hardly spotless.

But how could she refuse such a kind gesture? And to wear clean, new, unmended gloves again—she smiled with delight.

Lucy held the glove to her cheek. She would explain to the viscount, very soon, the impropriety of offering gifts to a lady with whom one had only the slightest acquaintance. But just this once, she told herself, the notorious viscount would have his way.

After Violet heated water, Lucy went upstairs to bathe and change. She wished for a cup of tea, but there was no tea left; Lucy sighed at the thought. If only she could collect part of that reward—

There would be tea enough at the salon, she had no doubt. Soon a bright-faced Violet appeared, ready to button her mistress into her gown. To Lucy's surprise, Violet brought a cup of steaming liquid with her.

"But I thought the tea cannister was empty?"

"H'it h'is, ma'am—"

"It is," Lucy corrected automatically.

"It is, but h'I—I picked some chamomile leaves from a bush in the square while I was buying the brandy, so h'as—as to make you some herbal tea," Violet announced, beaming with delight at her own sharp wit.

"How clever of you," Lucy agreed. Violet's smile widened even more.

Lucy took a sip of the tea, and winced. "Um, are you sure you selected the right bush, Violet?"

"I think so," her maid said cheerfully.

"Ah, then go down and check the door, please. I thought I heard a knock."

"I didn't 'ear h'it, ma'am," Violet said, but she hurried out, anyhow.

As soon as she was alone, Lucy poured the bitter brew into the slop jar and set down the empty cup, hoping that Violet had not picked a large supply of the unknown plant.

She was both excited and nervous. To be sure, she had been regretting her lack of social outings, but she'd never meant to start so high! What if she disgraced the elegant viscount completely? Lord Richmond would never want her help with the mystery, then.

And besides, for some reason she didn't care to examine too closely, the thought of earning his scorn troubled her. She wanted his respect; surely that was not unreasonable?

Lucy sighed, considering it, then picked up her hair brush. The viscount would be here soon. It would not do to be late.

"No one there, ma'am." Violet said, coming back into the room.

"Sorry, my mistake," Lucy murmured.

Violet dressed her hair. The little maid brushed Lucy's fair hair and smoothed it into a knot at the back of her head; Lucy gazed into the looking-glass and nodded. "Thank you, Violet."

"You should try the new crop, ma'am; the maid next door says short hair's all the fashion now with fine ladies."

Lucy shook her head automatically. Stanley had always preferred her hair long. But then, she no longer had to worry about pleasing Stanley, who had favored a demure, almost dowagerlike appearance for his wife.

Still, she had no time to consider drastic changes this afternoon. She inserted the small pearl eardrops handed down from her mother and pulled on a pair of gloves. She felt amazingly fine in her new gloves and hand-me-down dress. Lucy allowed herself another glance into the looking glass, then heard a rap at the front door.

This time Violet looked up, nodding. "I 'eard it, too."

"Go down, Violet, and be sure to check through the window, first, just to be sure it is the viscount."

"Yes, ma'am. You 'ave a lovely time, do," the girl told her, hurrying out of the bedchamber.

Lucy made her way more slowly down the narrow staircase, her heart hammering now that the moment had come. She found Lord Richmond standing in the hallway, awaiting her descent, and she was rewarded for all her efforts by the look on the viscount's face.

"You look splendid, Mrs. Contrain." He bowed. "That shade is most becoming."

Lucy flushed. "Thank you," she said. "I hope it is a suitable outfit for such an occasion. I confess I have little experience with this kind of social event."

He smiled slightly at her candor. "I have no doubt you will be the object of universal admiration."

Lucy raised her brows. "I may be gullible, my lord, but not green enough to believe that! However, as long as I do not embarrass you—"

He flashed his alluring smile. "Never," he assured her. "Shall we go? My carriage is waiting."

She felt exquisitely pampered, walking out of her unpretentious home to be handed into a handsome deep blue chaise by the viscount himself. Seeing a flicker of movement from an upper window across the way, Lucy wondered just how many of her neighbors were watching and speculating. Gossip would be flying along her lane before the carriage was out of sight! She pushed the thought aside, relishing instead the feel of the soft velvet cushions that lined the carriage seat. And neat wooden shutters at the window that opened and shut—she had never ridden in such a well-made equipage.

The viscount took his seat beside her—she was intensely aware of him, sitting so close—so aware that she made herself look deliberately away. She took a long breath, then found that not a wise idea. He smelt so lovely, all clean linen and musky male scent. She glanced up at him, and found that was a mistake, too. His dark eyes glinted with humor, but as always, the laughter that lurked in their deep brown depths had a feel of comradery to it. He never seemed to laugh at her, or rail at her mistakes, as Stanley had so often done.

She cleared her throat. "Ah, is there anything I should know before we arrive at the salon? About the duchess, for instance?"

The viscount considered. "Our hostess is a lady of good humor and middle years. She was once a favorite of the prince regent, but now I believe they are only good friends. He looks in on the salon occasionally, but not every week."

Lucy blinked; good heavens, this was moving in exalted company, indeed. She had never set eyes on the prince, except once years ago when she had glimpsed him from the street when he had been riding by in an elaborate carriage. Her mother had pointed him out to the young Lucy. She remembered the round good-looking face and the romantically long locks framing it, and most of all, his beaming smile.

"What do you think we can accomplish here? I mean, what do you wish me to do?" That he could not do very well by himself, she really meant. Of course, it had been her idea to help him find the ruby; she had just never expected the search to take her to a duchess's drawing room.

"Chat with the people at the salon—see if you can find anyone who knew your husband. I'd much like to know why he was at the salon, and who brought him," the viscount pointed out, his tone matter-of-fact.

This was so sensible that Lucy blushed that she had not thought of it herself. "Of course."

Talk to a large number of strangers . . . try to find out

what they knew about her own husband that she should have known and did not. Damn Stanley—even after his death, he seemed determined to thrust her into awkward situations.

Her stomach felt as if it were full of rampaging butterflies; she drew a deep, calming breath. Too soon, they had rolled out of Cheapside and into the more fashionable west side of London, where the townhouses were tall and elegant and well maintained. Some of the squares had small green parks in the middle, and Lucy almost forgot to be nervous as she gazed out the window at the passing scene. So many carriages, too, and such well-dressed ladies and handsomely tailored gentlemen who strolled or rode.

Not that she saw anyone who could eclipse the handsome aristocrat beside her. She turned her head and found that Lord Richmond was watching her.

At once she felt self-conscious—she must be gaping like a country lass come into the city for the first time. She felt the ready flush spring to her cheeks and tried to think of something sensible to say.

"What is the theme of the salon? Does the duchess enjoy the arts, or politics, or is this a purely social gathering?"

The viscount considered, then flashed his beguiling smile. "I believe you will hear more gossip and gossamer than affairs of state and substance, but our hostess enjoys a good joke and entertaining anecdotes."

Oh dear. Lucy knew no gossip and she certainly had no store of amusing stories. She swallowed.

And now the chaise was pulling up in front of a large handsome home, with a fanlight over the wide double doors. As the vehicle rolled to a stop, she heard the horses stamp their feet, and a footman hurried to open the chaise door. He put down the steps and stood ready to offer a hand as Lucy climbed carefully out. She rubbed her fingers together, feeling the delicate leather of her gloves, then lifted her chin. She could do this.

Think about finding the gem and paying off your debts,

think about saving your home, Lucy told herself. No, for this moment, just think of maintaining your calm and not disgracing yourself by some gauche and unmannerly action. This was no place to spill your tea!

Lord Richmond was beside her now, offering his arm. She was happy to rest her hand lightly in its crook, and she only hoped he would not detect the slight tremor of nervousness.

The butler accepted the viscount's hat and gloves and escorted them personally up the wide staircase and through the open doorway into the drawing room.

The viscount murmured her name to the servant in expensive livery who stood at the doorway, he himself obviously needed no introduction. The footman declaimed in echoing accents: "The Viscount Richmond and Mrs. Contrain."

Lucy flushed, did she imagine the stares? She wondered how many of the elegantly attired men and women in the big room remembered the details surrounding her husband's death.

A woman with a wide smile and wider hips came up to them, her gait unhurried and her expression gracious; this must be the duchess.

"My dear Richmond, how good to see you again. You've been absent far too long!"

He bowed over her hand. "I've been traveling in Europe on family business that could not be delegated. I'm happy to bask in your charming company again, your grace."

She beamed, then threw a glance toward Lucy. "And your friend, delighted to meet you, Mrs.—Contrain."

"Thank you," Lucy murmured, exchanging curtsies, making sure to dip low enough to defer to the other lady's exalted rank and more advanced age. "I'm very happy to be here."

"You'll find some amusing fellows here today, Richmond, but no one with your store of shocking anecdotes. Do come and sit by me on the settee and make me laugh; I've been amazingly bored this sennight."

With a bow to their hostess and a barely discernable wink to Lucy, the viscount followed the duchess to a nearby divan.

Left behind at the edge of the room, Lucy gulped. She faced a very large and elegant room, full of very stiff and intimidating strangers. Oh, dear, and it wasn't as if she were practiced in such affairs. For a moment, she felt almost frozen with fright, then the absurdity of the situation tempered her anxiety. After all that she had survived in the last year, threatening tradesmen and endless dunning, the gradual ebb of her tiny store of pounds and shillings, how dreadful could it be, after all, to attend a duchess's salon?

Lucy took another slow breath and noticed cups of tea and glasses of wine on the trays the servants carried here and there among the crowd, and three-tiered plates of delicious-looking sandwiches and cakes and other pastries. If the butterflies were rioting in her middle, at least they would be well fed.

She accepted a cup of tea and allowed a maid to serve her a delicate Wedgwood plate of petit fours and tiny sandwiches. Then she discovered that while one might actually balance a full cup of steaming tea in one hand and a plate of edibles in the other, it was then impossible to actually eat anything, nor did she have a hand to lift the fragile cup from its saucer.

Oh, dear. Lucy looked about for an empty seat, and at last saw a spot next to an elderly lady who wore deep puce and a dyspeptic frown. Steeling herself, Lucy walked across the room and sat gracefully down.

"May I join you?" She set her plate on the small table at her elbow and was able at last to sip the excellent tea. "How do you do? I am Mrs. Contrain."

"No doubt," the other woman said, her tone cool. "Lady Marible. You know the name, I'm sure. My family has sat in the House of Lords for seven generations."

"How wonderful," Lucy agreed, suppressing a grin as her companion proceeded to reel off a long line of distinguished forebears. Lucy took a bite of cake, oh, scrumptious! The sweetness of the delicacy almost ameliorated the sourness of the other woman's expression. And she soon found that the cucumber-and-creamed-salmon sandwiches were just as good. When the older woman paused at last, Lucy said, "A most impressive list of ancestors. I'm sure you do them proud. Do you come to the duchess's salon often?"

"Every week," the dowager said, the three ostrich plumes that adorned her headdress waving as she gestured. The lady wore an elaborate gown trimmed with flounces of purple roses and a thick choker of pearls that made Lucy feel naked by comparison. Lucy smoothed the sleek blue silk of her gown to reassure herself, and the feel of the lovely gown renewed her confidence.

"The duchess only invites the cream of society, the top of the Ton," Lady Marible added, her tone abrupt. "Usually."

Lucy decided she would not consider this a personal slight. "Perhaps you have met my late husband here, Mr. Stanley Contrain?"

The other lady grimaced. "Doubt it. I only talk to people I know."

The idiocy of that statement made Lucy almost choke on her last sandwich. She chewed and swallowed. "I prefer conversing with strangers, myself, so much more diverting."

The older woman stared at her, as if not sure if Lucy were assaying a jest. "Too much riffraff allowed into society nowadays."

Lucy sighed. This was going nowhere. "Perhaps you are acquainted with the countess of Sealey?" she suggested. "The countess has a weekly salon, too, and—"

"That woman? When she was younger, she—well—" Lady Marible's mouth pinched as if she had bitten into a sour plum. "I have heard some scandalous tales of her early years. I would not lower myself to visit her home."

Lucy stiffened. She could ignore personal snubs, but her friend would not be impugned. "How unfortunate for you! The countess is a lady of wit and refinement. And great kindness and loyalty, I might add. Her friends are privileged to know her."

Lucy's neighbor blinked at such outright rebellion. "But—"

"I shall leave you to enjoy your solitude, and to chat with those people whom you already know." Lucy took one last drink of her tea and rose. Anyhow, she had finished her tidbits, and sitting too close to this prune-faced, mean-spirited female would diminish anyone's appetite.

She walked away too quickly, and almost bumped into a stout gentleman crossing the room. "Oh, pardon me," she said.

He glanced at her, and then looked her up and down, smiling as if the prospect pleased him. "No, no, my fault entirely. Should have looked what I was about. Mr. Carley-Smyth, at your service."

"Not at all," Lucy assured him. "And I am happy to meet you. I am Mrs. Contrain."

He bowed over her hand, holding it just a moment too long. "You must be new to the duchess's salon? Don't recall seeing you before, and I would certainly remember such a fresh, lovely face."

Lucy blushed. "Yes, this is my first visit. But perhaps you met my late husband, Stanley?"

Mr. Carley-Smyth wrinkled his brow for an instant, then shook his head. "Don't believe so, my dear. But let me get you a glass of wine, we should certainly get acquainted."

He seemed as enthused about her company as Lady Marible had not. But he also claimed no memory of Stanley. Suppressing an inner sigh of impatience, Lucy chatted for a few minutes, then made her escape as soon as she politely could.

Moving across the room to choose another guest to question, Lucy was surprised to see a familiar face. Familiar, but not necessarily welcome.

"Fancy meeting you here," Marion Tennett said, her tone arch and her eyes as sharp and narrow as they had been at Mrs. Morris's dinner party. "I understood that you didn't go out into company much, my dear."

"I manage to unchain myself from my fireside occasionally. How do you do?" Lucy said, her tone carefully noncommittal. She trusted this woman about as much as a moth would trust a spider as it hovered an inch above a sticky web. At least the viscount was still monopolized by the duchess, and Marion Tennett could not blame Lucy for his lack of attention.

"I see you've put aside your mourning, how sensible of you," Marion Tennett noted, her tone honey-smooth.

"It was time." Lucy glanced down at her soft silk and kept her voice neutral. She would not permit this woman to induce unnecessary guilt. "After all, it's been over a year since my husband's death."

"I suppose so," Mrs. Tennett replied, as if reluctant to admit that Lucy had not committed a social faux pas. "Early March, wasn't it?"

"Yes, it was." Lucy looked at her more carefully. "Your recollection is very exact. I thought you did not know my husband, Mrs. Tennett? Has your memory sharpened? Perhaps you met him here at the duchess's salon?"

The other woman shrugged, her smile suggestive. "Perhaps, now and again. I hardly remember."

Was this the truth? Lucy tried to think of more questions that would decide the accuracy of this woman's remarks. "I suppose he came here to enjoy the gossip and bon mots?"

Stanley had enjoyed gossip, and sometimes, when his mood was good, had regaled her with stories of aristocratic scandals, though he usually refused to tell her how he had heard them. "At my club," he would say vaguely, "having a drink with the fellows, you know."

Mrs. Tennett looked arch. "You should know that better than anyone, my dear; he was your husband!"

Lucy flushed. If she had known Stanley the way a wife should know her husband, she would not be in this predicament now. But she could hardly confess this to a stranger, much less one as hostile as Marion Tennett.

"Yes, indeed," she murmured. "Is your own husband

here?" She glanced through the crowd for the short, portly man who had accompanied Mrs. Tennett to the earlier dinner party.

For some reason, this made the other woman frown. "I believe I see a friend I should speak to." She swept abruptly away, leaving Lucy blinking in surprise. On the whole, however, she did not regret losing a companion of such uncertain temper.

A servant passed with another silver tray, and Lucy accepted more sandwiches. She nibbled on one, and, when no one was looking, tucked the other inside her reticule to save for Violet.

Lucy chatted with several more people, but despite Mrs. Tennett's vague comment, no one else seemed to remember her husband. Yet the duchess's name had been in his appointment book. Had Stanley visited the salon only once? Why, and how on earth had he received an invitation. Had someone brought him along, as the viscount had done with Lucy, and if so, who?

Speaking of which, the viscount appeared to have been at last released from his duty to his hostess. Lucy looked up and found him at her elbow.

"Any luck?" he asked quietly.

"The only person I have spoken to who admitted to any possible memory of my husband was your old friend," Lucy said.

He raised his dark brows.

"Mrs. Tennett, who made such a fuss at the dinner party last Monday," she reminded him, keeping her tone bland.

He grimaced. "Ah yes, I saw her in the crowd."

"I'm sure she will be swooping down to claim you any moment," Lucy pointed out. "What about the duchess, did you ask her about Stanley?"

"She says she doesn't remember meeting him, nor does she have any idea how he came to be invited to her salon, if he was. On the other hand, Her Grace has the memory of a peahen," he answered, in a low voice meant for Lucy's ears alone. "That does not necessarily mean your husband has not attended this gathering."

"According to Mrs. Tennett, he may have," Lucy argued. "However, I can find no one else who can remember him. You might try to get more details out of her, since you're the one she has a tendre for."

He raised his brows again. "And that annoys you?"

She wished she could retract those last impulsive words. "Of course not, your social acquaintances are of your own choosing. I wish you every . . . happiness in your dealings with Mrs. Tennett."

His grin was wry, but it faded when she added, "And here she is, now!"

She saw the annoyance flicker in his dark eyes before he smoothed his expression into one of smooth urbanity. He turned and bowed to the newcomer.

"My dear Lord Richmond," Marion Tennett purred. "How delightful to see you again."

"Charmed," he said, but his tone was dry.

"Let us sit and have a lovely little chat," she suggested, her lashes dipping into a flutter of invitation.

"Of course," the viscount agreed, with a bland glance toward Lucy. "Would you like to join us, Mrs. Contrain?"

"No, no, I would not dream of disturbing a tête-à-tête between such old friends," Lucy said cheerfully. "I believe I see an acquaintance in the crowd, please excuse me."

She marched away, her back straight, although her excuse was only that. But now she had to speak to someone or look foolish indeed. She headed for a group of matrons at the side of the room, and paused on the edge of the crowd until one of the women caught her eye.

"How do you do?" the other woman said. "Mrs. Maldear. I'm sorry, I don't believe I recall your name."

"Mrs. Contrain," Lucy told her. "You may have met my late husband at the duchess's salon?"

"I'm afraid I don't recall him," the other woman said. "Did he come for the duke's card game in the library?"

That was the most sensible observation anyone had yet made. Stanley conversing with the upper crust was hard to imagine, Stanley playing cards with anyone at all made no strain on her imagination.

"Perhaps," Lucy suggested. "Does the duke play cards every week?"

"Oh yes," the older woman said, plying her fan. "Although the games are held on Tuesday and Thursdays, I understand, not today."

Lucy frowned. The date book had said Friday, quite clearly. If only she knew what to think, and what Stanley had been up to. How could he have been connected to a jewel robbery? It was too far-fetched.

She pretended to listen to the other women as the conversation resumed around her, lots of amusing stories about people she had never met and had no interest in at all. As she allowed her gaze to stray about the room, she saw an older gentleman emerge through a set of velvet curtains.

Was there a card game this afternoon, despite what the other woman had told her? If so, that would make Stanley's attendance a year ago more likely. She murmured a farewell to the group and drifted across the room to peer into the next chamber. But before she could part the draperies and take a look, a portly, middle-aged man of medium height and ruddy complexion strode through them, almost colliding with her.

"I'm s-so sorry," Lucy stammered. "I didn't mean—"

He gave her a brief but gallant bow. "Not at all, my dear girl, entirely my fault. Not looking where I was going, a bad habit."

Something about him teased her memory. She made her curtsy, sure from his easy self-confidence that this was a man of rank, though she wasn't sure—

Then she heard the viscount's voice. "Your highness."

Oh, dear! This was the prince regent himself! Lucy blinked and wished she had dipped even lower. He had aged since she'd seen him all those years ago, well, of course he would have. But the fast living intimated by the scandal sheets had added more lines to his face and more pounds to the rotund figure than might have otherwise accrued. Yet, his smile was as broad as she remembered, and he chatted with the viscount as if they were old acquaintances. The royal personage roared with laughter at some jest that she had not even heard.

"And your lovely friend?" the prince said, after his gulps of laughter at last faded. "You must introduce me, Richmond."

"Yes, your highness. This is Mrs. Stanley Contrain."

The stout prince beamed at her, but then his smile faded. "Contrain? That the fellow you think might be involved in—you know—"

"Possibly, yes," the viscount said, his tone quiet. "Mrs. Contrain is offering her help in deciphering the mystery."

"Oh, good show," the future king of England exclaimed. "You must find it, Richmond, or I shall be in such a stew—if the broadsheets learn of this—as if I haven't been roasted by them often enough!"

Lucy swallowed hard. The viscount made a subtle sign, and the prince lowered his too boisterous voice.

"Yes, yes, I know. If this gets out—" He paused and pulled out a large handkerchief, dabbing at his florid face, now a little shiny with perspiration. "I've got a dozen Bow Street runners on it, and some chaps from the Foreign Office, but they've come up with nothing at all. I know you're the one who can find it, Richmond, if anyone can." He sighed lustily.

"And if this lady is disposed to help us, well, I'm in your debt, ma'am." He gave her another courtly bow, and Lucy only hoped that his words were prophetic.

"You should both come along next Tuesday to my theater party, just a small intimate group," he added, about to turn away. "Bring her along, Richmond, you hear?"

"Of course, your highness," the viscount agreed. "We should be honored."

Honored? Lucy felt a qualm of pure disbelief. Flabbergasted was more accurate. Having tea with a duchess had taxed her nerves quite enough; now she was gadding about with a prince? What in the name of heaven had

Stanley been up to, to involve her in such complicated puzzles?

She swallowed hard and managed a smile. The prince lifted her chin as if she were a child. "A fetching gal," he murmured. "Bit of luck for you, Richmond, what?"

The viscount, thankfully, made no reply to this blatantly suggestive remark and merely bowed again. The prince swept off to greet the hostess of the salon. Watching him go, Lucy saw the crowd dipping into bows and curtsies, marking his progress through the crowded room like a swathe cutting through a field of grain.

"Surely he didn't mean—"

"Surely, he did," the viscount said. "Always has an eye for a pretty face, our Prinny, even though he himself prefers his amours older and more experienced."

Lucy blinked, trying not to imagine the stout form of the prince and the well-endowed duchess of Rockhaven in an intimate embrace. She didn't know whether to frown or giggle at such an image.

She gave herself a mental shake and pulled her thoughts back to their own particular entanglement. "Did you learn anything from Mrs. Tennett?"

He shook his head, looking as frustrated as she already felt. "Marion either denies all knowledge or hints at outrageous possibilities in which I have little credence."

"No doubt wanting more of your attentions," Lucy murmured, but this time she was careful to keep her tone bland. "Except for Mrs. Tennett, whose memory seems, um, undependable, I have had no luck finding anyone who could remember seeing Stanley here, even though I've spoken to more strangers this afternoon than I have in the last year."

The viscount seemed to take that as a hint. "Then we may as well take our leave," he suggested. They made their farewells, thanked their hostess, and were soon seated side by side in the viscount's luxurious chaise.

This time Lucy was less interested in the comfort of the carriage's padded seats, although she could never quite ignore the strength of Lord Richmond's masculine presence. But just now she felt thwarted and of no help at all. At this rate, how were they going to find out anything about Stanley's habits, much less the missing gem?

And if she could not earn the reward—Lucy shut her eyes and pushed away images of men pounding on her door, pushing two homeless women into the street.

She had to be helpful—she needed a thousand pounds!

Six

When they reached her home, the viscount helped her out of the chaise and then knocked at the door him-self, but there was no answer.

"Is your servant in?"

"She usually is, unless she's out picking more weeds to brew for me," Lucy muttered.

Lord Richmond looked perplexed. "Weeds?"

She waved the question aside and unlocked the door herself. "Violet must have gone on an errand."

Lucy opened the door, and the viscount followed her into the tiny hall. She sniffed. There was an odor in the house she didn't immediately recognize. Had Violet left a pot of onion soup too close to the edge of the fire? Something didn't smell right. Lucy needed to thank the viscount for his escort, but first—

"If you don't mind, let me just check the house," she told him. Not waiting for his assent, she hurried into the kitchen.

As she entered the room, a howl as deep as a foghorn

almost knocked her off her feet. She had forgotten about
Lucifer.

Lucy shrieked. Lord Richmond hurried into the kitchen
after her, only to come to an abrupt halt when he saw the
huge dog, which had jumped to its feet. The fiend had
apparently been napping comfortably in front of the
hearth—some watchdog! But now it seemed ready to
make up for its momentary lapse. It bayed again and took
a step forward, lifting its heavy muzzle and eyeing them
with suspicion.

"Good God," the viscount exclaimed. Grabbing Lucy's
arm, he shoved her behind him. He lifted one hand in
reprimand as the dog snarled. Its teeth were large and
slightly yellow, and its eyes glittered. "Back!"

Lucy peered around him, feeling much like a lamb confronting a ravenous wolf. She tried not to reveal her terror;
it would only encourage the beast. And the viscount did
not even have a walking stick.

"Down!" The viscount said, his tone forceful enough
to make up for his lack of a weapon, but instead of heed-
ing the admonition, the dog growled again and crouched.

Cold with fear, Lucy tried to remember the commands
that could control this beast. What words had Violet used?
Her mind felt clouded by panic.

"Sit!" she yelled.

The dog took another step closer. Its growl seemed to
fill the kitchen.

Lucy wracked her brain. "No, that wasn't it. Back, no.
Oh, I know, to earth!"

But instead of obeying, the dog lunged.

Lucy heard a ripping of fabric and a muffled curse. The
viscount, through some superhuman feat of strength,
pulled away from the big muzzle and the dog howled
again. Lord Richmond pushed her through the nearest
doorway, jumped in behind her, then slammed the heavy
door before the dog could follow.

It bayed again and sprang against the door, which shuddered under the animal's immense weight.

Lucy held her breath, and she felt the matching tenseness of the man beside her. The dog scratched at the door once more, then she could hear it pacing up and down, the nails of its massive paws clicking against the slate floor.

She leaned against the viscount, shivering with fear. Lord Richmond put one arm around her, and gradually her trembling stopped. In a few moments, she lifted her head from his chest.

They were in the pantry. A tiny chamber lined with shelves, it had only one small window high at the back. The light was murky, and although Violet scrubbed the shelves and the stone floor regularly, Lucy could make out a few motes of dust swirling in the faint beam that broke through the dimness. The tiny space smelled of long-eaten meat pies and salted fish, of cinnamon cloves and nutmeg, and of some smallish onions that hung in ropes from the ceiling.

The viscount was silent, but his body still seemed stiff. She glanced down at him and drew a deep breath.

"Heavens, you are wounded!" Well, of course, the dog had taken hold with its huge jaws. "I am so sorry, my lord! I should have remembered he was here. How bad is it?"

"Nothing to signify," he answered, his voice controlled. But she saw the blood staining one leg of his once buff-colored pantaloons.

"Let me see," she commanded, dropping to her knees and pulling off her gloves.

"Mrs. Contrain, this is hardly proper," he pointed out. This time his voice wavered it. Was he weak with pain?

Glancing up, she saw with annoyance that he looked more inclined to chuckle. His dark eyes glinted with suppressed laughter.

"I am a widow, my lord, if you recall. I have seen a man unclothed before," she told him, lifting her chin and keeping her tone dignified. "Besides, I do not wish to see you bleed to death in front of my eyes!"

She pushed apart the shredded knit fabric and bit her lip as she surveyed the damage the dog had done.

"It's only—ah—" Lord Richmond braced himself as she dabbed at the drops of blood. "A slight wound."

"I must beg to differ. It's still bleeding, I need to wash and bind it," she told him. "I regret, my lord, that I must ask you to lower your pantaloons."

She refused to meet his gaze, sure that the wicked humor still bubbled in the depths of his dark eyes despite the pain he must be feeling.

"I have seldom had that request made under such, um, unpropitious circumstances," he pointed out, but he did as he was bid.

His thighs were firm and muscular, she couldn't help noticing, and his olive-toned skin pleasant to look on. She kept her gaze carefully averted from the undergarments that covered his private area and concentrated on the lacerations the dog had inflicted. The bite did not look deep, though it had ripped open the skin in two large gashes.

"Nor with less pleasurable consequences," she agreed, grimly. "I do not have any water at hand to wash this with, until we are rescued from that monster, but—oh, the brandy!" She had spied the bottle, bought with the viscount's own funds, sitting on an otherwise empty shelf. And she had a stack of clean cloths that were used in the kitchen. She would make do with what she had.

"I'm going to clean this with the brandy and then make a bandage," she told him. "We really cannot leave this unattended."

The viscount eyed the bottle doubtfully. "A terrible waste of reasonably good brandy. Besides, it's going to hurt like hell."

"I'm afraid so," she agreed. She offered him a sip first.

"The condemned man gets a last drink?" His expression wry, he took a hearty swig, then returned the bottle to her.

About to pour it over his leg, Lucy paused; her hand still had a tendency to shake. She did not usually partake of such strong liquor, but considering the attack—she took a long drink straight from the bottle, the brandy burning its way down her throat and into her belly. She coughed, then went back to her task.

"Stand as still as you can," she told him.

He grimaced, but braced himself. Even so, when the sharp bite of the alcohol touched the open wound, he jumped.

"Just another moment," she told him, grimacing in sympathy. "The worst is almost over, truly."

"Easy for you to say, when you're the one holding the bottle!" The viscount muttered a few more words beneath his breath that she was just as glad not to distinguish. But in a minute, she was ripping up a clean cloth to lay against the shredded skin, then tying it in place as best she could.

"If you don't move too much, I think it will hold," she said in a moment. When she raised her head to regard him, she shook her head. "You're very pale, my lord. I think you need to sit down."

"Where?" he asked, succinctly.

There were no stools inside the pantry, not even a box or a barrel. Lucy looked around, not sure what to answer.

"I'll be fine," he asserted, but he was indeed very white. He leaned against the door. It creaked a little, and the beast outside growled, making Lucy shiver.

"I'll just stand," he said, his voice not quite normal.

Lucy watched in horrified fascination as, his legs folding neatly beneath him, the viscount slid very slowly down to the stone floor.

Oh, dear. He had slumped forward. She moved across to kneel beside him, putting her arms around him to steady him—she did not want him to bang his head against the stone floor if he passed out altogether. When she felt she had him secure, she shifted position and sat down next to him. The floor felt cold through her thin skirt—surely this was not good for an injured man.

"My lord, I am so sorry!" she murmured, not sure if in his present state he could hear her. But his answer came quickly.

"We shall have to take our enemies more seriously," he told her. "I knew they were murderous, but I didn't expect them to destroy us one bite at a time."

"Ah." Lucy hesitated, then decided it was no use putting off the revelation. "I regret to inform you—that thing outside is the result of a friend's efforts, my lord."

"You have dangerous friends, then," the viscount pointed out. This time his voice was stronger, she was glad to note. She turned her head to face him. He looked more like his normal self; his color was returning.

"Violet borrowed the animal from the butcher's boy," Lucy explained, her words coming out all in a rush. "She can make it mind, but it doesn't seem to heed my words—perhaps I said the wrong command."

"By all means, search your memory," the viscount suggested, his lips curving into a smile. "Or we shall be here for some time. I do not think we can overcome that beast by brute force. Not without a pistol—on second thought, make that an elephant gun."

Glancing at his injured leg, Lucy shivered. "No, no, we mustn't damage it. Violet should be back soon."

She saw his gaze scan the bare shelves, and, embarrassed that he should witness their destitute state, spoke quickly. "Are you feeling better?"

The viscount frowned. He felt like hell. His leg throbbed—he just hoped that beast was not rabid—and he had seldom been displayed in such a dismal light to a lady he had vowed to protect. But Lucy Contrain did not seem of a mind to chastise him for his shortcomings as a dragon—or dog—slayer. She watched him anxiously, and he tried to smile for her benefit. He felt remarkably uncomfortable; the door behind him was hard and had already, he was sure, inflicted a few splinters in sensitive areas of his anatomy. The stone floor was cold and dank, and the light was dim.

But the woman who squeezed herself so close to him—ah, now. That was another story. He felt his awareness of her surge into something close to genuine need. This was hardly the time for a little carefree seduction. But her cheeks were flushed and her fair hair slipping out of its pins. She leaned so close, her arms still wrapped around his chest to support him in his moment of weakness, that he could feel her firm round breasts pressed against him, and she had no idea just how tempting she was.

At least his wound should be good for something; he could no doubt use her natural sympathy to lead her to lower her guard . . . and then something he had almost forgotten he still possessed raised its hoary head—a twinge of . . . conscience.

It was hardly fair to use his injury to seduce an honorable woman. He had been spending too much time with termagants like Marion Tennett. Nicholas smothered a sigh.

"I think perhaps you should sit on the other side of the room," he suggested.

Shifting she looked up at his face. "Am I hurting you? I'm so sorry."

"No, rather the opposite." He smiled down into her warm blue eyes. "I'm afraid you feel altogether too—ah—appealing."

She gazed at him for a moment, her eyes widening, then an adorable flush swept over her face, all the way down to her neckline. "I didn't—that is, I don't mean—"

"Oh, I know. You meant only to sooth my fevered brow, not raise the beast, inside our refuge as well as out."

She could hear the click of the dog's massive nails against the slate floor as it prowled up and down outside their hiding place. And she understood the viscount's reference perfectly and did her best not to blush again. Of course it would be more proper not to sit so close to him.

But it felt so lovely, leaning inside his arm, feeling his hand on hers, laying her head against his chest. He felt warm and solid and strong, and it had been such a long time . . . well, that was hardly his concern.

And he had had the grace to warn her. She must not suggest that she was open to invitations for improper conduct.

"I only wished to keep you from passing out on to the hard floor," she explained, with as much dignity as she could muster. The fact that she had enjoyed their close contact could not be discussed.

"Of course, and you have my gratitude. Doubly so, for sparing my head a knock as well as for dressing my wound." His tone was suitably grave, but that spark of wicked humor lingered in his dark eyes.

Damn the man. He probably sensed exactly what her response to him was. Lucy's sympathy for him, fired by the injury incurred on her behalf, faded just a bit. "I'm not—I never—"

"Of course not," he agreed, and this time his eyes twinkled, she would swear to it.

Lucy slid a little way across the cold floor, putting a gap of at least six inches between them.

"Oh, that's much better," he agreed, his tone silky.

"Be serious, if you please!" Lucy snapped. "I don't have a great deal of latitude, you know. I'm sorry my pantry is so small, but—"

Outside the dog snarled and lunged at the door—she had spoken too loudly. Lucy jumped and put out one hand. It was only an instinctive gesture, but the viscount clasped it at once, his grip reassuringly strong.

She returned the pressure, of no mind to release him. If she had to face the canine monster outside the door, a door which seemed less and less sturdy the more the beast rattled its rusty hinges, she was glad to have an ally. Propriety be damned. What was that compared to being devoured by great drooling jaws?

"I've never cared for large dogs," she tried to explain. "When I was very small, a mastiff chased me up a tree. I was stuck there for hours." Her voice wavered just a little, and he shifted his body closer once more so that he could put his arm about her shoulders.

She did not resist. It seemed so natural to shelter inside his arm, normal to rest her head for an instant against his chest. Perhaps it was the brandy; something powerful surged inside her, and her thoughts seemed a little fuzzy.

"Mrs. Contrain? Are you ill? Don't pass out," she heard him say.

"It's my turn." Though she would blush for the words later, they seemed, just now, to make perfect sense.

She felt the sting as he slapped her cheek.

"Ouch!" She opened her eyes. "Why did you do that?"

"I don't want you swooning on me," he told her, his voice firm. "Over me, perhaps."

She opened her mouth to protest, but he interrupted before she could get her thoughts together.

"Would you like another sip of the brandy? I believe there's a bit left in the bottle."

That might not be a good idea, she thought, but she couldn't make the words come out; her brain was still strangely fogged and the room whirled around her. So she nodded instead and swallowed when he held the bottle to her lips, shivering as the potent liquid burned its way down to her stomach.

She blinked again, but at least now she could see his face. He looked genuinely concerned.

"Take slow, deep breaths. . . . Is that better?"

"Yes, thank you. I'm sorry to be such a milksop." She struggled to sit up straighter, but he did not remove the arm that supported her.

He glanced around the almost bare larder. "I think you're weak from a scanty diet and exhausted from worry."

She thought about arguing, but it would have taken too much effort. "No matter," she told him. "I'll be all right, presently."

"Yes, my dear Mrs. Contrain," he said, and his tone was different than it had been, though she could not identify the change, "I promise you, life will get better."

He lifted his other hand to touch her cheek very gently.

Lucy turned her head toward the feather-light contact, and the touch became a caress. She shut her eyes, shivering again but from a totally different emotion, as his fingers moved across her cheek, up her temple, and across her brow, slowly down the other cheek and then, sending tremors of response through her body, he traced the outline of her lips.

Lucy tried not to gasp. But she opened her lips instinctively, and when he paused, she pursed her lips around his fingertip, touching it with the tip of her tongue.

She felt the reaction in him, though he made no outward movement. For an instant, they seemed frozen, as if
this were a tableau from a theater pantomime, then he
moved his hand and used both to hold her face. He
pressed his mouth to hers.

His kiss was firm but questioning, asking more than
demanding. Her answer came at once. An immediate response rushed through her body, and she pressed against
him, eager for his kiss to deepen, which it did, for his
arms to pull her nearer, and they did.

She moved her own hands up and caught the dark,
slightly curling hair at the back of his neck and pulled
him even closer. She was as hungry for this as she had
ever been for a hearty dinner, and despite the rapid physical response inside her, she knew it was much more than
just her body's need.

This man felt right, from his teasing glance to his wry
wit, to his instinctive readiness to protect her. It could
have been Lucy whom the dog had bitten, but the viscount
had pushed her out of the way, without pausing for an
instant to consider his own safety.

And, God, he stirred feelings inside her that she had
not felt since—no, had never felt, not like this. . . .

The kiss lasted until at last they broke apart, both
breathing hard. Lucy could feel tendrils of her hair falling
out of the knot that had held them back—they tickled her
cheek. She tried to push them back, but they fell forward
again. The viscount pushed a curly lock gently aside.

"I think," he said, his voice husky, "that unless we are
released from this cubbyhole soon, you will be in jeop-
ardy from more than a belligerent beast."

"Or simply a different type of beast?" She lifted her
brows.

"Quite possibly," he agreed, bending closer.

"Thank goodness," she murmured, and lifted her head
to kiss him again.

Then a shriek from outside the door made them both
start. Lord Richmond pulled away and lifted his head, and

Lucy recognized Violet's voice. She sighed.

The maid was calling loudly. "Ma'am, come quick! Lucifer 'as caught an intruder in the pantry!"

"Lucifer has caught *me* in the pantry," Lucy corrected, trying not to sound as irked as she felt. Of course she had wanted Violet to return and release them, but did it have to be just now? Her lips still seemed to resonate with the impression left by her protector's kiss.

Glancing at the viscount, she could see evidence of a mixture of emotion on his face as well, though he soon smoothed his expression to its usually guarded urbanity. He got to his feet, moving a bit stiffly and favoring his injured leg, then put out a hand to Lucy.

She allowed him to help her up; they could hardly continue their lovemaking in the cramped confines of the pantry, with Violet and that horrid animal outside. Still, Lucy could not totally escape a pang of regret.

"Open the door, Violet," Lucy called. "And control that creature!"

In a moment the door creaked open—the dog's assault had definitely not helped the condition of the rusty hinges—and she emerged, with the viscount behind her.

The dog growled when it saw Lord Richmond, and Violet's eyes widened.

"I thought that creature obeyed commands." Lucy frowned at the animal.

"But it does, ma'am," Violet argued. "The butcher's boy—"

"I know, I know, but when I said, 'To earth,' it ignored me completely," Lucy pointed out. "Oh, be careful."

The dog was on its feet, and its lips were raised into a deep snarl. It seemed determined to consider the viscount in the form of a threat.

Violet looked puzzled. "I don't know why 'e didn't listen, ma'am. 'Ere, Lucifer, to h'earth!"

The dog sank back on its haunches.

"That's it," Lord Richmond said from behind her, his voice low. "It's 'to h'earth,' you see, not, 'to earth.'"

Lucy didn't know whether to laugh or scream. "Yes, I

see," she said. Violet's expression was still perplexed;
Lucy would not embarrass her by explaining just now.
"Violet, perhaps you would return this—this thing to the
butcher, with our thanks?"

"Yes, ma'am, if you want," Violet agreed, though she
looked disappointed. She led the big dog, loping along
quite peacefully behind her, out the back entrance.

Lucy drew a deep breath and turned to regard her—
almost—lover. If they had not been interrupted—well, it
was best not to consider that.

"You should return home and have a physician check
your wound," she suggested, even though she hated to see
him go.

He gazed at her. "I suppose the butcher's shop is close
by?"

"Yes," she agreed.

"And Violet will return almost at once?"

Lucy nodded, blushing a little. If he thought—

"Then I suppose I must. But I will return tomorrow,
Mrs. Contrain, and we will consult as to how next to
investigate your late husband's activities."

He was back to business again, and why should he not?
They had to find the ruby, to redeem the viscount's honor
and to ensure her survival. And they would; the interlude
in the pantry had been a—a—well, it was a mistake. She
must not allow her pent-up feelings to overcome her
again.

And mercy, she hadn't realized she had such strong . . .
feelings.

Lucy swallowed hard; she had been silent too long.

"Unless you don't wish to resume the search for the
gem? Perhaps you would rather I continued alone?" he
asked.

"Oh, no, I am committed, my lord, do not doubt it."
She put out one hand for him to clasp, telling herself it
was only a gesture of civility, not a desire to feel the
warmth of his skin one last time.

"Good." He bowed over her hand, lifting it unexpectedly to his lips. The touch of his kiss sent shivers all the

way to her toes. Before she could compose herself to make a polite reply, he had turned. She hurried after him and made sure that he climbed stiffly into his carriage without problem. The coachman lifted his reins, and the chaise pulled away.

Were her neighbors watching today? She hoped they had not made out the bloodstains and the torn pantaloons on her visitor. The rumors would be flying, indeed.

Shutting the door and bolting it, Lucy wrapped her arms about her in a solitary kind of hug and tried to rein in her unruly impulses. This would not do; she would end up without a reputation of any kind, except the worst. And if one part of her brain insisted that the viscount was just the man to throw away a reputation for, she could not afford to listen.

She sighed and returned to the kitchen, pulled up a stool to the hearth and gazed at the banked coals, waiting for Violet's return. If her thoughts lingered in the direction of the pantry, no one had to know.

When Violet returned, the maid put a few mealy potatoes on to boil for their dinner, and Lucy gave her the sandwiches she had smuggled out of the duchess's salon.

Lucy was pondering which of her hand-me-down clothes were elaborate enough to wear to the theater with a prince as one's host when Violet lifted her head.

"Someone's knocking at the door, ma'am," she pointed out.

Lucy picked up her stout walking stick and went to see, with Violet behind her. Lucy peered out the front window, first. "It's only a boy with a bundle—you can answer it."

Violet opened the door, and there was a mumble of conversation. When she shut it again, Lucy came to see. Violet held the wrapped package with both arms; she had her shoulders braced to bear the weight. And there was a wonderful salty aroma. What could it be?

" 'Ere's the note, ma'am," Violet said, nodding to a piece of paper grasped in one hand.

Lucy took it quickly. *"My dear Mrs. Contrain,"* it said. *"One of my tenants sent me a fresh-cured ham, and*

*since I will be out for dinner, I thought you might be able
to make use of it. Your servant, Richmond."*

What? She read the message again, aloud, then flushed
in mortification. That remark about her not getting enough
to eat, and he had seen their empty larder. Oh dear. She
really should send it back. It was dreadful to have to take
charity, even from the viscount, who was a much kinder
man than he liked to pretend.

Her stomach rumbled as if in protest. And there was
Violet to consider, too; how long could they go on surviving on watery soup and scraps of food smuggled out
of other people's parties? Lucy sighed.

"H'if that's not just like a man," Violet pointed out,
oblivious to her mistress's struggle with injured pride.
"H'it's not like a well-cured ham will spoil in one night!"

Lucy laughed reluctantly. "Mind your *h*'s, please. No,
indeed, but I supposed we must accept with thanks, do
you think?"

"Oh, yes, ma'am," Violet agreed, her eyes wide. "I'll
slice some of it for our dinner." She practically flew back
to the kitchen, despite the heavy burden in her arms, and
Lucy decided a little pride sacrificed for a hearty meal
was a small enough price to pay. Besides, when she got
the reward for recovering the ruby—which reminded her,
she had to pull her weight in that search.

She went back upstairs and steeled herself to open the
chest with her husband's things and go through them one
more time, just in case she found anything suggestive.

But she found nothing but the same worn clothing and
patched undergarments; her patches, her darns in his
stockings. Again, she marveled that Stanley had apparently been to a duchess's salon—how had he come to be
there? If they could figure out that, perhaps it would lead
to more information about her husband's unknown pursuits.

She heard a rap; someone else was at the door. She
shut the lid of the chest and returned to the small landing.
"Check the window, first," she called down to Violet, who
had come to answer it.

"Yes, ma'am," Violet agreed, ducking into the empty parlor. "It's another messenger," she reported shortly.

She hurried to open the door, and by the time Lucy had come down the steps, she found her maid struggling to hold an enormous basket filled with all sorts of foodstuffs.

"What has he done now?" Lucy exclaimed, not sure whether to be vexed or to weep with joy at the sight of fresh loaves of bread, jars of jams, crocks of pickles and other relishes, sugared fruits, and more.

This time the note said: *"My dear Mrs. Contrain, a few items to complement the ham. Your servant . . ."*

Really, the nerve of the man. She lifted her head as she heard a faint sizzling sound. "Violet, I think the potatoes are boiling over."

" 'O cares?" Violet said, then almost dropped the basket in her confusion. "H'I—I'm sorry, ma'am."

Lucy bit back a smile. "I know what you mean. Take this to the kitchen and rescue the potatoes. We'll have an early dinner."

"Oh, yes, ma'am." Violet's tone was rapturous. She hurried back to the kitchen, and Lucy paused to contemplate the annoying, exasperating, generous, arrogant man. Why did he hide his feelings under such a layer of cynical detachment? Perhaps most of his acquaintances might believe it, but she had seen—

Another rap at the door interrupted her thoughts. Really, now what? Had he sent linen and silverware, too?

She took the precaution of peeking through the front window, but again, it was only a skinny street urchin. His arms seemed empty, however.

Lucy opened the door herself and saw a slip of paper extended to her.

"Thank you," she said, but the boy in the ragged clothes had already darted away. A strange messenger.

She shut the door and bolted it, then unfolded the somewhat grimy paper. It said: *"I have a priceless object that belonged to your husband. If you wish to see it, I must have a hundred pounds."*

There was no signature. Lucy stared at the paper.

The ruby!

Seven

They had an early and most unorthodox dinner, and they both ate till they could barely move. Afterward, Lucy put away the remaining foodstuffs in the pantry—they had barely made a dent in the contents of the enormous basket despite their enthusiasm—while Violet scrubbed the dishes and pots. When the kitchen was clean again, Lucy sent Violet off to an early bed; the little maid looked heavy eyed from the unaccustomed largess of their meal.

"But, ma'am," Violet tried to say, her words interrupted by an enormous yawn. "I need to 'elp you off with your gown and brush your 'air."

"I'll manage, thank you, go to bed," Lucy said firmly.

She checked to be sure all the doors and windows were locked, and then climbed the stairs to her bedroom. In her room she managed to unbutton her dress and get into her nightgown, then she washed her face and unpinned her hair, shaking the long wavy locks free before brushing them absently, as she puzzled over the note.

Who could have sent it? She must send word to the

viscount first thing tomorrow. Her thoughts lingered for a time on which neighborhood lad they could persuade to undertake a long walk, on the hope that the viscount would reward him with a coin at the end of it. Oh, he would. Lord Richmond was a generous man. . . .

And all the while, Lucy tried to avoid the looming fact that she so dreaded to face. The note proved that Stanley must have been involved, after all, in the theft of the huge ruby. Oh, dear. How could it be true?

Her husband had been a thief.

It was impossible to believe. Certainly, Stanley had had his faults—he had kept secrets from her, and he had lived his life in a strange solitary fashion, not interested in taking his own wife out into company. Yet, he had also been so old-fashioned and stiff in some of his attitudes that she could not picture him as a larcenous man. They had attended church together every Sunday morning without fail, and he'd kept a prayer book by his bedside.

He had been so concerned with propriety that she was not allowed to wear dresses with low-cut necklines, no matter how fashionable or otherwise acceptable such styles were. She had acquiesced in his whim—it had not seemed important enough to argue about. There was so much more to weigh on his behalf—he had married her when no one else had paid her a second glance, allowed her to bring her mother with her into their tiny home, been unfailingly polite to his mama-in-law, and usually courteous, if sometimes strangely distant, to his wife.

She had much to thank him for, and she would never forget that. But the love, the true understanding she had wished for so deeply, had never developed between them. She had thought that liking and mutual respect might be enough to spark a joint attachment, that from the seeds of civility, love might grow. Instead, the longer they were married, the more distance had loomed between them, and eventually their relationship had withered into only the barest pretense of affection.

Not that he had seemed to hate her, or even dislike her—he simply wasn't interested. She served his tea and breakfast in the morning, and he thanked her politely. He bade her good day before he left, often not to be seen again until dinner, and sometimes not even then. After dinner, and the barest of conversations—about the weather, sometimes a few tidbits of gossip about Society people she had never met, gossip which Stanley claimed to have heard in his club—he usually went out again and did not return till the small hours of the morning.

And when he came home, tiptoeing quietly into the bedroom, Lucy never knew how to respond. In fact, she had tried everything, pretending to sleep and hoping he would wake her with a kiss . . . which he never did. His routine was invariable; he would shed his clothes and pull on his nightshirt in the dark, slide into bed very quietly, never touching her, and fall at once into an apparently deep slumber.

And if she sat up and lit a candle and smiled at him, hoping to welcome him with a kiss that might blossom into other—perfectly proper—marital relations, he would pat her on the shoulder as if she were a child, ask about her health, bid her good night most civilly, but never approach her.

She had felt so helpless, so unappealing, so bewildered. She was not the most beautiful woman in England, but surely she was not the ugliest, either? Why did her own husband have no desire for her—weren't men usually blessed with healthy carnal appetites?

But then, Stanley had been slight of frame, with almost no extra poundage on him. He tended to pick at the most savory dinner, his appetite uncertain. Perhaps his—his other appetites were as uncertain and as muted as his desire for boiled cod and roasted mutton.

Lucy sighed. How could he have been lured into stealing the ruby? It could not have been Stanley's plan— killing Lord Richmond's agent—her husband had had such mild manners. Something was so wrong with this image that she could not fathom it. This was nothing like the man she had known . . . or had thought she'd known.

Could it be that her husband had had another side to him altogether?

Lucy blew out her candle. These thoughts were fruitless; she refused to think about it any longer. Morning would be here soon enough. She tried to change the direction of her mind, to stop her thoughts going in circles, and endeavored to think of something pleasant. The lovely dinner she and Violet had had, the fact that there was actually an abundance of food in the pantry for the first time in weeks.

But that led back to the man who had sent it all, and then to their enforced stay inside the tiny larder . . . and the kiss, and the feel of his arms about her. . . .

Oh, dear. Sleep now seemed further away than ever. Lucy punched her thin pillow and turned to face the wall. No, no, this also would not do. Even if the viscount's very presence weakened her knees and made her heart beat faster, she could hardly permit herself the luxury of a brief affair.

There were too many risks—what if she was left with child?

Lucy sighed. She had once longed for a baby, but that was when she was a married woman. A widow could hardly come up with a belly swollen with child; she would be an outcast, and the child would suffer even more, a stigma attached to its name for life. And what Cousin Wilhelmina would say—Lucy shuddered at the thought. Besides, her mother would have been so disappointed. . . . No, no, it was too perilous. And worst of all, no matter how divine their tryst would be, and she had no doubts about its sweetness—

At some point, he would leave.

And that rejection would shatter her being. She knew instinctively that if she allowed herself to love the viscount, she would never be able to forget him. She could not, like his other lovers, welcome him briefly, enjoy the passion, and then blithely send him on to the next conquest. No, better to stay away from such dangerous temptation.

So she tossed and turned for what seemed like endless hours till at last she fell into a troubled slumber. And even then the dreams that stirred her sleep were such that she did not dare to examine them too closely when she opened her eyes the next morning.

And yet, she knew at once that something was different. As she blinked at the pale sunlight shining past thin curtains, she realized that for the first time since her husband's death, she opened her eyes with anticipation, not dread. The usual sense of apprehension that for so long had blanketed her with its oppressive weight had lifted. There were still debts looming, as well as the threat to her home, the dreadful thousand-pound debt to be settled, but she had a glimmer of hope that she could assist Lord Richmond in his search for the missing ruby and do what respectable females were so rarely able to do, unless they were governesses or companions or domestic servants working for a pittance—earn money!

It was a faint hope, but it was the first shred of it she had found to grasp, and it made all the difference.

Lucy sat up in bed. And when Violet opened the door of her chamber, the fragrance that emerged from the small china teapot on the wooden tray the little maid carried was enough to brighten Lucy's mood even more.

Tea, real tea! Oh, what a delight. A cannister of tea had been tucked into the basket of food; she had almost forgotten. And the plate held ham, and slices of bread spread with strawberry jam and wild honey.

"I hope you had a good breakfast, too, Violet?" she remembered to ask, sipping the hot tea with relish.

"Oh, yes, ma'am." Violet grinned broadly. "And there's plenty of ham left, enough for days, maybe weeks."

"Wonderful," Lucy agreed. "We may be heartily tired of ham by the time we finish it off."

Violet looked shocked at the suggestion. "Oh, no, ma'am. H'it's lovely!"

Lucy didn't argue. After she had bathed and dressed, she sat down to compose a note for the viscount, which began with a fervent thank-you for the ham and the basket of food he had sent, and then informed him of the missive she had received. She sent Violet to enlist one of the neighborhood boys to take it to Lord Richmond's residence. She was somehow not surprised to learn that Violet had already discovered where his house was located.

"I 'ad a chat with 'is coachman," her maid said, her tone a bit too innocent.

"*His* coachman." Lucy nodded. She felt as if she should issue a reprimand, but for what? "Very well."

When Violet went off to see the note on its way, Lucy sat down to her sewing box. She had a prince's theater party to attend in a few days, and the prospect was making her even more nervous than the duchess's salon. Of course, she had survived that affair, but still—

A knock at the door brought her back downstairs. It could not be the viscount; there had not been enough time for the note to even reach him. She peeked out the front window and was surprised to see one of her neighbors on the front step.

Lucy went to open the door. "Mrs. Broddy, how are you?"

The matron's expression was hard to read. "I have been remiss in calling, so I thought I must see how you are doing, Lucy, dear."

Lucy blinked, surprised both by this unexpected solicitude and the revelation that they had suddenly moved to a level of intimacy involving Christian names. "That's kind of you, won't you come in?"

She was forced to take her visitor into the dining room. "I'm afraid the front room is, uh, not in the proper condition for visitors," she explained. "Would you like a cup of tea?" Thank God she had some to offer!

"That would be nice," Mrs. Broddy agreed.

"I'm afraid Violet is out on an errand," Lucy said. "You'll have to excuse me while I put on the water."

"Oh, don't bother," her neighbor said. "You should hire more servants, Lucy dear."

"Yes," she murmured. "No doubt."

"I know you have remained in solitude after the death

of your husband, and I certainly didn't wish to intrude upon your grief," the woman told her. "But since I have seen you, just by chance, out and about several times this week, I thought I would check and see that all was well with you."

Ah, yes, the moving curtain in the window across the street. No doubt, just by chance. Lucy proceeded with caution.

"I have been asked to furnish some details about Stanley's former business, that is all," she said, trying not to blush.

"Business with a man of title? Stanley?" Mrs. Broddy looked unconvinced. "Lord Richmond is a man of dubious reputation—"

And how long had it taken her to trace his crest on the carriage door and discover his name? Gossip must have been flying up and down her narrow street for days. Lucy sighed. She should have known that such an unusual occurrence as a visit from a man of rank would stir up every old cat within miles.

"And spending time alone with him could suggest ideas of improper behavior. Since your dear mother is dead, my dear, I don't hesitate to offer advice in her stead—"

"I think I should put that kettle on to boil," Lucy interrupted. "I would not wish to be remiss in offering you refreshment."

But her neighbor was not to be silenced. She waved aside the offer.

"In matters of propriety, we cannot be too careful, you know. Your late husband certainly understood that; he was always the most proper of men. I know you would not wish to defame his memory—"

This time Lucy jumped to her feet. "I'm sorry I cannot chat any longer," she said, her tone firm. "I fear I have another appointment."

The older woman frowned. "There's no need to take offense; I am only considering your welfare. If your dear cousin were here, I'm sure she would agree with me."

Lucy suppressed a shudder. Wilhelmina? That would

be all she needed! "I promise you, I will remember your council," she told the spiteful old gossip. She did not promise to heed it, however. "But I'm afraid I must go upstairs and change my clothes. I am going out."

Mrs. Broddy made her departure, still frowning. As soon as she shut the door on the woman, Lucy stamped her foot. Oh, how infuriating! Yet, hadn't she known how it would be? She really should not be seen with a man of such uncertain reputation. . . .

No, that was her cousin talking, the disapproving voice echoing in her mind just as if Wilhelmina were actually here. The fact was that the viscount had such a kind heart, and despite his flirtatious manner, she could not believe that he would harm anyone intentionally.

Or was she simply telling herself that because she enjoyed his advances? Even if she hadn't had the pressing need for money that made her eager to help in his search for the ruby, the fact was that spending time in his company lightened her mood and made her heart beat faster . . . perhaps this was exactly how a practiced seducer worked.

Oh, damnation! Lucy went back upstairs and took out the maize-tinted dinner dress she was altering for the prince regent's theater party. Then, realizing that she did not want to be found here when the viscount arrived— she did not wish to receive him in a suggestive setting— she took the dress and her sewing basket downstairs to the dining room. So when Violet returned and looked in on her mistress, a broom and dust rag in her hands, Lucy was sewing virtuously, all alone.

"I'll start on the upstairs now, ma'am," her maid said, carefully minding her *h*'s. "I sent the greengrocer's lad with the note; 'e's—I mean he's—fast on his feet."

"Good," Lucy said. "Thank you, Violet."

The girl nodded, and Lucy heard her going up the stairs. Lucy bent her head over her sewing, and presently found she was listening hard to the street sounds. Every time a carriage or a cart went by, she strained to hear the hoofbeats and tried to detect a familiar rhythm.

This was silly. She must not allow her affections to become fixed on a man whose social position was totally unattainable, even if he had been interested in matrimony, which he obviously was not, and even if he were, he would hardly pick a penniless widow. . . .

She jumped—she had stabbed the needle into her finger. Bother! She put her abused thumb to her mouth and mumbled a few more words, none of which her cousin would have approved. Why was Wilhelmina so much on her mind today? Perhaps Lucy was feeling guilty, even though she had surely done nothing . . . well, she had kissed the viscount in the pantry, and worse, enjoyed it. One part of her longed to repeat the experience, and next time, next time if they were not interrupted, where would a kiss lead?

Her thoughts wistful, she forgot to listen for sounds of a carriage, and when the rap on the door came, she almost pricked her finger again. She jumped up, dropping the needle, then forced herself to sit down again calmly and allow Violet, whose footsteps could be heard descending the staircase, to answer the door.

In another moment Lord Richmond appeared in the doorway. Heavens, he made her heart almost stop, he looked so tall, so commanding, his dark eyes brilliant with intelligence and, always, that disarming spark of humor. And even the set of his mouth, that appearance of cynical indifference, which she was more and more learning to discredit . . .

"Mrs. Contrain?" He bowed.

She tried to pull herself together. "Please sit down," she said, with as much dignity as she could muster. "Violet, make us some tea, please."

"Yes, ma'am," Violet agreed. She bestowed a glance upon their visitor that was practically beaming and disappeared down the hall.

"I must thank you again—" Lucy began, but he waved her words aside, pulling out a chair and sitting down.

"It was nothing. Mending?"

Lucy tried not to flush. "Ah, just trying to get ready for

our next social engagement, that is, not exactly social, our sleuthing operation, rather." She stopped, afraid she would say too much.

The viscount frowned for an instant. Was he afraid she would not be dressed properly when they went into royal company?

Lucy wrinkled her forehead in worry, but then he spoke abruptly, and she forgot all about the difficult subject of clothes.

"The note," he reminded her. "May I see it?"

"Of course," she said. She put the dress aside and withdrew the wrinkled note from her pocket.

The viscount read its few words slowly, and then read them again.

"If this is blackmail," he said, "they seem to be setting you up first."

"What do you mean?"

"There is no direction about where to send the hundred pounds," he pointed out.

"Yes, I thought of that." Feeling more at ease, she bent closer to look one more time at the smudged paper.

"So you should expect to receive another note," he suggested.

Lucy shivered. The thought that someone out there was lying in wait for her, hoping to lure her to—to what?—was unnerving. Then she remembered that she was not alone, Lord Richmond would be by her side, and the fear subsided.

"What shall we do about their demands?" she asked, adding awkwardly, "I regret to say that I do not—I mean—"

"I don't expect you to pay a hundred pounds," he assured her. "I will take care of that, if it is necessary. The problem is, the figure they ask for is too small."

She gazed into his face, watching the concentration with which he attacked the problem. "Too small? It sounds like a lot of money to me."

"Yes, but for a priceless gem like the Scarlet Widow,

it's a paltry sum." He frowned, then shrugged. "But we will pay it, of course."

"And not suggest to the unknown thief that he should be asking for more," Lucy couldn't help pointing out.

The ready gleam of humor reappeared in his eyes, and his frown faded. "No, we will not encourage his avarice."

"Who do you think it can be?" she asked. "The writer of the note, I mean."

He shook his head. "I have no idea, but it's imperative that we find out. He must have some connection with the original theft, although . . ." He paused, looking deep in thought.

Lucy sighed. It all came back to the fact that her husband had, after all, been a criminal. Lord Richmond had been kind enough not to comment on the fact, but now she said, "I still find it hard to believe, you know. That Stanley really did take part in the robbery."

He nodded, and this time his expression was not in the least sardonic. "I'm sure it is a blow. I am sorry."

She nodded, annoyed to find that her eyes had suddenly dampened. The viscount lifted his hand as if to reach out, then paused. She blinked hard, determined not to succumb to a fit of hysterics. What would he think of her if she continued to fall into the dismals at any provocation? This was hardly reassuring behavior for a sleuthing partner. This morning she had counted up the days remaining until her house would be taken from her unless she could produce the thousand pounds and settle her husband's biggest debt—the others would have to wait. But remembering that ultimate threat clouded her mind with anxiety. She needed her wits about her now, and she tried to push her other worries aside.

"Do you think we should try to track the messenger when he returns?" she suggested. "Only, we don't know when he will return."

"And it will be hard to watch your door twenty-four hours a day," he agreed. "As determined as I am to find the gem, if I camp out on your street, it might be noticed."

Lucy nodded. "I'm sure. And I fear I cannot invite you

to stay, my neighbors would think . . ." she stopped, blushing as she remembered Mrs. Broddy's remarks.

"Yes, I can easily imagine," he agreed. "Neighbors do seem to assume the worst." His tone was wry, and his eyes glinted again.

She tried not to smile; a woman's reputation was a serious matter. Her mother had told her so often enough, as for her cousin . . .

"So if—" she paused. The viscount turned his head and motioned for silence. It had been a quiet tap, but they had both heard it.

She stood up quickly, but heard Violet's footsteps in the hall before she could get to the door. Lucy hurried out, but Violet was already shutting the door.

"Who was it?" Lucy asked.

"Just a boy, ma'am," the maid said, looking surprised at the sharpness of her mistress's tone. " 'Ere's another note for you."

Lucy almost snatched the paper. Behind her, Lord Richmond asked, "What did the messenger look like, Violet?"

The maid crinkled her forehead in thought. "Just a street lad, milord, a bit grimy around the edges, like. 'E didn't wait for no coin."

"Was he the same one who brought the last note?"

She nodded. "I think so. Ooh, 'cuse me, milord, the teakettle is whistling." She hurried away, and Lucy read the note one more time.

Bring the hunred pounds to the house wit the red door in Little Hedding, Hampstead Heath, tonight at 8 o'clok. Ask fer Eve.

It was not signed. Lucy frowned at the words, then handed the paper to the viscount.

He examined it closely. "Come back and sit down," he suggested. They returned to the dining room and the viscount spread out the new demand alongside the first note so they could compare them side by side.

"What do you see?" he asked.

"Aside from the fact that the writer's spelling has suddenly worsened?" Lucy answered. "The paper looks of the same texture and coarseness, and the ink on both is a greenish-black hue, but the handwriting is not the same."

"So there is more than one person involved." The viscount's tone was grim. "I like this less and less."

"But for a small outlay, you said it yourself, we shall retrieve the gem," Lucy pointed out. "That's the essential thing. And then, of course, we can receive the prince regent's reward!" She blushed a little, knowing she must sound greedy.

The viscount's glance was gentle. But when she spoke again, she saw his gaze sharpen. "When we go tonight—" Lucy began.

"Do not think I will allow you to accompany me," he interrupted. "I have an idea about this location. If I'm correct, this is a very dangerous vicinity and no place for a lady to be out after dark."

"My lord," she said firmly. "I am not some pampered society miss. I have been poor all my life, you know, or at least since my father died when I was a small child. Before we moved in with my cousin, my mother and I were forced to live in neighborhoods which were far from genteel."

"I doubt you have ever lived in an area quite like this," he insisted. "I'm sorry, Mrs. Contrain, but some things are not fit for a lady's eyes."

"Good heavens, you sound as prim as my husband!" Lucy snapped, then bit her lip. That observation was hardly chivalrous to either gentleman. "That is, what I mean—"

"It is a question not just of propriety but of safety," he told her, as if determined to hold on to his patience, though his eyes had narrowed again. "I regret that I must check your enthusiasm, but I will not allow you to go."

"And I regret that it is not within your provence to tell me what I can and cannot do!" Lucy's quick temper had flared. "Do you wish me to go alone?"

"Hardly!"

"That is one of the few advantages to widowhood, Lord

Richmond. No man can tell me what to do, or what not to do."

She suddenly remembered Lady Sealey's advice on the other benefits of a widow's condition, but she swept the memory away. She was too angry just now to be embarrassed over the suggestion of greater license available in affairs of the heart.

For a moment, he regarded her in silence, and she was reminded of the arrogance in his manner which had been so much in evidence in their first meeting.

"I doubt any man could control you, Mrs. Contrain," he pointed out, his tone hard to read. "Not through force, at any rate, and certainly not through logic."

She lifted her chin. "Oh, unfair! What is illogical about my plan?"

"I have just pointed out all the dangers attendant on your traveling to Hampstead Heath, a locale favored by footpads and other lowlife. If you were reasonable, you would admit the rationality of my argument."

"I fear your argument is lacking one vital fact." She leaned forward, trying to make him see reason. "Lord Richmond, the note was addressed to me. You have no business being involved in it at all, as far as the person or persons who penned this invitation know. In fact, if you go alone, you may scare off the writer. And we have to find the gem!"

He hesitated.

"Mrs. Contrain, you must understand how dangerous this is."

"I do!" Lucy tried not to shiver at the thought of some unknown villain who had already killed once and could likely to do again. "And I admit, I am happy to have your company. If you were not here, I should have to go alone—"

"I would not allow it," he repeated, too quickly.

She smiled at him; she couldn't help it. Her anger had faded as quickly as it had come. She was reminded how close he sat as they faced each other, both half turned away from the tabletop and the papers it held. He regarded

her with that wry expression, she was beginning to believe, he used to cover his thoughts when they became
too—too what?

He leaned forward just a little. The thick dark hair that
curled slightly over his forehead—she was tempted to
push it back, to touch the lock of hair and the olive-toned
skin which lay beneath it—

"Tea, ma'am," Violet said cheerfully as she entered the
room with a tray in her hands.

"Does she plan it?" the viscount murmured.

Lucy grimaced, trying not to feel frustrated by the untimely interruption. She shot him a speaking glance, then
pulled her own features into a polite smile.

Violet bustled about, setting down the tray laden with
teacups and slices of bread and butter and even some
fresh-made scones, which she must have mixed up this
morning. The maid seemed so pleased to be able to offer
refreshment to a visitor, even if he had provided the mak-
ings, that Lucy could not be angry. And anyhow, she had
no business wishing to be alone with the viscount, to be
tempted to pursue those scandalous thoughts and turn
them into actions which were not in the least proper.

"Then it is settled," she said as she poured him a cup
of tea. "We will go together."

He frowned again for a moment as he accepted the cup.
"On one condition: you will abide by my instructions exactly."

"Of course," she agreed, her tone demure. She pretended not to see the skeptical glance he gave her.

⁓

Lucy spent the rest of the day reworking the gown for the
prince's theater party, trying not to think of the voyage
into the unknown upon which she was about to embark.
But she would not be alone; it was amazing how the
knowledge of the viscount's presence steadied her nerves.

When a still sunny Violet brought a dinner tray into
the dining room, as if delighted to get back into a more

proper routine, Lucy sat in solitary splendor and ate another delicious meal of sliced ham and side dishes gleaned from the basket of foodstuffs. Then Violet brought her mistress's shabby cloak and helped Lucy change into her worn widow's weeds. Just for tonight, she had decided to look as demure and retiring as possible; besides, the unknown blackmailer might be expecting to see an obvious widow. Then Lucy paced up and down the small hall, listening for the sound of the carriage pulling up outside her door.

When she heard the sound of wheels and hoofbeats, she hurried to the front window to make sure it was the man she expected. But when she peered out, Lucy felt a distinct shock. Instead of the viscount's by-now-familiar chaise, she saw a small and slightly shabby hackney cab.

Who on earth?

Lucy went back to the front door and put one hand on the doorknob, but when the tap came, she hesitated.

"Mrs. Contrain?"

She would know his deep, rich voice anywhere. She pushed back the bolt and swung open the door. The viscount stood on her doorstep.

Even in the darkness, she recognized his hawk-nosed profile as he glanced up and down the street. Lit only by the faint light from her hallway and the flickering light of the carriage lantern, his face was shadowed, making it appear harsh and forbidding. Perhaps she should have been afraid—after all, she had known the viscount only a short time. But instead, she felt both shielded and exhilarated.

Still, she couldn't help asking, "Why did you come in a hackney?"

"Where we are going, a well-equipped chaise would attract entirely too much attention," he told her. "Despite my precautions, however, someone is already curious—I see a face peering at us from a window of the house across the street."

"Ah, Mrs. Broddy," Lucy muttered. "My dear inquisitive neighbor." She looked up, lifting her head just in case the woman had not seen enough to satisfy her, and gave a cheerful wave. The curtain dropped abruptly back into place.

Lucy would have sworn she recognized the driver, who doffed his hat as the viscount handed her inside. She took her seat. The cab was dilapidated but clean, and more cramped than the viscount's private chaise.

"Is that your coachman driving?" she asked.

Lord Richmond nodded. "I hired the vehicle for the evening," he said, his voice calm. "If things turn nasty, I want someone in the box I can depend upon. We don't want to see our cab driving away, leaving us stranded."

"No indeed!" Lucy agreed. Now that the time was near, she couldn't help feeling a certain uneasiness, which did not lessen as the viscount's driver drove their shabby equipage past the outskirts of London. Buildings grew more scattered as they rolled onto what seemed, in the early hours of evening, to be a decidedly deserted heath.

Tree leaves rustled in the night breeze, and the moon drifted in and out of clouds that obscured its faint light. She shivered. When Lord Richmond put his hand over hers where it rested upon the threadbare seat, she drew a deep breath.

"I'm all right," she assured him, but somehow her voice sounded too high. She swallowed and tried again. "I mean, I am perhaps a bit apprehensive, but not enough to—that is—I will not be a burden to you tonight. I do wish I knew whom we are meeting."

"Ah, yes, our mysterious penman," the viscount agreed.

Lucy suddenly sat up straight. "Oh dear, the hundred pounds!"

"I have it here," Lord Richmond assured her.

For the first time, she saw the large leather wallet that had been tucked discreetly beneath the seat, next to a slim walking stick.

The thought of handing over what—despite the viscount's disclaimer—seemed like a very large sum of money to a someone who had to be a scoundrel, disturbed her. Her instinct was to fight back, not to give in to blackmail. But they seemed to have no choice. The prince regent must have his gem delivered safely to him, and the viscount must identify the murderer of his friend and clear his own name. And since it had to be done, she must be brave; she would not succumb to her sudden awareness of the danger that swirled about them.

She pushed her shoulders back and tried to feel resolute. Whoever had the gem must have been allied with her husband in the robbery. He might be—must be, for she knew it could not be laid to Stanley's hand—the killer. At that thought, she could not prevent another slight tremor from running through her.

Lord Richmond seemed to read her thoughts. He squeezed her hand, then lifted it for the briefest moment to his lips. She sensed the warmth of his kiss against her palm, which, though the night was mild, felt cold even inside her thin gloves. "I do not wish to see you distressed," he said. "Shall I take you home? I can go on this errand alone."

Lucy shook her head. "Oh, no, whoever wrote and directed the note to my door is expecting to see me. It might alarm him if I were not there. He might slink away into the darkness and disappear before you have the chance to retrieve the stolen ruby." She drew a deep breath, determined not to allow her trepidation to be so obvious. "I am quite calm."

An owl hooted suddenly from the darkness, and she jumped. "Perhaps not totally calm, but close enough. Are we almost there?"

She thought he smiled; even in the darkness inside the carriage, she could see the pale glint of his teeth as he lifted his lips. "It's another dozen miles, at least."

"Oh," she answered. And nothing to do to take her thoughts away from the unknown danger they were about to encounter . . .

Then she smiled, glad that the viscount could not deduce that thought. There were plenty of things a man and a woman could do inside a carriage as they drove through the darkness, with, for once, no prying glances upon them.

But all these deliciously sinful activities came under the heading of temptations she had already foresworn.

Except that he was still holding her hand.

She debated as to whether she should quietly slide her hand out of his clasp, yet, the feel of his fingers grasping her own delighted her. His skin was warm and his grip strong, and through the slight touch, she seemed to sense the potent male energy that flowed through his whole body. He sat at ease in the shabby carriage, yet she could imagine how easily he would unfold his long frame, and the strength he would use to put aside any assaults leveled against them. If she had to ride through the dark to an unknown and dangerous destination, she could not, Lucy realized, have picked anyone else she would rather have had by her side.

Perhaps she sighed quietly at the thought, because she detected the motion when he turned his head to regard her more closely.

"Are you sure you're all right?"

"Of course." Yet, her voice quavered still. But now it was not fear, exactly, that made her heart race. The hackney hit a bump in the road and jolted its passengers. Lucy found herself thrown sideways against Lord Richmond, and she gasped.

"Oh, I'm sorry. I didn't mean—"

He put one arm about her shoulders to steady her. She lifted her face to stare at him in the darkness, then as the moon slipped out from behind the cloaking clouds and allowed a beam of pale light to enter the carriage, she saw him smile again.

"I know you didn't—more's the pity." And as she tilted her head toward him, as if in invitation, he lowered his own and allowed his lips to touch hers.

It was a tantalizing kiss, the barest whisper of a caress, then he pulled back. But instead of scandalizing her, as it should have done, Lucy felt her pulse quicken. Something stirred inside her, and all the excitement of their brief stolen embrace inside the pantry returned with a rush. This man lit fires inside her, fires she had never suspected existed.

She knew she should retreat, knew that the viscount would accept her withdrawal and not force the issue, but the problem was—she longed for his kiss, yearned with a passion that had been growing all through her own unfulfilled, almost chaste marriage—and now, alone in the darkness, she found that she could not find the fortitude to deny her unmet hunger.

She kissed him. She kissed him hard, pushed herself closer, allowed her lips to open to better taste the salty warmth of his mouth. For a long moment she focused on nothing but the kiss and the firmness with which he returned it, and then his tongue slipped inside her mouth, and Lucy jumped. Her husband had never done this!

But Lord Richmond probed again, gently, and she found it a very sensual sensation. Soon, with desire racing through her, she was emboldened to meet his exploration with her own. He put both arms around her now and pulled her even closer, and Lucy felt the blood roar in her ears. All the careful speeches she had made to herself, the admonitions against improper behavior, melted away like butter left to sit in a ray of warm sunshine.

She raised her arms to clasp his neck and allowed herself to lean into his embrace. Their kiss seemed to last for years, and then when they fell apart, Lucy breathless with pleasure, the viscount brushed his lips over her cheek and her temple and the edges of her hair. Every touch only excited her more; it was lamentable—no, it was marvelous—to find that instead of sating her hunger, every touch only deepened it. If this was how intimacy could be, she had been missing so much!

Then she felt the carriage slow, and the viscount lifted his head from his delicate exploration of the curve of her neck. Lucy sighed.

Damn the coachman—why did they have to approach their destination now?

But her companion was looking out, and Lucy tried to

push her hair back into place as she stared, too, out into the night.

"Where are we?"

"Approaching the village."

"Hampstead?" she suggested.

He shook his head. "No, we are not going to taste the spring waters for our health, you know, or visit with artists and writers. Our goal is a more secluded and much less reputable village on the edge of the heath; highwaymen rode here years ago, preying on passengers bound for London. This quiet patch of forest has seen its share of blood spilled and innocents slaughtered."

"Oh!" Lucy shivered and looked about her with an almost morbid fascination, though, so far, all she could see were tall trees lining the road, their leafy branches swaying in the night breezes, and a dark sky with clouds scattered gray against black. The almost full moon flitted among the clouds, and she heard the sweet, poignant notes of a nightingale, its melody aching with an unearthly beauty.

Then another sound floated through the darkness, one much less melodic. It was laughter, drunken laughter she suspected, and then she heard the sound of a door slamming. Now the trees fell away, and she caught a glimpse of the heath itself, a rolling green vista scattered with occasional shrubs and copses of tall trees. A small village came into view, a few cottages huddled along a narrow lane with one house larger than the rest. Somehow she was not surprised to find that their rented carriage pulled up in front of this house, and, yes, in the flickering lantern light and the glow of the brighter flambeaux that sat on either side, she saw that it had a red door.

The hackney rolled to a stop, and she heard the horses stamping their hooves and snorting, and from inside the house more sounds of rowdy merriment. Someone yelled, and others laughed and cursed, and, oddly, a pianoforte tinkled an uncertain, faltering tune. Lucy drew a deep breath.

"Do you wish to remain in the cab?" Lord Richmond

asked. "I can tell them I have come on your behalf. This is truly no fit place for you."

"No, I must show myself." Lucy braced herself. "This is our most promising lead, and we cannot allow it to slip away from us. I will go in first, and you should follow, staying a little behind me."

He lifted his brows, but he tucked the wallet stuffed with money inside his coat, picked up the walking stick and then, looking about him before he emerged, stepped out of the carriage. He helped her down and crossed to the house, pushed open the rough wooden door, and allowed her to enter before him.

Lucy crossed the threshold and into a world she had never even dreamed of. It might have been a tableau out of one of the storybooks her mother had read her as a child—the scene was just as strange and exotic. She had never glimpsed an alehouse of such licentious appearance. Half a dozen men, who all seemed much the worse for drink, sat around a large room crowded with chairs and settees and small tables. Several women shared the settees with male companions, and they sat just as close as Lucy and the viscount had been pressed in the privacy of the hackney.

The man nearest to the door stared at Lucy, blinking as if trying to make his drunken eyes focus. He was short and stout, his stomach rounded, and his thinning hair stood up from his head. There were ale stains on his white shirt, and when he finally brought her image into focus, he grinned broadly.

"Wanna glass of wine, sweetie? Wanna kiss?"

"No thank you," Lucy answered quickly, backing up a little and glancing about her as she tried not to show her distaste and her amazement.

The men were well-enough dressed, but several had their vests unbuttoned and their neckcloths loosened in a most unseemly fashion. The women's dresses were amazingly thin and revealing, their necklines cut so low as to be hardly decent. The closest female looked up, pushed her companion's wandering hand away from her bosom, and stared boldly at Lucy. The woman's cheeks were so flushed that Lucy wondered if she had a fever. Her hairpins were slipping out and her coiffure disordered, and a dark bruise shadowed the base of her throat.

"What's a woman doing 'ere?" she said, her voice loud and coarse. "We don't need no more—" Then her gaze slipped away from Lucy, as if drawn by an irresistible force. The woman's eyes widened, and her mouth parted in an O of admiration. Lucy knew that the viscount had entered the room behind her.

"Ooh, lovey, you want to come upstairs with me? I'm the best woman 'ere, I promise you!"

Another woman sprang up from her couch and slipped around the first one. She had bright red hair and hard dark eyes. She wore a diaphanous green gown that showed the outlines of her figure with distressing clarity as her nipples pressed hard against the thin cloth. "No, no, you should choose me," she almost shrieked. " 'E looks like a man 'o knows what 'e wants! And I can give it to you, dearie."

Swallowing hard against her dismay as she realized just what type of establishment this was, Lucy drew herself up. "Excuse me, but—"

Another woman had approached; were these women of the night going to engage in fisticuffs to determine who was allowed to dally with the viscount? He might have to beat them off with his stick. Lucy should have told *him* to stay in the carriage! Thrusting a man of such potent masculine appeal into this house of ill repute was like dropping a ripe ear of corn into the midst of a flock of hungry chickens.

The corn had a mind of its own, however. "No thank you," Lord Richmond said, his voice cool. "I am here with this *lady*." If there was a slight emphasis on the last word, it went unnoticed.

"What'd you bring your own doxy with you for?" one of the women demanded. "What kind of queer bloke are you?"

Lucy tried her best to interrupt. "Is anyone here named Eve?"

They stared at her, their expressions reflecting varying degrees of disgust and unslaked avarice, and two shook their heads.

But the first woman asked, her tone suspicious, "Naw. And what you want with 'er, any'ow?"

"She sent me a note. It's very important that I see her," Lucy persisted. "Do you know where I might find her?"

"It's worth a shilling to you," the viscount added quietly, passing over a coin.

The woman's eyes gleamed. "She's upstairs—I'll tell 'er you want 'er. Though she don't do odd stuff, dearie, I'll just warn you. But me, on t' other 'and, I'd be 'appy to try a threesome, if that's what you be wanting."

Lucy had no notion what the other woman was suggesting. She didn't answer, and she felt a moment of relief when the woman, with a suggestive sway to her hips and a provocative glance back over her shoulder, headed for the narrow staircase.

Lord Richmond moved closer to her, and a skinny man, who had seemed to be heading her way with an unsteady gait, turned aside and threw his arms about the woman with the bright red hair. Giggling, she led him toward the stairwell. In a moment, although their progress was slow due to the man's inebriation, they disappeared around the bend in the stairs and into the dimness on the next level.

Lucy's shoulders were rigid with tension, and she tried not to show her unease. She wanted nothing more than to slip out the front door and be driven safely back to London. But to save her home, she needed the prince's reward, and for that, they must locate the ruby. They would be away from here soon, but just now, she must find the writer of the note. Thank God for the viscount, standing quietly beside her, his expression a mute warning to the other men in the room.

The wait seemed endless, but then a new face appeared at the top of the stairs. This woman was younger than the trio downstairs, Lucy thought, though her eyes looked hard, and her mouth was pressed together into a tight line. She held a flickering candle as she stared down at them.

"You wanted me?" she asked. Her voice was not un-pleasing. If Lucy had shut her eyes, she could imagine the speaker to be a farmer's daughter from Kent. But see-ing the hard edge experience had given this woman, Lucy judged that whatever rural hamlet she had sprung from had been long left behind.

"You're Eve? I have come to speak with you." Lucy took the note from her pocket and held it up.

The woman's eyes narrowed. She glanced over her shoulder for an instant and hesitated. A burst of laughter erupted from the group in the big room, and she seemed to make a decision. "Best come upstairs," she said.

Lucy glanced at the viscount, whose expression was grim, and then hurried up the stairwell, secure in the knowledge that he was close behind. On the next floor, Eve lead them down a hall lined with shadows into a door halfway down, which opened into a tiny chamber. The room held only a bed, its covers tumbled and stained, and little else.

"We can talk here," the woman called Eve said. She put down the candle, which stank of cheap tallow, and leaned against the wall. Unlike the others below, she seemed to be most interested in Lucy. Folding her arms, Eve looked her visitor up and down, making Lucy feel awkward and almost assaulted. But this was no time for social niceties, so she pushed the idea aside.

After all, she was curious, too. This woman, though young, was generously built with wide hips and a deep bosom. Her hair was brown, and it glinted with reddish streaks that Lucy suspected came from henna. And her cheeks were very red, perhaps from rouge. The light was dim, but it did not conceal the dark circles under the woman's eyes, or her attitude of veiled desperation.

Lucy glanced at the bed and discovered she had no inclination to sit down. The blankets smelt musty, and the whole room held an unpleasant odor. There were no chairs. So she stood in the middle of the bare floor, her back erect and her chin up.

"You wrote the note?"

Eve nodded. "It's only fair I should get something," she said, her tone truculent. "I ain't asking for a lot, not from flush coves like you."

Lucy couldn't help reflecting that the woman would have waited a long time if Lucy had had to come up with the hundred pounds. Flush, she was not.

"And what can you give us for the money?" Lucy demanded. "Do you know where it is?"

"What? That's a stupid question." For some reason, the inquiry seemed to make the other woman nervous. She looked away for a moment, and her glance seemed furtive.

"It's very important. We need to locate the—the valuable object that my husband left with you," Lucy hurried on.

"You want to take it away?" Eve sounded alarmed, her eyes had widened.

"Of course, we do."

"Why would you do that?"

Lucy felt perplexed. "It's not yours, you know. We must return it to its rightful owner."

"Did you expect to take the money and keep what you've stolen?" Lord Richmond added. "We're not quite so gullible as that!"

The girl cowered a moment under the authority of his tone, but then she shook her head. "What do you mean, stolen? I don't want to give it up—why else would I write to you? I won't let you—I just wanted some funds, it's only right that Stanley should leave me something to help—"

Lucy forgot the illogic of the woman's argument. "You knew my husband personally, then?"she interrupted.

Eve smirked for a moment. "Oh, yeah, I knew him all right."

Lucy swallowed. She knew she should probably feel shock and outrage and hurt, but her husband had been such a stranger to her, and his disposition now seemed to become more inscrutable with every new revelation, that she wasn't even sure how she did feel. Yet she could not envision Stanley, fastidious in his personal habits, almost pious in his attitudes, here in this den of iniquity.

"Did he come to see you often?"

"How you think I got the—what I tol' you about in the letter?" Eve demanded, rolling her eyes.

It would be much more dignified not to comment on the depraved actions that occurred in this house, Lucy told herself. But the words burst out of their own volition. "But why did he come?"

"What you mean, why?" Eve stared at her again. "Don't be simple. What you think any man comes for?"

Then a heavy tread sounded in the hall, and Eve lowered her voice. "Oh, bloody hell. You listen good, hand over the money and I'll get you out down the back stairs. I never told 'im your street, you know, even when he made me send the second note. I knew Stanley wouldn't want you hurt. It'll be worth it to you, and Stanley would want you to—oh, hell!"

The door burst open.

"Why didn't you tell me they 'ad come, you worthless whore!" the man on the threshold snapped. "Trying to keep it all for yourself, eh?"

Lucy felt as if her heart had stopped beating.

Eight

*T*he viscount stepped forward. He raised his brows, as if it were only a drunken peddler who accosted them, instead of a man who seemed to be built like a brick oven.

The man in the doorway wore once fashionable, now slightly too well worn clothes. He had a wide torso, and his arms were long, ending in big broad hands. His legs were short in comparison, giving him the look of an overgrown dwarf, even though he met the viscount at eye level, and Lord Richmond was a tall man. The other man's dark eyes were almost hidden by a wide, heavy brow that seemed to run in one straight line across his jutting forehead, giving him a bestial look that made him seem hardly human.

Lucy felt fear billow inside her. She wanted to scream for help, but she knew they could expect no assistance here.

She was astonished to hear the viscount speak in a voice as calm as ever. "I do not believe we have any business with you."

The other man guffawed. "Any business that 'appens

'ere is my business, and I get the lion's share of it, you understand?"

"Oh, I believe I do." Lord Richmond nodded. "Whether I concur, however, is another story."

"Huh?" The other man's features screwed up, for a moment, into an almost comical expression of incomprehension. Then he blinked and stepped even closer. "You can take your fancy words and put 'em where they belong, milord, and I will take the blunt you're 'olding inside that fancy coat!"

Lucy could not keep herself from taking a step backward. Her legs hit the edge of the bed, and she barely kept her balance.

The viscount, on the other hand, moved forward, standing in front of her and facing the host of the house, whatever he called himself, squarely.

"I will hand over the money when I have something to show for it," he replied, his tone still controlled.

Eve spoke, her voice thin with fear. "Jace, please. Don't do nothing stupid. I'll give you half—"

" 'alf, my grandmother's ass, I want it all, you stupid girl. Why you think I even let you write to these coves in the first place?" The snarl on the man's face made him look even more savage.

They would never get out of here alive, Lucy thought, cold with fear. Jace was enormous, and she was sure he had others like him to call upon. They had only their driver, too far away to hear them shout, and anyhow, he was an older man, past his prime.

"I suggest you control your greed and allow us to depart peacefully," the viscount suggested. "It would be best for all concerned."

"Best for you, maybe!" Jace stepped forward again, standing almost face-to-face with Lord Richmond.

Lucy held her breath.

The big man put out one of his hamlike hands and gripped the viscount's lapel. "If you want to get out of 'ere alive, I suggest you 'and over the blunt, and any other little valuables you may be carrying. And if I'm feeling really generous, like, I might even let the lady go. Though she would make a nice addition to my girls 'ere."

Lucy gasped.

"You will refrain from bringing this lady into the conversation." The viscount looked at the other man as if he were an annoying insect. "Also, I suggest you take your dirty hand off me. My tailor would not approve. Tell me, where is the prize we came to find?"

Jace emitted a deep rumble, perhaps the sound was meant for a laugh. "I'll be 'appy to tell you, your lordship—when I meet you in 'ell!"

The viscount sighed, glanced at Lucy as if in apology, then he moved so swiftly she could barely follow the action. His left hand, still holding the walking stick in an easy grip, brushed aside the man's hold, and his right hand jabbed hard into Jace's midsection.

The other man grunted and bent over, his face dark with pain.

Lord Richmond stepped around him, motioning to Lucy to follow, which she hastened to do.

The viscount glanced at Eve. "I think it might be best if you left with us. I fear your—ah—patron's temper is not to be trusted."

Lucy suddenly remembered the bruise on the woman below stairs and repressed a shudder.

"Yes, do," she urged.

But the other woman, though she watched the prone figure of her employer with obvious fear, shook her head. "I can't."

Lord Richmond wasted no more time in argument. He held the door for Lucy, and for an instant she thought they would make it to safety after all.

But the man sprawled across the dirty floor suddenly found his breath, and yelled, "Homer, to me! The mark's getting away!"

The viscount gripped Lucy's arm and pulled her into the hall. They made it to the top of the stairs before two men appeared from below. Neither was as large nor as fearsome as Jace, but they were alarming enough, and there were two of them. The closer man had a balding head and small mean eyes; his stomach was rounded but his arms were thick with muscle; the second was slighter in form and bore a purplish birthmark on his temple. They blocked the narrow staircase quite effectively.

Together, they were as good as an army, Lucy thought. Despair clouded her thoughts and panic was not far behind. But having hysterics would hardly help. She pressed her lips together to prevent any rash cry that would further distract the viscount.

" 'and it over," the first man growled.

The viscount showed no sign of the terror that weakened Lucy's knees. "I'm not sure what you mean," he said.

The other man scowled. "Course you do. Give the blunt 'ere, or I'll peel it off your dead body."

"Kill 'em anyhow," the other man said from behind. "I like the looks of the woman."

Lucy swallowed hard, and the viscount drew a deep breath. "Perhaps you should come and take it," he suggested. For the first time, his tone sounded truly grim.

The balding man took another step up the staircase. Lucy stiffened, but the viscount, in one smooth movement, slipped his walking stick beneath the man's legs and tripped him up, knocking him backward. The villain lost his balance and bumped the second man, and both tumbled to the bottom of the stairs in a cursing, yelling whirl of flailing arms and legs.

"Let's go," the viscount muttered, grabbing Lucy's hand. They hurried down the stairs, but the two men lay in a heap at the bottom, still blocking their exit.

Any thought of stepping over them was obviously futile; a burly arm emerged from the tangle of bodies, reaching for the viscount's leg. He withdrew a step.

"Very well, let's find those other stairs Eve spoke of."

Lucy needed no urging. They remounted the stairs in record time. She was afraid they would find Jace at the top, but for the moment, the hallway was empty.

The viscount turned to the left and began to open doors.

"Hey, get out," a drunken, but refined voice called from one room.

Lord Richmond ignored the curses, but he seemed to have no luck finding the other exit. How long till the two men came back up the stairs, or Jace recovered? Lucy steeled herself and opened the nearest door.

She saw only two squirming bodies upon a small bed. She slammed the door hastily and tried another. This room was empty, with only a neatly made bed and a small chest beside it. She hurried on.

Then she saw that Eve peeked out of the half-opened door of the chamber they had been inside earlier. Eve's eyes widened when she saw them. She didn't speak, but she jerked her head toward the other end of the hallway.

"This way," Lucy called to the viscount.

He came quickly to join her, and they headed toward the far end of the dimly lit hall. Eve's face jerked back inside the room, out of sight, and there was the sound of a blow. Then, to Lucy's horror, Jace stepped back into the hallway, blocking their path.

And this time he pulled a small, lethal-looking dagger from his belt, holding it easily in one hand. "I think it's time to 'and over that blunt, milord," he jeered. "And then you'll find what 'appens to anyone who crosses Jace of the 'eavy 'and."

They were doomed, Lucy thought. The viscount's walking stick would be no match for that sharp blade. The villain who faced them knew it, too. He smirked, and the look in his eyes made her shiver.

Lord Richmond ignored the man's boasting and eyed the weapon in Jace's hands. With a fluid movement, the viscount pulled apart the walking stick, revealing a slim sword that had somehow been hidden inside.

"Perhaps this makes the contest more equal?" he suggested, his tone as urbane as always. "I think you should step aside."

Jace roared and plunged forward. The viscount thrust with the sword, and the other man bellowed again, this time in pain. Blood seeped from a wound in his arm, and he dropped the dagger. It fell with a clatter against the bare floorboards, and the viscount kicked it backward.

Lucy saw it slide past and, without any conscious plan, scooped it up.

Meanwhile, the viscount held his sword to Jace's throat. "I suggest," he said, his voice almost a whisper but still somehow menacing enough to make the other man go pale "that you step aside."

Jace moved back, his unwillingness palatable. "I'll find you, you bloody namby-pamby, and next time, you're a dead man!" he mouthed.

"My sentiments, exactly," Lord Richmond shot back. "If you cross my path again, you will not live to report it. And if you kill that girl, I will hear of it, and you will join her in hell!"

Jace backed against the wall, and the viscount motioned him on into the next room. Someone inside protested in a bleary voice, but no one took any heed.

"Stay inside until we are gone," the viscount warned. He slammed the door on Jace's murderous expression as the man clutched his bleeding arm.

"Come."

Lucy needed no urging. She hurried after him toward the end of the hall, where they opened the last door and found an even narrower set of steps that twisted and turned into the darkness. But as they took the first step, a small light appeared at the bottom.

It was too much to hope this might be a friendly face, Lucy thought, and uttered a prayer. How many escapes could they hope for from this hellish place?

No, the candle came into view, carried by the balding man whom they had already faced. This time, his expression was dark as the shadows around him, and he held a small pistol, pointed straight at the viscount's heart.

"Nowhere to go, milord," the man below them pointed out. "Me mate's at the other stair. Now h'I'll kill you, and maybe cut out your 'eart and feed it to you, if you live long enough after the bullet."

He was too far below for the viscount's sword to reach

him. The man raised the gun, and Lucy remembered the small dagger she still clutched in her hand.

She threw it.

Her aim was poor. It slid off the man's shoulder, leaving only a slight slit in his dirty shirt. But the man shouted and recoiled, lifting the pistol's muzzle slightly.

Lord Richmond did not hesitate; he sprang forward, and the sword knocked aside the gun, then slid down to pierce the man's chest.

Gasping, the ruffian fell backward. Could they make it around him?

"He still has the gun, and he's not dead," the viscount said into her ear as if he could read her thoughts. "We have to go back."

"But Jace will be there," she tried to protest. The viscount had already taken her hand to pull her after him up into the small hall. For a moment she found she could not move; her cloak had snagged on a nail protruding crookedly from the rough staircase. She pulled against it, and, if their case had not been so desperate, would have exclaimed in annoyance as she heard it rip. But they had more to worry about, just now, than ruining her cloak.

Pulling the cloak, now half off her shoulders, after her, she sped up the stairs. But as they reached the hallway again, she stiffened. It was beginning to feel like one of those farces in the theater, where droll characters run round and round the same room. If the situation were not so serious, she might have laughed. But right now, comedy was the farthest thing from her mind.

And sure enough, Jace was already peering out of the room into which they had put him. He grinned when he saw them.

"Look out!" she exclaimed.

The viscount didn't answer, but he jerked open the nearest door facing them and pulled her inside.

"Want a tumble, good-looking?" a woman who sat on the side of the bed asked. She wore only a soiled shift, and her lank hair, streaked with gray, tumbled about her shoulders.

Lord Richmond ignored her and glanced about him.

"Can the door be barred?" Lucy asked, trying to think. She inspected the rough door, but saw no sign of a latch, much less a lock. Perhaps Jace didn't allow it. She could hear his tread in the hallway. "He's coming!"

The viscount pushed the bed against the door. The woman squeaked in alarm and retreated to a corner. Then he took two steps to the window and pushed up the sash.

"Mason, here!"

What was he doing? The door moved inward an inch, then stopped when it met the bed's frame. But now it trembled as if someone's shoulder had been put against it.

"Mrs. Contrain, come here," the viscount called. He was still peering out the window. Lucy stepped back, but she kept her gaze on the door. The bed frame was too slight to hold for long against the brute strength of the man outside.

Sure enough, the door squeezed further open as the bed was shoved back. Jace rammed his way into the room. His expression was enough to turn anyone's blood cold. Lucy could make no sound, but she gestured toward the viscount, in the process pushing the damaged cloak further off her shoulders. She tugged at it, then gasped as she saw that Jace had somehow acquired a pistol. He took aim at Lord Richmond.

She had no dagger this time, only the cloak bunched in one hand. Lucy tossed it, and for a crucial instant, it covered Jace's face. The pistol spat fire as he pushed the cloth aside. The woman on the bed screamed.

Who was hit? Lucy looked around quickly, but the viscount showed no sign of injury, and the prostitute also appeared unhurt. A large hole on the wall confirmed the impact.

The viscount took two quick steps, and his fist smashed into the other man's face. The sound was quite satisfying. Jace fell again, into a heap, and Lord Richmond took Lucy's hand.

"To the window!"

But they were a floor aboveground, how could they jump without risking broken limbs or even death?

Lucy looked out and saw that their hired carriage now stood directly beneath the window. She began to understand the viscount's plan.

"I will go first, but you must follow quickly." Lord Richmond, glanced back at the groaning figure of the ruffian he had hit.

She nodded.

He pushed the window open as far as it would go, then slipped over the sill. He let go of the top of the window, his wide shoulders barely scraping through, and slid out of sight. She heard a muffled sound of shredding canvas and the thump of impact.

Lucy gasped and ran closer to see if he had landed safely. The hackney's cloth top had a ragged split, and the coachman fought to hold the startled horses. They shook their heads and made the carriage shake as they tried to bolt. But the viscount appeared unharmed; he held up his arms to the window.

"Now!"

The woman on the bed reached forward and grabbed at Lucy, who shook off her clutching hands. "Don't even consider it!" she snapped.

Lucy pulled up her skirts—this was no time to worry about modesty—and climbed through the window's opening, using the frame to steady herself. She hesitated for only an instant, then held her breath and jumped.

The viscount reached up and grabbed her, pulling her into the safety of the carriage. "Go, Mason," he yelled. Their carriage moved forward with a lurch as the coachman at last gave the horses their head. In another moment, they were pounding down the narrow road, heading away from the bawdy house.

Shouts came from behind them, but the hackney was moving at a smart pace, and unless Jace and his cohorts had horses already saddled or hitched to a carriage, they should be safe. Even so, she would be relieved to be back in London.

Already the shabby little village was behind them, and trees rose alongside the road. The moon was out, but the narrow road was littered with potholes, and the hackney lurched and bounced along it.

Lucy prayed the carriage would not fall apart. However, knowing the viscount, they would simply climb aboard the pair of horses and keep going. Dear God, what a night!

She shivered, thinking of the evil men they had left behind. Lord Richmond reached to put his arm around her. She leaned against him.

"I will not insult you by asking if you are all right," he said. "You are a most remarkable woman, Lucy Contrain."

She looked up at him, and was surprised to see how calm he looked. "Then you must allow me to note that you are an amazing man," she answered. "I did not think we would leave that place alive."

"But we did, due partly to your efforts," he told her.

"But we did not get the ruby!" Lucy sighed. "All that, and nothing to show for it."

He pulled her tighter. "I wouldn't say that, exactly."

She looked up at him, not sure of his meaning. "Do you think this was only a wild goose chase? Does that woman really know where the gem is hidden?"

He frowned. "Eve knows more than she is telling us, I'm sure of it. I fear I will have to go back."

"Oh, no!" Lucy protested. "You cannot. With that murderous crew about him, how can you face that devil again? I think we should—"

"There will be no 'we.' You will not be with me, next time," he told her firmly, and his arm tightened even more. "I should never have allowed you to come. I cursed myself many times during the past hour for exposing you to such peril."

"But we're safe now," she reminded him, unable to resist glancing outside at the dark trees skimming past their carriage. She was happy to hear nothing more than the pounding of the horses' hooves against the dirt road, and the occasional hoot of an owl.

"Still, I was wrong to allow it. I will come up with a plan, and if Eve knows anything, I will uncover it."

We will uncover it, Lucy thought, but this did not seem the time to argue. For one thing, she relished the feel of his closeness too much. And for another, she was sure of what his response to her debate would be. They would discuss this later, she thought, closing her eyes and allowing herself to enjoy his embrace.

❧

What a fool he had been, Nicholas thought. He felt the warmth of her, nestled inside his arm, and pushed back the desire that surged inside him.

He was more shaken than he cared to show. On his own, that little romp inside the second-rate whorehouse would have only exhilarated him; the awareness of genuine danger cut through the dull ennui that sometimes threatened to overwhelm him, that had dogged him for years.

But with Lucy Contrain beside him, sharing the danger, it had not been in the least amusing. Allowing Lucy to be hurt—it didn't bear to think of. Something stirred inside him, not simple lust this time, although God knew her luscious curves fit so nicely against him that it was hard to remain altruistic, but more. A glint of emotion emerged, one that he had buried long ago, buried so deep that he had never expected it to arise again.

So despite the hunger inside him, he restrained himself during the ride back to London. He knew he could have kissed her again, opened the gate to all the passions that waited inside her, tapped the sweetness that he hungered to taste. But not now, not until he could puzzle out the conflicting emotions that swirled inside him.

So they rode in silence through the darkness, and he refused to examine too closely just how content he felt with Lucy beside him, and how natural it seemed to have her pressed against him, totally sweet, completely trusting. . . .

~~~

They had another argument when the hackney arrived safely at her door.

"You should collect your maid and come away," the viscount suggested. "Eve knows your whereabouts. Jace might come to London or send hired thugs to avenge his lack of success tonight."

Lucy shook her head. She had an overwhelming desire to retreat to her own room, her own bed, and push aside all thoughts of this nightmarish excursion. "Eve said he doesn't know my location."

"And you would trust your life to a prostitute?" His tone was grim. "I can take you to a respectable hotel, if you like, you will have your maidservant with you. No one would wonder at it."

And allow him to pay for her room and board? Lucy could not accept more charity, and she herself certainly had no money to pay for lodging. "No, I do believe her. And I really want to stay in my home, please."

This small, unpretentious dwelling had been her only refuge for years of uncertainty; she was not ready to leave it. Perhaps this instinctive reaction was one of the moments of illogic he had accused her of before, but just now, Lucy was too weary and too shaken to reconsider.

The viscount frowned, but after more debate was eventually forced to concede. "I will send one of my servants to stay here, you must allow me that."

She nodded, wanting only to fall into her own bed. And yet, when he drove away, Lucy felt an irrational wave of loss. But no, tonight she needed to be alone, to sort out the feelings of dismay and betrayal that had descended upon her during the carriage ride home, distressing emotions that plagued her after confronting Stanley's mistress.

She bolted the door behind her. Violet, a shawl clutched about her shoulders had appeared in the hall. She watched, her expression perplexed.

"Are you all right, ma'am?"

"Yes, thank you," Lucy said. She explained about the viscount's manservant who would arrive shortly. "As soon as he comes, let him make a pallet in the kitchen and then you get back to bed, it's very late."

Violet insisted on going up with her to unbutton her dress and brush out her hair, which seemed to be in a sad tangle. When Lucy sent Violet away, instructing the maid to sleep as late as she pleased on the morning, and climbed into bed herself, the darkness was already softening with the first faint flush of dawn. She yawned and pulled the thin covers up to her chin. Yet her mind would not relax into sleep.

What a terrible place that bawdy house was! Jace, the man who ran it, was a villain, pure and simple. Poor Eve, to spend her life in such a place. She hadn't seemed such a bad woman, not really—she had tried to get them out. What did she know about the missing ruby? Lord Richmond was correct—they had to find out.

The thought of Eve in her husband's arms provoked strange feelings. Mostly disbelief—it was so hard to imagine. Why had Stanley gone there? What lack had he found in his own wife that he could not find pleasure at home? It wasn't as if she were not willing, one of those wives she had heard whispered about who disliked bedroom sport. She had often wished that Stanley were more interested in lovemaking. Perhaps the women who frequented those types of establishments knew things that a proper wife did not know. But how was she to find out what those secrets were, the ones that would entice a man, if no one would tell her?

Not that she had a husband now, but still, Lucy wished she knew just what she had done wrong. She turned restlessly in the bed, pounding her pillow and trying to find a comfortable spot where sleep would claim her. And yet, despite her feelings of sadness and flashes of anger over Stanley's lack of constancy, the oppressive despair that had been her constant companion for months remained at bay.

She had a sudden poignant realization that it was good

to be alive. During the long year after Stanley's death she had sometimes wished, in the darkest and most hopeless hours of the night, that she had died, too, when her husband did. Just one step into the road in front of a speeding coach would do the trick. . . .

But something had always held her back, some nagging, stubborn refusal to give up on life, to relinquish all hope of a better future. And now she knew that she had been right to struggle on. If she had given up, succumbed to the depths of her despair, she would never have met Nicholas. . . .

No, even in the privacy of her bedchamber, she could not think about Lord Richmond, or sleep would never come. Anyhow, what good would a liaison with the viscount do—he had had so many women that he would be quickly bored with her. She had failed Stanley, she did not wish to disappoint another man. Again, she wished for some insight into what it was that she lacked. . . .

Suddenly, she thought of the countess. Lady Sealey must be nearly as well versed in love as any courtesan, Lucy would bet on it. With a surge of relief, she promised herself that she would seek a private conversation with the older woman and beg for her insights.

At last, her eyes grew heavy, and Lucy could allow her tangled thoughts to slip away. . . .

~~~

She did not have the luxury of sleeping late, after all. Church bells pealed only a few hours after she had shut her eyes, and Lucy woke to a sudden awareness that it was Sunday. She could, of course, skip church service, just once, but her conscience would nag her, and besides, life had been so confusing lately that she felt the need for some quiet contemplation in a house of worship.

So she struggled out of bed, and a sleepy-eyed Violet helped her pin up her hair—which increasingly seemed such a nuisance that Lucy thought of the new modern crops with a sigh of longing—and then she dressed quickly, pulling on her new striped day dress. Leaving behind the brawny footman whom the viscount had sent to guard the house, the two women hastened through the streets and made it through the church doors just in time.

Lucy slipped into her usual pew, and Violet went up to the upper loft to join her friends, fellow servants from the neighborhood. Lucy opened her prayer book and tried to follow the service. She certainly needed to ask for forgiveness, not so much for the trip to the house of ill repute, for which she had had a logical reason, after all, but for her secret temptations when it came to the viscount.

Where was he this morning? Sitting properly in a church pew, or still in bed asleep? And if so, was he a bad person? Stanley had shown up in church every Sunday, and now it seemed that he had had plenty of human frailties. . . .

She suddenly remembered how, one Sunday walking home from church, she had glimpsed her husband peering hard at an attractive young woman on the other side of the street, a woman with a low-cut dress and swelling bosom. Stanley had looked hungry, for an instant, and his leer had startled her. But when he saw that she had turned her gaze his way, he'd colored and pulled his countenance back into its usual bland expression. Should she have suspected that he had secret longings? How much of Stanley she had not even known, and how much the thought pained her now. . . .

And yet how could she judge even her late husband? She was feeling rather imperfect herself, these days.

Lucy sighed. Perhaps God understood and forgave the shortcomings of his creation, man and woman alike. Faith, as the vicar said, was a comforting thing.

They stood for the Gospel reading, and Lucy pulled herself to attention. Then, when she sat again, she tried to heed the sermon that followed. After the service ended, she was about to leave the pew when a piercing voice cut through the hum of conversation around her.

Lucy stopped in shock. Good heavens, that couldn't be—

Nine

"Men are to be enjoyed, not understood."
—MARGERY, COUNTESS OF SEALEY

*I*t was.

A few feet away, Cousin Wilhelmina blocked a good part of the aisle as she chatted with Lucy's neighbor, the gossipy Mrs. Broddy. What on earth was her cousin doing here?

Lucy ducked instinctively, trying to hide herself behind a smiling matron who had emerged from the next pew. But it was too late.

"Good morning, Lucinda," her cousin boomed, moving forward through the crowded aisle like a ship cutting effortlessly through a harbor of smaller boats. "I was wondering if you were here. I hope after some Christian contemplation, you have conquered your ill temper."

"Of course I am here," Lucy said, ignoring the reference to her last outburst. "I'm surprised to see you, however."

"The inn where I was staying was not to my liking," Wilhelmina told her. "The beds were not aired, and the food was indifferent. When I happened to call on Mrs. Broddy, she offered me her spare room for the summer.

I accepted. I see you have put off your mourning, Lucinda. About time, though your hair is badly done. You must train that girl of yours better," her cousin added.

Lucy ignored the criticism, so typical of her cousin, still too preoccupied by Wilhelmina's awful news. Of course Lucy had known that Mrs. Broddy and her cousin were friends—two of a kind, in Lucy's opinion—and for the parsimonious Wilhelmina, the proposal of a free room would have won instant favor.

"How generous of Mrs. Broddy," Lucy said, her voice faint. Her cousin across the street, so that both women could now spy on Lucy's every movement? She was tempted to pinch herself. This must be a bad dream—worse, a nightmare.

"I will come to call on you soon," her cousin added. "I spent yesterday settling in. I do not wish to be remiss in the civilities."

"Of course not." Lucy was still having trouble with her voice. She took a deep breath. It could be worse, she told herself grimly. At least Wilhelmina was not staying under Lucy's roof, God forbid!

"We will be happy to come to dinner any evening. Perhaps today?"

"I'm afraid I'm not ready to entertain just yet." Lucy spoke more firmly. "But I will certainly keep your suggestion in mind."

"Not entertaining, really? I understood that a certain titled gentleman has been visiting you quite often," Wilhelmina said, her tone repressive. "Another reason you need an older, wiser relation close at hand to advise you. I'm sure you would not wish to start gossip—"

"And I'm sure you would not wish to spread it!" Lucy snapped.

Wilhelmina actually paused for an instant, blinking in surprise. "I—really, Lucinda—this is unlike you."

"Excuse me, I believe we are blocking the aisle," Lucy said. "Good day." She turned and walked quickly toward the front doors, trying not to allow the anger to overwhelm her. She was in church; she should strive for some Christian charity.

But Wilhelmina would provoke a saint!

After saying her farewells to the vicar and his wife, Lucy found Violet waiting for her. They hurried toward home. Lucy was of no mind to wait and walk side by side with her cousin and her neighbor.

Violet had already heard the awful news from Mrs. Broddy's cook. "Eats like a 'orse, she does, Maddy told me," the maid muttered.

Lucy shook her head. When they reached home, she went straight up to her room and peered into her small looking glass. It was true, her unruly hair was slipping out of its pins again, and she looked hot and flushed from the brisk walk home.

Lucy sighed, tugging at one straying tendril, then suddenly made up her mind. "Violet!"

"Yes, ma'am?"

"Bring the scissors!"

Wide-eyed, her maid hurried to comply, and Lucy sat down in front of her small dressing table. "Take it off," she directed.

"Ma'am?"

"I want a nice, short, fashionable, cool crop. Cut my hair, please."

Violet's eyes sparkled with enthusiasm. "Oh, yes, ma'am. What a good idea!" She lifted the scissors, then paused, looking suddenly uncertain. "But I ain't 'ad a chance to practice on anyone, ma'am. What if I make a mess of it? It's your 'air, I mean."

"Hair," Lucy corrected. "And whom do you think we can practice on?" she asked, practical as always. "No, I'm willing to chance it. Go ahead."

Nonetheless, she braced herself as Violet drew a deep breath and made the first cut. A long lock of fair hair fell to the floor. She was committed.

A half hour later, they both peered into the glass.

"Is it all right, ma'am?" Violet asked, her tone uncertain.

Lucy ran her hands through her hair. It certainly felt, well, short! But the wavy blond hair that had always been so hard to pull neatly into the somber buns that Stanley preferred now had been released. Unconstrained, it curled wildly about her heart-shaped face. She thought it looked rather becoming, on the whole.

"You did a fine job," she told her maid firmly. "I am most pleased."

Violet beamed. "Oh, thank you, ma'am. I think you look very nice, really, I do." She left to fetch a broom and dustpan to sweep up the hair that cluttered the floor, and Lucy fluffed her hair again. Yes, she thought she liked it, though it felt strange to have her head so light and so free.

If it were only as easy to obtain her liberty from the lowering thoughts that still lurked at the back of her mind. Cutting her hair had been a momentary distraction. But now thoughts of Stanley and his mistress returned, and her own illogical but inescapable feelings of guilt, of having failed him, in some way that she could not even begin to understand.

She had thought he was a decent enough husband despite his eccentric ways, though they had not managed to achieve any genuine closeness. But she knew plenty of wives in the neighborhood who did not see that as unusual. Lucy thought of Mrs. Broddy and her taciturn husband, who withdrew into his study every night after dinner and left his wife to her own devices. Lucy had been in the Broddy house only a few times, but it had been easy to see what the pattern was.

But not only had Stanley left her at home, left her out of his confidence while he was alive, he had taken his secrets to the grave with him. She wanted to weep, and she wanted to rail at him, but he had escaped that, too.

Lucy made a small exclamation of frustration. Perhaps she should just sit down and cry, but she had wept enough. And Violet would be back at any moment.

Keep busy, that was the thing. Lucy retrieved the dress she was altering for the prince regent's theater party and took it and her sewing basket down to the dining room, where the light was better.

So she was sitting at the table, trying to think only of small stitches, when the doorbell rang. Lucy jumped, but Violet was already clattering down the steps.

"Check out the window first," Lucy called, more out of habit than fear of more intruders. Their borrowed footman was still close at hand, and he did add to her peace of mind. Still, one never knew.

But perhaps she had already detected the sound of the carriage, because she was not really surprised when she heard Violet announce, "The viscount Richmond, ma'am."

Violet curtsied, and the glance she threw toward the viscount was downright coy. Lucy blushed. Was she as obvious as all that? The fact that her heart lifted when she saw his face, which no longer seemed so severe and forbidding as it had at their first meeting, was totally beside the point.

When had she stopped thinking of him as intimidating and stern? Somehow, her attitude had been changing all along, and going through the life-threatening adventure at the bawdy house made it seem as if they had been friends forever. She had seldom trusted anyone as she did this man, even though she still knew precious little about him.

She had trusted Stanley, too.

Nicholas observed the change in her expression. He had not yet uttered a word—what had made her withdraw like that? The first look she had given him had been full of warmth and welcome, and it hurt to see it vanish.

Careful, old man, he told himself sternly. You'll be in over your head with this one if you're not prudent. He tried to armor himself with the usual cynicism, but in the company of Lucy Contrain, it was strangely hard to achieve. That way she had of lifting her chin, as if awaiting another blow from fate; the lack of bitterness and the charity with which she spoke of her late husband, even though Nicholas himself found his opinion of the man— jewel robbery aside—dropping lower and lower; the warmth of her smile; the whole-hearted way she threw herself into every endeavor—really, she was the most delightful, delectable—

And that way led to ruination for them both. Hadn't he sworn never to allow another woman to enter his heart, never allow a female to gain his trust and his love and leave him painfully, achingly vulnerable to her loss?

There was a reason he usually dallied with more sophisticated women, whether bored wives or world-weary widows seeking mutual amusement. He never flirted with young ladies who were just out, telling himself he did not wish to break any hearts by suggesting attachments that would not materialize. It was his last remaining vestige of gentlemanly honor, he sometimes told himself mockingly late at night after yet another meaningless assignation. Yet perhaps it was more than that; perhaps he had been protecting himself, too, more than he knew.

"Mrs. Contrain." He bowed, playing for time, and when he raised his head again, she had smoothed her face into a bland and polite welcome. He didn't want politeness, not from her, damn it!

"I hope this is not an inconvenient time to call?" he suggested. "I trust my footman has been of help to you?"

She smiled. "He has so little to do—we have no silver for him to polish or visitors to escort into the empty drawing room—that Violet has put him to work peeling potatoes," she told the viscount. "But yes, thank you. His presence here has been comforting."

"I'm pleased to hear it. I was afraid you might still be troubled after the escapade last night."

She shivered, putting down the fabric that filled her lap. "It was disturbing, but I am recovered, thank you."

She didn't look it, but he forbore from pointing out the dark circles under her eyes. Something else was different; he realized she had cut her hair. It made her look even younger, like an enchanting street urchin, although seldom had he seen one with such velvety cheeks and smooth rosy skin. He found that the new style enhanced her beauty most effectively—she seemed more alluring than ever. Before he realized what he was doing, Nicholas reached out his hand toward a curling tendril.

She blinked at him in surprise as he touched the pale-hued lock, then his hand brushed her cheek.

It was as if a spark jumped between them. He heard her gasp, and Nicholas stood very still. Oh, God, he wanted this woman. He could see her breasts rising and falling beneath the thin muslin of her gown, and the way her eyes had widened just a little. He thought of how she would look flushed with passion, and how he could make her eyes shine with pleasure and delight.

Lucy Contrain needed more delight in her life, he would have sworn it.

But she drew back, a perceptible movement that caused him to withdraw his hand.

"I—I—" She picked up the pile of fabric again and dropped her gaze to it. "I was just working on a gown for the prince's theater party."

Earlier, she had started to put in a bit of silk to fill in the low-cut neckline. She had been so accustomed to concealing as much flesh as possible, as Stanley always demanded. Now, after seeing the dresses that the women had worn in the bawdy house, the dress that Eve wore, the woman her husband had preferred, she had decided she would do no such thing.

But, flustered by the viscount's nearness and the feelings his slightest touch evoked inside her, she pulled too hard at the bit of silk. Some of the careful stitches she had already put in loosened, but the rest clung to the original neckline. Hearing the rip of the fabric, she exclaimed in dismay.

"Oh, and I have been working on this for three days!"

Absurdly, tears filled her eyes. It was only a gown, Lucy told herself fiercely. She knew she was weeping for many other reasons entirely. Still, it was a nuisance; this was the last dress in the countess's box, and the most suited for this important occasion. Could it be fixed? It must.

She sniffed. "It's no matter, I will mend it." But she

put the gown aside and faced the viscount squarely. He was her nemesis or her salvation, she could not have said which—only that nothing in her life had been the same since he entered it.

"And I must return with you when you go back to Little Hedding," she told him.

He regarded her gravely, and it took him a moment to react to her words, as if his mind had been on something else. He shook his head. "No."

"I must," Lucy tried to persuade him. "I have thought for hours about our encounter with—with Eve, and there is something else, something she is holding back. I know there is, and I don't believe she will trust you enough to tell you the truth."

"Am I so untrustworthy?" he asked, his voice low.

For some reason, Lucy looked away. "Of course not, but you're a man, you see, and I suspect in her life she has had little reason to trust the male portion of humanity."

Nor had Lucy, Nicholas thought, despite her higher and more respectable status in society. Her father had died, her husband had betrayed her, and Stanley Contrain's unexplained and apparently endless debts now threatened even the roof over her head. When had a man ever stayed the course for her?

She deserved better. . . .

Yet while Nicholas longed to aid her, comfort her, she did not want his touch.

Strange how much that hurt. He told himself she was simply a woman of propriety, with scruples that must be respected. He was a reprobate; she was not. He was not so cynical that he did not believe that some people observed strict rules of behavior. Yet, with Lucy, he knew her hesitation came from more than just a proper code of conduct, and he felt amazingly rejected.

He wanted to reach out to her so badly that it was hard to restrain himself. He wanted to hold her hand, pull her into his arms, kiss away that lost look, the look of pain and bewilderment that clouded her eyes. He wanted to caress the determined thrust of her chin that revealed how stubbornly she refused to give up.

Lucy Contrain would be no man's victim. And he would not be allowed to succor her, damn it, much less lead her down passion's primrose path.

He found his fingers flexing; his hands would not be still, as if they still hungered to reach out to her. He took a step backward before he betrayed himself.

"I will not take up your time any longer. After the prince's theater outing, we will discuss our next step regarding the ruby, and what we will do. I will be here at seven-thirty Tuesday evening to pick you up."

She nodded. Of course, every time his elegant chaise rolled up to her door, it offered more gossip for the neighborhood mill, she thought, but she would not allow the Mrs. Broddys of the street to govern her actions. Nor her cousin.

"Thank you," she told him.

He made a rather hasty exit, and the room seemed suddenly very empty without his presence. Had she offended him? No doubt he simply had more interesting ways to spend his time than with a poor widow in Cheapside. She tried to be practical, reminding herself not to dream of possibilities, of connections which the world would frown upon, which any rational woman would know could never happen.

Only in fairy tales did a princely fellow sweep a poor girl off to a palace and into his loving embrace. In real life, marriage was at best a matter of practical and polite expedience, at worst, a purely business arrangement. That was what her cousin Wilhelmina had declared often enough while Lucy was growing up.

"Nor are you pretty enough, Lucinda, to hope for anything more than a pity match," her cousin had said once. The recollection was piercingly, painfully clear. They had been sitting in her cousin's overheated parlor while Wilhelmina sipped tea and Lucy's mother worked on a large pile of mending, trying to keep their clothes looking halfway respectable so she didn't have to go to their cousin to ask for a few pounds for a new frock and endure a long lecture about the importance of economy.

Lucy gritted her teeth at the memory. And the men that Wilhelmina had pushed her toward—she shuddered to remember. Lecherous, old, ill . . . no wonder that Stanley had seemed so appealing, when he had been introduced at church one summer while he visited an acquaintance in a nearby village, even though she barely knew him when she accepted his proposal.

Only her mother had murmured to her, that day in the parlor glancing at the miniature of Lucy's father that she kept always near her, "Love is a miraculous thing, Lucy, darling, and it has little to do with wealth or consequence."

Lucy had not been granted love, but she had made her escape from her cousin and the invisible bondage of life as a poor relation. She glanced about her, comforted as always in the knowledge that this house, small as it was, poor as it was, was hers now . . . at least, it was hers if she could keep the creditors at bay. She felt no obligation to her cousin; Lucy's mother had worked hard enough during her lifetime to repay Wilhelmina for the paltry board and shabby rooms the woman had extended to them.

This house was Lucy's home, and she would keep it, by the grace of God and her own resolution. If it took every ounce of effort in her body, if it took a dozen trips into the hellish bawdy house on Hampstead Heath, she would not give up!

And having to rework this lovely dress once again was only a minor inconvenience, given all that. Lucy rubbed her eyes and picked up her needle with renewed determination.

Violet brought her a cup of tea an hour later. Lucy took a long sip, relishing the strong taste, sweetened just as she liked it. When the tap on the door came, she lifted her head.

Violet went to the door. She came back carrying a large box. "Oh, ma'am, look, it's for you!"

Violet set it on the table, and Lucy, curiosity replacing all other thoughts, hurried to open it. The name of a renowned dressmaker graced the lid. When Lucy took off the top and pushed aside the paper, she saw the note.

"To replace the cloak you sacrificed to aid our escape," it said. It was signed simply, *Richmond.*

Lucy pulled it out. "How handsome," she murmured. "And so gentlemanly of him to remember that I left my cloak behind."

"Ooh, ma'am," Violet said. "Try it on, do."

It was constructed of the finest black wool, trimmed in smooth velvet and lined in silk; it draped her with easy warmth and elegance, ten times finer than the shabby cloak she had abandoned at the bawdy house, and to which she had given barely a thought since they had made their rushed exit. Lucy rubbed the soft wool between her fingers and smiled in appreciation. What a lovely wrap.

They hung her new cloak carefully in the clothes press in Lucy's room, and somehow she seemed to take its warmth with her to bed, and even her dreams of housebreaking thieves occurred less often than usual.

❧

On Monday Lucy threw herself into final preparations for the royal theater party. Violet brushed her curly hair as they practiced hairdos for the big event, and Lucy worked steadily with her needle; the dress was almost complete. She thought the tear in the neckline would not be observed, unless someone looked very closely indeed.

And the knocks at the door continued. Quite early in the morning, the boy from the local butcher shop delivered the fattest goose that Lucy had ever seen.

Violet came to show her, hugging the big plucked bird in her arms as if it were an overlarge baby. "Ma'am, just look!"

"Good heavens, did he mistake the house?" Lucy exclaimed. "I did not order such a thing—it must cost a fortune."

Violet shook her head. "No, I asked, but he said a swell cove stopped at the shop yesterday. His coachman banged on the door till the butcher himself looked out from his rooms above the shop. And the gent tossed him half a crown and said send the best bird 'e—he—had to this 'ouse."

"House," Lucy corrected absently. She exchanged a telling glance with her maid. "The viscount!"

"Yes, ma'am," Violet agreed without surprise. "But what are we to do with h'it? It, I mean."

"Cook it, of course," Lucy murmured, though she understood Violet's dilemma. The days were warm now, and the poultry, unlike the cured ham, would not keep long even when roasted. They could certainly not eat all of this enormous bird themselves, and it was a shame to waste any of the rich meat. She made a quick decision.

"Put this on the fire to roast—it will take hours to cook it. Then, since Mrs. Broddy and my cousin think they should be entertained, and we should not wish to be behind in the *civilities,* run across the street and invite the Broddys and my cousin to dinner. Tell them it will be a simple family affair, since we have little to prepare as side dishes, and they may find the courses a bit sparse. Though, lord knows, my cousin will be delighted to have occasion to criticize something!"

"Yes, ma'am," Violet said, her nose wrinkled in dismay.

"And then go up to Mrs. Smith's house."

"Mrs. Smith?"

"The widow with seven children who owns the cobbler's shop on the next street, that Mrs. Smith. Invite her, too, and tell her to bring *all* the children." Lucy smiled as Violet gaped at her. "We do not wish to waste any of this delightful bird."

"No, ma'am," Violet agreed, a reluctant grin supplanting her frown.

Lucy and the footman helped Violet prepare for their impromptu feast, and though it made serious inroads into the pantry's bounty, she thought the resulting dinner was a tasty one.

Her cousin raised her brows when the footman showed the two women into the dining room, already nicely laid with every dish of Lucy's china, also a bequest from her mother. "Really, Lucinda, a male servant? His wages will be twice a chambermaid's, such extravagance! I thought you were short of funds?"

"Yes, but Mrs. Broddy advised me to hire more servants," Lucy couldn't help saying.

Her neighbor coughed as Wilhelmina threw her a lowering glance. "Ah, well . . ."

Wilhelmina turned back to peer at Lucy. "Why on earth did you chop off your hair in that ugly modern style? I should have advised against it."

But I didn't ask you rose unbidden to Lucy's lips. She swallowed the retort as she heard another knock at the door.

"I believe the rest of our company has arrived."

When Mrs. Smith entered, followed by a bevy of children, ranging in age from a tall, nicely-spoken lad to a youngster of five or so, Wilhelmina looked even less pleased. They all sat down, although Lucy had had to borrow extra chairs from Mrs. Broddy, earlier, to crowd around the table.

Several times, as the widow Smith's smallest boy jumped out of his seat to chase his next-oldest brother around the table, wailing, "I wanted that piece, Mama. Make 'im give it to me!" Wilhelmina demanded loudly, "Why are these children not in the nursery where they belong?"

Lucy ignored her comments as a girl of about twelve grabbed her brother and pushed him back into his seat. He soon jumped up again. Violet, who was bringing in a dish of pickled eggs, almost collided with the child.

"Charley!" his mother admonished. "Do sit down and finish your lovely dinner!"

Charley subsided for the moment, looking angelic as he chewed on a drumstick almost as big as his arm, while

Cousin Wilhelmina muttered darkly, "Children should be seen and not heard!"

But the cheerful bedlam of Mrs. Smith's brood made even her cousin's words hard to decipher. On Lucy's other side, Mrs. Broddy spent her time trying, and failing, to draw out scandalous information about the viscount. "But does he have honorable intentions?" she asked. "Really, Mrs. Contrain, you must consider your reputation."

"Oh, I do," Lucy agreed, her voice calm. "I consider it at least twice a day, before breakfast and after tea. Such a shame your husband had another engagement tonight. Another serving of goose for you?"

"No, thank you," Mrs. Broddy snapped. Looking peeved, she and Wilhelmina departed as soon as dinner ended.

Afterward, Lucy said good night to Mrs. Smith and her crew, and with the footman to help Violet clean up the dishes, she went up to her room and fell, exhausted, into her bed.

The next morning Lucy woke, her stomach a little queasy. Not from the goose the night before, which had been excellent, but from the prospect of the amazing social scene she would glimpse tonight. Lucy Contrain, going off to the theater with a prince. What an unprecedented occurrence. She drew a deep breath and told herself that all would be well. Somehow. She would not spill her tea, she would keep her mouth shut and say nothing stupid, and the state of her nerves would improve. Surely they would.

She looked over the mended dinner gown, chose long kid gloves from the stock the viscount had sent her, and polished her mother's small ear drops with a soft cloth while the footman cleaned the velvet evening slippers.

Later that morning Mrs. Smith sent her middle son over with an armful of lilies of the valley along with renewed thanks for Lucy's hospitality. Lucy regarded the small white flowers with pleasure; most of them she put into a vase on the dining room table, but some could be used to decorate her hair, since she had no pricey ostrich feathers or diamond tiaras to finish off her coiffure. She was set for the night.

Or so she thought.

While they ate a light luncheon, savory soup made with the last bits of the goose, and Lucy chatted with Violet about how early she should be ready, another knock came.

Violet went to answer the door. In a moment, she was back bearing a square box.

Violet beamed. "Ma'am, more surprises!"

Feeling that she was past astonishment, Lucy opened the large package, but she was wrong. She gasped when she pulled the shimmering fabric out of the paper in which it was cocooned.

"It's beautiful!" Violet whispered.

Lucy had no words at all. Speechless, she touched the lightly woven shawl, with its gold-colored threads sparkling through the filmy fabric.

"Ooh, try it on, ma'am, do," Violet suggested.

Lucy needed no urging. They hurried up the stairs to Lucy's bedchamber, where Lucy quickly shed her muslin day dress to put on her gown for the theater party, and, with Violet's assistance, tied the evening wrap about her shoulders. It covered the damaged neckline and seemed the perfect accessory for the maize-colored gown.

Glancing into the looking glass at all her donated splendor, Lucy barely recognized her own image.

Fairy tales, indeed!

"You'll be the most beautiful lady there!" Violet vowed, her eyes wide.

Lucy laughed. "I hardly think that will be the case. There will be many well-dressed, elegant guests, Violet." But she would be able to walk into the theater with the assurance that she was as well garbed as any aristocrat there. Lucy felt a rush of gratitude at her benefactor. She looked back at the empty box and found the calling card that had slipped to the side.

The Countess of Sealey.

Of course, Lucy should have known, what a generous

friend the countess was! There was no message on the card, but Lady Sealey was always modest.

What had made the countess think of an evening wrap? Perhaps the viscount had whispered into her ear news of their impending royal outing. Whatever the cause, this was amazingly generous, even for the countess.

This time, a note of thanks was not enough. This generosity could not wait for acknowledgment until the countess's weekly salon, and anyhow, Lucy preferred greater privacy for such an occasion. Besides, a walk would be a good way to distract her from her nervous qualms; she had hours yet before it would be time to leave for the dinner party.

Violet put away the wrap, and Lucy carefully disrobed and donned her day dress, suitable for making calls. She told Violet of her destination.

"I'll just take off my apron," the maid suggested, "and I'll be ready, ma'am."

But when Lucy came downstairs, she found that their borrowed footman, whose name was Chudley and who took his role of protector seriously, insisted on accompanying her.

"Lord Richmond would 'ave my 'ead if anyone assaulted you on the street, ma'am," he told her.

Lucy agreed. The day was warm, and Lucy set off at a brisk pace, Chudley a pace behind her. Even with her escort, Lucy kept a sharp eye about her, but she encountered no unruly beggars today. After she left her own neighborhood behind and crossed into the west side, the streets became wider and the houses larger. Carriages passed, with well-groomed horses showing off their paces, heads held high. Children with their nursemaids played in the green parks in the middle of large squares of houses, and their shouts and laughter suited Lucy's mood exactly. Her mood was still sunny when she reached the countess's residence and banged the brass knocker.

The butler admitted her promptly, and one of the house's footmen took her up to the large salmon- and gold-hued drawing room. Lucy found the countess sitting alone, with a bit of fine needlework in her hands.

The older woman put down her needle at once. "My dear child, what a lovely surprise. Come in, please. I was feeling quite overcome with ennui. Bring us a tea tray, Watkins."

The servant bowed and departed, and Lucy sat down in one of the gilt-armed chairs.

"I just had to thank you for your generous gift, it is so beautiful!"

But Lady Sealey waved her thanks aside. "Oh, that's quite enough of that, dear child. Now, tell me what amusements you have planned. I hope you are getting out more?"

A bit perplexed, Lucy explained about the amazing invitation to the theater as part of the prince's party.

The countess acted unaware of Lucy's plans, though perhaps she was simply being tactful. She smiled. "How lovely. I dined with the prince a week ago—his cook's sauces are superb. I'm sure you will have a wonderful time, though it may be a bit of a crush. The dear prince does enjoy the theater, and he likes playing host even more."

Lucy laughed. "I'm looking forward to it. And it will certainly be a change from my last outing."

Oh dear, she had not meant to mention the trip to Hampstead Heath. No, that wasn't true; she had longed to talk the whole thing over with a woman she could trust not to gossip, a woman wise in the ways of London's polite—if not always moral—society.

"Really?" her hostess inquired, lifting her elegant brows.

"I would not tell anyone else this, but I know you will not be shocked to hear that my husband had—had a mistress," Lucy blurted. She drew a deep breath.

The countess nodded, her expression unaltered, and Lucy continued more calmly. "For reasons having to do with my late husband's business dealings, I arranged to meet this woman."

Lucy paused again.

"Oh, my, how brave of you. I hope this person was not unpleasant towards you? Courtesans can be very bold."

"Not exactly."

The countess leaned forward, the diamonds in her rings flashing, and patted Lucy's hand. "But you were distressed?"

Lucy considered, then answered slowly. "I—I hardly know how to say what I felt."

"It would be natural to feel shocked and angry," Lady Sealey suggested. "Or, of course, hurt that your husband should take his favor elsewhere. You know that many men make a habit of just such indulgences, my dear. If you were deeply in love with him—"

Lucy sighed. "Not precisely, but I had hoped that our attachment would grow."

"Then try not to allow this news to wound you. Some perturbation over such a discovery is natural, of course, but I hope you will not permit your husband's straying to unsettle you overmuch."

"It does," Lucy said in a rush of candor. "The worst part is, it's not as if I had been reluctant to share his—his passion, you see. I always wished for us to be closer. But Stanley came to me so seldom, and now that I know he had a liaison elsewhere, I can't help but wonder what I did wrong, where I was lacking."

The countess gazed at her, her fair skin dusted with powder to soften its fine lines, and her hazel eyes hooded. Lucy could not read her expression.

"It haunts me, that I could be so inept as to drive him to another woman!" Lucy went on, determined to admit it all now that she had started. "I feel that I must have failed him, and now it colors all my memories of the marriage."

"Lucy, you must not say this, nor think it!" Lady Sealey said, her tone unexpectedly firm. "There is nothing wanting with you, I am sure of it."

"But why—"

"This is simply what men do, dear child. Who can fathom their motives?"

Lucy sighed. "And to see her—she was not a terrible slattern, but she was still so—so different from me, I felt very strange."

Lady Sealey gave a small ladylike snort of laughter. "That's often the point, my dear."

"I don't understand." Lucy looked back at the older woman, who waved her hand.

"This type of woman—"

The footman entered with a tray, and the countess fell silent until the tea had been poured and Lucy had been enticed into taking some dainty sandwiches and cakes.

"No, it's more than that. Some men prefer women who are not ladies, dear child. And such a man may find it hard to feel passion for a lady who is his wife. Not that he would consider marrying someone who was not a lady, of course."

Lucy felt even more confused. "But that makes no sense."

"Who said it should be logical? Men claim logic as their province, but they are as often befuddled as females, in my experience! No, as I said, some men want their wives to be saintly and untouched, even by them. Meanwhile, the only type of woman who can arouse them to ardor is a woman who is most certainly not saintly. It was your husband's problem, my dear, his failing, if you will, but not yours. Please do not reproach yourself."

She patted Lucy's hand again and urged her to drink her tea before it cooled.

Lucy took another sip, as much to occupy herself as to satisfy any thirst. She still did not understand why Stanley could have desired another woman simply because she was a wanton, while his own wife, whom he had chosen freely, held no physical attraction for him.

"Then, you don't think there is some trick or method I need to study—" Lucy blushed. "Just in case I should ever form an attachment, that is . . ."

"My dear, if you develop a fondness for a man of healthy appetites, and if you find yourself longing to re-spond, I am sure you will have no problem meeting his expectations. When two people are well suited and have genuine affection and trust between them, all the rest will sort itself out in a most enchanting way. I promise you it is so." The countess smiled, as if at memories of her own.

Lucy tried to believe the older woman's words, but doubt still lingered deep in her heart. It was all very well for the countess to utter such comforting theories, but Lucy would bet her best buttonhook that *she* had never had a husband who shunned her bed. Sighing, Lucy changed the subject and finished her tea and cake.

Then she walked home, a little more slowly, her faithful escort trailing just behind. They reached home safely, and Violet unlatched the door.

The sun had dropped in the sky, and the afternoon's warmth was waning. "I have water 'eating—heating—for your bath, ma'am," Violet said.

Lucy put aside her nervous qualms and threw herself into preparations for the grand night to come. She bathed, washing off the dust of the street, then dried her hair before the fire, enjoying how quickly it dried, now that it was short and fell into natural curls all about her face.

Violet helped her tease the tendrils into the most becoming shape, and added small white flowers from the lily-of-the-valley blooms to adorn her hair. Lucy put in her ear drops and clasped her grandmother's small pendant around her neck. Then she donned the dress and carefully placed the filmy wrap about her shoulders. When she stood, she felt like a princess.

Tonight, she would not be surprised if a pumpkin pulled up to her door!

But there would be only—only!—the viscount's elegant chaise. Oh, when this mystery of the ruby was solved, how hard it was going to be to go back to her real life, with no royal invitations and no rakish noblemen to escort her to intriguing parties and make her heart beat faster.

Lucy shook her head at herself. They would be there tonight to search for answers—she must pull her head out of the clouds and remember what she was about. Illusions were dangerous things; hadn't she learned that already? What business did she have dreaming about any man? She had thought, for a while, that she could be happy with Stanley, and he could be happy with her. . . .

Oh, drat the memories. Tonight was only for tonight! No matter how brief it would be, she made up her mind to enjoy every moment. And with that decision, the nervous quivers that had troubled her stomach for days as she anticipated the prince's theater visit suddenly faded.

Tonight was her night, and Lucy would seize it.

So when the viscount's carriage stopped in front of her small house, Lucy was ready to allow Lord Richmond to help her up into the cushioned seats. She was intensely aware of his touch as he handed her into the carriage.

He looked even more severely elegant than usual, in his dark evening coat, taut pantaloons, and spotless white linen. He was not such a dandy as to sport gold watch fobs or diamond studs; he wore only the uncut emerald signet ring that he always wore, and his neckcloth was a masterpiece of apparent simplicity.

And the look he gave her made her blood roar in her ears.

"You look ravishing," Lord Richmond said. "I am honored to be your escort tonight."

He was such a gentleman, making it sound as if he really wished for her company, and not as if they were only linked by their joint desire to retrieve a stolen treasure. Lucy smiled, and without thinking, put out one hand.

Not one to miss an opportunity, Nicholas took it at once, then brought it to his lips, kissing it tenderly.

Lucy shivered, but to his disappointment she drew her hand back, shaking her head. "I   that is—we are already acquainted, my lord, there is no reason—that is—"

She stopped, looking flustered. At least he did have an effect on her, Nicholas told himself, trying to repress the desire that rose inside him when he sat so near to her . . . if only she were more open to his advances. . . .

It was just as well the ride was a short one. Lucy found when they drew up before the theater that she was stiff with tension. Not that she feared the viscount would ravish her in his carriage. She trusted him implicitly, and of course he had dropped her hand when she requested it.

The problem was, she did desire his attentions, longed for him to kiss her hand, her cheek, her lips . . . yet something held her back, even now, when she had promised herself that tonight would not be haunted by past regrets. Lucy drew a deep breath and tried to think of other things. And heavens, she was here as a guest of a prince!

Ten

*W*hen they reached Covent Garden and the chaise pulled up in front of the large theater, the viscount helped her out. Lucy found she was almost trembling with excitement. She had never been to a real theater—she hardly counted the Punch and Judy shows at the local village fete that she used to enjoy as a child!

Lord Richmond offered his arm, and they entered the theater. It was crowded with people, among them several women dressed in the same dissolute style as the women she had seen at the bawdy house on the heath. Lucy stared, then blushed and turned her gaze away as they passed. The viscount nodded and spoke to several well-dressed acquaintances, the men smiling and nodding, the women flitting their fans and looking coy, but did not pause. He led her up a stairwell to an upper level, where eventually they were shown, with due ceremony, into the prince regent's box.

"There you are, Richmond! And the lovely young gal, too, how jolly!" Their royal host greeted them effusively as Lucy sank into a deep bow.

As she rose, the prince pulled the viscount aside for a whispered conversation, leaving Lucy free to stare, entranced, down at the theater floor.

It was a cacophony of noise and color and movement; few people were still, and almost no one listened silently. The lower level was jammed with men and the occasional woman in working-class clothing, most of them talking, drinking, shouting, or singing ragged snatches of tune, for the most part drowning out any hope of hearing the orchestra, who sat just in front of the stage itself and just now had their instruments lowered. The sides of the theater were lined with several tiers of boxes, and here turbaned matrons peered through their lorgnettes less at the stage than at other patrons, as if on the watch for possible gossip-inducing behavior; in other boxes, men and women of fortune flirted and talked, their behavior little different from the poorer patrons in the pit, except for their richer apparel and gleaming jewelry.

It was such a spectacle of sight and sound that Lucy found it hard to take it all in. With a start, she realized that the play was already in progress on stage; the actors were declaiming, and at a particularly effective line, some of the audience noise—though certainly not all—faded, and Lucy could make out what was being said.

She sat down quietly—the viscount was still occupied by the prince, who wiped his brow and waved his handkerchief, looking agitated—and tried to follow the play.

"It is the east, and Juliet is the sun . . ." the actor below belted out, lowering his voice a little as the audience paid more attention, continuing to rattle off his lines with assurance and the appearance of real emotion.

The play tonight was *Romeo and Juliet*! Her father had left her a leather-bound set of Shakespeare, which Lucy cherished. She had read this play many times, sitting alone in her small sitting room in Stanley's absence and dreaming about the love she did not seem destined to reap, but she had never seen the drama performed. She had not even thought to ask the viscount what they would be seeing, but this was a treat. Lucy sighed with pleasure and prepared to enjoy herself.

"See how she leans her cheek upon her hand . . ." Romeo paused dramatically before adding, "O, that I were a glove upon that hand, that I might touch that cheek . . ."

The actress playing Juliet stood on a balcony in a fetching blue gown, but for a moment, Lucy's attention wavered. She glanced down at the lovely, long gloves she had donned to wear for the evening, new gloves that the viscount had sent her. And he had certainly touched her cheek . . . For a few moments the memory held her much more intently than the scene being enacted on the stage.

To be in love, with the passion and the delight that the actors on stage were emoting . . . No, surely that was not what Lucy was feeling now. It would be the greatest folly if she were to forfeit her affections to the viscount. Even the countess of Sealey had not advocated that. "Amuse yourself," she had advised. "Lighten your mood, my dear."

She had never suggested that Lucy should lose her heart.

The scene below continued, and Lucy tried to pay attention. But now more visitors were being admitted to the royal box, and Lucy pulled her chair backward to make room. As Lady Sealey had noted, the prince was obviously fond of playing host.

Oh, dear. With a sinking heart, Lucy recognized Marion Tennett and her round, reticent husband. This was not the company she would have chosen, but of course, she was not in charge of her royal host's party, and it was ungrateful to even think such thoughts.

With an inner sigh, Lucy resigned herself to a polite welcome. At least Mrs. Tennett seemed in better humor. Her narrow lips lifted as they exchanged greetings.

"My dear Mrs. Contrain, how sweet you look tonight! I am so happy to see you here. I have been longing to spend more time in your company."

Lucy tried to hide her surprise. "How kind of you, Mrs.

Tennett," she answered, with total untruth, trying to decipher this sudden change in mood.

"Oh, address me as Marion, do, and may I have leave to address you as Lucy?"

"Of course," Lucy was forced to answer. "I take it you enjoy the theater?"

Marion threw a quick glance at the stage, then settled herself into the chair beside Lucy. "Oh, I adore it." And she proceeded to prove her assertion by ignoring the actors and pouring into Lucy's ear an endless stream of spiteful gossip that barely allowed Lucy to hear an occasional line from the stage. Lucy tried to hide her disappointment. If anyone could ruin such a rare treat as a night at the theater, it was Marion Tennett.

Below them, Juliet was saying, "My bounty is as boundless as the sea, my love as deep; the more I give to thee, the more I have, for both are infinite."

Oh, how lovely. Lucy wished intently to be free to attend the play more closely. If only this silly woman would stop nattering in her ear. And why was Mrs. Tennett suddenly determined to make Lucy a bosom friend? To make sure that Lucy spent as little time alone as possible with the viscount? To impress Lord Richmond and lure his attention back to Mrs. Tennett herself? Lucy found she had precious little trust in this woman's apparent tender of friendship. So she nodded and murmured soft replies to the comments the other woman made, and strained to hear snatches of the play.

On stage, the doomed romance proceeded rapidly into the secret elopement, and then the combats and fatal mistakes that led to the young lovers' untimely deaths. When the nurse broke the awful news of Romeo's death to her youthful charge: "He's dead, he's dead!" Lucy found unbidden tears spring into her eyes. She blinked hard, determined not to show such weakness in front of the woman who still sat beside her.

But the rush of feeling that flowed through her could not be stemmed. Lucy knew too well the shock of that pronouncement, the anguish of sudden loss, even though—

perhaps in some odd way, more intent because—her fondness for Stanley had possessed nothing like the depth and passion of Juliet's love for Romeo.

And when Juliet, in fading accents that managed to briefly silence even the crowd in the pit, proclaimed, "O, break my heart! Poor bankrupt, break at once!" Lucy found a tear sliding down her cheek. She reached into her reticule for a handkerchief.

"Really, my dear, it's only an illusion," Mrs. Tennett exclaimed, her brittle laugh ringing out.

Had she no imagination, no sensibility at all?

Lucy didn't trust herself to speak. She wiped her cheeks quickly and with great effort pushed back more unshed tears, though it made her throat ache. "Have you never lost someone you loved?" she asked, her voice quiet.

Mrs. Tennett's eyes glinted, and Lucy could not determine the emotion that flashed there, but she felt its intensity.

"Oh, I have known loss," the other woman agreed, lowering her voice, too. "But I suspect I am stronger than you. If the deprivation of a dear one pains you, then I must advise you to take care. If you become too attached to Nicholas, I must warn you, dear Lucy, he will surely break your heart, just as effectively as any dead husband. And we would not wish you to end up cold on the bier like poor Juliet, now would we?"

Hateful woman!

"I have no interest in Lord Richmond," Lucy said, knowing her voice sounded stiff.

"Really, my dear, you expect me to believe that? No woman ever graced with his attention has been immune to him, no more than he can resist the fleeting attractions of any pretty woman who crosses his path. I have observed him for years, and I can assure you it is true." Mrs. Tennett's expression exhibited only an apparently sincere solicitude.

Lucy was almost too angry to find words to reply. "I will mind my heart, thank you for your—" she paused to draw a deep breath "—kind, and I'm sure, unbiased concern."

Mrs. Tennett's gaze hardened. "You think I am still desirous of attracting Nicholas myself? Of course I am. He's much more exciting than my husband, and the best lover I've enjoyed in years."

The bluntness of her declaration left Lucy speechless for a moment, and the other woman plunged ahead.

"But if he can throw me over for newer pursuits, what do you think he would do to you, Lucy, dear?" Mrs. Tennett smiled, but her thin lips seemed stretched too wide. "It's not as if you have the beauty to hold him, you know."

Feeling as if she had been slapped, Lucy flushed.

"Oh, you're pretty enough, in a common sort of way, but hardly a beauty of the first rank, as Nicholas is accustomed to having his pick of. Dark hair is in style this year, not fair, and besides, I doubt you have the talent in bed to hold an accomplished lover. Your husband may have been content with your moderate charms, although I heard rumors that he had other interests himself, but I am certain you'll never hold Nicholas. I would advise you not to try, and save yourself the grief of his going." She patted Lucy's hand. "I'm only thinking of your welfare, my dear."

In a pig's eye!

Pulling away from the touch, Lucy jumped to her feet. "Your advice is certainly something I will remember. Excuse me, I think I need some air."

The viscount had his back to her as the prince continued to talk, tugging at Lord Richmond's sleeve when he was not waving his hands in the air. So Nicholas did not see her go. No matter, she did not want to face him just now, flushed as she was with embarrassment, anger, humiliation—the emotions that raged inside her were almost impossible to define.

She left the box and strode a few feet away into the corridor behind it. She would not weep, she would not; she had been embarrassed enough by Marion Tennett's

heartless comments. Lucy would not demean herself further. But the rush of anger and regret that flooded her
now was almost impossible to contain. She paced up and
down, not even noticing the other patrons who ambled
here and there, visiting friends in different boxes.

So she didn't recognize a familiar face until she almost
collided with another woman.

"Mrs. Contrain, are you unwell?"

It was Julia Blythe, and she put out one hand to gently
touch Lucy's arm.

Lucy shook her head, but she found it impossible to
speak. She feared she would burst into tears, and she
could not, she must not disgrace herself in this public
place.

"Here, come into our box." Mrs. Blythe drew Lucy
gently into one of the nearby enclosures. Inside, Mr.
Blythe and a couple of men were discussing bare-knuckle
matches with total disregard for the closing scenes of the
play, and they paid little heed to the two women.

Mrs. Blythe drew Lucy down into a seat at the edge of
the box. "The play must have induced distressing memories for you."

Lucy nodded and bit her lip to stem any tears. "I'm
sorry. It's very kind of you, Mrs. Blythe—"

"Oh, call me Julia, please. I understand you have few
acquaintances in London. Do you have family nearby?"
She sounded genuinely concerned, so Lucy did not mind
the question.

Lucy shook her head. "My parents are both dead, and
I have no close relations." That was true enough; Lord
knew that cousin Wilhelmina didn't count as such.
"Please call me Lucy, too, if you would."

"Then your bereavement is that much harder to bear,
alone. I hope you will come and call on me, when you
wish it. I should enjoy getting to know you better." Julia
looked into her beaded reticule and handed Lucy one of
her calling cards.

Lucy found that the extension of genuine empathy
eased her turmoil, just as Marion Tennett's vicious com-

ments had magnified it. "I should enjoy visiting with you," she told Julia. "And when I am prepared to entertain again, I would be delighted to see you at my house, as well."

"Then it is settled." Julia gave her an impulsive hug. Lucy smiled, wishing she had the other woman's artless ease and self-confidence. "And look, they are beginning the farce that follows the play, so you can laugh for a while instead of weep."

Lucy grinned. "Definitely a more attractive option," she agreed. "And I suspect I should return to my host's box before someone wonders where I am." Or before Marion Tennett felt confident that she had vanquished Lucy so easily. Was she flirting with the viscount right now? "But I thank you, more than you know, for your enormous kindness."

"Oh, fie, I have been hoping to see you again," Julia protested. "I was only happy for the chance to chat."

Lucy made her farewells and walked slowly back to the royal box. But before she could enter, a tall, familiar form emerged. It was Lord Richmond, his expression concerned.

"There you are," he said. "It took me an eternity to get free of the prince—his highness is most anxious about recovering the object. But I was uneasy about your abrupt departure. What is wrong?"

"Nothing," Lucy said, squaring her shoulders. "I am quite all right."

"I must dispute that." The viscount touched one finger to her cheek. The light touch was almost a caress, and his warmth and strength soothed her. "Have you been weeping?"

"The play is a sad one."

"Perhaps a poor choice for a widow," he suggested. "I'm sorry that it has distressed you."

She managed to smile up at him, though she knew it was a weak effort. "You were not the one who chose the night. We were bidden here by a prince, after all."

"And I suspect that Mrs. Tennett's company did not

increase your ease. I regret you had to endure her—I did not know they would be here tonight. However, the prince does not ask my approval for his guests, and Tennett is often in the prince's company." Nicholas's dark eyes looked genuinely concerned.

"She seems to resent any demands on your attention, even those as impersonal as my own," Lucy answered, knowing that her tone sounded stiff.

To her surprise, he frowned. "You know her character enough not to lend credence to her words, surely?"

"It is not my affair," she said, then wished she could rephrase her answer. Still, her remark was true in more ways than one.

"My dear Mrs. Contrain—"

"We should go in," Lucy interrupted, though her lips felt stiff, and she braced herself for more catty advice from Marion. "We will be missed, and that will only add fuel to Mrs. Tennett's jealousy."

To her surprise, the viscount shook his head. "I have made our farewells to the prince. It's not necessary for you to be pestered by that woman any longer."

Lucy felt an amazing lift of relief. "The prince doesn't mind?"

"He has more than enough company to amuse him," Lord Richmond pointed out, keeping his voice discreetly low. "People will come and go all night. Prinny loves any excuse to make merry."

She nodded, and when he offered his arm, she took it gladly. Royal invitations were more fatiguing than she could have imagined. They descended the stairs. Lucy could hear laughter and occasional raucous shouts from the theater pit as the farce continued on stage, apparently more popular with the audience that the Shakespearean drama had been.

With a word to a footman the viscount summoned his carriage, and very shortly she was being handed into its luxurious confines. She settled back against the padded seat and kept her gaze turned determinedly away from Lord Richmond. He seemed to notice entirely too much, and she knew she had never been able to keep her face from revealing her emotions.

So she watched the street as other carriages passed, and peddlers pushed their carts wearily home after a long day. She was intensely aware of the viscount, sitting quietly on the other side of the carriage. She could feel his gaze upon her now and then, but he seemed to respect her wish for solitude and did not speak. After a few moments, she shut her eyes and allowed the roll and sway of the well-sprung chaise to lull her almost into a light sleep.

When the carriage paused again, Lucy opened her eyes, and then blinked in surprise. This was not her street; this was not—from the look of the elegant townhouses lining the thoroughfare—even her neighborhood.

"Where are we?" she blurted.

Lord Richmond stirred, and she felt the strength of his presence again. How had she forgotten, even briefly, with whom she shared this small space? She blinked and tried to marshall her thoughts.

"This is my residence."

Lucy swallowed hard. He surely didn't mean to take advantage of their time together—had all her trust been misdirected?

"I thought you needed a little quiet time, a glass of good wine in front of the fire, a friend perhaps to speak to. But it is entirely at your discretion. If you would prefer to go straight home, I will instruct my coachman."

He watched her hesitate, and could observe, even in the dim light from the flambeaux outside, the first spark of alarm fade almost as soon as he had detected it. She took a deep breath and wrestled with herself; he could see the struggle clearly.

Nicholas sat very still, not wishing to frighten her, nor to suggest that she was in peril of either her honor or her person. It was scandalous behavior, yes, to bring her here, but his servants were loyal and well trained, and no one would find out from his staff if she spent an hour or so here in his company.

He couldn't bear the hurt he had seen in her tonight—at first the renewed signs of an old sorrow, then a new humiliation—that last was the crowning motivation that had led him to take action in his usual imperious style to bring her here.

She needed cherishing, the fragile and courageous and too much put-upon Mrs. Lucy Contrain. She needed tender handling and a shoulder to lean on—she had soldiered on alone long enough. And he wanted badly to offer that shoulder, to be the one she turned to for support as well as many other things he shouldn't want from her.

For a small eternity he needed all his control to sit apart, not touching her, not influencing her, not—be truthful, man—seeking to seduce her when he knew perfectly well that he could do it if he tried. It would be wrong. She was too wounded, too vulnerable. So, holding himself in check when all he longed for was to reach out, he sat very still and waited.

At last she nodded slowly. "Very well," she said. "It has been a trying night. I admit I—I do not wish to be alone."

The simple truth of her words shone in her eyes, the poignant loneliness that she was so brave to admit. He ached for her and with her. At last, with infinite relief, he could reach out and push open the carriage door. At this signal the footman who had been waiting outside sprang to help, unfolding the steps, and Nicholas—still with careful economy, touching her only as much as bare civility would allow—helped her step out.

Without any further words, he led her into his house. While his bland-faced butler bowed, Nicholas said, "Wine in the library, and some light refreshment, please, Hodges."

The servant nodded and disappeared into the back of the hall. Her eyes wide, Mrs. Contrain glanced about her.

"Your house is quite lovely," she said. "What a magnificent tapestry."

Its colors were exotic, and the hunting scene depicted on its fabric field revealed a vibrant energy, even though the figures had a unique style. She dropped her gaze to the table. "What is this statue?"

"Buddha, in one of his poses," the viscount answered.

The design was unusual to her eyes, but she could sense its serenity. Lucy looked from the brass shape to the bright, stylized painting behind it, which depicted several women in colorful Eastern costumes and a figure with blue skin whom she suspected must be some kind of local deity.

"A Hindu god, with a princess and her handmaids behind him," Nicholas explained.

He led her into the library, his favorite room in the house, the one that spoke most clearly of who he was. He had a strange perception that she sensed this, and again she gazed, wide-eyed, at the Indian carvings and vases, the painted screen with its exotic bright colors, the bright-colored silks that had been made into pillows for the deep leather chairs.

"It must have been fascinating, to travel to India and the East," she said, running her hand along the smooth line of an ivory elephant whose upturned trunk seemed to greet them. "I should like to go there."

"No!" he exclaimed before he thought, and when she looked at him in surprise, he lowered his voice. "That is, it is a beautiful country, yes, but with its own dangers. I have not been back in some years."

Obviously puzzled, she stared at him, and to distract her he crossed to the large globe in the corner and twirled it. "I have traveled a good deal. My family had business holdings in several countries, and I still own an interest in the East India Company," he explained. "It's not quite the thing for an aristocrat to dip his hands in trade, I know. It has given some of the sticklers for propriety another bone of contention to toss at me."

"And why should you care?" Lucy suggested, her tone indignant. "As if they could do without their tea! What hypocrites!"

Her quick defense should have amused him—he cared very little what most of society said about him—but instead her words moved him more than he cared to show. She was so honest, so full of warmth and compassion . . . and dear God, he wanted her so.

To steel himself, he turned away again until the servant brought in a tray with wine and glasses and a platter of sandwiches and small savories. He nodded dismissal to the footman and served her himself. He was glad to see her take a sandwich and some of the pickled relish; he still worried that she was eating properly, though her color had improved in the last few days.

He poured her wine. Even brushing her fingers as he handed her the crystal goblet made his pulse leap. He forced himself to sit down in a chair across from her, keeping a discreet distance between them. He glanced at the fire in the hearth, leaping and snapping, and tried not to stare at his guest, when all he really wanted was to watch how the flame's light played in her fair hair and reflected in the clear blue of her eyes whenever she looked his way.

Only when she had finished eating and put her plate aside, taking another sip of the wine, did he speak again.

"Now," Nicholas said. "I want the truth."

Lucy felt her heart jump and hoped she did not look as guilty as she felt. An absurd feeling, she had not lied to him—exactly.

"I don't know what you mean," she said, her voice low, but she found his commanding gaze hard to meet. She glanced down at the Oriental rug, bright with blues and reds, upon which her feet rested.

"I'm sure you do. What did Marion Tennett say tonight that distressed you so much? It was more than the play, though that drama may not have been the best choice for your first outing after a year of mourning. But Marion has been her usual manipulative self, I am quite sure, and I wish to know what poison she attempted to fling into your face."

She heard anger in his voice, and other emotions harder to read.

"I do not wish to speak ill of one of your friends," she

murmured, darting a quick glance toward his face.

"She is not my friend," he said.

When Lucy raised her brows, he added, "Yes, we had a brief liaison. I soon realized that she was not the kind of person I wished to spend time with. What was between us ended long ago."

Lucy found that she believed him. The gleam in his eyes—she felt suddenly abashed again, and looked away, once more studying the intricate patterns of the rug.

"It is a Sehna rug from Persia," he pointed out, a hint of laughter in his voice. "A very nice one, too. But that does not answer my question. What did Marion say that upset you so?"

"She—was trying to be my friend, or so she claimed." Lucy knew that she still did not credit Mrs. Tennett's sincerity. Lord Richmond might be sure that he had no more interest in Mrs. Tennett—that did not mean the other woman agreed! Still, Lucy did not feel she should vilify the woman just because Mrs. Tennett found it hard to let go of the viscount. Would Lucy feel the same way, if she had lost his attention? It was just as well not to answer that thought.

"She simply warned me not to allow myself any illusion of—of feelings for you. She said it was the quickest way to a broken heart."

Silence. Lucy braced herself and met his gaze again. Some emotion smoldered in his dark eyes that she still could not read. But she felt a stirring of feeling prickle up her spine, and she had to remind herself to breathe slowly and normally. She must ask him to call for his carriage, very soon. To stay too long, alone in such an intimate setting, would be the utmost folly.

Yet, she was glad to have had this glimpse of his home. She had learned a great deal about the elusive viscount tonight, more than he might have realized.

"And you believed her?" He did not move a finger, yet she had the impression of a sleeping lion whose lids are about to lift, whose great power is about to be released. She felt her pulse quicken.

"Well, yes. I think I—that is—any lady would feel bereft of your company when a liaison ended. You are more charming than you know, my lord."

God, what an adorable innocent she was. How had she lived over a score of years to still be so guileless? And yet, how could she not? She had been marooned at home while her feckless husband sought out whores and dens of iniquity, leaving the sweetest, warmest woman Nicholas had met in a decade to sit alone, solitary and unloved. . . .

The silence stretched—did he not believe her? Lucy blurted the rest of her new "friend's" advice, although she had meant to leave these comments unsaid. "She told me I had not the beauty nor the allurement to interest you, and I knew—"

He moved so suddenly, like a spring uncoiling, that she gasped. Kneeling before her, he reached up, his hands clasping her arms with almost painful strength.

"And you believed that!"

Was he angry at her? Lucy blinked in dismay, and he must have read some of the confusion in her eyes because he loosened his grip and raised one hand to touch her face, as he had touched it at the theater when he had seen evidence of her unshed tears.

"My dear Mrs. Contrain—surely I may now call you Lucy? My dear Lucy, how can you value yourself so lightly?"

She was so aware of his nearness that it was hard to think, much less answer coherently. The strength of him, the male power that hung about him like smoke about a fire, drew her closer despite all her intentions. *Like a moth to the flame,* some part of her mind suggested. *And you can be burned just as badly.*

She tried to marshal an ounce of dignity. Sitting very straight, she told him, "I did not say I was the ugliest woman in London, my lord—"

"Nicholas," he interrupted.

"My lord," she repeated firmly. "But it would be foolish, not to say vain, to pretend to the kind of matchless beauty that makes some women the toast of the Ton."

"Have you seen these women?"

She flushed. "No, of course not, I did not go out enough to—but I have heard the stories. Stanley often said . . ."

Her voice faded, and he nodded. "And what did Stanley say, bringing home stories of these matchless beauties? Did he explain their vanity, their pride, or their artifice?"

She didn't answer, but he did not wait for a response.

"When did he talk about you?" He spoke almost too loudly, and Lucy winced.

The viscount lowered his voice, but his tone was insistent. "When did he tell you just how lovely is the curve of your cheek, and how your eyes shine in the candlelight, bright and clear and honest. Did he ever tell you just how refreshing your candor is, when one is surfeit with the facades and silly pretenses of so many in the Ton? How your warmth eases a man's loneliness, and your natural courage and good humor brighten the day . . ."

His voice faded, and he looked a little surprised, himself. But he could feel nothing like the astonishment that Lucy was experiencing. She swallowed hard. How could he say such sweet and nonsensical things? Was this how a practiced seducer worked? Small wonder no woman could resist this man, if he spoke such lovely balderdash to each new prospective lover. To bask in his intent, understanding gaze and to believe, just for a moment, that even half of his words could be true . . .

No, she knew better. She told herself she must pull away, she must admonish him to go back to his chair, she must put more distance safely between them . . . And even while these good intentions ran through her head, she lifted one hand and, for the first time, she touched his face.

His olive-toned skin was smooth, and as she ran her hand lightly over his cheek, she felt him tense. A small scar at the corner of his mouth stopped her hand—she had a sudden impulse to kiss it, as if the pain it had once caused could still be eased. . . .

He pulled her closer, and Lucy stiffened. "No, we can't, I shouldn't—"

"Why?"

"Because all the things Marion said are true. You would not—I am not—"

He brushed her lips and smoothed her frown away. "I am, and you are."

Before she could tell him this, too, was nonsense, he had slipped his hand to her throat, tracing its contours.

Something strange was happening to her body—she felt like a wax candle melting in the sun. Lucy found she was holding her breath; she inhaled with an effort. She should speak, but—

"I love the way your throat curves, just so, and your shoulders are perfect, neither too broad nor too narrow."

He ran his fingers lightly over the slope at the base of her throat, then stroked her shoulders. She felt his touch like gentle fire against her skin.

She tried again to make her voice heard and, this time, croaked out a few words. "Are you—are you trying to seduce me?"

He had—oh, dear, oh dear—untied her wrap and slipped her gown off one shoulder. She made a small sound deep in her throat.

He regarded her, those deep brown eyes brimming with enigma. Yet despite that, his gaze was surprisingly mild.

"Yes, Lucy, I am."

She tried to answer, but this time, no sound at all emerged. Her stomach had turned to jelly. She could get up and run away—if her legs would support her. She could protest, remind him of his honor and her own. She could—if she did not want so desperately to stay.

But she managed to mutter, "We can't—"

The viscount shook his head. "I have held myself back for days, but tonight I think—"

"Yes?"

"I think you need to be loved, sweet Lucy. You have no idea of the effect you have on a man." He took one of her hands and lifted it to his chest, slipping it beneath his coat and pressing it against the smooth linen of his shirt. Yes, she could feel his heart beating, surely beating faster than normal. For her? Because of her? Or was this the effect that any woman had on him?

He smiled at her, and again she knew her doubts were reflected on her face. "I want you to believe that you can do that to a man, any man of sense and taste. But most certainly to me, Lucy Contrain."

"My lord—"

"If you do not call me Nicholas, I—shall do some very pleasurable things to you, dearest."

She bit her lip, feeling a wild urge to laugh, to cry, to protest her total disbelief that this could be happening.

To her surprise, again, he released her hand, and for an instant, though he remained very close, still kneeling in front of her most improperly like a suitor asking for his lover's pledge, he did not touch her.

"Unless you truly do not want my affections, in which case I will see you home, safe and untouched."

And unloved.

Lucy knew the smart thing to do, the proper thing to do. She should rise now, dignified and ladylike, just as she had always behaved, and walk to the door. Go down the hall and step into the carriage. She had no doubt he would keep his word and see her home, without more beguilement.

The bloody hell with being smart and proper!

Lucy moved her hand, slowly and deliberately, and placed it back upon his chest. She was sure she felt his heart thump even faster.

"I think," she told him, her voice low and tremulous, "I think that I would like to be seduced, my lord."

"Nicholas," he corrected.

"Nicholas," she whispered, looking into the depths of his eyes, knowing she might drown there, and yet having no desire to pull away.

He lifted her hand to his lips and kissed the palm; his warm touch made her shiver. Then, as his lips traced their way up her arm and onto her shoulder, she quivered again in delight.

He loosened the buttons in the back and pushed her gown further down, and now he could trace light patterns across her chest, his hand rising and falling, but never going too far.

She was breathing quickly—her skin seemed more sensitive than it had ever been.

At last, he dropped his hand further, and by now every fiber of her longed for a more intimate touch. And when he cupped one breast, she jumped, feeling the contact like a spark of pure desire. Inside her she sensed long dormant responses ready like kindling to burst into flame. Oh, heavens, she wanted this man. If anyone interrupted them tonight, servants, dogs, villains, she would surely die of frustration.

He caressed the soft skin, touched the nipple, and Lucy drew a long breath. Stanley had never—

Then Nicholas bent his head and kissed the top of her breast, just where it swelled outward, and in her shock, Lucy lost the rest of that thought. Oh, my—

His mouth dipped lower and captured the nipple, now erect and straining against his firm lips, and Lucy made a most unladylike sound. She glanced down at him, afraid she would witness his repulsion, but his gaze on her was as warm and caressing as always. And he kissed her again, his mouth soft and firm, warm and smooth against her breast, and she felt the shock waves travel up and down every inch of her skin.

When he pulled away, she made an inarticulate sound of protest, but she found he simply rose in order to kiss her lips. This time, Lucy returned his embrace with a fervent energy of her own. She felt him react to her new response, his kiss becoming more urgent, more demanding. And she relished every moment of it, delighted in the firmness of his mouth against hers. When his tongue pushed through her half-opened lips, she responded in kind. Her hunger for this easy exchange of passion surprised her, and perhaps him, though she could not really judge. And she wanted more.

When he broke the contact again, she moved toward him instinctively. "Patience, my love," he told her, his voice low and intimate. "Slower is better, I promise you."

So, throwing her arms about his neck, she allowed him to lift her from the narrow chair and carry her across to the wide, cushioned divan. Lowering her carefully, he kissed her again, then pushed her gown further down and bent over her.

Lucy felt herself opening to him like an unfurling blossom. Whatever happened now, she would see this mad act to its glorious conclusion. She wanted him, and for the first time, she had the nerve to allow him to see her desire, beginning to understand that he would not draw back in disgust, as Stanley had.

Again, Nicholas stroked her breasts, first one, then both, and she quivered from his touch. Then he moved his hand to her feet and slipped off her evening slippers, running his hands up the smooth curve of her shin, then her thighs, and up into the private areas that no man, most certainly not her husband, had ever caressed in such a way.

Lucy found she was beyond coherent thought. She ached for him, and he didn't mind; he stroked the sensitive parts of her that she had no words for, had never dared ask Stanley to touch. And his contact sent her swirling into a maelstrom of feelings that she had never been close to experiencing before, sucked her in like a leaf into an eddy, into currents too powerful to resist.

She did not want to resist. She wanted him closer, she wanted to come together in that most intimate union that she had always suspected should be more than she had known. She wanted *him*.

So while he paused to shed his clothing, she pushed away the rest of her own, and when he came to rest his body over hers, she was more than eager for him to ease inside her. He slipped into the warmth that awaited him, and she gasped with pure joy. The feel of him inside her was a surprise, too, everything was a surprise. He felt so much firmer and larger, this was so different—she pulled him to her, and he took her mouth in a roughly passionate kiss and then again, with more deliberate, delicious movement. She moaned as he moved deeply inside her, and then when she saw that the rhythm itself was part of lovemaking, she moved her hips to meet him, matching his tempo with her own, sometimes trying to hasten it. Again he slowed, and smiled at her, kissing away her protests.

"Enjoy," he murmured. "There is no need for haste."

So he caressed her, met her passion with his own strength, and then at last his steady movements accelerated, carrying her with him along a rushing wave of passion that took her to places Lucy had never dreamed of. Words were too little, the small cries she uttered were not enough to express the intensities of feeling that seemed to flood through her, over and over, joy after joy, sensation after sensation.

She had never in her life felt so close, so connected, nor so alive. With this man. With Nicholas.

When his passion neared its peak, she was ready, more than ready to burst with him into fulfilment, soar with him, explode with pure ecstatic delight. When he pulled out and slipped his hand inside her until her passion crested, she barely noticed the change, too overcome with these new and overwhelming sensations.

Then she was floating, free and untrammeled, sure that she had touched the hem of heaven itself. She gave a small cry, then sighed very deeply. He pulled her into an even tighter embrace, and she lay secure in his arms, almost surprised that her body was still intact; she felt as if the pieces of it might have burst apart, like a blasting cannonball but without the pain. But the sensations Nicholas had evoked—never had she imagined lovemaking could be like this.

She leaned her head against his chest, damp with a fine film of perspiration, enjoying the solid strength of his body and his particular masculine scent. His arms were firm about her, his eyes still alert, still caressing, even when his hands lay immobile. He still accepted her, enjoyed her response, had never once looked repulsed or shocked by her reactions.

She had never felt so complete.

Nothing in her marriage, those few, brief, awkward joinings in her marriage bed, had ever been like this. Stanley had barely managed to get inside her before the lovemaking would end, and more often, he had refused to try. For an instant Lucy shut her eyes against tears, for the sadness of the marriage that had been so unhappily barren in its physical and emotional relationships, and, too, in genuine sympathy for Stanley and his inability to love his own wife.

She had suspected that things had not been as good as they could be. She'd never known there were mountains to scale that would lift her soul as well as her body, thrilling her, fulfilling her in so many ways.

For that, she would thank Nicholas, or she would when she could utter the words. For now, she rested her cheek against his chest, hearing his heartbeat gradually slow, and stroked the damp hair that lay against the back of his neck.

When he raised his dark brows, she smiled into his eyes.

"No regrets, sweet Lucy?" he whispered.

"None," she told him, her voice still husky. "Never."

His smile widened, and he kissed her again.

And then, one more surprise in a night of surprises. He stroked her still-sensitive breasts, kissed her still-eager lips, drew her to him again, and then—then there were even more delights. . . .

⟡

Later, she had dozed. When she opened her eyes, she drew a deep breath. Why did she feel so relaxed, so calm, so—happy! It was such an unfamiliar feeling, this moment of ease. She smiled, without for a moment even remembering why, then everything rushed back.

"I enjoy seeing you smile," he said. He had eased off

the settee and now, clothed again, sat in a leather chair a few feet away.

Lucy blushed a little, but her smile broadened. It was lovely to have something to smile about, something as special as this night, this man, this coming together.

She raised her head from the pillow and found that Nicholas had covered her with a wide soft strip of brightly colored silk. She fingered the smooth fabric. "How beautiful this is."

"It's a sari," Nicholas told her. "The Indian women wear them, wrapped about their bodies in a rather ingenious fashion."

"With no buttons," Lucy observed. "How resourceful." A sudden thought distracted her, and she glanced at the window and the darkness beyond the heavy draperies, frowning in concern. "What time is it?"

"Only a little past midnight," he told her, his tone reassuring.

"I must get home!" Lucy sat up, clutching the silk to her naked body. "My neighbors—I have had gossip enough already."

He frowned at that. "Inquisitive tabbies, are they? Any evening engagement would keep you out this late, my dearest Lucy. Don't let them terrorize you."

Lucy thought of the nosy Mrs. Broddy, and her dreaded cousin Wilhelmina, and suddenly she laughed. "I will not," she promised. "But truly, it's time I returned home."

So she dressed quickly, or as quickly as she could while savoring this curious, enchanting sense of lassitude, hating to let go of the relaxed, easy feelings that lingered after their lovemaking. This, too, was new to her, and it was like the afterglow of the fire that had raged inside her earlier, slowly fading embers as warm and comforting as their earlier passion had been tumultuous.

Nicholas helped her button her gown up the back and fetched an ivory-backed brush and a small looking glass when she refused his offer of a bedroom upstairs in which to redo her hair. Fortunately, her new curly crop was easy enough to rearrange.

When he tied her new wrap about her shoulders, she was ready to go to the carriage, putting aside the reluctance she felt to leave him.

She paused at the door of the study, trying to hold this hour with her forever. Behind her, Nicholas leaned down to kiss her briefly. "This was the first time, not the last," he whispered into her ear.

Lucy smiled back at him, cherishing the feel of his lips after he opened the door, then they proceeded decorously down the hall and into his carriage.

On the ride home, he put one arm about her shoulders and she sat close to him, treasuring every moment of his nearness. There was no need to talk; the easy communion she felt with Nicholas imbued the silence with its own message.

When the carriage slowed again, Lucy smothered a sigh. Would they, indeed, share more nights of passion, or was Nicholas as fickle as his reputation, and Marion Tennett's warning, had suggested?

Either way, Lucy was sure she would never regret this night, and she would never ever forget it. She felt a different person, a new woman, with new perceptions and new confidence. And those she would carry with her forever.

So when the carriage drew up in front of her small house in Cheapside, her mood was still serene. But her composure lasted only until she stepped out. In the light of the carriage's lamps, Lucy's eyes widened.

Her front door, battered and splintered, hung ajar.

Eleven

"*Nicholas, look!*" *Lucy ran forward, thrusting aside* the damaged door.

"Lucy, wait," she heard him call after her, but instead, she bolted into the darkness.

What had happened? Who had entered her house? She bumped into a wall and, using her hands, felt along its rough plastered surface till she came to the dining room.

She stood in the doorway, blinking, waiting for her eyes to adjust to the faint glimmers of light that came through the uncurtained windows. Heartsick, she expected to see an empty room; some creditor or other who had finally made off with the last of her furniture.

Instead, she made out dim shapes of upturned chairs thrust to the side and the table pushed back out of place, as if someone had scanned the floor itself.

What on earth?

As she stood there, trying to understand what had happened, the room lightened. Nicholas had brought in a carriage lamp, which cast a flickering circle of pale light about them.

"I don't understand—" Lucy began, when she suddenly felt her heart seem to stop. "Oh God, Violet! And where is Chudley?"

They found the footman's crumbled body lying in the hall just beyond the dining room.

"Is he dead?" Lucy whispered, one hand to her mouth.

Nicholas stooped over the servant and parted the man's blood-soaked hair. "No, but he has a wide gash on his head. I must stop the bleeding."

Lucy rushed up the stairs, stumbling in her haste and banging her shin painfully on a corner of a narrow stair, all the way calling her maid's name. But no one answered, and the silence hung menacingly in the narrow hallway.

She found some linen towels in a heap in the hallway and brought them back to give to Nicholas as he tended the footman. Then she returned to the upper floors, climbing all the way to the attic floor and Violet's small bedroom. It was empty. Usually painfully neat, the bed had been pulled apart, the covers tossed here and there and the mattress cut into slits, its straw spilling out and littering the normally clean floor. But Lucy saw no sign of her servant and friend.

"Oh, dear Lord, please let her be safe," she breathed. She bolted back down the steps, glancing into her own bedroom to see the same confusion and disarray, then hastened on. Nicholas rose and tried to slow her, catching her when she stumbled again. With the viscount holding her arm, they both hurried into the kitchen.

The last embers of the fire burned on the hearth, and the stools had been tossed aside, one with legs shattered violently. Flour littered the floor, as well as grains of sugar and loose tea. Lucy saw, her heart sinking even further, that the pantry door was half open, and obviously her newly restocked larder had been pillaged, too, and the foodstuffs ruined. But nothing mattered except Violet's safety—where was she? If she had been taken away, murdered—

Lucy blinked back tears of panic. "We must put out the alarm," she told the viscount, grabbing his arm again. "We must—"

"Quiet," he murmured, his head to one side. "Listen."

Lucy paused, and then she heard it, too. A muffled sound—Lucy sprang toward the pantry and pushed open the door. The figure on the stone floor moved, despite the ropes that bound her arms and legs and gagged her mouth, and moaned inarticulately.

"Oh, Violet! Are you hurt?" Lucy dropped to her knees beside her servant.

Nicholas produced a knife and slashed the girl's bonds. In a moment they both helped Violet sit up, and Lucy rubbed her cold hands and touched her face anxiously where a smear of blood stained her cheek.

"Are you hurt?" she repeated, and this time Violet croaked an answer.

"Bloody 'orses' arses! T'was at least three of 'em, ma'am. I 'eard the door smashed, and the sound of blows. When I ran downstairs, poor Chudley was on the floor, and they threw a dirty blanket over me 'ead and then tossed me into the pantry and tied up me arms and legs. I tried, ma'am, but I couldn't stop 'em!"

"Of course not. I'm just glad you weren't—" She couldn't bring herself to finish the horrible thought. Lucy drew a deep breath, feeling dizzy with relief.

Who had done this? Was there some creditor so angry that she had not paid Stanley's debts that he would stoop to such malicious and useless damage? She could hardly credit such anger. Or had Jace forced the information about Lucy's location out of the hapless Eve?

Nicholas frowned. "Stay here while I check the rest of the house," he told her, "to be sure no one lingers in hiding to catch you unprepared."

Shivering, Lucy nodded. She found her stout walking stick and, with it nearby, looked through the rubble until she located a pot to heat water over the coals, and a rag to clean the cut on Violet's forehead, then she tended to Chudley and tightened his bandage.

When Nicholas returned, he brought reassuring news. "There is no one lurking inside the house," he told Lucy, after drawing her aside. "Chudley is stirring, and I do not think his wound is mortal. The back door is secure, and my coachman is watching the front. How is she?"

"Shaken and bruised." Lucy glanced back at Violet, who sat on the one stool which still had all three legs intact. "But there seem to be no bones broken, thank God."

Nicholas nodded. "Can you leave her long enough to go through the rooms with me? I would like to see just what has been damaged."

She wasn't sure why he should wish to look over her shredded household goods, but she nodded. "I will return shortly, Violet."

The servant managed to grin, though her voice still trembled a little. "Yes, ma'am. Shall I come and help you clean up?"

"Not now," Lucy said, her voice firm. "Just rest."

The little maid sighed, obviously still weak with reaction from the assault, and did not argue. She held her hands out to the fire, which Lucy had rekindled, and seemed content enough. Lucy followed the viscount back through a tour of her poor, ravished home.

In the dining room the chairs were indeed upside down, thought at least still whole, and the table was pushed out of place. The china that had been stored on the shelves beside the fireplace had been reduced to shards of glass, and they had to step gingerly around the damage. Her spirits sinking even further, Lucy wondered if even one intact teacup remained. It wasn't as if she had the funds to replace all this, either. There would be no more dinner parties in her future.

Sick at heart, she led the viscount up to her bedroom, which was more disrupted than Violet's. Feathers from her thin pillows dusted the floor like new-fallen snow, and her newly donated clothing had been slashed.

Lucy swallowed hard. Then she saw even worse; the set of Shakespeare, which had sat in a small bookcase against the wall, had been tumbled about the floor and pages ripped from their bindings. Her father's books . . .

even her mother's Bible and prayer book had not escaped untouched.

She bit back a sob. "How could anyone do this, just because I have not been able to pay off my debts? Such viciousness—"

"I don't believe it was a disgruntled creditor," Nicholas told her, moving the lantern from side to side as he surveyed the damage. "Look at how thorough the destruction is, the smallest item not escaping notice."

Lucy stared at him, trying to read his expression in the flickering light. "You think—you don't think this was someone searching for the ruby?"

Nicholas sounded grim. "Yes, I do. Otherwise, why so much destruction? They took nothing away—they took everything apart, instead. That set of books would have gained a thief quite a few pounds, but the intruders did not try to sell it."

Lucy swallowed hard against the lump in her throat. "They were my father's," she explained, trying not to weep. "And the Bible was my mother's."

Nicholas put one hand on her shoulder, its touch infinitely comforting. "They can be repaired," he promised her. "The pages can be restored, and new bindings stitched—they will be made whole again. I will see to it."

His generosity made her blink hard. "You're too kind to me," she said, her voice low. "But I cannot sink deeper into your debt—"

"Nonsense! What could you owe me?" he interrupted, his expression almost formidable in the flickering light.

"The forty shillings you gave those men who tried to take my dining table and chairs," she reminded him, surprised that he did not remember.

Nicholas relaxed. "My dearest Lucy, I am not in want of forty bob. Allow me to help you this time. Surely, a friend can help another in distress?"

She smiled at him and allowed her doubts to slide away—who could resist the warmth in his dark eyes or that intimate smile? Dimly, she recalled that she had, at first glance, thought him cold and stern. What a difference a few days and several glorious hours could make!

"Besides, when we find the ruby and you collect the prince's reward, you will have ample funds at your disposal," he reminded her.

Lucy sighed. "We do not seem to be making any progress, and I have been of no assistance at all, my lord— Nicholas. I hardly see why you require my continued help."

"On the contrary," he said, his voice firm. "You have, with your presence, allowed me to make greater strides in the last week than I have done in a year."

"How?" Lucy demanded, startled at such a rash claim. "I have had very little response to my questions about Stanley."

"You're wrong. I think this is precisely the result of your inquiries." He gestured to the destruction all about them. "It came at a high cost to you, and I will not forget that, but it has helped us immeasurably in our search."

"I don't see how," she confessed.

"Someone else is searching for the ruby," he explained.

"Yes, I see that, but—" Lucy paused to consider the implications.

"Just so," he agreed. "Either we have two separate sets of villains, which seems unlikely, or the first set, the ones who stole the ruby in the first place, have somehow managed to misplace it. They are looking for it now, with increasing desperation."

"Then Stanley was not involved after all!" Lucy blurted. When Nicholas remained silent, she felt her flash of relief fade as quickly as it had come. "No, in that case, why would they be interested in searching his house. I see what you mean. But why now, Nicholas? Why wait a year to take apart his home?"

He shook his head. "I don't know. But this seems to have started after our trip to the brothel on Hampstead Heath. I think I shall have to make that return trip we talked about."

Her earlier suspicion might be true. Jace could have sent men, or come himself, to search.

"*We* will have to," Lucy corrected, though her heart sank at the thought of returning to that adders' nest. "You need me to try to convince Eve to tell us what she knows. I think there is more she has not said."

She held his gaze firmly, and her tone held a new confidence. She knew that he understood why.

Nicholas's answering look was both affectionate and concerned. "I will not dictate your actions, but I don't have to tell you how dangerous that place is."

Lucy shivered, remembering their near-fatal battle. "We shall have to be prepared, that is all."

He nodded, looking thoughtful. "And I think we shall go in the daytime, this time, and catch them, hopefully, by surprise. But first let us tend to the injured servants, then we all need a few hours of sleep."

Lucy could not argue with that. Not only did poor Chudley need to be seen by a physician, and perhaps Violet as well, but the evening, with its sights and joys and fantastic events, seemed to have stretched for days. She thought of her shredded mattress upstairs and wondered if she and Violet would now be sleeping on the floor. How could her financial state possibly get any worse?

As if following her thoughts, which he had an uncanny habit of doing, Nicholas said, "You cannot stay here. We know it is not safe. You and Violet will come home with me tonight, until your house is put back into order and we're quite sure the danger is past."

"I cannot: With no chaperone my reputation would be ruined!" Lucy bit her lip in alarm.

"My servants are most discreet. And even if your presence is remarked upon I will not allow you to come to grief, Lucy, I give you my word, but I cannot leave you here in a ruined house, awaiting the assassin's return." For a moment his brooding eyes lit with a spark of humor. "If you do not return with me, I will be forced to stay with you. Your reputation will be just as impugned, and our sleep will be considerably less easy."

She was too fatigued to argue further. "Very well." She went to the kitchen to explain the news to Violet, whose eyes widened. "But, ma'am, I'm in me nightdress! I 'ave to change, first," she protested.

"I regret to tell you that your other clothing is in shreds," Lucy told her. She untied her scarf and wrapped it around her diminutive maid; it hid little of the nightdress, but it was the best she could do. "This will keep you respectable," she said, trying to sound confident.

While Violet still gaped, Lucy ran upstairs once more to see if anything at all could be redeemed from the mess. But even her hairbrush had been pulled apart, though she did locate her toothbrush on a pile of shredded silk that had once been a new hand-me-down gown. Lucy touched the shards of fabric, sighing. What a lovely gown it had been, too. Now she was even more restricted in her wardrobe than ever; what on earth would she do? If they didn't find the gem quickly, Lucy was going to end up naked!

Thank goodness she had been wearing her mother's ear drops and her grandmother's gold cross. And her diningroom table and chairs looked miraculously unscathed. Her precious books could be repaired, Nicholas said. Had the unknown despoilers expected the ruby to be somehow hidden within a book binding? It was a faint hope, if the ruby was as large as she understood, but perhaps Nicholas was right, and they were becoming desperate. She shivered.

Desperate men were dangerous men.

Nicholas found her standing there, her toothbrush in her hand, and called to her from the doorway. "Come, my dear, before the sun rises and all your neighbors discover more to gossip about."

She hurried downstairs, gathered up Violet, and allowed Nicholas to put them both into his carriage, where the wounded Chudley lay back against the other seat, supported by Nicholas. Worried, Lucy glanced over her shoulder at the shattered front door, which Nicholas had eased to, though it could not be locked. There were still a few pieces of furniture intact.

"I will have some of my men return to stand watch,"

he assured her. "And the door will be repaired, with a new and better lock."

Reassured, she settled into the carriage. With Violet by her side, eying the plush interior with amazement, and the wounded footman, she and Nicholas were forced to sit apart, but Lucy could enjoy the mere fact of his presence.

When they reached his home again, Nicholas saw Chudley helped away by two astonished footmen, then he called for his housekeeper. A plump, pleasant-looking woman appeared promptly, with a tall housemaid at her elbow.

"Mrs. Contrain," the viscount said, "this is Mrs. Mott, who will take good care of you and your maid. Mrs. Contrain is my guest, Mrs. Mott. Her house has suffered a disaster, and she has lost all her clothing and personal effects."

"A fire?" the housekeeper's expression contorted in sympathy. "Oh, you poor dears!"

"More like a whirlwind," Nicholas said grimly, while Lucy hesitated, not sure how much she should explain.

"Opal, you take Mrs. Contrain's maid up to the servant's level and see she gets all that she needs," the housekeeper told her housemaid.

The young woman smiled at Violet and waited for her to follow. Standing very straight, Violet glanced once at Lucy for reassurance, then disappeared after the other servant.

Mrs. Mott turned back to Lucy. "Let me show you to a guest chamber, ma'am. Would you like a glass of hot milk, to settle your nerves, like? And a little something to eat?"

"Milk will be quite enough, thank you," Lucy answered. "You're very kind." She followed the woman up the broad staircase to a guest room larger than her sitting room at home. As Mrs. Mott flung open the door, Lucy paused in the doorway.

Everywhere was neatness and order. The bed, reassuringly whole, was draped in soft rose-colored silk, and draperies of the same color covered the windows. Behind the drapes, the first faint rays of dawn lightened the darkness.

Lucy felt the tenseness in her shoulders relax. She sat down in a chair beside the bed.

"I've called for hot water, ma'am, and we can fill the hip bath if you wish to bathe," the housekeeper told her, lighting the candles on the nightstand and bureau. "There's soap and towels there on the dressing stand."

Lucy glanced at the large china basin. "I will wait till later," she said, not wishing to put such a charge on the servants at such an early hour. "Washing my face and hands will be enough for now, thank you. But I fear I have no nightdress."

Mrs. Mott screwed up her mouth, as if trying to consider. "And there will be no shops open as yet. Let me see what I can do, ma'am."

She bustled out of the room. Lucy shut her eyes, becoming aware of just how weary she was, now that the initial shock over the invasion and damage to her home was ebbing. She tried to consider all the things she needed to do, but her thoughts seemed to blur. . . .

Mrs. Mott sailed back into the room, carrying a glass of milk upon a tray, with a white linen garment folded over one arm and something else in her other hands. What, had she flown down and up the stairs to return so quickly? Lucy blinked, realizing with a start that she had drifted off to sleep while still sitting upright.

"I'm afraid this is the best I can do just now, ma'am. It's my own best nightdress, and just washed and ironed, though I know it will be an ill fit. We shall have a dressmaker in to see you by the time you're ready to get up," the housekeeper promised. "And his lordship has sent you two of his silver-backed brushes to use."

"You're both very kind," Lucy repeated, feeling a secret relief that the viscount did not, after all, maintain a closet full of nightclothes to clothe his string of ladies. Perhaps there had been some slight exaggeration of the number of Nicholas's affairs.

But later she would have to explain, as delicately as

possible, that she could not afford a dressmaker. Nor would she allow Nicholas to purchase her wardrobe, as if she were a kept woman! Perhaps Lady Sealey had a few more cast-off dresses she could donate. Lucy sipped the warm milk and found her thoughts harder and harder to keep in focus. She yawned widely as a new housemaid slipped into the room with a ewer of warm water.

"Is Violet all right?" Lucy managed to ask, while Mrs. Mott gestured to the servant to pour warm water into the china basin. "My maid? And how is Chudley?"

"He's in bed, with his head bound up like a heathen, ma'am. And your maid's had warm milk, too, and a bite to eat, and is tucked into bed, already asleep," the housekeeper answered. "Now, is there anything at all that I can fetch for you? Would you like me to brush out your hair?"

"No, thank you, I will be fine," Lucy answered. As soon as they departed, shutting the door behind them, Lucy forced herself to rise from the chair—she had never felt so tired in her life—and, shedding her clothes, she made a quick wash in the basin, then pulled on the borrowed nightgown. The loose-cut garment was too wide and too short, but little matter. She found a nightcap included, but the night was mild, and Lucy didn't bother to don it. She crawled between the linen bedclothes and was asleep almost before she touched the pillow.

~

*When she opened her eyes again, Lucy blinked in sur*prise. Where was she? This luxurious room was quite unfamiliar, as was the smooth, unpatched sheets and soft down pillow beneath her head—then it all came rushing back, and she shut her eyes again for an instant, sighing. Oh, her poor house. She felt almost a physical pain at the memory of the destruction, then admonished herself. She was safe, and so was Violet and Chudley. The house was still in her possession, technically. If the viscount had said he would send men to watch it, she felt sure he had kept his word. Now—

A very faint knock at the door interrupted her train of thought. Lucy pushed herself up to one elbow. "Yes?"

The door opened, and Violet peeped in. She wore someone's hand-me-down black uniform with a white apron, and a trim white cap perched on her neatly dressed brown hair. She looked conscious of her impressive appearance, and indeed, she looked very well, aside from several purpling bruises and the healing scrape on her forehead, left from her rough treatment last night.

" 'Ow are—I mean—how are you feeling, ma'am?"

Lucy managed not to smile. "I am quite fit, Violet, the question is, how are you?"

"Much better, ma'am, the maids 'ere—here—have been smashing, and I got a new outfit that's terribly elegant." She came closer so that Lucy could admire it. "Me cap has lace on it!"

Lucy nodded. "You look quite splendid, and I am glad the staff is kind to you."

"Oh, my lord gave orders, he did, and they're treating me like a queen. I only got to attend to your wants, which I would do, anyhow, of course, but no scrubbing the floors or cleaning out the hearths. I'm a *lady's* maid, in this house." Violet seemed to consider this the equivalent of a blissful holiday. Lucy was simply happy to find the little maid had regained her equanimity after her painful treatment at the hands of the vandals.

"And Chudley?"

"He's still abed, ma'am. Those awful men banged him up terrible, but Mrs. Mott says he'll recover."

"I don't suppose you remember anything more about what those men looked like?" Lucy asked.

Violet's smile faded, and she shook her head. "I'm sorry, ma'am, but it was dark, and they was so fast, like, and then they had a cloth over me head—"

"It's all right," Lucy reassured her. "I only wondered."

"Are you ready to get up?" Violet asked. "I'll fill the hip bath for you and order you a tray, ma'am."

Lucy had to bite her lip again. Violet sounded as dig-

nified as Mrs. Mott herself; perhaps she was enjoying
having the chance to emulate such an impressive role
model.

"That would be lovely," Lucy said. "Perhaps you can
get some assistance—the water jugs will be heavy."

"Oh, yes, ma'am, I got an undermaid assigned just to
help me, and I'll call a footman if need be," Violet said,
obviously trying to be casual about her enormous jump in
status, but just as clearly reveling in it. "Would you like
tea or hot chocolate, ma'am, or both?"

Lucy couldn't help laughing. "Tea will be fine, and
some toast, please."

She found a robe, as short and wide as her nightgown,
ready for her, and when she went into the dressing room
and found the hip bath prepared with warm water, she
couldn't help feeling just like Violet. Out of such a terrible invasion, what luxury, what kindness the viscount
had extended to them.

Friends—she refused to affix any other description to
him, she had to remember that their connection would be
only temporary—were a wonderful blessing.

The water enveloped her like a warm cloud, and she
sank into it with a sigh of pleasure. It seemed to ease the
tension in her shoulders and take away the lingering stiff-
ness of weeks of worry. Then, after she had shut her eyes
and enjoyed a comforting soak, there was perfumed soap
to lather herself with, and more warm water to rinse her
hair and her body, then thick towels to use to dry herself.
Donning the robe, she rubbed her short hair dry by the
fire. Then came the question of clothes.

She had none, except the evening dress she had worn
to the theater last night. Oh, dear.

But Violet had returned, beaming. "There's a dressmaker waiting in your bedroom, ma'am. And I have your
breakfast tray laid out."

Lucy frowned. How could she explain to the dressmaker, and to the viscount, that she could not afford this
luxury and would not allow him to assume the cost, which
she had no doubt he was ready to do?

She went back into the bedroom, still pondering this delicate issue, and found a trim, older woman with an assistant standing ready behind her, both with measuring tapes in hand.

"I understand your house was damaged by fire, ma'am, and all your clothes destroyed."

So that was the official story, was it? The viscount's staff no doubt knew better, with Chudley and Violet to share their tales, but perhaps the truth would not leak out of the house.

"So I know that your need is most urgent, and we are happy to put aside our other customers' orders and make sure you are taken care of," the dressmaker assured her.

Nicholas must be an excellent customer, indeed, Lucy thought, not sure whether to laugh or frown. Or else he had simply promised this woman a handsome bonus for her special efforts. And Lucy hated to disappoint a hard-working tradeswoman, but—

"I—I thank you for your prompt attentions," Lucy began.

She paused, startled when the other woman motioned for her to lift her arms. Without further ado, she measured Lucy at all pertinent points, efficiently and impersonally.

"His lordship says I must waste no time, ma'am," the woman explained.

Lucy waited till the assistant had jotted down her measurements, though she was sure that this shrewd-eyed woman would have them in her memory, as well. But when the dressmaker motioned for her assistant to bring up a packet of fabric samples for Lucy to choose from, she shook her head.

"I fear I cannot order a new wardrobe, just yet—" she began, then faltered as the woman blinked at her in surprise.

"But you have no clothing!"

"No, of course, but—but I also have some urgent business that must be completed first, then I will—I will see to my needs." Lucy tried to explain. If the viscount was determined to help her, she would borrow a small sum and search for some inexpensive muslin from the warehouses and get to work herself with needle and thread.

The seamstress raised her brows. "Very well, ma'am. For the moment, I have brought an assortment of linen shifts and nightclothes, which do not require as precise a fitting as outerwear and will do for the time, until your own can be made. Also, as it happens, we had a riding habit almost completed for another client, whose need is not as pressing as yours. Now that I know your measurements, and after some slight adjustments, I can have that ready for you by noon."

"You're very kind," Lucy said, weakly.

"As soon as you are ready, I will return and we can plan the rest of your wardrobe," the other woman assured her.

After thanking the seamstress again, Lucy had Violet see them out. Then Lucy sat down at a small table and drank her tea. Violet had brought up an assortment of delectables, light scones with delicious strawberry jam and clotted cream, fresh-baked bread spread with butter, coddled eggs and thick ham, much more than Lucy could imagine having room for.

But she ate what she could, then when Violet returned, allowed her maid to brush out her curls, now quite dry, and she changed into a new shift and robe, sending back the housekeeper's borrowed clothing with expressions of her gratitude.

Not long after Violet took the tray away. Lucy's new habit arrived, and she donned it quickly.

"You look splendid, ma'am," Violet told her, grinning.

Lucy stared at herself in the mirror. It was a handsome outfit, and it fit quite well. The navy jacket with gold embroidered lapels and gray skirt made her look trim and shapely. She blushed a little when she realized she was considering what Nicholas would think when he saw her in it, and if he would approve of her appearance.

"Have you seen Lord Richmond this morning?" she asked her maid.

"Oh, yes, ma'am. He says as soon as you're ready, he

will escort you on the ride you 'ad—had planned."

Violet was working hard on her *h*'s, Lucy thought absently. She would have been amused if she had not had more pressing matters on her mind. Oh dear, the visit to the bawdy house loomed, with its treacherous host who had tried his best to murder them the last time they had set foot inside it. Lucy drew a deep breath.

"Are you going riding in the park, ma'am?" Violet asked, her gaze innocent.

"I believe we're going a little further," Lucy answered, trying to keep her expression even and wishing that this excursion were indeed as simple as a romp in the park.

Bracing herself, she picked up the hat that had come with the habit. Violet helped her adjust it, and, bidding her maid good-bye Lucy made her way slowly down the staircase. She must remember to maintain her dignity. She did not wish to embarrass Nicholas after all his kindness.

In the front hall, a footman bowed to her, and the butler, his elderly countenance smooth but his eyes kind and fatherly, told her, "His lordship is in the library, ma'am, if you are seeking him."

"Thank you," she said. It was the room she had thought to check first, anyhow. It was obviously Nicholas's favorite spot.

She found him giving orders to two burly servants, by their lack of livery perhaps gardeners or stable lads.

"And be quick about it," Nicholas finished.

The two men departed, their expressions intent and their pace rapid; they seemed to be taking their employer at his word. Lucy had stepped to the side of the room until he finished; now she came forward.

Nicholas leaned forward and kissed her, a long, delicious kiss that made Lucy tingle down to her toes. She threw her arms about his neck and kissed him back with hearty abandon, then, as he pursued the embrace, his lips moving to her cheeks, her neck, pushing back the high collar of the jacket, she blushed.

"We must not," she whispered. "Someone might come in."

"My staff are too well trained," he assured her, a wicked twinkle in his eyes. But he straightened and allowed her to step back and readjust her hat, which had slipped out of place in the enthusiasm of their embrace.

Lucy was sure that her cheeks were flushed, but hopefully, the color would fade and not attract remark from the servants. "Are we going to—you know—that awful place?"

"If you are feeling uneasy, you do not have to accompany me," he reminded her, reaching to take her hand, though this time he only held it firmly inside his own.

Lucy allowed her hand to rest inside his; the strength of his grip was always reassuring. "No, I think I should," she said. "In fact, I must. If I can make a difference with Eve, I must be there. It's only that last time—last time was most unnerving."

Nicholas nodded. "I have taken some precautions," he assured her. He let go of her hand and walked back to his desk. She saw a large carved box upon its top, and from this case, Nicholas withdrew two wicked-looking pistols. He checked their priming and then replaced them, picking up the box and motioning for her to precede him through the doorway.

They went out the big front doors. Lucy was startled to find a rather nondescript small brown carriage awaiting them, instead of either the usual midnight-blue chaise with Nicholas's crest on the doors or the hired cab they had used—and pretty well destroyed—last time.

"It's bigger than a hackney," Nicholas explained, "while slightly less obvious than my own chaise."

Anything would be less obvious than a chaise with a nobleman's crest on its doors! Trying not to smile, Lucy commended him on his foresight.

Nicholas grinned. "We shall see if it helps."

A footman hurried to take the case of pistols from his master and place it carefully inside the carriage, then turned to help her in. Lucy settled herself inside, and Nicholas took his seat beside her.

Soon the London streets whirled past them. This carriage was not as well sprung as the bigger one, and Lucy felt the jar as its wheels hit a pothole. She shifted in her seat, and Nicholas put one arm about her shoulders.

"You really do not have to make this trip," he told her, apparently reading her movement as one more sign of nervousness.

"I wish to." She reached up to touch his cheek tenderly. "I am your partner in this investigation, and I have as much at stake as you." Which reminded her, she had to explain to him about the dressmaker, and her refusal to allow him to foot her dress bills, but——but not just now. Just now, he was kissing the small of her neck, and it was altogether too delightful a sensation to interrupt. . . .

This time the trip passed much more quickly than the last. When Nicholas straightened and Lucy glanced out the window to see how far they had come, she gasped and sat up straighter, too, pulling her jacket back into place and retrieving her hat, which had somehow ended up on the other seat.

"You did that on purpose!" she said, her tone accusing.

"I should hope so," the viscount agreed, his eyes gleaming with mischief.

"No, I mean, to take my mind off—to keep me from feeling apprehensive—"

"An excellent excuse," he agreed, grinning, "for my otherwise natural tendencies when alone in a carriage with a lady whom I—a lady who furnishes such delectable temptations. Did I succeed at this altruistic mission?"

Cheeks red, she tried to frown at him. "You know perfectly well you succeeded admirably."

"Then you cannot chastise me for my lack of self-restraint. That was your next comment, I take it?" His tone was bland.

Lucy shut her lips firmly. "Not at all. I think you may desist now, my lord. We should be discussing our strategy. We have a formidable and well-supported foe to confront."

Thinking of that awful man who hosted this bawdy house made her shiver, from much less happy emotions than the ones the viscount had been inducing.

"I have been giving some thought to our design, I promise you, and I have taken certain measures . . ." Nicholas had opened the case and now was slipping both pistols inside his jacket.

Lucy watched him. "How many bullets do they hold?" she asked.

He glanced up at her. "One—one each, that is."

She considered pointing out how many men Jace had at his disposal, and sighed. Nicholas knew it perfectly well. They would have to hope for the best. At least she had Nicholas by her side; no one else could make her feel more secure, even in this place.

When the carriage paused, they stepped out to see the small house looking even more shabby and rundown in the daylight. Lucy looked around and was startled to see a small cart just behind them, with two men sitting on its crude seat.

"Nicholas," she hissed. "Are those his men?"

"No," he answered, his tone also low. "Backup troops."

She recognized, then, the man in the nondescript clothes who handled the reins of the cart—it was one of the servants she had seen in Nicholas's study. Of course, how obvious; he had taken steps, as he had told her repeatedly.

Feeling much better, she took the viscount's arm and they approached the bawdy house. At Nicholas's signal the driver of the cart came behind them, while the other man waited with the vehicle.

The door was shut. Without bothering to knock, Nicholas tried the handle, and it swung open. Did Jace feel himself so secure that he did not even lock his door, or had some minion been careless?

Nicholas stepped over the splintered threshold, and Lucy hastened to follow; the servant remained at the doorway, perhaps to guard their exit.

Eyes wide, Lucy gazed about her. This time, the house looked very different. In the middle of the day, the room was deserted. Several overturned chairs and some sticky, empty mugs showed that last night's revels had gone on as usual. A few buzzing flies hovered over the mugs, and dust darkened the corners of the floor and grimed the tables.

No one seemed overly concerned about housekeeping in this place; obviously, the host did not, and the women who labored here, joined in sweaty and loveless union with any man who walked through the door, probably had little energy left for scrubbing floors or washing mugs. Lucy shuddered, thinking what a hellish life they must lead.

How had Stanley come to be here? Her fastidious, finicky husband, who could not bear crumbs in the butter or wrinkles in his precisely tied cravat . . . as worn as his linen might be, it was always pressed just so. She could not imagine him here. Perhaps he had been a different man with Eve. . . .

That was not a productive line of thought. Lucy pulled her reflections back to focus on their current dangerous endeavor. Nicholas had already peered into the back hall and apparently found it empty of lurking rascals. Now he motioned to her for silence as he proceded to the narrow stairwell.

He did not have to remind Lucy of the need for quiet. But how on earth would they find Eve on the next level without awakening the wrong woman, who would most likely shriek and alert everyone to their presence?

But apparently Nicholas remembered which small room Eve had taken them to the last time they were here. He led the way down the narrow hall and eased open a middle door.

The room was empty. Lucy felt her heart sink. Now what?

Nicholas frowned, and Lucy dared to whisper, "Has Jace killed her?"

Because they had come to see her, to ask questions . . . if Jace was the leader of the gang who had stolen the jewel, he was already a murderer. It made Lucy tremble to think they might have brought about the woman's death.

She prayed it was not so. Eve's life must have been hell enough, to think that they might have—she frowned, trying to identify a small noise.

"Nicholas!" Lucy whispered. "This way!"

His brow creased, he followed her lead this time. They went further down the hall till Lucy located an even steeper stair, almost a ladder, which led up to the attic. She picked up her skirt and climbed quickly, even though she shivered at the thought of Jace or his men blocking their exit. From this level, they would be too high to dare the jump to safety that had saved them the last time.

But they had come here to find Eve, and Lucy had a sudden suspicion. When the steep flight of steps culminated in a small, cramped space at the top of the house, Lucy found two doors at each side of the tiny landing. Without hesitating, following the continuing sound, she chose one and turned the knob.

Inside, she found what she had expected. A woman lay on a tiny cot, which looked somewhat cleaner than the musty, stained beds on the floor below them. Her face was dusky with fatigue, her eyes shadowed by dark circles, and she wore only a patched shift, just now pushed down to expose one swelling breast.

It was Eve, and in her arms, she held a baby.

Twelve

*L*ucy went rigid with shock. And yet, somehow, some-how this was not totally a surprise. Suddenly many things fell into place.

Eve stared at them, looking astonished to see them appear without warning.

"What're you doing here?" she demanded. "Jace will kill you for sure, if he finds you back! Didn't he come close enough last time? He beat the bloody hell out of me after you got away. I weren't even sure if you lived to make it back to town, jumping out of the window like madmen!"

"I'm sorry to hear about the abuse you endured at his hands. I regret that we made it worse," Lucy said, keeping her voice gentle and its timbre evenly pitched, though her chest still felt very tight and queer.

A baby.

She glanced back, and the darkness in Nicholas's face showed her the depth of his emotion. He must be very disappointed. He looked almost ill with shock, but he remained silent. He seemed to trust her to find the right

words to persuade this woman that she should aid them.
And that wasn't all Lucy had to do, not now.

"But we still need your help, and more than that—"

She was interrupted by a fretful wail. The baby had
released its grip on the nipple it had been suckling. It
whimpered again, a fading cry that somehow seemed less
strong than it should have been.

Eve sighed. "My milk is going, and I don't have nothing else to give the mite. She ain't growing the way she
should be."

Despite the need for haste, for a moment Lucy could
not concentrate on anything else. She stared down at the
baby—how old was it? Stared at the narrow shape of the
face, the too-thin nose, and knew she didn't even have to
ask the question that was foremost in her mind.

"He was real pleased when I tol' him, Stanley was,"
Eve said, her voice defiant and at the same time, very
weary. "He promised he would take care of me, and the
baby, too, so I didn't have to get rid of it before it was
born, like women who—women in my place usually do.
But after he died, well, the money ran out—"

Lucy had no doubt of that! She had suffered enough as
her small stock of funds had dwindled, and she had had
only herself and Violet to worry about, not a helpless
infant.

"And then Jace wanted to . . ." Eve paused and shivered.

Lucy shuddered as well. She had no doubt how easily
the black-hearted Jace would dispose of anyone in his
way, even a baby.

"So I thought, if I could get some blunt, and it was
only right that Stanley should—that you—you probably
had plenty, then I could keep my baby." Eve swallowed,
for an instant. "I never thought you'd want to take her."

"I didn't know—" Lucy started to speak, then hesitated.
The misery in Eve's face jumbled her thoughts. "That is,
we thought your note was about something else."

She could almost feel Nicholas's frustration, although
he still stood silently behind her. If Eve did not have the

ruby, given to her for safekeeping by Stanley, then who did?

Eve seemed to be hardly listening. She gazed down at the baby, her expression twisted with conflicting emotions. "But you could take care of her, see she's fed and clothed, and Jace couldn't get to her. When she's old enough to take to bed, or even before, I know what he'll want to do w' her—"

Oh, God, Lucy thought, shaking her head at once. "No, that must not be allowed."

"So take her." Taking a deep breath, Eve thrust the baby into Lucy's arms.

Startled, Lucy looked down at the baby, who began to cry in earnest. It was a smelly little burden, so slight, so innocent, despite the less-than-reputable beginnings the child had had. But none of that was the babe's fault! Still—she thought how she would feel, if she were lucky enough to have had a child, and then someone had taken it away.

Lucy looked back at Eve, and blurted, "You must come with us."

"Me?" Eve looked at them in shock. "But—"

"You cannot want to stay here, with such a man as your—your employer, under such horrible conditions!"

"But I don't—"

"And the baby needs you, she needs her mother," Lucy finished, her tone quiet but firm, and she gently settled the child back into her mother's arms.

Eve's eyes glistened with tears. Gasping, she hugged the baby to her.

Then a shout from below made them all jump.

"They have seen the carriage," Nicholas warned, his voice still tight with suppressed emotion. "We must make haste!"

Lucy grabbed Eve's hand and pulled her up. "Run!"

The other woman needed no urging. Pulling a thread-bare blanket about her thin shift, she hastened after them, and they descended the narrow flight of steps so rapidly that Nicholas had to brace them both when they hit the next landing.

But they were not fast enough.

A familiar form appeared at the other end of the hall. Most of Jace's hairy torso was exposed as his stomach jutted over his waistband; he'd hastily pulled on a pair of trousers and was still trying to button them. His feet were bare. His heavy brow beetled over his narrow eyes, and he glared at them, rage growing on his face.

"You! You dare to show yourselves 'ere! You'll not live to tell the story, me namby-pamby lordship, not this time!"

He shouted several names, and Lucy shivered with fear. She glanced at Nicholas, who held a pistol ready in his hand; she had not even seen him draw it. He held the weapon steady, pointed at the pimp's heart.

Jace came closer, then hesitated at the sight of the pistol.

"You will step aside and allow us to leave," Nicholas said, and his tone would have struck fear into hearts more valiant than this bully's. Lucy swallowed hard.

"You can't take the woman!" Jace argued, his heavy line of brow still knitted. "She's me bread and butter; what you want with 'er? You already got the other 'un!"

Nicholas's voice hardened even more. "You will keep your muck-laced thoughts to yourself, sir. And 'the woman' is free to do what she wishes. If she wants to leave with us, she will."

"Don't do it, Sadie, you'll end up out on the street, starving, with no roof over your 'ead and no one to keep you as nice like I done!" Jace spoke directly to Eve.

The prostitute sniffed and clutched her baby even closer. "As if you was so kindhearted and generous? Any woman here would leave, in a minute, or the ones with any wits left, if they weren't so afeared of you."

Jace snorted, an ugly animal sound. "They got reason. I'll find you, slut, and have your throat cut, and maybe the other fancy woman, as well—"

Nicholas interrupted. "If you make any attempt to harm

either of these women, I'll see you strung up on the nearest gallows. You can bet your wretched existence on it."

His tone was so cold and menacing that Jace stammered his reply. "I—I'd not—"

"I'm sure you've plenty of crimes in your past. Convicting you would be an easy task for any magistrate, stolen rubies aside."

The big man's nostrils twitched, like a dog who has scented fresh prey. "Rubies, what rubies? Sadie, you got rubies? If you're 'olding out on me—

Then he stopped, and something in his eyes warned Lucy. She glanced over her shoulder. "Behind you," she cried to Nicholas.

A man stood in the other end of the hall—she remembered, her heart sinking, that there were stairs at both ends of the hallway—with an old-fashioned blunderbuss in his hands. He lifted it.

Lucy threw herself in front of the baby in Eve's arms. Eve shrieked, and there was the sound of a gun firing, an explosion which in the narrow hall felt almost deafening. Coughing at the acrid scent of the gunpowder, her ears ringing, Lucy felt herself for bullet wounds. Who had the discharge hit?

Looking about, she saw that it was Nicholas who had fired, and the man with the long weapon now slumped back against the wall.

Jace charged forward, but Nicholas had already drawn out the other pistol, switching the now empty weapon to his left hand. He lifted the new pistol in time to slow Jace's advance.

The stout man, his hands clenching and unclenching, stood a scant three feet in front of them. Lucy could smell the stench of old sweat and almost feel the anger emanating from the twisted face and narrowed eyes.

Eve was whimpering with fear, and the baby wailed, too. Now other women poked tousled heads into the hallway, clutching blankets to near-naked bodies. They disappeared from view almost as soon as they appeared, as soon as they detected the guns and the ongoing conflict, retreating for cover from more flying bullets.

Lucy heard the heavy tramp of feet approaching rapidly on the wooden stairwell. More of Jace's men were coming. They would be outnumbered; what about the viscount's men waiting outside? They needed help, now, though Lucy was not sure if even two more men would be enough, when Jace seemed to have a small mob at his disposal.

Nicholas handed her the empty pistol and reached back inside his jacket. More weapons? To her surprise, he withdrew a silver whistle, put it to his mouth, and uttered one piercing note.

"Don't matter 'ow many men you got," Jace warned him. "Mine are meaner and bigger and stronger. I'll have your head on me doorpost, this time!"

Lucy strained to hear, and she thought she could detect sounds of a scuffle, bodies slamming together, on the lower level. She was cold with fear—what if Jace was correct? She shuddered at the commotion. Something slammed into a wall, and the thump resonated throughout the house.

Another of Jace's men appeared, thrusting aside his wounded comrade. This one held a pistol, too, smaller than Nicholas's weapon but surely just as lethal. He inched forward.

"Nicholas!" Lucy whispered. "A man with a gun, behind us."

Nicholas did not take his eyes off Jace, but she felt his tension.

"Not enough bullets, me stinking lordship?" Jace taunted. "You can't stop us all."

"You're first on my list, however," Nicholas replied. Then, even as the man behind them crept closer, his gun held ready, Nicholas returned the whistle to his mouth and gave two blasting peeps.

Lucy jumped. The man behind them hesitated, swinging his pistol toward Lucy for an instant. Eve was still sobbing with fear. Lucy put one arm around the other woman and faced the gunman, holding her breath.

Jace was less impressed with Nicholas's strange response. "Shoot 'im, you fool, we can deal with the women," he commanded.

The underling shifted his weapon once more and pointed it straight at Nicholas. No, no, not Nicholas! Lucy thought of rushing at the man, trying to divert his aim.

Nicholas, as always, seemed to read her thoughts. "Be very still," he muttered, his voice low. "We are not done for, not yet."

As the man pulled back his trigger, an immense dark creature bounded up the steps. It snarled at Jace, who shouted in surprise and stumbled back against the wall.

With a low-voiced command Nicholas stepped aside and the big animal, looking like something out of a nightmare, sprang at the man with the pistol. Jace's minion screamed and fired. But though again the hallway reverberated with the explosion, he had jerked the gun up, and the bullet seemed to have gone wild, missing everyone.

Even the enormous dog looked untouched. In the tiny corridor he appeared even bigger, if that were possible. Jace's narrow eyes were wide with panic, and he tried to crawl away, but the animal sprang forward again and grabbed the man by his foot.

Jace screamed in pain.

"Lucifer?" Lucy demanded, hardly trusting her own eyes. "I don't believe it. How on earth did he get here?"

Nicholas looked as mischievous as a boy. "I had a chat with Violet and asked leave to borrow him from her butcher friend," he said, reaching for Lucy's arm. "Come along, we must make haste."

"I am only sorry I did not have an excuse to put my bullet into your miserable hide," he told Jace, who now huddled against the wall, his face contorted with agony.

"Take 'im away, please, take 'im away," the rascal begged.

Nicholas looked at the man and shook his head. "Lucifer, to h'earth," he commanded, and the dog, almost as if with reluctance, released Jace's bleeding foot. The man groaned and crawled further away.

The viscount led them down the staircase. Below, two more of Jace's gang shrank away, though Lucy thought it was the dog loping after them, more than the pistol still in Nicholas's hand, that made them pale with fear.

With Nicholas's servants limping after them, somewhat the worse for their fight with Jace's minions, they all hurried to their vehicles. The two servants returned to the cart, and the big dog leaped into its wagon bed. A cart, of course; the animal had been hidden beneath the canvas cover on their trip out of town, probably dozing peacefully until called into action.

Lucy shook her head, even as she pushed Eve and the baby up into the carriage and followed quickly. When Nicholas joined them, the coachman flicked the reins, and they took off at a fast trot.

Lucy did not breathe easily until they had covered several miles. Then she glanced at Nicholas, sitting silently beside her. He eyed Eve and her baby—both seemed to have fallen into a restless slumber, despite the bouncing of the carriage—with an expression that was hard to read. Lucy wondered about it, but then he felt her gaze and turned to meet her eyes.

"I had to take them away," she said, quietly. "I could not leave her, nor the child, to the mercy of that horrible man."

"I know." His tone was as enigmatic as his expression.

She wondered if he resented the fact that she was thrusting more responsibility upon him. "Of course, you do not owe any obligation to Stanley's child, Stanley's dependants, but—"

"You feel that you do?" His brows lifted.

"I wanted a child badly, once, when I still had hopes for our marriage." She paused, trying to sort out her feelings.

He reached to press her hand. "I'm sorry, this discovery must pain you."

She grimaced. The knowledge that Stanley had given another woman a child, when he would not, or perhaps could not, impregnate his own wife, might have shattered her if she had found out a few months ago. . . . But now, now she was armored by having found Nicholas, a man who did respond to her, who had taught her that she was not flawed, not distasteful to a lover who, unlike Stanley, had a healthy appetite of his own. So somehow this new discovery from Stanley's past was easier to bear, even though she would likely never have the freedom now to hope for a child of her own. She sighed, but was able to meet Nicholas's gaze.

"I'm all right."

"Do you wish to adopt his child?"

Lucy shook her head. "Oh, no, I would not take her from her mother, too much has been stolen from Eve already. And she seems to have genuine feelings for her, just as any mother would. And yes, I do feel I should help them, if I can figure out how. The problem is, I have no funds, right now." She looked away from his eyes, which looked dark and brooding somehow, in the carriage's dim interior.

"You know I will do anything you wish," he told her. "Though I do wonder just how many unclothed women I can persuade my staff to accept without eliciting comment."

She was surprised into a laugh. "Yes, I can see how that could present a problem," she agreed.

They discussed what was best to do with Eve and her baby, and when the woman stirred, it seemed sensible to Lucy to ask the woman what she herself would wish.

Eve fingered the blanket draped around her shoulders and shifted the baby in her arms. "I got no blunt—" she said, her tone anxious.

"I understand that, we will help you," Lucy said, her tone gentle. "Stanley would have wished it, I'm sure. But what would you choose? For example, if you had an alternative, would you prefer to live in town or in the country?"

For a moment, a spark of life, perhaps even hope, flashed in Eve's eyes. "I grew up on a farm in Kent, me lady. Sometimes, when Jace had beat me, or one of the customers, I used to dream of being back in me own garden, tending the potatoes and the beans." She sighed, her expression for an instant far away.

"Do you have family to return to?" Lucy asked.

Eve made a face. "Me mum died when I was ten, and when me dad married again, his new wife didn't want me around. She was so mean, my brothers left. One went into the navy, and we never heard from him again, the other went to London, but I don't know where. Then me dad died, too, a couple years later, and his wife told me to get out. So I went into the nearest town, hoping to find a place as a housemaid, but no one would take me on, and I— well, I drifted into—into—"

Into the only trade she could find to keep herself from starving. Lucy sighed at the thought.

"What if we find you a cottage on a farm, where you could safely stay?" the viscount asked, his tone a little gruff.

Eve glanced down at the child, and Lucy added quickly, "And the baby, too, of course. How old is she?"

"I—she was born at the end of last summer, me lady," Eve said, her voice softening for an instant. "I still had a few pounds left, then, and I couldn't give her up. I hoped—well, you know."

Lucy knew perfectly how illogically one could hope for something good to happen; she had spent the last year of her life in much the same fix, sliding closer to ruin, praying for a way out. She looked over at Nicholas. He seemed to be gazing out the window, watching the countryside slide past. He leaned forward and tapped on the windowpane. When the carriage slowed and rolled to a stop, he spoke to the coachman.

The vehicle moved forward again. In half an hour, they came to a small inn along the road, and the carriage slowed.

"Wait here," Nicholas told them. He went inside the inn and returned shortly, a portly host behind him, beaming at the distinguished and unexpected guests.

"We will have some refreshment," he told Lucy and

Eve. "There is no private parlor, but the host has agreed to empty the taproom so that we may enjoy some privacy."

And how much had he paid to ensure this courtesy, Lucy wondered. The viscount's tone was imperious, as it often was, but since it benefitted them all, she could hardly complain about his tactics.

"Are we far enough removed to be safe from Jace and his men?" she asked quietly, as Eve looked curiously around her.

Nicholas nodded. "My men will sup outside and keep watch," he said. "Not to mention Lucifer! But I hardly think that villain will try to follow us, after the vanquishing we gave him."

So Lucy stepped out of the carriage, followed by their new charges.

The innkeeper's eyes widened a little when Eve emerged from the carriage, the blanket wrapped awkwardly about her barely clothed body, but he made no comment. Instead, they were ushered inside with as much bowing as if they were each duchesses, and in the small, smoky ale room a table was soon loaded down with simple but hearty fare, shepherd's pie and roasted chicken, potatoes and stewed turnips, brown bread and home-churned butter.

There was only ale, bitter to the taste, to drink, but Lucy managed a few swallows as she ate, and she enjoyed watching Eve's astonished response to the bounty before her. The woman ate heartily, if not daintily, chewing on a drumstick and pulling off a large hunk of bread. It would help her milk supply, Lucy thought. She spoke quietly to the host, and he nodded, returning soon with heated milk so that Eve could soak bread in it and offer the child some pieces to suck on. The little girl, whose face was shaped so much like Stanley's, was older than Lucy had first suspected; perhaps poor diet had slowed her growth. With plenty of food, fresh milk from a farmer's herd, and a mother at peace to care for her, the child would have a chance to grow and thrive.

Lucy owed Stanley that much.

But what a generous man Nicholas was, to be willing to help with an affair that was not his own. He had no obligations, no loyalty to her dead husband!

She looked across the table at him. "If—when we find the ruby, I will repay you, I promise," she told him, worried. "You do understand I could not leave them there?"

Nicholas answered, his voice low, "I understand that your heart is generous and loving, and I am only happy to be of some small service to you."

She blushed. "It is a great charge, I know."

He shrugged, brushing off her thanks with his usual abruptness. "A few pounds a year, at most."

"It will change her life and offer the child a chance to grow up healthy and unharmed," Lucy corrected. "It is an enormous thing you do now."

For a moment his guard slipped, and she saw emotions chase themselves across his face. What caused him to look so drawn with pain?

His next words distracted her.

"I fear we will have to begin again," he said.

"What do you mean?"

"Jace seemed to have no knowledge of the ruby," Nicholas reminded her. "We know now that the note, the brothel, it was all a wrong turn."

"But the vandalism, the damage to my house," Lucy objected.

Nicholas looked grim. "I know, if not Jace, there must be someone else."

When they finished the meal, they returned to the carriage and rode another hour until they came to a stretch of farmland belonging to Nicholas, one of his smaller properties, he explained to Lucy. He got down from the carriage and spoke with the farmer, a genial-looking man who hurried out to meet his landlord.

After a space, Nicholas came back to the carriage. "It is arranged," he said. "Come and see."

He handed Lucy down, then turned aside to speak to his driver. Lucy offered an arm to help Eve, who held the child, to emerge after her. The farmer's wife, stout and red-cheeked, curtsied. A trio of healthy-looking children clung to her skirts or ducked behind them, giggling, as their mother said, "This way, my lady, I will show you the cottage. I think it will be just the thing for your servant and her babe. You poor thing, to have lost your home and all your belongings in a fire."

Another mythical fire, was it? Lucy bit her lip, but she followed the farm woman past the larger farmhouse to a small stone cottage that lay a space behind it.

"We was using it for extra help, now and then, but this will be a nice little retreat for a widow and her child," the farmer's wife said brightly. "And we'll be sure she has plenty of good foodstuffs, and I'll get her some muslin and linsey-woolsey to make up some new clothes, my lady, as his lordship has asked."

Lucy tried to think how to tactfully disabuse the woman of her mistaken assumption about Lucy's rank, but she was distracted. As they went inside, Eve gazed around the modest room, with its stone hearth, plain furnishings, and nice tight windows, as if she were a wandering soul getting her first glimpse of heaven.

After years on the street or in Jace's horrible establishment, this cottage must look like paradise.

"Just for me?" Eve whispered. "All of this?"

Lucy looked from the simple collection of crockery and pots and pans on the shelves beside the fire to the bed pushed into the corner of the one big room. "Yes," she said, her voice gentle. "Yes, indeed. You will be safe, here, and you and your daughter will not go hungry."

"I'll just fetch a new loaf of bread, baked this morning, and some butter and milk," the farmwife told them, and she bustled out.

Nicholas glanced into the cottage, ducking his head at the low doorway. He motioned to Lucy, who left Eve still staring blissfully at her new home, and she crossed to meet him.

"Tell her to pick out a new name. I doubt Jace will try to look this far, if he looks at all—he probably will assume we have taken her back to London—but just in case, I think a new identity would be a wise precaution."

Lucy nodded. "I will suggest it. You didn't tell them about her past?"

He shook his head. "Better to allow her to make a fresh start, I should think. So I said she was a former servant of yours, fallen onto hard times after her husband's death." He didn't quite meet her gaze, but Lucy nodded.

"A sensible stratagem," she agreed.

Nicholas passed back under the low doorway and out of sight, while Lucy explained the ruse to Eve.

"It warn't my real name, anyhow," the woman said, with no apparent qualms.

Lucy remembered that, at the bawdy house, Jace had called her Sadie. "Why was that?" Then she blushed, wondering if Eve had changed her name because of shame at her profession. But the answer was even more surprising.

"Stanley called me Eve, a pet name, like," the woman explained, touching a rough-hewn chair with appreciation and not looking at Lucy. "So I kept it, after he died."

"How long was it before you heard—I mean, how did you come to hear of his accident?" Lucy wondered for the first time. It had been in the newspapers, but she wasn't sure if Eve knew how to read.

"He'd been to see me, that night," Eve said, seeming quite unself-conscious about how Lucy might feel about such confidences. "And one of the publicans in the neighborhood, who lived above his tavern, saw the carriage that hit him, never even stopped, they said, such unfeeling coves!"

It was the first time Lucy had heard such details about the accident, and for a moment, she shut her eyes as she remembered the shock and horror she had felt when first informed of Stanley's death.

The farmer's wife returned—she seemed to move at a fast trot wherever she went—and brought the conversation to an end. Her arms were full, and the children also carried foodstuffs. The woman placed a crusty loaf of round bread on the scrubbed tabletop, with a pitcher of milk, a crock of butter, and a large yellow cheese, while the oldest child stood on tiptoe to set his handful of potatoes and string of onions beside them.

"The cheese is my own," the farmwife told them, her tone proud. "Your woman can help me in the dairy, later, if she likes. I have the best dairy in the county, if I do say so, and good workers are always welcome."

Eve looked pleased at the suggestion. "Oh yes, and I can put in a garden, too, behind the cottage, if you please, ma'am?"

The other woman nodded. "Of course. I'm Mrs. Taylor, Cora Taylor. What's your name, dearie?"

Lucy waited, too, to hear Eve's choice. Eve thought about the question for a moment, then announced, "Lizzie—ah—Smith."

"Well, Lizzie, you have a nice rest, now, and I'll check on you later," Mrs. Taylor told her, apparently accepting the identify without any suspicions.

"Thank you, ma'am," Eve said, and she whispered as Lucy pressed her shoulder in farewell, "and thank *you*, ma'am, most of all. You're a saint, you are! Stanley always said as much, as pure as his own mum, he said."

Lucy blinked at the irony of this statement, but she smiled and followed the farmer's wife out of the cottage.

"Not to worry, my lady," Mrs. Taylor told her, pausing to call after her small son, "Robbie, you leave those chickens be! They won't give no eggs if you chase them like that!" She turned back to Lucy. "Lizzie will be just fine now."

"I think so," Lucy agreed. "I do appreciate you looking out for her. She's had a hard time of it."

"I'm happy to do it, my lady, not that his lordship weren't most generous as well," the farmwife admitted.

They made their good-byes, and Nicholas handed Lucy into the carriage. After they were under way, she sighed and leaned her head against his shoulder. "You are a wonderful man, do you know that? If you could have seen her face when she saw the cottage! And the baby will be safe now."

She glanced up at him, and again she saw the darkness pass over his face, and felt him tense.

Lucy sat up, alarmed. "Do you suppose they will not be safe?"

"No, I think they will be quite all right," he told her, his expression once more controlled.

But she had glimpsed—what? What troubled him so?

He did not seem to want to speak, or even to continue the light lovemaking they had enjoyed earlier in the day on their way out of town. Now, he simply put one arm about her shoulders, and they sat silently until they approached the outskirts of London. The sun was sinking low in the sky by this time, and Lucy felt her stomach rumble with emptiness. How soon one could become accustomed to regular meals again, she thought, smiling at herself.

"Are you very fatigued?" Nicholas asked suddenly.

She sat up straight. "Not terribly. I have recovered from the fright at the bawdy house. Why?"

"I thought perhaps we would go by your house and look through the damage more carefully. If we are ruling out Jace, we need to search for the real villain."

Lucy nodded. "Of course."

So Nicholas tapped on the carriage window and instructed his coachman of the new location. The carriage turned toward Cheapside and the narrow street where Lucy's house was situated.

When she reached her own street and the carriage drew up in front of her home, Lucy was pleased to see that a new front door had already been installed. It looked reassuringly stout, and the new shiny brass lock was also impressive.

Nicholas helped her down as the cart with his servants and the big dog went on their way to return the animal to its owner. The viscount rapped on the door. In a moment, a sturdy young man opened it. "My lord! I weren't expecting you."

"Is all well?" Nicholas asked. He waited for Lucy to precede him, and she stepped inside.

It felt like an age since she had been here, though it was less than twenty-four hours. Today, the hall looked serene, again, and when she glanced into the dining room, the table and chairs were back in their usual positions.

She looked into the kitchen, and found that the flour and food that had littered the stone floor had been cleared away—Violet would be most appreciative, Lucy thought, hiding a grin—and although the pantry was empty again, at least it was clean.

Upstairs, she found her bedroom looking very bare. The tatters that were the only remnants left of her clothing had been taken away, and only her bed frame, the empty clothes press, a small chair, and the shattered bookcase remained. She touched the splintered shelves sadly. Her books were gone. She glanced anxiously back toward Nicholas, who had followed her into the room.

"They have gone to the binders to be repaired," he reminded her.

She drew a deep breath. "Of course."

"My men have put all the loose paper into a basket," he told her. "I wish to look through the pile one more time."

His tone was grim. They were grasping at straws, and they both knew it. But there had to be something—

Lucy knelt on the bare floorboards and looked at the scraps of paper without much hope. With Nicholas kneeling beside her, she took out each fragment, one at a time.

"What is this?" Nicholas demanded.

Lucy peered at the ragged sheet. "It is the notice that my house will be claimed, unless I can repay the thousand pounds in—in less than three weeks, now."

"Your late husband's debt?"

"I assume so." She flushed slightly.

"Of what type?"

She stared at him, not sure of his meaning.

"What do you mean? I assumed it was a gaming debt, perhaps."

"But debts of honor are rarely claimed after the gambler's death," Nicholas told her. "They are most difficult to collect at all, legally, but most men pay them to avoid the social ostracization that would result from not honoring one's obligations."

She blinked. "I didn't know that. But then, what else could it be?"

"A business debt?" Nicholas persisted. His gaze looked beyond her, as if he were thinking hard.

She shook her head. "I doubt it. He didn't really have a part in any business venture, or none that I know of. Early in our marriage, Stanley had a small income from his late mother, who'd inherited shares in a vineyard in Portugal, but it had already begun to dwindle when we wed, and it faded away as the war with Napoleon ran on."

"Then, if he had no investments, from where did his income derive?" Nicholas asked, adding, "I am sorry to be so inquisitive about such private matters, but—"

"No, I understand." She sighed. "He gambled, of course. And sometimes he mentioned discharging commissions, for which he said he was paid small sums."

Nicholas's gaze was sharp. "And for whom did he carry out these errands?"

"I don't know." She flushed again. "Stanley was very secretive." She thought she saw anger flash in the viscount's eyes, and she sighed. He must be feeling very frustrated. If only she could tell him more. If only she knew more!

What a bastard the man had been, Nicholas thought, but he could hardly remark as much to Lucy. Treating his wife no better than his housekeeper, keeping her in the dark, neglecting her for a woman as common as Eve of the many names. Stanley should have been drawn and quartered—if there had been that much left of him after the carriage accident. Nicholas took a deep breath. This did not advance their search. He glanced back at the paper and spoke at last, his tone determined.

"I think we must find out more about Thomas Brooks."

Thirteen

*"Knowledge is power,
and women need all the power they can grasp."*
—MARGERY, COUNTESS OF SEALEY

*N*icholas saw Lucy safely back to his townhouse and departed almost at once to start the search for the elusive Thomas Brooks.

Inside, Lucy made her way past a footman, who bowed solemnly, then paused to smile at Mrs. Mott, who had hurried out to the front hall apparently as soon as she detected the sounds of Lucy's return.

"A lovely day for a ride, ma'am, I hope you had a pleasant time?"

"Yes, indeed," Lucy agreed a bit absently, thinking of their adventure at the bawdy house and trying not to laugh. "It was very—quiet."

"How nice," the housekeeper said, her tone placid. "It's nearly four, ma'am. Would you like your tea in the drawing room or upstairs in your room?"

"In my room, please."

Lucy climbed the two flights—with a start, she realized that the guest chamber already seemed comfortingly familiar to her—and took off her hat. She washed the dust off her face and hands and was drying them with a soft linen towel when Violet appeared, carrying a silver tray with careful attention to the dishes it held.

"How was your ride, ma'am? It must 'ave—have been a long one." She set down the tray, which contained a teapot, a china cup and saucer, and plates of sandwiches and scones and cakes.

"Yes," Lucy said, then paused to stare at the enormous amount of food her maid had brought up.

"Cook made these lemon cakes special,'cause I said you liked 'em, ma'am," Violet said proudly. "I remembered the recipe, and I 'elped her beat the cake batter."

Lucy looked at the riches laid out for her afternoon tea, more than she had often had for her evening meal, and swallowed a lump in her throat. All the servants here seemed determined to pamper her every whim.

"That was most thoughtful of you, Violet. I haven't had lemon cake since—since two years ago on my birthday."

She took a deep breath. She could not become too accustomed to such luxury. As soon as her house could be made habitable again, she would have to return to her real life, with all its poverty and penny-pinching. But if by then they had located the ruby, perhaps she could afford a small delicacy once in a long while. . . .

"Wouldn't you like a piece of the cake?" she suggested to Violet, who was pouring the steaming tea into a cup.

"Oh, no, thank you, ma'am. We already sampled it, so to speak, just to make sure it turned out right," Violet confessed. She took the tray away.

Hiding her grin, Lucy took a big bite. While she ate, she considered their current impasse, and wondered if Nicholas was having any luck. Then, taking a bite of the sweet tangy cake, Lucy almost choked. It was Wednesday!

Coughing, she sat up straight and took a sip of tea to wash down the food. It was the day for the countess's salon! She was rather late, but if she hurried, she could still get there in time.

Lucy jumped to her feet—the riding habit was not what

one would generally wear to a tea party, but she had no choice—and rang for Violet.

When her maid reappeared, Lucy was already adjusting her hat. "I have to go out," she said.

"But 'is lordship said you wasn't to go out alone," Violet reminded her, looking anxious.

Lucy frowned a moment. "Very well, if you would accompany me, please."

"Of course, ma'am," Violet said.

Happily, the walk from Nicholas's home was much shorter than from Lucy's Cheapside residence. They were admitted to the foyer of the countess's townhouse a short time later, and Violet adjusted her mistress's hat before curtsying and disappearing to chat with the household servants until Lucy was ready to leave.

"Lucy, how lovely to see you," Lady Sealey said after Lucy climbed the stairs and joined the cluster of women in the drawing room. "Have you been riding? A lovely day for it."

"Ah, it is a beautiful day." Evading the central question, Lucy sat down and accepted a cup of tea from the servant offering it. "As to that—I have had some disturbing times since I last saw you."

The countess's carefully plucked brows knitted. "What has happened?"

Lowering her voice, Lucy explained about the damage to her home and its contents. Despite her attempt at discretion, several of the other widows stopped to listen, wide-eyed, as Lucy explained about the vandalism.

"All your clothes cut to ribbons? How appalling!" another young woman announced. "I don't know how you are bearing up so cheerfully, Mrs. Contrain."

"I am happy that the only servants who were at home survived without serious injury, unlike my property," Lucy told them. "But yes, it was a terrible shock."

The countess was frowning. "And you have no idea what could have induced such an attack?"

Lucy hesitated; she had agreed with Nicholas that some parts of the story should not be repeated.

"La, the crime in London is getting out of hand," a middle-aged woman in black crepe snapped. "My cousin's London house was broken into while she and her mother were spending a few weeks at Bath, and every scrap of silver and plate taken. You cannot leave your house empty for an hour, nowadays!"

Several women had tales of burglary to share, and the talk became general again, to Lucy's relief.

The countess shook her head. "I am most unhappy for you, Lucy dear. We shall have to see what we can find to help you in your plight. I hope you are not staying there, now, with so much to be repaired? And with no man in the house, too. Why don't you come and spend a few weeks with me?"

Lucy hesitated. It was on obvious solution, so why did it not appeal to her more? "Thank you for such a generous offer," she said. "But . . ."

"But?" The countess prompted. I have already moved out and am staying briefly with—ah—a friend."

The countess's hazel eyes looked shrewd for an instant, and Lucy felt her cheeks flush.

The older woman nodded. "A particular friend? I am so glad to hear it," she said, satisfaction tinging her voice. "I thought you were looking much more cheerful than on your last visit."

At that, Lucy blushed in earnest and took another sip of tea so she could look away. But after a long drink of the warm brew, she had recovered enough to catch her hostess's eye again. "Perhaps I should be more circumspect. In fact, I'm sure that I should. However, you did advise me," she murmured, "to seek more amusement in my life."

The countess threw back her head and laughed. "So I did, so I did. I'm so pleased you were sensible enough to heed the words of your elder. As long as you are discreet, my dear." Her eyes twinkled as she patted the smooth knot that crowned her head and pushed a tendril of silver hair back into place.

After a few more minutes, Lucy moved away so that another guest could have a private chat with the countess. From the murmur of words and the younger woman's occasional dab at her cheeks, she suspected that the countess was offering her usual warm solicitude to a new widow still struggling to cope with her grief. Lucy remembered those times well.

Amazing how much brighter life had become since she had met Nicholas. Was she being disloyal to Stanley, to allow her sorrows to fade?

"Why so glum?" Roberta demanded as the handsome redhead joined Lucy on a settee on the other side of the room.

"Wondering that I could feel so happy again—it is a most unfamiliar sensation. And wondering, too, if—if—"

"If you must feel guilty about it?" Roberta demanded bluntly. She raised her brows in a gesture similar to the countess's. "Life is short, my dear, you know what Lady Sealey says. And wearing black for the rest of your life will not bring your husband back, which is sometimes a pity, and sometimes—ah—just as well."

Lucy nodded, trying to sort out the conflicting emotions inside her. "I have learned that my husband had—had another interest," she said carefully. "Perhaps it colors my feelings, I am not sure."

Her circumspection was wasted on the more worldly woman.

"Had a mistress, did he? Lots of 'em do," she said. "My own Harvey was a real lady's man, but I didn't mind, too much. When he was home, we made merry together, and we both enjoyed every minute of it." She sighed a little at the thought, then added more briskly, "But that doesn't mean I intend to sit home chained to my fireside and prick my fingers with a crewel needle for the rest of my life. Many agreeable men are happy enough to enjoy an occasional romp with a widow who knows what she wants, and how to give it back."

Lucy blushed at the other woman's bluntness. "If so,

what do you do about—" she hesitated, and the other woman waited, looking inquisitive.

"I mean, at the last tea I heard one of the women speaking of methods to avoid, ah—untimely consequences. A woman without a husband cannot discover herself with child. I heard something about a sponge soaked in red wine?" Lucy stared down at her teacup, embarrassed at this intimate subject, but Roberta sounded unfazed.

"Oh, yes, I know what you mean. It's a French technique. You take a small square of sponge, soak it in wine, and then attach a string to it and insert it . . ." She lowered her voice and explained the procedure, while Lucy tried in vain not to turn even redder.

"Thank you," she said later, feeling as if her cheeks were on fire. But she had learned a great deal that she had never been told.

Roberta shrugged. "My dear, you can always ask me anything. The French are much more practical about such things than we English."

After this unprecedented discussion, Lucy had no doubt of it. The other guests were beginning to take their leave, and she said good-bye to Roberta.

Before Lucy took her departure, the countess motioned her aside and whispered, "My dresser has a hat box for you, child. She has given it to your maid."

"Oh, thank you, my lady, you are much too kind," Lucy answered, aware of what the box most likely contained.

As usual, the countess waved away her thanks. "Nonsense. Now, have a good week and keep yourself safe, my dear."

On the way out, Lucy summoned Violet, who appeared with the promised box in her arms. Lucy could not peek at its contents in view of the countess's footman, so she would have to wait till they were back at the viscount's house and inside her own chamber before she could raise the lid. But they walked briskly, as she was eager to see what sartorial delights were contained inside it.

When they entered the hall of the viscount's home,

Hodges came to meet her. "You have a visitor in the drawing room, ma'am."

But no one knew she was here. Alarmed, Lucy motioned to Violet to go on, and the maid disappeared into the back hall. Lucy herself hurried up to the drawing room, but she paused on the threshold in surprise and dismay.

Dressed in bright purple and wearing a matching turban, Cousin Wilhelmina was planted on the largest settee, looking as solid as a battleship moored in the harbor. The viscount's servants had obviously been tending to her needs, as she held a cup of tea in one hand, but even so, her expression was dour.

Lucy conquered a sharp urge to turn and run the other way. Taking a deep breath, she proceeded more slowly into the room.

"Cousin," she said, her tone cautious. "How nice to see you."

"Indeed," Wilhelmina retorted, her own manner curt. "I wonder that you do not blush to see me, instead!"

"Excuse me?" Lucy braced herself, recognizing Wilhelmina in one of her worst moods. "I'm not sure what you mean."

"I mean that you are brazenly living in sin with a man to whom you are not married. I thought that even you, Lucinda, had more scruples than that!"

Lucy blinked, feeling as if she had been struck. So much for being discreet! She glanced over her shoulder to see that, thankfully, the footman had departed.

"Lower your voice," she snapped.

Wilhelmina paused, looking surprised at the unexpected vigor of the response. Lucy did not wait to allow her irascible relative time to recover.

"I should think you would have more confidence in me, *Cousin*," Lucy continued, keeping her tone level with great effort. "I am staying here, with my maid, because my house has been ransacked. Do you think it improper for one friend to help another?"

The older woman snorted, an inelegant sound. "That's

one way to put it! If you wish to make excuses—"

"Have you seen my house?" Lucy demanded. "I am most surprised you and Mrs. Broddy—I know her husband is as deaf as a post, but she certainly keeps up with all the happenings on our little street—did not hear the men who broke down my front door on Tuesday night and savaged all my belongings."

Wilhelmina had the decency to look a little self-conscious. "I did hear some sounds of turmoil. We wondered about such raucous visitors, at such a late hour."

"But you raised no alarm, did not even make an inquiry to see if I was being murdered in my bed?" Lucy pointed out. "I must thank you for your solicitude."

Wilhelmina reddened. "I had no idea—and where were you, then, if you were not at home at a respectable hour?"

"I was at the theater with friends, part of a party invited to the prince regent's box," Lucy retorted.

Her cousin's eyes widened. "Such a wild tale, Lucinda—"

"Merely the truth," Lucy interrupted. "You may ask anyone at Covent Garden, his royal highness is always observed. But anyhow, when I returned, I found my whole house a shambles, quite unlivable."

The other woman looked perplexed, as if for once not sure how to continue her tirade. "I—I—"

"Yes, thank you for your concern," Lucy said, trying to keep the irony out of her tone.

"Why did you not come to me, or your neighbor?"

Oh, dear, good question. Lucy thought fast.

"Since I knew that you are staying in Mrs. Broddy's only spare bedchamber, I did not wish to inconvenience her," Lucy said, as smoothly as possible. The very thought of living under the same roof with two such censorious women made her nauseous, but she could hardly confess that.

"She has an extra attic room, as she's currently short a housemaid. I'm sure that if I spoke to her—"

"And I'm sure you would not wish me to live in such straitened conditions when I have other friends with more space to accommodate guests," Lucy said, cutting her off. Amazing how good it felt, to interrupt her bossy cousin, instead of the other way around. "Unless you would like to give me funds so that I can reside for a few weeks in a nice hotel?"

"Of course not! That would be a ridiculous extravagance. But this, this is not proper!" Her cousin repeated, chewing on her thin lower lip stubbornly. "You under the same roof with a single man—"

"His cousin is chaperoning us, of course," Lucy said, her tone airy, hoping that Mrs. Broddy, with her inquisitive ways, had not found out too much about the viscount and just who made up his household.

"I didn't know he had a cousin," Wilhelmina argued.

"Everyone has a cousin," Lucy retorted. *Like it or not,* she thought. "She came in from the country just recently."

"And where is this woman?" Wilhelmina looked about her, like a bloodhound straining to pick up a scent.

"Lying down for her usual afternoon rest." Lucy was a little alarmed at how easily the lies seemed to rise to her lips. Perhaps she was being corrupted, after all. But if it stymied her cousin's domineering actions, she welcomed corruption with open arms!

"I should like to meet her."

"I'm sure you will, in time. I will not interrupt an older lady in need of her repose, however, just to satisfy your curiosity. In fact, the afternoon is slipping rapidly away, and I will not keep you, Cousin. I must go up and change for dinner."

Looking frustrated, Wilhelmina frowned again, but she took a breath and hoisted her considerable bulk to her feet. "I shall return soon, Cousin. I should be remiss if I did not check on your welfare."

Lucy, unfortunately, had no doubt of the seriousness of her intent, nor on what Wilhelmina would really be checking.

"You're too kind," she said for the second time that day, and this time with much less sincerity.

But at last her cousin made her departure. Sighing,

Lucy headed for the stairs. She met Mrs. Mott on the way up.

"I have had hot water sent up for your bath, ma'am. Dinner is at eight. His lordship said there will be no extra guests tonight."

Lucy nodded. "You've been lovely, Mrs. Mott. If you treat all his lordship's guests this well, I wonder that they ever leave."

"Oh, ma'am, he don't ever have guests," the housekeeper said. "In fact, I was so glad to see you, that is—it's so good for him to be seeing a nice young lady." Her tone suggested that she had some hints of his lordship's less reputable liaisons. But he did not bring the women home . . . Lucy felt warmed by the revelation.

Probably he would not have brought her here, either, if it had not been for the disaster at her own house, she reminded herself sharply. She could not allow herself to feel special, or to believe that Nicholas might be developing genuine feelings for her.

As much as she might wish to believe it.

Upstairs, Violet was waiting, and Lucy crossed the room quickly to examine the two dresses the countess had bestowed upon her, and which Violet had now laid out upon the bed.

"This green silk is lovely," Violet said. "And if we tie the sash tightly, I think it will do for tonight. There isn't time to alter it properly, but I will get right to it, first thing in the morning."

Lucy nodded and pulled off the riding habit for Violet to brush and clean while she surrendered to the luxury of another real bath, the warm water scented with bath salts that left her skin feeling smooth and silky. What a household to live in! Did Nicholas have any idea just how fortunate he was?

Sighing in appreciation, she leaned back against the rim of the copper tub and shut her eyes.

∽

Nicholas frowned.

"I don't know what you mean, your lordship," the man in front of him said, his tone just a little too obsequious, his eyes a tad too shifty.

Except for the wily gaze, the man appeared quite innocuous and vaguely familiar. He was short of stature and portly and possessed the round face and chubby, apple-red cheeks of an overaged infant. Perhaps this look of childish innocence served him well in his line of work.

Nicholas glanced around the small room; the shelves were lined with stacks and rolls of paper, tied neatly with black ribbon. Everything was dusted and orderly; the office presented the normal appearance of a work-place inhabited by any man of affairs. A rash young man of property, who had spent a little too much at the gaming tables, might think this man safe to deal with.

And he would find out his error only when it was much too late.

Nicholas met Mr. Brooks's inquiring stare and kept his own expression bland. The other man, who had risen quickly from behind his desk when Nicholas had been announced by the clerk outside, now frowned in his turn.

"You seem to be accusing me of—of—"

"I simply said that I understand your reputation is somewhat questionable, even for a moneylender."

The pale blue eyes blinked, and Mr. Brooks looked pained. "Now, surely, your lordship, you would not tar all men of—men of my profession with the same tainted brush?"

"I have made inquiries," Nicholas repeated. "And I regret to say I was not impressed by what I was told."

"A man in my line of work will have his detractors, my lord, but I hope you will not listen to gossip. If you wish to make a transaction, I shall be only too glad to assist you. I can assure you that I have dealt with scions of some of England's finest families, including those with titles loftier even than yours."

"Indeed."

Looking encouraged by the noncommital answer, the

man rushed on. "Not that your rank is not most impressive, of course. In addition, you will find that I can accommodate sums of any magnitude that you should require."

"Then you must be most successful, indeed," Nicholas commented, keeping his voice even. "I know men who lose their entire fortunes at cards or dice or other rash wagers. Or perhaps you have backers of even more wealth than your own?"

The gaze shifted, again, and then the blue eyes focused on Nicholas's face. "I am quite ready to do business with you, my lord, you need not question my resources. I assure you they are ample. Now, what amount are you in need of—that is, what amount do you desire to borrow?"

"How much would the interest be?" Nicholas inquired.

Mr. Brooks smiled, but his eyes were still hard. He meant, no doubt, to look friendly. "That will depend on the amount you require, my lord."

"No doubt. I suspect it's just as well that I come in search of a different currency," Nicholas told him.

The other man looked confused. "I fear I don't understand."

"Information is often more valuable than money. I'm sure you understand that, too," Nicholas said. "I want to know about your dealings with Stanley Contrain."

Behind their pale lashes the blue eyes looked down, then rose to meet Nicholas's gaze, this time with obvious effort. "I fear I do not recall that name. Perhaps he did business with a different firm?"

"Then your current claim against his property, his house in Cheapside, is unfounded? I will be happy to inform the magistrate on your behalf." Nicholas raised one brow.

"Ah . . ." The moneylender hesitated. "That—that Mr. Contrain."

"Yes," Nicholas agreed. "Just how many poor widows are you currently working to evict, that this fact strains your memory so?"

Mr. Brooks looked pained. "It is a business matter only,

my lord. You do not expect me to pretend to be running a charity, here."

"No, I don't think that. What I wonder, however, is why you lent money to a man of such a small and uncertain income."

The lender shrugged. "Perhaps he misrepresented the facts, my lord."

"And you have become so prosperous by accepting every potential borrower's claims?" Nicholas allowed his skepticism to color his tone.

Brooks looked irritated. "Anyone can make a mistake! Anyhow, he did have resources, he owned a small house."

"I doubt that this loan was a mistake. I have been told that you will give rash young men more time to pay their interest-swollen debts if they bring their friends to you, so that you always have a new supply of gullible victims," Nicholas pointed out. "Just what else do you require of the men who owe you money?"

"My lord?" A faint sheen of sweat showed on the moneylender's forehead. He made a motion as if to reach for a handkerchief, then restrained himself. "I don't—I don't know what you mean."

"I'm told that Stanley Contrain sometimes carried out commissions for his . . . patrons. What did he do for you, to stave off some of his debt?"

The man hesitated, as if not sure of the extent of Nicholas's knowledge. "I don't—I think you have been misled—"

"Oh, I think not." Nicholas steeled his tone. "Now, answer my question. What did he do for you?"

Brooks looked close to panic. "Some small errands, perhaps, I hardly remember."

"That," Nicholas murmured, holding the pale-eyed gaze with his own hard stare, "I do not believe."

The moneylender opened his lips, but could only stammer. "B-b-but—"

"And I shall find the answer, whether you are prepared to offer it, or not," Nicholas finished. "Good day. I shall see you again."

Without waiting for a response, Nicholas turned and left the inner office. Outside, a swarthy-skinned clerk gaped at him as Nicholas passed through the anteroom. When the door banged behind him, he left the building and retraced his steps down the narrow street, without rushing but very aware of his surroundings.

A man with the rolling gait of a sailor came out of a tavern, his face flushed from too much ale, and a coal cart lumbered by. Nicholas tarried at the intersection till two more carts and an overloaded coach passed, then crossed, stepping around a fresh pile of steaming manure and several puddles of dirty rainwater.

He walked slowly for two more streets, ignoring an empty cab that passed, before suddenly quickening his steps and turning abruptly into a side alley.

The man who had been following him had to run to catch up—he entered the alley at a trot. It was easy enough for Nicholas to reach out from the shadows where he had been waiting and grab him by the lapels of his shabby coat.

It was the clerk from the outer office. He gasped in surprise and tried to break free, but Nicholas's grip was too strong.

"Let go o' me!"

"First, tell me why your master sent you to trail after me?" Nicholas demanded, his voice stern.

The man tried to shake his head, but Nicholas tightened his grip.

"Don't bother to tell me you were only going out for a stroll. You have followed me since I left Brooks's office. Why?"

"He—" the clerk faltered, looking uncertain.

Nicholas shook him, handling the slighter weight as easily as if the clerk were a punching bag in Nicholas's favorite boxing salon.

" 'E didn't tell me, me lord," the other man blurted. " 'E just told me to find out where you went, after you left."

"Why this intense curiosity about my movements?"

"I don't know, me lord."

"Is this your usual practice with new applicants?"

The man shook his head, looking both miserable and bewildered.

Smothering a curse, Nicholas released his grip. The clerk stumbled backward, gasping in relief.

"Go back to your employer and tell him to beware of what he tries with me," Nicholas warned. "I am no witless calfling, ready to be slaughtered and hung up to drip my lifeblood out for his profit!"

"Yes, me lord, sorry, me lord," the man muttered, then took to his heels before Nicholas could change his mind.

Nicholas walked another block, and when he was sure that no one else was following, hailed a hackney cab and rode back to his own residence.

Not that it would take long for Brooks to discover where Nicholas lived, if that was the lender's purpose. The man had connections in Society, that was obvious enough, just from the brief list of his victims which Nicholas had elicited by making some discreet inquiries at his club. But Nicholas suspected that Brooks wanted more.

Still, when he reached home, Nicholas had a word with his butler about increased security, then, after a glance at the grandfather clock in the hall, strode up the stairwell and to his room to change for dinner.

When he returned, the clock was chiming the hour. He found Lucy waiting on the landing, and he offered her his arm as they went down to the dining room side by side.

She had changed out of the riding habit and into a pleasing dinner dress of pale green silk, which suited her fair good looks even if it seemed a bit too large for her slender figure.

"I hope you had a pleasant afternoon?" he asked as he seated her, then took his own place at the head of the polished walnut table.

She nodded. "Did you find anything?"

He gave a glance toward the footmen, who were offering dishes from the first course. "A little. I will give you the details later."

She accepted the warning with good grace, nodding. "Of course."

Lucy kept her expression even, controlling her impatience with effort. She was eager to hear what he had learned about the mysterious stranger who threatened her home. She dipped her spoon into the soup before her and was distracted at once by the skill of the viscount's cook. She savored the thick turtle soup; then, when the servants removed the soup plate and replaced it with the next dish, she tasted the broiled trout; then the chicken flavored lightly with rosemary, its skin tender and juicy; and finally the pork with fresh plum sauce. With these culinary delights, not to mention all the vegetables and side dishes, it was hard not to simply enjoy the meal.

And Nicholas was being a most gracious host, making innocuous conversation about the best plays he had seen last Season, and what might be offered at the London theaters this year. It was all light and pleasant, and Nicholas looked relaxed enough that she ventured, after a space, a more personal question.

"Why have you not returned to India in so long, my lord?"

They had maintained a formal address in front of the servants, and Lucy kept the practice, now. But she almost regretted her question when she saw the old barrier veil Nicholas's expression.

"Why do you ask?" He glanced down at his plate, toying with a forkful of meat.

"Only that it seems to be a place which you cared for. I see beautiful objects from the East all around your house," she pointed out, glancing at the rich colors of the Oriental rug that covered the floor, and the carved ivory that graced the sideboard. "Yet you said you have not been back in years. I only wondered—"

His eyes glinted with the old reserve, a look she had observed at their first meeting and had almost forgotten. But she knew him better, now, much better, and perhaps it was harder for him to hide his true thoughts, or at least easier for her to interpret them.

"Perhaps I have simply found too much to amuse me in England," he suggested, his tone light. But a look of pain flashed briefly behind the mask he used to hide his feelings, and for an instant she remembered the last time she had seen that glimmer of emotion.

Feeling a sudden hollowness in the pit of her stomach, Lucy looked away from his face. This, too, was a conversation that would have to wait for a more private time. What a man of mystery the viscount was. . . .

Trying to regain the ease which they had enjoyed during the beginning of the meal, she told him of the visit from her cousin, trying to make the tale funny.

The viscount did not smile. "Your cousin and your neighbor are most determined in their efforts to remain informed about your actions. Nor does their inquisitiveness appear to be motivated solely by concern for your well-being, although perhaps I wrong them. You have known them both longer than I—"

Lucy nodded. "Having known them longer, especially my cousin, I regret to say that you are quite correct. Wilhelmina enjoys censure much more than compassion."

He frowned. "I do not wish you to be harassed, nor to suffer embarrassment."

And a woman's reputation was a fragile thing, Lucy thought. "Do you think I should take up my neighbor's offer of—of hospitality?" She tried to keep her tone even, although her heart sunk. "Or Lady Sealey kindly offered—"

"No, indeed, it sounds like a most ungracious invitation," Nicholas suggested. "I said I would look out for you and I will. Unless you are not content here?"

There was no way to answer that, to offer a polite lie, without her too transparent face giving away her true feelings. Lucy had never been so happy in her life. However—

"I know that my presence is a charge on your household—"

"Don't talk nonsense," he interrupted, his tone gruff. Once, his brusqueness might have alarmed her—now she was learning that he assumed that tone to hide his moments of compassion or to mask his acts of kindness. So she gave him a wide smile.

"It will not be forever. No doubt my house will soon be in shape so that I can return," she suggested. "And if we find the thief, so that he cannot trouble me again—"

"No doubt, but not yet," he agreed.

Lucy found she had not resolution enough to argue. The question of her current lodgings could wait, they had more pressing matters to discuss. Or perhaps she did not wish to think of leaving him.

At any rate, Lucy found she had no appetite for the desserts that the servants brought out to tempt her, and Nicholas, too, waved away the cakes and trifles, even the tray of cheeses that the footmen offered.

"Shall I withdraw and allow you to enjoy your brandy in solitary splendor?" she teased gently when a footman brought in a new decanter.

He raised his brow. "I have a better idea—we could both enjoy it in the greater comfort of the library."

His favorite room, where they could speak candidly. Lucy nodded and rose. She was eager to hear his report of his day, and eager just to be alone with him so that she could touch his sleeve, lift her hand to his face, or slip it inside his shirt to touch the warmth of his chest and feel his heart pounding . . . that thought led to others which caused her own heart to race and made her glad that she could turn away and walk, with a dignified gait, to the door, hiding her no-doubt too obvious moment of confusion.

When they had crossed the hall and were safely inside the library and a footman had brought a silver tray with two goblets and the decanter of old brandy, Nicholas nodded a dismissal. The servant bowed and left them, shutting the door quietly as he went.

Nicholas poured the brandy, and Lucy accepted the glass, though she gazed at it doubtfully. She seldom imbibed such strong spirits. She sipped and felt the potency of the liquid as it burned its way, deep and smooth, all the way down to her stomach. Goodness! She set the glass still holding the rest of her portion of brandy carefully on the nearest small table and turned an expectant gaze upon her host.

"Tell me."

Nicholas recounted the tale of his visit to Thomas Brooks.

Lucy gulped. "He's a moneylender! I should have considered that possibility." She had known well enough, after her marriage if not before, how precarious Stanley's income had been. She had worried with him, although he had refused to discuss the details with her, only haranguing her at times about keeping the household budget as small as possible.

She had stewed and basted tough, cheap cuts of mutton so that they would be edible, skimped on expensive sugar and white flour, and done everything she could to economize. Her own clothing bills were very small; Stanley's tailor and bootmaker and other sartorial indebtedness she had had no control over.

She had offered to let their cook go early on, willing to take on the work herself, but it was Stanley who had refused, afraid the neighbors would talk. So the cook and the scullery maid had stayed, until Lucy had been forced to give them their notice after his death, when there was truly no money for their wages.

"I knew he was gambling often, after his income dwindled," she said slowly. "I even thought that that might be why he was at the duchess's salon, to take part in the card games. But I was told they are held on Tuesday and Thursday afternoons, not on Wednesday, and his diary notes that he went to the salon on a Wednesday, so—"

"Not when the prince regent is present."

"What?" Lucy did not understand.

Nicholas frowned. "When Prinny graces the duke and duchess with his company, there is always a card game, no matter what day it is."

Lucy blinked. Of course, schedules were easily altered to suit a royal guest's preference. "But if that was what happened, who brought Stanley along? He cannot have had an invitation on his own, without someone's introduction."

Nicholas pondered the question. "Perhaps someone connected with Brooks, someone seeking to lure your husband into further debt. The games that the prince indulges in are played for very high stakes."

"So that Stanley could then be blackmailed into helping steal the ruby?" It always came back to the missing gem, about whose whereabouts they still had no clue.

She sighed and put one hand to her temple, which threatened to throb. If this speculation were true, it had been a dastardly plot. Not only had it caused her husband's disgrace, but now she owed this man, this Thomas Brooks, a thousand pounds, or he would take her house.

"Do not concern yourself," Nicholas told her. Again his tone sounded curt, but she knew the kindness concealed behind it, the compassion he did not seem to know how to express more openly. "I will not allow anyone to take away your home."

She stared at him. "But a thousand pounds! It is an immense sum, and—oh, I know that to you, my lord, it may not seem so, but I could never allow you to assume such a charge. And that reminds me, it was very kind of you to bring in a dressmaker for me, but—but I cannot allow you to pay for my clothing. I would feel like—like—"

She couldn't quite bring out the term.

He lifted a hand toward her cheek, flushed with earnestness, and the adorable lips that he yearned to meet, then dropped it again. It took all of his self-control, especially now that he knew how receptive she was to his touch and how much she could enjoy the act of lovemaking, not to take every excuse to touch her, not to slip away morning, noon, and night to strip off her clothes and his and join their bodies in the same elated passion that they had shared only once.

He ached for her now, at dinner, at breakfast, every day, every hour. He feared that the effort to keep himself detached made his tone even more curt than usual, but fortunately Lucy did not seem to notice.

And now he restrained himself, yet again, though it took every ounce of his self-discipline. He would not risk her thinking that he had brought her here for his own amusement. He feared that, despite her growing assurance, she still had too little confidence. She might rush back to her own bare house and into harm's way.

"My dear Lucy," he told her, keeping his tone controlled. "You must have something to wear. The vandals who assaulted your home made rags of your entire wardrobe. What will your censorious cousin say if you stroll naked down the street?"

She laughed, a spontaneous peal of merriment that made his pulse leap. To make her laugh, to make her happy—he could spend his whole life doing nothing more than that, and what could be more worthwhile? He took another sip of the brandy, allowing it to linger on his tongue while the fiery liquid filled his throat and nostrils with its potent mist, then he swallowed, feeling it flow into his very blood, taking its fire with it. As if he needed more incitement to passion . . .

He wondered if even his control would last much longer. Perhaps he should suggest bed—oh yes, that was exactly what he wanted to suggest!

Setting down the brandy, Nicholas shut his eyes for an instant. Control yourself, he told himself; you are not a green boy, led only by passion.

More's the pity!

Lucy watched the subtle play of emotions behind the impassive expression he habitually wore. There was no doubt that she could read him so much more clearly now. What caused him so much turmoil? And that thought led to another, the question that had been growing inside her for some time.

"Nicholas," she said, impetuous as always, "why does the baby trouble you so?"

Fourteen

His expression froze, and he looked as if he had been punched in the gut.

She bit her lip, wishing she could take back the impulsive words. "I'm sorry, I didn't mean to pry. I—"

She paused, because he had wheeled. He strode across the room to stand in front of the hearth and gaze down into the fire, his back to her, his face safely hidden.

The silence stretched.

Oh, dear, oh, dear. Why had she blurted those incautious words? She would not hurt him for the world. Twisting her hands together in her lap, Lucy hesitated. She wanted to follow him, soothe that tense line of shoulder, caress his cheek, now turned away. But perhaps he was angry at her for invading the private spaces that he guarded so ferociously.

The fire popped and hissed, but no one moved, and no one spoke. Lucy felt all the agony that he could not, despite his best attempts, hide from her any longer.

"I'm so sorry," she said finally. "I should not have spoken. Please, forget it all. Your—it is your choice, and I had no right to ask."

Silence again, then he slowly turned. The shadows played upon his face, creating illusions, making him appear very old for a moment, his skin stretched taut over bare bones.

She put one hand to her mouth, rocked by the misery now naked before her gaze. It etched his normally smooth expression into a twisted mask that she hardly recognized, while his dark eyes reflected a pain so old, so enormous, that it must have threatened his sanity, much less his self-control.

"Oh, my dearest," she whispered. She found that she had crossed the space between them without even being aware of her steps. She put both hands up to his cheeks, wanting only to caress, to comfort. She touched the lines of pain, smoothed them, her touch as gentle as a baby's breath. Babies, that was his weak point, that was why he could not look at Eve's child without that black veil crossing his face. But what had caused such anguish?

She would not risk asking again.

Instead, she stood on tiptoe to encircle him with her arms. She pressed her face against his chest, pulled his cravat aside without compunction for its usual fashionable tautness, and kissed the smooth skin of his throat, her lips warm against his skin.

Groaning, Nicholas lowered his head and found her lips, his own mouth hard and demanding, his kiss extending both need and surrender.

Lucy was too busy returning his kiss, meeting his thrusting tongue with her own, to smile, but inside, her guilt eased and pleasure grew. Not just the pleasure of her body responding to his, but the crowning delight of knowing that she could bring him respite from his troubles, perhaps even afford him joy. And if she could, she would offer him the world, knowing that he had brought all the stars of heaven down to present to her, the first time they had made love. She still felt their shimmer inside her whenever she recalled that night.

Their kiss stretched on for measureless moments until he lifted her easily into his arms and brought her to the divan where they had experienced such delight the first time they had come together. He lay her down carefully and loosened her gown, but, to his surprise, she sat up and put his hands away.

"This time, this time is for you," she whispered.

He thought he had not understood her. But the light in her clear blue eyes shone like a candle in the dark, brightening even the self-imposed isolation in which he had dwelt for so long. Did she really comprehend what she was saying?

Lucy slipped her hand inside his shirt, touching his bare skin, touching the center of his chest where his heart beat now with a quickening rhythm. Then she pushed the linen shirt aside and allowed her hand to slide, with enticing slowness, down his chest. She paused to caress the flat nipples, and he drew in a sharp breath.

Encouraged by this sign, she leaned forward and pressed her lips against them, kissed first one, touching it lightly with her tongue, then the other. He felt his pulse leap. Trying not to groan, he reached for her, but again, she shook her head.

"You, first," she said, her tone mischievous.

Now she lowered her hand further, tracing a path over his groin with such a deliberate pace that he almost shouted. He had to brace himself, the sensation was so intense, and now she touched the most sensitive area of all, caressing him, there—

Perhaps she did understand!

"Lucy," he said, the word as much a groan as an endearment. "Lucy, my love—"

She raised her hands and pulled off his cravat, unwrapping it slowly from his throat and dropping it to the floor, then with the same deliberate motions lifted the white shirt.

Too impatient to wait, he pulled the garment off and tossed it aside, not looking to see where it landed.

Next, she unbuttoned his tight-fitting pantaloons, and

with tantalizing slowness pushed them down.

"The hell with that," he muttered, and tugged off the rest of his clothing. "And now, dear heart, you must do the same."

She had already loosened the back of her gown so that she could stand and step out of it. Pausing to smile at him—the sweet vixen!—she stripped off her shift and her stockings and the rest of her underthings, but while she tossed the other garments aside, she held up the thin linen shift in front of her, as if this were a game, holding it like a screen to hide the final glimpse of her nakedness.

Dear God in heaven, she did learn fast! Nicholas drew a deep breath, feeling the need for her in every fiber of his being. He hardly needed to push aside the concealing garment; the vision of her unclad body was delightfully affixed in his memory. Her swelling breasts, the narrow waist, the slim, curved hips that drew him like a bee to an enticing flower . . . His usual self-control was deserting him rapidly, making a mockery of the man who was so practiced in his casual lovemaking. . . . But there was nothing casual, nothing easy about this.

This was Lucy, and who else had ever made him feel this way? Not even—the forbidden name drifted to the front of his mind, and, out of long habit, he pushed it away.

No, that was a lifetime ago. This was now, and he ached for Lucy, wanted her more than he had wanted any woman in recent memory, wanted to push himself inside her, release his seed into her, dare the Fates to strike him down yet again. Dare he be so brave, so rash?

And yet he wanted more, more than even that. He wanted to please her, delight her, protect her, make her dizzy with joy, see her laugh and put away for all time the tiny lines of worry that sometimes wrinkled her brow.

He wanted her, but he also wanted her to be happy.

"Oh, Lucy," he said again, hardly aware of the words he spoke. Now her hands had returned to his cheeks, caressing them gently. She touched his face, his shoulders, the bare skin which seemed so sensitive to her light strokes, massaged his neck and his shoulders until he felt like melting butter. And when again her touch moved, reached down, circled his chest with its light sprinkling of dark hair, and then dropped lower still, he groaned aloud.

She stroked lightly, then with more strength, and he could hardly contain the pure animal response that she elicited. Then she circled him with her fingers, held him inside both palms in a firm, easy clasp, stroking his flesh into even more pulsating life as if she was totally at ease with his body as well as her own.

He could hardly restrain himself. Awash in sensation, he swallowed hard. The slow, caressing movements were more than any man, even one as controlled as Nicholas, could endure.

"No," he said, putting aside her hands, knowing his voice sounded hoarse. "No, love, now we do it together."

And he sat beside her, pulling her onto his lap to face him, allowing her—she grasped his intent very quickly and positioned herself just so—to slip himself inside her as she sat easily upon him, gasping a little with the pleasure of the feel of his body inside hers.

Oh, heavens, Lucy thought, not even trying to hold back a deep sigh of delight. Oh, my, oh, my, what amazing sensations this position induced.

It had never occurred to her that men and women could enjoy love in any position other than the one she and her husband, on their few rare encounters, had always assumed in bed. Even in the first heady, exhilarating lovemaking that she and Nicholas had shared, they had lain upon the wide divan with him over her, as she had expected.

But this—he moved inside her, and she gasped, then moved her hips and found how to control the rhythm even more than he. And how intense a pleasure it was! She felt ripples of sensation slide over her skin, waves of sensation, like ice and heat, like joy made solid, washing over her in waves that grew and crested, and still she moved, sliding her body, gripping his with her most private parts, and the ecstasy she felt was mirrored in his own expression, for once totally unguarded, totally open.

They rose together, emotionally and physically, until at last the pleasure blossomed into the final explosion of passion that could no longer be contained. This time he did not try to withdraw from her, this time he held her close and she returned his embrace while his body spasmed and hers moved in the same climatic throes, her wordless, breathless sounds echoing inside her mind like soft cries of a lost bird coming home to its nest.

And when at last he was still, he held her tightly, refusing to allow her even to slip down to sit beside him on the leather-upholstered divan. So, still resting in his lap, she wrapped her arms about him and lay her head on his shoulders and felt the bliss of complete and utter contentment.

"My dearest love," she whispered into the smooth olive skin of his shoulder, but the sound was the merest breath, and she did not think he heard. It was just as well—she would not burden him with expectations that he might feel honor bound to fulfill. Now was enough, the future she would worry about later. Whatever happened, no one could take this from her, this hour, this union, complete and joyous.

So when Nicholas spoke, she started a little, not expecting to hear his voice. "Lucy," he said. "You continue to astound me."

She laughed a little at that, then paused.

"Oh," she said.

He lifted his head to regard her, as if hearing the moment of alarm.

"I forgot the sponge!"

"Sponge?"

"Nothing," she said, though she had to suppress an inner sigh. If he was so disturbed by babies, and if she should become—well, she'd worry about that later, too.

"It's not for you to—" He cleared his throat. "If I seemed—"

There was another pause, and when he spoke again, she

hardly recognized his voice, its tone was so raw.

"Once," he said, very low, "once there was a young man who went out to India, to manage his family's varied business ventures. It was an adventure, that beautiful and exotic land, and he was heady with the excitement of his new life. He loved it all, the spice-scented bazaars and graceful minarets and Hindu temples, the jungles teeming with strange wildlife and echoing with shrieking birds and snarling leopards, even the sacred cows stopping traffic on city streets. Oh, there was ugliness, too; poverty and disease, crippled beggars and homeless, orphaned children wandering the roads, but he was young enough to ignore all of that, sure that disaster would never touch him."

Lucy held her breath, entranced by this glimpse into Nicholas's past, afraid to respond lest the wrong word should stop these unusual confidences.

"And then he met a young Englishwoman with dark hair and merry eyes, as young as he and just as naive. Her name was Anne, and she had come out to visit her uncle, who was a government administrator at one of the British colonial stations. And the young man fell in love and wooed the young lady, and they married, selected a house for themselves on the outskirts of Bombay, with a garden filled with bright tropical flowers. They were sure they had found their own private Eden. Then, a year later, she bore a child, a boy, named after her father . . . and everything seemed perfect. . . ."

His voice faltered. Lucy's eyes widened. Nicholas had had a wife, a child! But she held her too-reckless tongue, afraid to say the wrong thing, waiting for the rest of the story, though now she braced herself against the tragedy she felt was coming.

"Until the fever came, racing through the city, striking down first the baby, who lived only a day after the illness ravaged his tiny body. Then, in her grief, his mother fell ill, too. Within a week, they were both gone, buried. And the young man longed for death as well, but the fever refused to take him, and he thought he would go mad with grief. . . ."

"Oh, Nicholas!" The pain in his voice was too much for her. Lucy bit her lip against more words, and waited.

"When he was strong enough to leave the house, he threw himself into work, and sometimes, being no saint, he sated himself with alcohol or with kisses from local dark-eyed women, who seemed happy enough to come to his bed. But nothing helped, not for long. Months later, when some of the fog had lifted, he made a decision. He sailed home to England and vowed never to go back to that beautiful, lethal land. . . . And in his native country he made for himself a life of selfish pleasures . . . as if he were the only person who'd ever experienced grief and heartsickness."

The rough tone twisted, transformed itself into the more usual cynical lightness. Yet now she knew what lay behind his pose.

"Oh, Nicholas," she repeated, this time more deliberately. "That does not mean that your pain was any the less, simply because others have lost loved ones, too. You had—you have—your own particular agony. No one with any heart would deny the vastness of your loss, nor your right to do whatever you had to do to protect yourself from more hurt."

He sat very still, though he continued to hold her close to him. She could not see his face, which was pressed against the top of her head. For another long moment he remained motionless, then she felt the sigh ripple through him, as if he had expected a different response.

Did he think she would rail at him for keeping his personal anguish private, that she would berate him for his licentious behavior in the years since. Who would be so heartless? If Nicholas had found a little ease in brief liaisons and a detached and ironic cynicism, who could judge him?

Not Lucy.

And now she felt something else, the slight tremor that he tried to contain, then the touch of dampness against her hair, as if his cheeks were wet from tears held inside for far too many years. She did not move, did not try to observe him weeping, if he still wished his grief to be unseen. But she held him even more tightly, laying her head against his chest and offering herself as pillow, refuge, comforter, as little or as much as he wished.

When finally the paroxysm of grief passed, again they remained entwined, sitting close, arms wrapped around each other until Lucy found that her legs prickled with numbness, and the fire in the hearth across the room had faded to glowing coals, and even the candles threatened to gutter into their pools of melting wax.

And nothing mattered, if her nearness brought solace to Nicholas.

When the clock in the hall struck one, Nicholas roused himself and whispered to her, "You must want your bed."

She smiled up at him, relieved to see that he was calm again, and more, his eyes reflecting some measure of inner ease that she thought perhaps she had never glimpsed in him before.

They dressed quickly, then he took a candle, snuffing out the rest, and led her up the stairs through silent, shadowy, happily untenanted halls—the servants must have gone to bed long since—and showed her to her room, lighting a candle on her bedside table so that she could prepare for bed.

And he kissed her once more, a long, lingering, bewitching kiss. Passion lay behind it, ready to rise again, but for now just the touch of his lips, warm against hers, was enough.

"Good night, sweet Lucy."

She watched him leave, closing the door very softly behind him.

Sighing, Lucy shut her eyes for a moment. She felt wonderfully tired, exhausted even, from the pleasures of the love they had enjoyed together and the emotional turmoil she had also shared. Poor Nicholas. Perhaps now he would began to heal, now that he had opened the festering wound that had poisoned his soul for so many years.

She tried to picture him with a young wife, holding a baby, but shook her head. It was another lifetime, as he said, and almost impossible to bring into focus. Nicholas young and naive . . . she could not grasp the image.

The Nicholas she knew now, she ached for. Even though he would lie in his own bed a few rooms away, she already missed him, missed his touch, his nearness, the warmth of him beside her. . . .

Scolding herself for such foolishness, she undressed, washed quickly with the tepid water from her ewer, and pulled on a nightdress. Without even bothering to button it, she crawled into the big bed, whose covers had already been turned down. Blowing out her candle, she lay her cheek upon the soft down-filled pillow.

If only Nicholas lay next to her . . . But though she smiled wistfully into the darkness, very soon, she found her eyelids grew heavy, and she slept.

～⌘～

She woke to find sunlight streaming into the room. What time was it? She must help Violet clean out the grates and bring in the coal, if enough remained in the cellar. . . .

Rubbing her eyes, Lucy sat up, then remembered with a start where she was. No scrubbing today, no worrying about a bare larder or an empty coal bin. Sighing, she lay back against the pillow. She could not continue very long commanding such luxury; it would be too hard to leave. And just because the viscount had come to her rescue did not mean that she had any claim upon him. She did not wish to be a beggar maid rescued by a prince; how on earth could a poor girl maintain any dignity in such circumstances?

Now, if they could just find that blasted ruby, which had caused everyone so much trouble to begin with, at least she would have a small nest egg to make her feel less destitute, less unequal. Of course, even then, she would never approach Nicholas's status in life, neither his rank nor his fortune. So there was no need to think that he might consider any permanent connection. So why did she continue to envision, with a longing approaching the physical hunger of her most straitened days, having Nicholas beside her, always?

Frowning at her own thoughts, Lucy heard a knock at the door.

"Come in," she called.

Violet entered, carrying a well-filled tray. She beamed with contentment, and she had a garment hung over her arm.

"I been altering the other dress the countess gave you, ma'am, and I'll have the dinner dress fitted by tonight, as well."

"Violet, you are a marvel." Lucy allowed her maid to set the tray upon the bedside table, then pour out a steaming cup of tea. Lucy sipped, relishing the taste, then took a scone and spread it with butter and strawberry jam.

"The viscount has a wonderful cook," she observed.

"Oh, yes, ma'am, the dinners in the servants' hall are wonders, they are," Violet agreed.

The girl already looked less scrawny, Lucy thought, as if she had gained some needed weight in the few days they had resided here.

"And so nice to me, everyone is. The cook is showing me 'ow—how—to make these little strawberry tarts, ma'am, and I've just about got the knack of it."

Violet seemed to be settling most happily into the household. Lucy considered warning her maid, as she had cautioned herself, that their sojourn here must of necessity be brief, but she decided not to dim the little servant's radiant mood.

"I'll just see about 'ot—hot water for your bath," Violet said now, after hanging the dress carefully in the clothespress. She bustled out again.

Lucy ate a leisurely breakfast, then went into the dressing room for her bath. More luxury, more delights.

Afterward Violet helped her into the morning gown. It was a pleasant-looking muslin, white sprigged with blue, and after Violet's work it fit much better than the unaltered gown she had worn for dinner last night.

Violet brushed her mistress's fair hair and produced some blue ribbon to thread through Lucy's blond curls. Lucy gazed into the mirror. She looked quite presentable, she thought.

Smiling to herself, she thanked Violet and made her way downstairs. As she expected, she found Nicholas in his library. He was sitting behind his large mahogany desk, sifting through a large pile of mail.

As she entered, he handed a note to his footman. "See that this goes out at once, by special messenger," he told the man.

The footman bowed and departed.

Was it something to do with the ruby? Curious, Lucy came closer.

Smiling at her, Nicholas rose and came round to kiss her, a quick, hard kiss that made her pulse jump and her stomach go weak.

She clung to him, then, aware of sounds in the hall as servants crossed on their various errands, drew back reluctantly.

"Is there anything new?" she asked.

"About the matter you mean, no, I'm sorry to say. We have to find a new line of inquiry, however, our need is too pressing." He paused.

Another footman entered, with more gilt-edged cards to add to the stack of letters and notes. Heavens, how did the viscount deal with so many invitations?

Nicholas reached for the largest card at the top of the pile and broke the wax seal. He lifted his brows. "Ah," he said. "We are bid to a royal ball."

Lucy gaped at him. "Surely not," she protested. "I mean, I'm sure you are, but as for me—"

He held out the card. "See for yourself. Prinny seems to remember you well. It will be held a week from tomorrow, which is more notice than he often gives his long list of friends. And he will want answers about our investigation, I fear."

Answers about the ruby. Where could it be? Someone had ripped apart her home to find it, she and Nicholas had searched for it, and every clue seemed to go up like smoke, with nothing of substance left behind.

Though it had led them to Eve, and to Stanley's child. They, at least, had been aided by Lucy and Nicholas's so far fruitless quest.

"I should check on Eve soon," Lucy murmured, as much to herself as to Nicholas. "And make sure she has settled comfortably on the farm."

He nodded absently, his thoughts obviously elsewhere. "You are sure that Stanley had no office in the city?"

To do what in? Lucy almost answered, but that seemed unkind, so she pushed the words back. "Not to my knowledge," she told him, "but there was so much that I did not know about Stanley's habits."

"I will make inquiries," Nicholas said. "And oh, I have something for you. One of my men found it beneath a loose board in your house."

Lucy raised her brows. It was obviously not the missing gem, or he would have told her at once, so what could it be?

He held out a small cloth bag, which jingled a little as he handed it over.

Lucy took it and poured out the handful of silver and copper coins onto the desktop. She touched the shillings and half pounds and pennies with one finger as she calculated swiftly; there were several pounds here, altogether.

Biting her lip, she glanced back at him.

Nicholas had returned to his pile of correspondence and was perusing a long sheet filled with numbers and lists written in heavy blue ink, but he seemed to feel her gaze. He looked up.

"Surely you do not think I would create such a shabby stratagem? If I were going to try to foist money upon you, Lucy my dear, I would not be so cheap!"

Flushing—she could never keep her thoughts out of her face, more's the pity—Lucy smiled reluctantly. "I suppose not. But who could have put it there, and why?"

"Possible Stanley had a few caches of money to use for future antes, that is, to enter a card game, when all other resources were used up," Nicholas suggested, his tone bland. "Many gamesters have such habits." He opened another letter and concentrated on its contents.

Perhaps. Lucy stared at the coins. She couldn't help thinking of days when she would have been more than delighted to have come across this small but useful stash. She started to ask exactly where it had been found, then decided Nicholas might suspect that she was questioning his story, so she shut her lips firmly. When she returned home, however, she would certainly check all the floors in the house!

"I should really send this to one of my creditors," she said, thinking aloud. "Although, with the exception of Brooks, I think you may hold the biggest debt at the moment, my lord."

"Surely not." He sounded startled.

"Oh, yes. Between the original forty shillings with which you saved my dining room furniture, and the nightgowns, and, um, other linen that the dressmaker brought with her, not to mention the riding habit—"

"Just try to hand over money to me," he said without raising his eyes, his tone low, and his lips curving a little despite his efforts to look stern.

Lucy shook her head. "And you accuse me of being stubborn? However, I admit if I don't use the funds in that way, at least this will be some help in replenishing my almost nonexistent wardrobe."

Nicholas did look up this time. "Lucy, if you have not visited a good couturier lately, let me warn you that this small sum will not buy even one dress in any shop on Bond Street. If you would only let me summon the dressmaker back—"

"Oh, I know that, but Violet is quite good with her needle, as am I," Lucy assured him. "If I went down to a linen draper or one of the big warehouses that sell cloth cheaply, I could likely get several lengths of muslin, and then she and I could stitch some additional gowns."

He frowned for a moment, then nodded and put down the sheet of paper in his hands. "Very well, I will accompany you."

"You are surely not interested in such a boring errand," Lucy objected. She glanced at the desk. "You appear to have plenty of work to do, my lord."

"Yes, Mrs. Contrain," he agreed, his tone gently mocking, "I do. And I have already set into motion inquiries to see if your husband had an office or room anywhere in the City. I hope for some answers, soon. But I also am most interested in keeping you safe."

Even she was not so stubborn as to quibble with that. And although he could perfectly well send a footman along with her, she much preferred Nicholas's company, so Lucy decided not to argue.

He called for his carriage, and they were soon on their way toward the river, where many of the warehouses full of linens and muslins were located.

"I will warn you that I have taken the liberty of having a new assortment of gloves ordered for you. The first ones should be delivered by this afternoon," he told her.

"Nicholas!"

Lucy tried to look stern, but as he was currently stroking her cheek with one finger, it was hard to achieve a suitable expression of reproof.

"If some villain had the temerity to destroy my original gift, which was only a trifle anyhow, I have the right to replace it," he argued.

She gave up. She had had only the one pair she had been wearing the night her house had been ransacked, so the restoration of a selection of gloves would be most welcome. But—"You are much too good to me," she murmured.

He lifted her palm, peeled off the glove, and kissed her palm. His lips were warm upon her bare skin. She shivered with delight.

"My dearest, I have not even begun to show you what I should like to do for you," he told her. His dark eyes twinkled, and she could not be sure if he referred to additional clothing, or to something much more pleasurable. So she laughed and stroked his cheek. When the carriage drew up in front of a large, plain building, she drew her glove hastily back on and prepared to step down.

When they were ushered inside, the clerks bowed deeply, and Lucy looked at Nicholas in suspicion. "They know you."

"Yes," he agreed, even while a young clerk, whose absurdly high collars almost obscured his cheeks, hurried up.

"Matthews, Mason, this lady would like to see some of our finest muslins, if you please."

"Of course, my lord. If you would follow me, madam." He bowed again and hurried toward the counters at the front of the long room.

"Nicholas, this is your warehouse?" Lucy stared at him.

"Didn't you know that the finest muslins come from the East?" He offered his arm, and she took it as they moved in a leisurely manner to follow the young man.

"But I am going to *buy* this cloth," Lucy insisted. "I cannot allow you to—"

"Of course you are. Did you think I would wish to see your custom go to a rival firm?" Nicholas's expression remained smooth.

Lucy, however, made a face at him. As if a few pounds would make any difference to his trading empire! She admired his nonchalance about his holdings, however, since most of the Ton would not admit to any contact with the world of business.

She said as much, keeping her voice low, and Nicholas shrugged. "My grandfather built it up. Why should I blush over the commerce that kept my parents, and now me, in easy comfort? I care little about empty-headed gossips."

No, that was Nicholas, true enough, unimpressed by anyone else's opinions, whether about his profligate life or his involvement with trade.

They had reached a wide table, and the clerk, with assistance from several other young men, brought out bolts and rolls of lovely cloth for her to examine. The muslin they lay before her was white and sprigged and checked and tinted in pale colors, all of them quite enticing. Lucy fingered one of the fabrics, enjoying the fine weaving and trying to make up her mind which ones she should select.

The young clerk hovered at her elbow and did not rush her.

An older man in a dark suit appeared, and Nicholas walked aside to speak to him. Perhaps one of his managers?

Lucy returned to the cloth. She selected a clear pale blue, a white sprigged with lavender, a soft green, and then, not sure of the cost, decided that this must be enough. She still had thread to buy, and buttons, and she hoped to have enough shillings left to purchase a plain straw bonnet, to which she and Violet could add trimming.

When she announced her selection, the clerk marked the lengths with the aid of a long wooden measuring stick, then motioned to one of his fellows to help him with the large bolts of cloth. They hurried off to have her dress lengths cut.

"I will put it into your carriage, madam," he told her.

"Thank you for your help," Lucy said, "And the total for the muslins I have chosen will be?"

He blinked. "Ah, I will have the bill included in your parcel, madam."

Lucy nodded, not wanting to commit a solecism by insisting on paying on the spot. Obviously, anyone the viscount brought would have ample credit extended by his employees, but she was still determined to discharge this obligation herself.

She lingered by the table, glancing through all the variety of patterns and colors while she waited for her fabric to be cut, and then became aware that another man stood beside her. Had the clerk returned with a question?

She looked around. "Yes?"

It was a different man. He had a pleasant, round face, though his eyes looked shrewd. He reached forward, but to Lucy's surprise, instead of taking up one of the bolts of fabric, he seized her hand.

His clasp was hard, almost painful.

She gasped and jerked her hand back, but his hold held true. What was he about?

"You know where it is," the man said, bending closer to speak into her ear. "It will be the worse for you if you do not tell us."

He kept his voice low, but she sensed the strong emotion he could barely contain, and she believed in the potency of his threat.

Lucy felt her heart beat faster—where was Nicholas? She had seen him step into an office with his manager, she remembered, the last time she had looked around. She considered screaming for assistance, but she hesitated to act the hapless victim. Surely the stranger wouldn't dare to hurt her here, in such a public place.

"Where is it?" the man repeated, and his grip tightened.

Lucy winced at the pressure, but she raised her eyes and met his gaze firmly. "Who is *us*?" she demanded.

Looking astonished that she would resist him, the man blinked, pale lashes shuttering the shrewd gaze for an instant. "Never you mind, just tell me, where is it?"

"I don't know what you mean."

The man's grip grew more and more painful. Surely, Nicholas would return to check on her soon. If not, like it or not, she would make a commotion.

"You have no right to it!" he muttered. "You want to expire like your husband?"

Lucy felt the chill run all the way to her bone. Did he, could he, mean—"Stanley's passing was not an accident?" she demanded. "You had a hand in his death?"

The man's expression hardened, and she saw more clearly the baseness beneath the surface charm. "You think he just happened to be run over by a carriage, two nights after he stole the biggest gem to come into England in decades?"

"Murderer!" The word was hardly more than a sigh. Lucy was having trouble getting out any sound at all; her throat seemed to close up with the emotion that surged through her. The realization staggered her. This man had killed her husband. "You dare to admit your crime!"

"He had no right to it, trying to double-cross us," the man repeated. He pulled her wrist back, twisting until Lucy flinched again. "But he didn't have the ruby on 'im—we checked—so I got to know. Where is it?"

His grip was too tight; she could not disengage her hand. So Lucy kicked him in his shin, hard, and although the impact hurt her toes, she thought that it affected him more. Exclaiming, he bent slightly, his expression pained, and she was at last able to free her hand.

Lucy grabbed the stout ruler with which the clerk had been measuring the cloth and thrust it into her attacker's stomach, and again in the direction of his groin.

His strangled groan pleased her enormously.

"Nicholas!" Lucy called, stepping a little away from the stranger so that he did not grab her again as he struggled to straighten himself. "Nicholas, I need you!"

Her assailant, his face pale and his eyes wide, glared at her and took a faltering step forward.

She brandished the long measuring stick, and the man backed away, then turned toward the outer doors.

"Nicholas, he is getting away!" Lucy shrieked.

Nicholas emerged, and while the men behind him gaped, he hastened to her.

"There!" She pointed to the man's blue-clad back. "Hurry! He's going out the door. He threatened me, he knows—he admitted—"

Nicholas did not wait to hear the whole story. "After him," he commanded, and half a dozen young men followed as he charged out the door.

Lucy ran after them, too.

Outside, she stepped around the viscount's waiting carriage and looked around the busy thoroughfare and jammed walkway. If her assailant managed to disappear into the crowd, they might never find him. No, she recognized the round face.

"There he is!" she yelled, waving her arm.

Nicholas ran, and the small army of clerks, looking almost comical in their tall collars and proper coats, scampered after him. But perhaps the number, if not the quality of his pursuers, was enough to rattle the man who had attacked her.

He had traveled half a block along the pavement. Now he edged around a cluster of merchants who blocked the walkway and approached the street, which was densely packed with brays and carts and carriages of all description.

"Hold on!" Nicholas commanded from just behind—he was narrowing the gap between them. "A reward for that man's capture!"

Several passersby turned to look, and one roughly clad coal tender abandoned his cart, which sat at the side of the street, to hurry forward from the opposite direction.

The round-faced man looked close to panic. He slipped past a waiting coach, then darted into the first opening in the heavy stream of traffic. But in his urgent need to escape, he was too precipitant.

A woman in a shabby shawl and gown screamed, and several men shouted, but it was too late.

The heavy wagon filled with grain was pulled by four big-footed dray horses. The fleeing man went down beneath their hooves.

"Wait, stop!" Nicholas called, but in vain. No one, not even the driver who pulled frantically on the driving reins, could halt the vehicle in time. The big wheels rolled squarely over the stranger's body. If the team's pounding had not already been lethal enough, the wagon carried his death knell.

Lucy put one hand to her mouth, too horrified to utter a word. She ran closer to the street.

"Lucy!" Nicholas shouted, looking back over his shoulder at her.

She caught herself at the edge of the pavement. There were still carriages milling and horses rearing and stamping. Anyhow, she did not want to examine the man's battered body too closely. She nodded and stayed where she was.

Nicholas drew a deep breath, then knelt beside the man, touching his throat, then his temple, which seemed to have been crushed by a blow from the horse's big hooves. He shook his head.

Lucy found it hard to breathe. She would not be ill on the street, she would not. But her legs felt curiously wobbly. She took hold of one of the streetlights.

One of Nicholas's clerks hurried to her aid. "Madam, you should go back inside."

"In a moment," she muttered.

She waited while Nicholas gave directions to his men, and until the body was lifted by several sets of hands and taken away, then at last Nicholas came to her.

"Are you all right? Did he hurt you?" His expression was dark. Nicholas gripped her hands so tightly that she winced, then he eased the pressure.

She was still grappling with the bigger horror, the sudden death, and—

"He said that Stanley's death was no accident!" she exclaimed.

The clerk, who had been standing nearby, stared at her, his expression inquisitive, and she lowered her tone. "We must talk."

Nicholas offered his arm, which at the moment she was happy to accept as more than just a polite courtesy; she still felt very tremulous. Side by side, they returned to the warehouse. He led her into a private office and called for wine.

"Now, what did he say?" Nicholas demanded, his expression stormy.

"He threatened me." Lucy shuddered, now that it was all over, and rubbed her sore wrist.

Nicholas reached for her hand, his touch gentle this time, and caressed the purpling bruise that was already forming.

He frowned. "I searched his pockets before I sent the

body away to be dealt with, but he had nothing on him that related to the ruby."

"Oh, no. He wanted to know where it is," Lucy explained. "That was what he was asking, why he was trying to frighten me. He seemed to think that I knew its location. And, oh, Nicholas, he said that Stanley was murdered."

The viscount did not react with the surprise she had expected. "Did you not consider such a possibility?" he asked, his tone gentle.

A clerk came in with a dusty bottle and plain glasses, and Nicholas poured for her. She sipped the liquid, wincing a little at its bitterness, and considered. "Not really," she admitted. Obviously, Nicholas had. "But to hear him admit it—how could anyone do such a thing? And now he's dead, too, just like Stanley—such irony. Who on earth was he?"

"That, my dear, was Thomas Brooks, who wanted to claim your house in repayment for Stanley's debts," Nicholas told her. "I met him very recently, and I thought then he knew more than he would say."

"I wish I had kicked him harder!" Lucy blurted, then flushed, remembering the current sad condition of the late Mr. Brooks.

Nicholas grinned at her, however. "I agree."

She sipped the wine until she felt recovered, and they discussed what steps to take next. "I know from what he said that there are more of them," Lucy suggested. "But we shall have no answers now from this man. And was Brooks the ringleader, or just a hireling?"

"An excellent question," Nicholas told her. "You should have taken up detecting earlier in your career, my dear. Unfortunately, I do not know the answer."

And he had considered it all, already, she was sure. Tempted to frown at him, even though his tone was quite serious, Lucy restrained herself; clerks came and went in the office, and the manager hovered at arm's length, looking anxious at all this unusual commotion.

She stood up, and Nicholas escorted her to the carriage,

where she found a bundle wrapped in brown paper and string waiting on the far seat: her muslins.

It had seemed like such a simple errand. Sighing, Lucy allowed the viscount to assist her into the carriage. He was about to enter after her when a shout on the street made him pause and turn his head.

"Prinny's folly! Cursed ruby worth a king's ransom is missing! Prinny's lost a fortune!" A boy carrying an armload of broadsheets shouted.

Nicholas's expression was black.

"Oh, dear God," Lucy whispered.

Fifteen

Nicholas strode across to toss the boy a coin, then returned to the carriage carrying the broadsheet, telling his driver to get home as quickly as he could. The carriage jolted forward, but in the press of vehicles they could proceed only at a leisurely pace.

"What does it say?" Lucy demanded, distressed to see Nicholas so grim. He pulled off his gloves to hold the broadsheet as gingerly as if it were poisoned meat and quickly scanned the narrow lines of print.

"A lot of this is balderdash, but the core of it is true: Prinny has bought an enormously valuable gem, and then lost track of it. The rest is concocted to make the most mischief; they hint at spies and master thieves, or even that Prinny might have had his pocket picked by some conniving mistress, or have been seduced, then enticed to give it to her outright."

"Oh, no," Lucy said. "Surely he could not!"

"Of course not, the prince has not even, as yet, set eyes on the Scarlet Widow." Nicholas tossed the sheet aside, then pulled out a handkerchief and wiped the smudges of cheap ink off his fingers.

Lucy gazed at the crumpled paper as it were an adder, ready to bite. "It didn't say anything about . . ." She couldn't finish the question.

He took both her hands in his; his fingers were warm even through her light gloves, and his grip comforting. "It never mentions Stanley," he told her.

Lucy drew a long breath of relief. "Thank heavens for that." For a moment, that was all she could comprehend, then her mind began to work properly again.

"Nicholas, who could have leaked the story of the missing ruby?"

His dark brows knitted, and she felt almost sorry for the person who turned out to be responsible.

"That, we must find out."

They rode the rest of the way in silence—he seemed preoccupied, and how could she blame him. Through the noise and clatter of the street, she twice more heard other lads bellowing news of the latest scandal. At the shouts Nicholas's expression hardened, if that was possible, even more.

When they at last reached the townhouse, he handed her out and motioned to a footman to take the parcel inside. Nicholas walked with her to the front door.

The butler barely had the door open before a servant she did not recognize, wearing heavily gold-trimmed livery, rushed forward.

"You must come at once, my lord," the man blurted.

"A special messenger from Carlton House," the butler told his master over the footman's shoulder.

Nicholas grimaced but nodded. "I shall be there immediately," he told the servant. To Lucy he bowed and added, his voice low, "I shall return when I can."

Lucy gave him a rueful smile. She did not envy him his job of trying to calm a distraught prince. Yet, she could not wonder at the prince regent wanting Nicholas's reassurance. Nicholas was the kind of man whom one trusted, especially when circumstance seemed blackest.

Hadn't she?

They had to locate the ruby, now, or the deaths of her husband and of Nicholas's courier would go unavenged. Even though one of the villains had met a similar fate, she was sure more guilty parties remained at large. Not only would these private injustices rankle, but the prince regent might find his future rule imperiled.

He had weathered public disgrace before, but that hardly helped now—if anything, it made him more vulnerable. How many scandals would the people, and the government, tolerate? If the ruby was not found, and soon, would they ask for him to give up his claim to the throne and step aside for one of his brothers?

England's future could be in their hands.

Lucy shivered. She was only guessing. Her grasp of governmental procedure and the details surrounding the succession of kings was hazy. She would discuss it with Nicholas later. He would know.

Just now, she took off her gloves and directed the footman to take her parcel of muslins up to her room. Violet would be in transports over the fine woven fabric, and they could begin measuring and cutting out her new dresses.

But before she could follow her purchases, the butler caught her eye. "We have a visitor, ma'am—" he began.

Just then, another footman interrupted, "The lady in the drawing room wishes for your presence at once, ma'am."

The butler glared, and the younger servant faltered. "If you please," he added, his expression meek.

Oh, no.

"But, ma'am, I must inform you—"

Not waiting for the butler to finish his speech, Lucy hurried up the wide staircase toward the drawing room. Not again!

Her intimations of doom were correct. Cousin Wilhelmina, today wearing a hideous shade of yellow green in addition to her usual scowl, sat firmly ensconced upon one of the settees, and she had brought along reinforcements. Mrs. Broddy, her skinny frame bedecked in a lavender dress that would have been quite unexceptional except for the addition of two rows of coral-colored flounces, perched on a nearby chair. They both regarded her with determined glares.

Oh, dear.

Lucy braced herself for battle. For an instant she wished she could simply run away. Seeing her cousin's forbidding expression made Lucy feel five years old again, a small girl who had dared to help herself to a fistful of jam from the larder. Remembering her punishment, and the others that followed, she repressed a shiver. Perhaps she had never been very good at following the rules. That had been her cousin's pronouncement, at any rate.

But she was a child no longer, nor would she retreat before her cousin's displeasure. Squaring her shoulders, Lucy marched into the room, taking the precaution of motioning to the hovering footman to close the double doors behind her. She had no desire to have the servants witness the confrontation she was sure was about to ensue.

"Good afternoon," she told both the women, not bothering to offer any social fiction about how pleasant it was to see them. "I hope you are well."

"Lucinda, we must bring an end to this." Raising her heavy brows, Wilhelmina put down her teacup with a clatter.

Lucy sat down on the chair furthest from her cousin. "If you say so. Are you finished with the tea tray already? I shall ring for its removal, unless you would like more cake? The viscount's cook has an excellent hand with them."

"You know perfectly well that is not what I mean." The older woman's voice rose. "I am beginning to believe that your wits are as addled as your moral judgment!"

"You can conduct yourself like a lady, if you please, and not a brawling fishwife," Lucy retorted. "Lower your voice!"

Her cousin gasped and for a moment seemed too offended to speak.

This condition, of course, was too propitious to endure.

Lucy took a deep breath and awaited the next sally.

"Really, Lucy," Mrs. Broddy said into the moment of silence. "I should never have expected this of you. This is your only surviving kin. Do you not owe her obedience and affection?"

"Affection must be earned," Lucy said, her voice barely above a whisper as she threw a telling glance toward Wilhelmina. "And as for obedience—"

"But I'm sure your cousin has only your best interests at heart."

"Do you?" Lucy switched her gaze to her Cheapside neighbor, who fanned herself with a lavender-tinted fan. "I am a grown woman. I think I can decide the best and most proper course of action for myself."

"Obviously, not." Her cousin had found her voice again, much too soon. "If you persist in residing so improperly with this—this infamous man, our family name will be impugned. I have come to take you back to Mrs. Broddy's."

Lucy forced herself to breath slowly. "And make you relinquish your cozy guest room? I should not dream of it."

"Certainly not." Wilhelmina snorted. "You may take the attic chamber."

"Wilhelmina is senior to you—" Mrs. Broddy began at the same time, then faltered beneath the other woman's glare.

"Yes, of course, she is older than I and no doubt could not readily traverse the extra flights of stairs," Lucy agreed. "But it really doesn't signify. I and my maid are settled quite comfortably here, so I must refuse your kind offer."

Her cousin transferred her steely gaze to focus it again on Lucy. "This is nonsense! If you will not listen to reason, I will call for a maid to pack up your things."

"You do not give the orders in *this* house," Lucy pointed out, managing to keep her tone composed.

"But I am your relation! With your parents dead, I have the right to command your situation!"

"Debatable. Anyhow, none of the servants will heed you, so do not embarrass yourself." Lucy met the angry gaze without flinching.

"But this is intolerable, we must be on our way!"

"I will not keep you," Lucy agreed, wishing nothing more than to see their backs. "But I will be not be going with you."

"Lucinda! Do you not understand? I am merely thinking of your well-being."

"As you did after the death of my husband? I do not recall you rushing to rescue me from my creditors or my penury, then," Lucy was annoyed enough to respond.

"You never told me you were in distress, nor did you ask for assistance." Wilhelmina pursed her mouth.

"I knew what your reply would have been," Lucy told her. "In fact, you made it quite clear when I called on you at the inn. You said I should not expect you to discharge my obligations. . . ."

"Nonetheless, you cannot stay here, with no chaperone to guard your reputation. I shall be the laughingstock of the shire when I return home!"

"And how will your neighbors even know? Who will tell them?" Lucy demanded.

Her cousin hesitated.

"You have already spread the gossip, have you not?" Lucy shook her head. "And then it occurred to you that by tarring me, you might be blackened by the same brush. A bit imprudent of you, Cousin."

Wilhelmina's cheeks were flushed. "It can still be repaired. Only, you must leave this house, now, at once!"

"I have a chaperone. The viscount's cousin—" Lucy tried to say.

"Oh, no more of that pathetic fiction," Wilhelmina interrupted. "You cannot expect me to believe such a tired tale. This man may have pulled the wool over your eyes, Lucinda—you were never very bright. But I know better! This man may bear a title, may have money to spend upon you, even, but his reputation is of the most reprehensible, most debauched—"

Lucy's ready temper, which she had so far kept in check by marshaling every scrap of self-control, suddenly surged like a torrent-swollen river bursting its banks.

"*This man* has offered me nothing but consideration and solicitude," Lucy cried, jumping to her feet. "Quite unlike my only remaining relation! He has shielded me from danger and distress, and if you think you may impugn him with such reckless abandon, I must inform you that he is a thousand times better than you, or anyone else that I know! He is the kindest, most chivalrous, most unselfish man that I have ever met!"

Too late, she heard the sound of the double doors being thrown back. It could not be Nicholas returning already. Had one of the servants overheard her emotional tirade? Putting one hand to her flaming cheeks, Lucy turned, and then stood, motionless with surprise.

A petite, gray-haired woman, her expression beaming with goodwill, glided into the room, not even waiting for an invitation. Ignoring the tense atmosphere, she put out both hands to Lucy.

"My dear Lucy, am I late for tea? Oh, and you have guests. I do hope I am not interrupting?"

Lucy knew that her mouth was open, but as to words— her mind had gone quite blank.

The tiny woman didn't wait for her to answer. She turned easily to the two other guests and offered them a slight curtsy. "How do you do? I am Lord Richmond's cousin, Lady Van de Meer. And you are?"

The silence stretched. Wilhelmina's cheeks had puffed out, and her eyes bulged; she looked as if she might have an apoplexy on the spot. Mrs. Broddy had flushed quite as purple as an over-ripe cabbage.

Lucy found her voice and her manners. "Forgive me, this is my cousin, Miss Flowers, and her friend, Mrs. Broddy."

"How lovely to meet you," the new arrival said.

Wilhelmina seemed to have turned to stone. She did not stir. Mrs. Broddy stood and made an awkward curtsy as she stammered, "I thought—I was t-told that the viscount lived alone."

"Oh, yes, I normally reside on my own estate in the country, but I enjoy coming into town now and again." Her tone perfectly composed, Lady Van de Meer sat down. "And of course, I would not have denied myself the pleasure of Lucy's company."

Silence again. Wilhelmina still looked stunned.

Lucy didn't know whether to laugh or to weep with relief. Not even sure if this woman was real, or an illusion conjured up by some fairy expressly to aid her, she could only throw her a quick look of gratitude.

"Do sit down, dear," the tiny woman said gently. "I have instructed the footman to bring fresh tea, since I am so shamefully tardy."

Lucy moved toward her chair but paused as Wilhelmina stood so abruptly that she shook the settee. "We must be going."

"Yes, I'm sure you have letters to write. Good-bye, Cousin." Lucy crossed to the side of the room to ring for a footman. "Mrs. Broddy. I am sure you will both be content now in knowing that I am so safely, and properly, provided for."

Wilhelmina glared and turned on her heel, almost bumping into the arriving footman, who stepped aside hastily. Mrs. Broddy, who seemed more in awe of the new arrival than her contentious houseguest, curtsied again and muttered a farewell.

The footman had to hurry to stay ahead as he showed them out.

Lucy waited a few moments, then allowed herself a deep sigh as she took her seat. "Pardon me, but are you—"

Lady Van de Meer laughed delightedly. "Am I really who I say I am? Yes, indeed, I admit I am that rapscallion's cousin." The twinkle in her eyes told Lucy that Lady Van de Meer was very fond of the rapscallion. Lucy grinned at her and then shook her head.

"I cannot imagine what you must think of such a scene," she began.

Lady Van de Meer smiled, but did not reply until the butler himself appeared with fresh tea and a new platter of cakes.

"Thank you, Hodges," she said.

He took away the used cups and plates, and when the doors had been shut again, the older woman turned her bright brown eyes upon Lucy.

"I received a summons from Nicholas, in his usual imperious style. I was surprised by his insistence upon such urgency, but it seems he was not exaggerating when he said he needed my presence here at once."

So that was the nature of the mysterious mission entrusted to the special courier. Lucy drew another deep breath. "It's very kind of you to—to—that is, you must think it very strange that I agree to visit when there was no one here to properly chaperone."

"Oh, my dear." Lady Van de Meer sipped her tea. "I was young once, too. And Nicholas wrote about the pillage of your house—you must tell me the whole story presently. But it is true that a lady's reputation is a fragile commodity, so a little care is in order. I am quite pleased with Nicholas that he should have remembered to be solicitous of your good name."

"You're very kind," Lucy said again.

"And by the by, I do not wish to speak ill of your relations, but that is a most unpleasant woman." Lady Van de Meer added, in her crystal-clear voice, "Would you like a cake?"

Lucy was surprised into a laugh. Nicholas's cousin had all his directness, though covered by a slightly more decorous polish. She had a sudden suspicion that she was going to like Lady Van de Meer enormously.

"Thank you." She accepted the small plate. Perhaps now that the altercation with her cousin was behind her, the knots in her stomach would loosen, and she could enjoy her tea.

Nicholas did not return until just before dinner, and when he strode into the drawing room, his expression seemed strained.

"My dear Nicholas, you look most fatigued," Lady Van de Meer exclaimed.

"I am sorry I was not here to welcome you properly, cousin," he told her. "It was very good of you to come, and so promptly." He bent to kiss her cheek.

She reached up to pat his arm affectionately. "Not at all. Lucy has explained the reason for your absence. Of course I understand that you cannot decline to answer the prince's summons. Is the prince regent terribly upset?"

"He is as perturbed as I have ever seen him, and that is saying a great deal. He is at one moment ready to retreat to some distant country estate to try to ignore the commotion, and the next, on the point of fleeing for the Continent, as if he were Prince Charles with a murderous army of Puritans at his heels—"

Lucy gasped. "He would not!"

"Oh, no, he won't do it. I spent a lot of time today helping him see reason, and counseling patience and fortitude. But he is truly in a panic, and he is pressing me severely to find the ruby and find it now." Nicholas rubbed his forehead as if it ached, making Lucy wince for him.

"You poor boy. We have been more happily engaged. Lucy and I have spent the afternoon chatting—she is a delightful young lady," Lady Van de Meer said.

Lucy blushed. "You're too kind."

"No, indeed, I am happy to find that Nicholas is exercising such good taste."

Nicholas's aspect lightened, and his glance at Lucy danced with mischief; making him look more like his old self. She blushed harder and was happy when the butler entered to announce dinner.

Nicholas gave his cousin his arm, then offered Lucy

the other, and they went into the dining room. While they enjoyed the usual savory meal, Lucy was able to induce the older woman to tell stories of Nicholas as a child.

"There was the time on his parents' country estate when he climbed the apple tree," she began.

"Every child climbs trees," Nicholas interposed. He took a bite of roast beef and chewed slowly.

His cousin chuckled. "Yes, but when the gardener came out to remonstrate because Nicholas was taking one bite out of each piece of fruit and then leaving them on the tree to rot, the boy not only refused to come down—he pelted the poor man with the damaged apples. His father was most displeased."

"Ah yes," Nicholas admitted. "He made me, most properly, apologize to the gardener and work off my punishment under his watchful eye. I spaded beds of carrots for three days! But I was only six, you understand."

Lucy laughed, but she added, "And perhaps already as peremptory as the man you grew into?"

"Certainly not," the viscount answered. But he did not meet her laughing gaze, as usual, and he seemed strangely distant. What was wrong? Perhaps only his preoccupation with the prince's crisis, Lucy told herself.

But afterward, when they chatted in the drawing room until Lady Van de Meer went up to bed, she found that he still seemed withdrawn.

Even though she longed to be close to him, Lucy was too aware of his cousin's presence to be disposed toward more reveling in the library. But she was a little surprised when Nicholas did not press her, nor seem interested in further lovemaking. He only bowed over her hand when she said good night, not even bending to kiss her, and his mind seemed far away.

So Lucy followed his cousin up the stairs, and in her room Violet was waiting to help her prepare for bed. And although her maid chattered about the new muslins Lucy had brought home, Lucy's replies were vague.

Was Nicholas, once reminded of the proprieties, losing his interest in her already?

Feeling worried by more than just the elusive gem and its effect on England's future monarch, she found it hard to fall asleep, and even then, her slumber was troubled.

～⌒～

The next day Nicholas left early to pursue his search for any office or room that Stanley might have kept in the city. Unable to sleep, Lucy came downstairs in time to see him donning his hat and gloves in the front hall.

"Do you wish me to accompany you?" she asked.

He shook his head, not meeting her gaze. "Ladies come so rarely into the financial district that I think your presence would only detract from my questions," he told her. "And I have promised to check in on the prince at lunchtime. He is likely still abed just now, which is why I am taking advantage of the morning."

Poor Nicholas. How did the prince expect him to search for the ruby and hold his future king's hand at the same time? She said as much, and Nicholas shrugged.

"He is not exactly rational just now. If I find out anything new, I will let you know at once."

Lucy had to be content with that. She went into the dining room and sat down. A footman brought her a fresh plate, and she helped herself to eggs and ham.

From the dishes that the servants were clearing away, she was afraid that Nicholas had eaten little, and his appetite last night had been poor.

Something was wrong, even more than the heightened hue and cry over the gem. Lucy sipped her tea and tried to puzzle out both mysteries.

After Lady Van de Meer rose, Lucy put aside her worries to spend time with her new acquaintance. They were by this time so much at ease together that Lucy could show the older woman the muslins she had purchased.

"Lovely," Lady Van de Meer pronounced. "And I know just the shop to get the thread and buttons for your new dresses."

She called for the second carriage in Nicholas's stables,

and they went out together on a shopping expedition. After checking several emporiums, Lucy used the rest of her coins for the notions she needed and to buy a simple straw bonnet.

"I should come into town more often," Lady Van de Meer commented, as she peered into a looking glass and adjusted a stylish new hat. She nodded to the clerk and added it to the two she had already selected for herself. "But it is little fun to shop alone. I have thoroughly enjoyed the morning, my dear."

"And I," Lucy agreed, warmed by the good-natured friendship that the older woman seemed ready to offer.

On the way home they drove through the park, then arrived in time for a light luncheon. Nicholas, of course, had not returned.

After lunch Lucy and Lady Van de Meer sat in the drawing room turning the page of a copy of *Le Beau Monde* and examining the latest fashions. Violet held up lengths of muslin as they considered exactly which style to emulate. Lucy looked up when the butler entered.

"Yes, Hodges?" Lady Van de Meer inquired.

The butler motioned to the two stout footmen who followed him. They carried in a large trunk, then lowered it down carefully upon the Oriental carpet.

Lucy stared at the big chest. "What is it?"

"Oh, my," Lady Van de Meer murmured. "How nice."

"His lordship thought you might find some pieces of fabric inside that you could make use of, ma'am," the butler explained.

He motioned to one of the footmen, and the man took out a cloth and dusted the top of the chest. Then Hodges himself, with a pause as if he were enjoying this small drama, opened the lid.

All the women came closer to peer inside and to exclaim over the contents. Lucy blinked at the vivid colors and gleaming silks. "How beautiful!"

"They are from his time in India," Nicholas's cousin explained. "This is a good sign. I don't think he has opened any of these boxes since he returned."

Someone, perhaps the housekeeper, had long ago placed dried mint inside the chest to discourage damage from insects, so the fabrics appeared in good condition, despite the years they had sat undisturbed in the attic.

Lucy drew out a length of green silk, laced with a golden pattern, and beneath it lay a roll of bright turquoise. The silk draped over her hand like a curving waterfall. As the servants withdrew, she fingered its silky surface, then shook her head.

"I cannot use these."

"My dear, why not?" Lady Van de Meer asked as Violet's eyes widened in dismay; she had been gazing in appreciation at the riches inside the trunk.

"They must have been bought for his wife," Lucy explained, swallowing hard at the thought of Nicholas's years of grief. "I would feel—"

"But that is why you should accept them, since he has offered. He has shrouded himself against his tragedy for long enough," the older woman argued. "This is a good sign that he can consider moving forward. You have been a good physic for him, Lucy. You must not fail him now."

"You really think so?" Lucy stroked the soft smooth silks. They were certainly tempting, but she would not hurt Nicholas. Still, it *had* been his idea.

"I am sure of it," Lady Van de Meer said, her voice firm. "And think, you have the muslins for day, now you can stitch some dresses for dinner and evening wear. It's a wonderfully provident notion of Nicholas's."

And it would be rude to reject it, Lucy told herself. She nodded slowly. "Very well."

"Oh, good," Violet said, then blushed. "I mean—I'm sure these will look so nice, made up, ma'am."

So they all plunged back into discussions of fashion, and when Nicholas returned, slightly late, for dinner, Lucy offered her thanks for such a splendid gesture. As usual, he waved away her gratitude.

"Someone should make use of them," he said, his tone gruff. "I should not want to have to waste them on my cattle."

"What?" Startled, Lucy looked up from the mint sauce the footman was ladling over her roast pork.

"In India, they sometimes drape the saris over the cows, you know," Nicholas told her, his tone solemn. "And they hang bells on their horns."

"They dress up their animals with saris?" She thought he must be jesting.

"As a thank-you for the milk the cows have bestowed upon the family. It occurs during a harvest celebration called *Pongal*."

Apparently, he was serious. Lucy recalled the brilliantly colored fabric she had held so carefully. "Are you saying that a cow has worn those silks?"

"Oh, no, not those," he assured her, grinning at last. "I should not give you the hand-me-downs from the cattle."

"I should hope not!"

Lady Van de Meer's crystalline laughter rang out as Lucy twinkled at her unpredictable host. And Nicholas met her smile, relaxed for just a moment, but he looked away too soon.

Despite his continued generosity, something had come between them, and it nagged at her, distracting her even from the discussion about his continuing search. He had explained the problem of the ruby's disappearance to his cousin, though he had left a bit vague the question of Stanley's role in the theft, and his cousin appeared too tactful to press him for details.

While his cousin chatted now about her new hats, Lucy ate her dinner slowly, wishing that Nicholas would do more than pick at his food.

Later she suggested ideas to Nicholas when she could think of any—he still had found no office let to her husband.

"There has to be somewhere else," she told him quietly while his cousin was pouring tea for them in the drawing room. "We have taken apart my house, not to mention the intruders who also did their share of searching. Yet they could not have found it, or Brooks would not have threatened me at the fabric warehouse. Do you think he was truly the only one involved in the theft, except for my husband?"

She waited anxiously for his answer.

"You said that he mentioned 'us' when he spoke to you," Nicholas reminded her.

"I know, but we have heard nothing more, no demands or threats. In fact, I think I should return to my own home, soon, if I can get it back into order. I hate to trespass upon your kindness."

"Nonsense," he told her, though his tone was more abstracted than commanding. "Besides, my cousin came up just to meet you. You would not wish to rush away when she has just arrived."

Lucy nodded. "No, of course not. But as for the ruby—"

"I am checking all the men's clubs to see if Stanley had any memberships or billets there that we do not know of," he told her. "After that, I don't know. Check every inn and hostel in the city, maybe—that could take us a while! You are sure he had no relatives that he might have left something valuable with?"

Instead of his own wife? Lucy sighed. "Not that I knew of," she told him, adding impulsively, "Nicholas?"

The barrier was there, every time she gazed at him. It veiled the dark eyes that had just begun to open to her. What had caused this setback?

"What is wrong?"

He looked away. "Nothing, my dear, except my frustration over our lack of success in finding the ruby. You should hear the prince rant over it every day."

Lucy sighed. She had seen more broadsheets when she and Lady Van de Meer had gone shopping, bearing crude cartoons and caricatures of the prince regent, his bloated body flung upon a tumbled bed while a poorly drawn harpy drew a great jewel out of his pocket. PRINNY CUCK-OLDED OVER ACCURSED EASTERN RUBY! the captions taunted. The *Times* was demanding, CAN WE TRUST OUR FUTURE KING'S JUDGMENT? And the other newspapers were even worse.

Yet, as troubled as Nicholas must be over the ruby, she was still sure it was more than that. They drank their tea, and Lady Van de Meer played upon the harpsichord for them. After they had applauded her skill, she shared stories of her time on the Continent, where she had spent most of her married life. After her husband's death, she explained to Lucy, she had returned to her English estate, where she'd grown up.

"I grew homesick," she noted. "And as we were never blessed with children, I did enjoy seeing Nicholas occasionally, the dear boy, when he came down to visit."

Lucy glanced at the "dear boy." So many of his benevolent acts he had done quietly, while his acts of wanton pleasure had been public knowledge among the Ton. The more she knew of him, the more she thought his reputation as a cynical man-about-town was highly exaggerated.

After Lady Van de Meer went up to bed, Lucy lingered to savor a moment alone. But when she touched his cheek, Nicholas drew back.

"I should not keep you," he said, his voice low.

Lucy looked at him, flushing. "I do not mean to press you, my lord," she said formally. "I am only concerned—" then she paused. How could she spell out, with any dignity at all, that these last few days he did not take any excuse to touch her, nor gaze at her with that special warmth she had grown to expect. She would certainly not act like Marion Tennett and hound him like another disgruntled, discarded lover if he had tired of her charms already.

Yet, somehow, she felt deep down that this was not the real cause of his detachment. She still felt the flux of emotion, even desire, that vibrated between them; he simply would not allow himself to express it. And as to why—

She could not help herself. Even as she was vowing to behave in a manner as polite and noncommittal as he, Lucy found that she had reached up to touch his cheek.

Desire flashed in his eyes, then he stiffened. He caressed her hand, kissing the fingers lightly before gently putting it aside. By then he had lowered his lids, but it was too late; she had seen the change in his expression.

"What?" She looked at her own hand, at the wrist still mottled with the yellowish, fading bruise left by Thomas Brooks's rude handling. And she remembered Nicholas's shout and the alarm in his face when she had stepped off the curb during the pursuit of the moneylender.

"That's it, isn't it?" she said. "Oh, my love. No one can predict who will stay completely safe. Love comes with no guarantees."

He hesitated, and, slowly, she stepped back. Only Nicholas could decide if he had the courage to open his heart again, to love a mortal woman who could be taken from him by accident or design, illness or violence.

Her heart ached for him; her entire body and soul mourned his absence. But he was the only one who could make this choice.

Kissing him lightly on the cheek, she went up to her chamber. And if her bed seemed very empty tonight, she suspected that Nicholas was feeling the same.

Would he reach out to her? Could he conquer his long-standing fears? She had no way to tell. Lucy pummeled her pillow, which had once seemed so comforting, and, her body tense with unresolved questions, tried to escape into forgetful sleep.

Sixteen

*T*he next day Nicholas had left the house by the time
she rose, heavy-eyed and weary. She and Violet
sewed for most of the day, with occasional pauses for
Lucy to try on the new garments. At tea Lucy chatted
with Nicholas's cousin, and afterward they took a drive
through Hyde Park, where Lady Van de Meer came across
a childhood friend, to the delight of both.

While they chatted, Lucy idly watched a slim girl of
about ten sitting on a bench and sketching, her dark hair
escaping its braid as she frowned, intent upon her pencil
work. Nearby, a governess plied her knitting needles, and
two ladies of middle age strolled along the pathway. Further away, a young man of medium height stopped to
examine a flower, almost losing his hat as he bent over
to peer closely at the bloom. Close by, a young couple
walked hand in hand. Watching the young lovers, Lucy
sighed.

When Lady Van de Meer made her farewells and promised to call upon her friend, they drove on.

"Many of my old friends have died," Nicholas's cousin

explained to Lucy. "Or I have lost track of them, after so many years abroad. It is a bit lonely for me now."

"I know someone you would enjoy meeting," Lucy said, delighted to think she could give something back to this kind-natured woman. "On Wednesday afternoon, when she has her weekly tea, we will visit Lady Sealey."

Nicholas did not return for dinner; he sent a note of apology. The prince wanted him close by, the future monarch was suffering more spasms of anxiety that could be quieted only by the strength of Nicholas's presence.

On Sunday she and Lady Van de Meer attended morning services with Nicholas's escort. Lucy bowed to her cousin and Mrs. Broddy but did not linger to chat.

The week continued in the same gentle pattern. On Wednesday, as promised, Lucy took the viscount's cousin along to Lady Sealey's tea and was pleased to introduce the two women.

They were soon exchanging stories of Paris in their youth, before the war against Napoleon had closed the city to the English, and several scandalous French noblemen who had delighted in ogling the English ladies. Lucy listened and laughed with the other younger women.

And on Thursday, when Nicholas was called away again, Lucy decided that she could not sit home and wend her needle any longer, even if her new dresses were not all complete. She needed to do something! And if she had no plan to search for the ruby, at least she could keep a promise.

"I should like to take a drive into the country," she told Lady Van de Meer. "There is a—a dependent of mine I should like to check on." And that was true, mostly; any charge of her late husband's was also hers.

Nicholas's cousin was amenable to an outing, so she called for the coach and loaned Lucy a shawl to put about her shoulders, as the day was somewhat windy.

The coachman knew the route, so Lucy had little to worry her, except private reflections about Nicholas's continued air of detachment, which pained her even more than his physical absences. Perhaps after his youthful tragedy he would never again be able to love fully. If so, there was little she could do except step gracefully aside. And if that thought sent an ache clear though her—Lucy sighed and tried to respond properly to Lady Van de Meer's comments about the pleasant countryside sliding past their carriage window.

They reached Nicholas's property by the middle of the afternoon. Several dogs barked to mark their arrival, and Mrs. Taylor hurried out, wiping her hands on her apron and giving them deep curtsies.

The farmwife greeted them both with enthusiasm and presently took Lady Van de Meer off to show her a promising new quartet of lambs.

Excusing herself, Lucy was able to make her way to the cottage at the back and knock on the door. The woman who opened the door seemed a stranger. With a start, Lucy recognized Eve.

The young woman had replaced her coarse shifts and low-cut dresses with a simple, plain round gown which she had surely sewn herself. Its pale green-checked muslin was not as finely woven as the dresses that Lucy and Violet had just completed, but beneath a tan apron the gown was neat and becoming. Eve herself, with her hair drawn simply back and no rouge on her cheeks, which nonetheless seemed to have acquired more color in her more wholesome surroundings, looked years younger than the last time Lucy had seen her.

"Oh, ma'am." Eve dipped a deep curtsy. "It's you!"

"May I come in?" Lucy asked. "I only wanted to make sure that you and your daughter are comfortable here."

"Oh, of course, ma'am," Eve said, flushing. "Please, do." She opened the door further and Lucy stepped inside.

She was pleased to see that the cottage was swept and neat, and it smelled appealingly of baking bread. The bed in the corner had its covers pulled smoothly across it. A small fire burned on the hearth, and a safe distance away, a crude cradle held the sleeping baby.

Lucy walked closer.

"Mrs. Taylor was kind enough to lend me the cradle," Eve explained.

Lucy peered down at the child. She, too, was dressed in a clean but simple gown, and she also seemed to have a better color. Her pale lashes lay against her cheeks, and she breathed lightly.

Lucy felt a pang, but she refused to dwell on it. If she had had a child . . . well, it did not seem likely now to happen. She remarked on how well the child appeared, and Eve beamed.

"Yes, ma'am. I think she's grown already. Mrs. Taylor has lots of fresh milk for her. And I'm learning to be a help in the dairy, Mrs. Taylor says my churning is coming along nicely. I did it when I was a girl, you see, and I hasn't lost the knack, nor that of milking. I have a nice easy hand with the udders."

"That's splendid," Lucy told her. "I am so pleased that you are happy here."

"Oh, ma'am, it's heaven, it is." Eve sighed. "I can never thank you enough." She blinked hard, and Lucy felt almost embarrassed at the depth of the woman's gratitude.

"And that it should be Stanley's wife who is so good to me, I mean—" she raised her apron to dab at her cheeks. "I'm thinking I should tell you how sorry I am, ma'am, that I should have—that I was the one he—" She faltered.

Lucy patted her arm. "I do not condemn you, honestly," she said. "We were not able to achieve the union I had hoped for, but I do not lay that blame at your door. Stanley had his weaknesses, and if it had not been you, well . . . and I believe that you cared for him."

"Oh, I did, ma'am, he was kind to me when so many of 'em were rough and heartless." Eve wiped her eyes again.

Lucy remembered the early days of her marriage and how grateful she had been to Stanley for taking her away from her cousin's house. "Yes, he could be kind," she agreed, sighing at the innocent girl she had been, dreaming of so much that had never come to pass.

"Our days in our little bird's nest were so sweet, and—well, I shouldn't be saying such things to you, I'm sure, but I just pray God will bless you, as you have me," Eve told her.

Lucy pushed aside her own bittersweet memories. "I am only happy that you have escaped the—the difficulties you were facing. And that Stanley's baby will have the chance to grow, healthy and unharmed."

As if on cue, the child stirred and gave a hungry wail. Lucy watched as Eve rushed to the cradle and lifted her into her arms.

"I will leave you," Lucy said. "But I will check on you from time to time, so do not fear for the future."

Eve gave her a deep curtsy, then held the door for her.

Lucy sighed. The viscount would look after Eve and the child, she was sure, even if Lucy's resources were not enough. He was too good a man not to. Why did he pose as such a selfish scoundrel, when anyone who looked beneath the surface would know that his pretense was untrue?

Perhaps he was afraid to be that trusting boy again in any way, the young man who had seen all his hopes dashed.

She returned to the farmhouse, and, after chatting with Mrs. Taylor, she and Lady Van de Meer returned to the carriage and were driven back to town. Nicholas did not return for dinner, and Lucy thought that she would tell him later about her visit with Eve.

The next morning Lucy realized with a start that tonight was the prince regent's ball. Oh, heavens.

It was Violet who reminded her. "You 'ave to choose which dinner dress you are going to wear, ma'am, so we can put the finishing touches on it," her maid told her, a little anxious that the big event was upon them.

Was the prince still holding the party when he was under so much criticism? Nicholas had told her that a special debate in the House of Lords had been announced to discuss the debacle of the missing ruby, so she was almost surprised the prince regent had not canceled the event.

But Nicholas, on his way out of the house after a hasty breakfast, shook his head when she asked the question.

"No, after changing his mind several times, he has decided to confront his detractors and carry on as usual. And I suspect he is right," Nicholas told her. "This is one time he must act the role he is destined to assume. I will be home in good time to escort you to Carlton House, my dear." And he gave her a polite bow—a bow, when she wanted to be pulled into his arms and smothered with kisses!—and made his departure.

Lucy went upstairs to consider the crucial question of a dress for the ball. The green silk had turned out very well, she thought; the blue had proved a bit difficult to drape properly in its bodice, but the color was also very nice.

She could not make up her mind. "Let's take them downstairs and ask Lady Van de Meer," she told Violet, who scooped up both. The three women were arguing each gown's merits in the drawing room, when a footman came in carrying a long box.

"For you, ma'am," he told Lucy.

As soon as he had put down the box and departed, Lucy pulled off the string and slid back the lid.

She gasped. Violet cooed, and Lady Van de Meer said, "Oh, my, how nice."

The dress that lay inside was a dream, a deep scarlet satin, the bodice exquisitely cut, with only a hint of sleeves, the skirt covered with an overlayer of gold netting which caught the sunlight and reflected it over and over. The bodice was fashionably low-cut, and the bottom of the skirt was adorned with a slim flounce.

A matching reticule and a lacy white fan lay beneath the dress when Lucy lifted it out. She felt quite stunned. This was no hand-me-down, this dress looked quite perfect for Lucy's own measurements. And the artful design and skilled workmanship that had gone into crafting this ball gown made Lucy's other dresses look crude by comparison. This was the work of an artist, and it must have cost a small fortune! But who—

She looked at the baroness. "My lady, did you—"

Lady Van de Meer shook her head. "No, dear child, though I wish I had thought of it. This dress will become you amazingly."

Was it the countess of Sealey who had been so generous? Lucy threw another glance toward Nicholas's cousin. Had Lady Van de Meer whispered the news of Lucy's invitation to a royal ball, and had the countess— but if so, how had such a dress been made up in time? It was only yesterday that they had visited Lady Sealey. This dress would not have been crafted overnight.

"I don't know if I can accept such an expensive gift," Lucy said slowly, although she still held the ball gown, hating the thought of putting it back into its box.

Violet made a face, and Lady van de Meer shook her head. "My dear, whoever sent you this sent it with love. You cannot refuse such a thoughtful and handsome offering."

"Oh, yes, ma'am," Violet agreed. "You'll look like a princess, you will."

Lucy laughed a little at the exaggeration, but she held it up to her body and felt the soft graceful folds of the skirt fall about her. Oh, just this once, she told herself, knowing that she was being weak.

She spent the afternoon getting ready. After a long bath, she carefully donned the ball gown and sat in her room while Violet brushed her curls into a riotous display that framed her face.

Lady Van de Meer came to the door carrying a small velvet case. "This would match your dress nicely, I think," the older woman said. "I would be pleased if you would borrow it for your special night."

Lucy opened it and gazed at a gold comb, encrusted with pearls. "It's beautiful, you're much too generous."

Violet eased it into her hair and adjusted it, then beamed at the picture she made.

Lucy smiled and added to the older woman. "I wish you were going with us."

Nicholas had offered to procure an invitation for his cousin, but Lady Van de Meer had declined. "I'm past the age for late nights and riotous parties, especially those thrown by royal hosts," she had said, adding, "But you look delightful, Lucy, dear. I hope you and Nicholas enjoy a wonderful evening."

"So do I," Lucy murmured. She turned to stare into the looking glass, astonished at the creature she saw there, all in scarlet, fair hair in curls about her face. She was going to a royal ball. A month ago, who could have imagined such a strange turn of events? Tomorrow, she would worry about the ruby, about Nicholas, about the future. Tonight—tonight was a fairy tale, and she meant to enjoy it. Violet brought her the glittering bronze shawl to drape about her elbows, and Lucy made her way down the wide staircase.

At the bottom Nicholas waited and the expression on his face eased the anxiety she had carried inside her for days.

Nicholas gazed at her without any barriers between them, and his dark eyes gleamed with warmth.

"You look beautiful," he told her. "As I knew you would."

He had known, had he? He had shown no surprise at all at her splendid appearance. Lucy blinked in realization. "The box," she said.

He raised his brows. "There is a problem with the box?"

"The dressmaker's box—it was the same as the one that held the cloak you had made for me, days ago, when I lost my old one at the bawdy house on the heath," she told him, her tone accusing. "I knew it. You sent the ball gown!"

He smiled, just a little. "Since you would not allow me to aid you with your costumes earlier, you must simply mark it up to my usual arrogance."

"Oh, Nicholas, you are not at all arrogant," she protested, forgetting all the times she had accused him of just such an irritating habit. "You are the kindest, most generous—"

She leaned forward to kiss him. But he met her embrace with a light peck, instead of pulling her closer, and she felt him stiffen.

Feeling as rejected as if he'd shoved her away, Lucy drew back, biting her lip. "I'm sorry," she whispered, blinking hard against the tears that dampened her eyes.

She was glad to hear the footman announce, "Your carriage is ready, my lord." She walked ahead of him and did not look back.

Outside, Nicholas handed her up, and they rode off in silence. Lucy smoothed her satin and net-covered skirt and refused to look at her escort, sitting so quietly beside her. Don't make a shambles of this, Nicholas, she thought, her hurt deep enough to approach anger. I will not allow this evening to be ruined. Can you not see how foolish your actions are?

"I did not mean to force upon you any—any—" she began stiffly.

The carriage passed out of the streetlight's range, and they were plunged into near darkness. And out of the dimness, she heard his voice, ravaged with pain. Unable to see his face clearly, his hawkish profile shadowed, she found his tone even more revealing.

"Lucy, I do feel for you. But—"

But he was afraid to acknowledge his love, his dependence on the vagaries of fate. It was as she had feared. He might never again risk his heart to life's uncertainties.

" 'Hostages to fortune,' a famous writer once called his wife and children," Nicholas said, his tone twisted. "And the greater the love, the greater the risk. I—perhaps I am a coward after all, my dear."

She drew a deep breath. She would not win him through pity, nor through the depth of her own need. If he came to her, he would have to make up his own mind, or their time together, as well as whatever relationship they were able to achieve, would be doomed before it ever began.

The rest of the ride, as they rolled along Pall Mall, went by without either of them speaking. When Lucy saw the imposing facade of Carlton House, its wide expanse and row of tall columns, she would not have been surprised to feel a return of her nervous qualms.

But with much more important concerns on her mind, how could she fret over a fancy gala, even if it were given by a prince? She found herself strangely calm as they drew up behind a long line of carriages, and, eventually, a lavishly liveried footman handed her out. The viscount offered his arm, and she walked inside, past the uniformed Hussers and through the gate, her head high.

When she entered the royal residence, Lucy did feel a moment of awe. Such gold and gilt and rich furnishings— she had never glimpsed such a sight! The rooms seemed enormous; Nicholas had told her of the forty-foot library.

She gazed at rich tapestries and thick draperies that adorned the windows, gilted chairs, and tableware so embellished with gold engravings that it was almost hard to see what the objects were really intended to be.

Had she expected the future monarch to be a man of simple tastes?

They followed a line of other guests up the staircase. The large room was already crowded with people, and the noise that emanated from it was enormous, a wave of sound that pressed against them as they paused and waited for the footman to declaim their names, as if anyone could hear!

If there had been a receiving line earlier, it had faded away, and their host was nowhere in sight.

"Are we late?" Lucy whispered to Nicholas.

"Only fashionably so," he said, glancing about him. "If I am pulled away by the prince, you have my apologies in advance."

Lucy tried not to show her dismay. There was such a crush of strangers here—but no, she would cope. "Of course," she said.

He led her further into the room, and she detected a hint of the tune the musicians were playing, hidden somewhere behind the throngs of people.

"But before he sees me, before I pay my respects, we can steal one dance, at least," Nicholas said.

Behind the wall of party goers she could now see couples moving in easy circles around a polished wood floor. It was a waltz.

Before she could protest that she did not know the steps, he pulled her into his arms, and she found they had moved out onto the dance floor.

"Nicholas!" Lucy tried to object, but she found his left hand holding her right, his other hand on her waist, as he guided her firmly, smoothly through the steps, up and down, to the side, around.

It was not as hard as it looked, and she soon grasped the cadence of the dance, just as she had learned so quickly the more intimate rhythms he had led her through, his body pressed even more closely against her own. The music swirled around them, and some of the crowd's chatter faded; Lucy felt as happy, almost, as she had felt in his more private embrace.

She and Nicholas, hand in hand, facing life together. Why could he not see that this was the only way to brave the unknown twists that life had in store?

No, don't think of that now, she told herself. Just move, follow his practiced lead, hear the clear notes of the violin defining the tune, and the deeper notes that chased the melody, and feel as if she floated through clouds of a golden sunset, instead of across the gleaming floor of a gilt-embossed ballroom.

When the music died, she stood, immobile in his arms, for another long moment. Nicholas gazed down at her, and she almost thought she could detect—

Then a hearty voice called, "Richmond, there you are!"

Nicholas sighed, and surely it was regret she now saw in his eyes. "We must go make our bow to the prince. Come along, my dear," he muttered.

He led her through the crowd to the center of the room,

where the prince regent, his complexion even more ruddy
than usual, held an informal court among a thick knot of
friends and sycophants. Nicholas bowed, and Lucy gave
a deep curtsy.

"Good to see you, my dear," the prince said, then
turned at once to Nicholas. "Any news, Richmond?"

"No, your highness, not yet," Nicholas answered patiently.

Prinny sighed. He lowered his booming voice and
pulled Nicholas closer, and Lucy stepped back. She saw
no need to linger here, so she slipped away, and when a
servant offered her champagne, she accepted a glass and
took a sip of the bubbly wine.

All about her were elaborately dressed matrons and
stiffly correct gentlemen. The old Lucy would have been
in a panic, feeling as unprepared as the unpolished country
girl Wilhelmina would have called her. But not now—
she glanced at a gold-framed looking glass on the wall,
and the woman who stared back was almost a stranger. It
was more than just the beautiful dress and the gems in
her hair, it was the look of confidence that so altered the
expression in the blue eyes, smoothed the old lines of
worry on the face, as the reflection in the glass stared
calmly back at her.

Lucy sipped the wine, and a young man with dark hair
came up to her, bowing deeply. "Good evening, I believe
we met at the duchess's salon. May I have the honor of
this dance?"

Lucy glanced at the dance floor—it was only a country
dance, this time, and her mother had taught Lucy the steps
as a girl. "Of course," she said, and placed her hand
lightly on his arm.

They danced two sets, and then Lucy instructed her
partner to lead her back to a gilt chair at the edge of the
room. They made polite conversation, while Lucy stole a
glance toward the prince's entourage—yes, Nicholas was
still effectively trapped.

When the young man made his farewells, Lucy remained sitting. A stout older lady sat down next to her;

she was dressed in an elaborate deep green ball gown and heavily bedecked with diamonds. But she also shone with perspiration, and she panted from the exertion of the dance.

"A bit warm, isn't it?" Lucy said, and the other woman nodded.

"A dreadful crush." She plied a painted fan.

Lucy opened her reticule, which had hung over her wrist by its cords while she danced, and drew out her own fan, and they chatted for a few minutes.

Then a new figure emerged from the crowd, and Lucy tried to keep her expression from reflecting her dismay. It was Marion Tennett, in a low-cut yellow-green gown, with opals gleaming around her neck and in her ears.

"How nice to see you again, Lucy dear," the other woman said. "And you, Mrs. Barton."

The other woman replied in kind, then stood. "Ah, I see someone I need to speak to. Do excuse me."

Lucy, before she could think of a similar pretext for escape, found Marion sitting down beside her as if they were truly old friends.

"Are you enjoying the ball?" Marion asked as she watched the couples twirling through another dance set. "Nicholas is a marvelous dancer, is he not?"

"Indeed," Lucy agreed. Did this peevish woman miss nothing? "It's certainly a glorious occasion."

"You've come up in Society quite rapidly, my dear." Marion fanned herself. "Nicholas's friendship does have its advantages."

Lucy bit her lip. She would not rise to this—what had Nicholas called her?—termagant's bait.

"Your gown is delightful, more of the couturier's skill?"

"I thought it turned out well," Lucy said, cautious as always with this unpredictable woman.

"I'm glad your fortunes have improved so markedly. Perhaps you have come into some unexpected inheritance?"

Lucy raised her brows. "What makes you think that my fortunes were in need of improvement?"

"Stanley was always so low on funds—"

Lucy stared at the woman. "I thought you barely knew my husband. Surely he would not have shared such a private detail?"

"He played cards with my husband, now and then." Marion shrugged. "I heard about his losses."

Lucy's mind spun with new ideas. "Really," she murmured. "They played together . . . at the duchess's salon, perhaps?"

"Here and there. He was a boring little man, really. I am happy to see that you have managed to forget his horrible accident on Bird's Nest Lane," Marion snapped. "Not that Nicholas's company could fail to make any woman forget such a loss."

Lucy lifted her chin, determined not to flinch before these waspish comments. Then suddenly, Lucy forgot the woman's petty insults, and her mind raced. Bird's Nest Lane? Eve had mentioned a "bird's nest," the place where she and Stanley had been happy together. Lucy had thought it just a figure of speech, but—oh, dear God.

Marion Tennet eyed Lucy narrowly. "What?" she demanded.

Lucy cursed her mercurial face; she could never hide her thoughts. But at least this woman could not read her the way that Nicholas could. Nicholas, she must tell him—

She turned to go and was startled when Marion grabbed her wrist. Lucy winced; it was still sore from her encounter with Brooks. "Excuse me! I must find Nicholas—I must—he will be looking for me."

"I think not," the other woman said, her thin lips tightening.

How spiteful and jealous could she be? Lucy braced herself to break free of the other woman's grasp. She was shorter than Lucy, and could not be that strong.

But Marion reached into her green satin reticule, and, as calmly as if it were a fan or a handkerchief, pulled out a small but lethal-looking dagger.

Seventeen

Lucy stiffened with shock.

Marion flicked the lace of her long sleeve over the weapon to hide it, allowing only the tip to show as she pushed Lucy toward a curtained alcove.

Lucy stumbled backward and in a moment found herself shoved through the curtains and pressed against a brocade-papered wall.

"Tell me," Marion said. "You have thought of something, I can see it from your face. Where is the ruby?"

"It was you?" Lucy stared at Marion's pretty, vapid features. "You helped Stanley and Thomas Brooks steal the ruby?"

"How do you think he even knew about it? Your precious Stanley had no entry to the best Society," Marion hissed. "It was my husband whom the prince told about the gem, bragging about how it would adorn his coronation robes! And it was I who saw the chance to seize a fortune, once and for all, before our erratic prince lost his fondness for William and tossed my husband aside as he has done to so many of his friends."

"But he trusted you!" Lucy retorted. "The prince trusted your husband. How could you repay him so?"

"All we have gotten from his friendship are too many gaming debts," Marion snapped back. "Living up to Prinny's notion of the good life takes capital, and William is too poor a card player to keep us out of debt. So when William came across your husband in a low-class gaming club, he saw his chance to recruit someone to help us pull off the theft, someone who had lost enough to fall into the clutches of the moneylender William recommended. And he was so insignificant, your husband, no one would miss him if the theft went awry, or if we were forced to cut his throat to keep him silent forever."

Lucy felt as if she had been plunged into an icy lake. How could anyone be so callous? She stared into Marion's eyes, her cool gaze so lacking in compassion or regret. "But he decided to turn the tables on you," Lucy said slowly. "Perhaps he had some hint of your plans for him after the robbery. So after the gem was in his hands, he struck out on his own, instead of bringing the ruby to you."

Marion's eyes flashed, and she shoved the knife against the tender skin just beneath Lucy's chin. Lucy tried not to wince.

"Tell me what you have thought of," the woman insisted again. "Or it will be the worse for you!"

"You're going to murder me in the middle of the prince's ball?" Lucy shot back.

"No one can see us!"

"Someone will have seen us enter this recess," Lucy spoke slowly, trying to bring some reason back to the frantic eyes that stared so intently into her own. "This is no isolated, dark street. You will not get away with murder, this time!"

She had said too much. Lucy saw the awareness dawn in Marion's glazed eyes. "Bird's Nest Lane! It was what I said—there is something on that street, is there not? Some hideout of Stanley's?"

Lucy cursed beneath her breath, then she felt the prick

of the tiny knife as it broke the skin. She would stand here and be slaughtered by this woman who seemed on the edge of madness.

Dropping her shawl, Lucy struck at the hand that held the knife and winced as she felt the blade break the skin again. But she had knocked Marion off balance, and she pushed again, hard.

The woman wavered, and Lucy shrieked. "In here, someone help me!"

Cursing like a streetwalker, Marion suddenly wheeled and disappeared through the heavy curtains.

Lucy dabbed at her stinging throat and felt the dampness of blood. Taking a deep breath to steady herself, she followed.

The press of the ball closed around her as she took a few steps away from the alcove. Almost at once she was jostled by chattering guests, and then bumped by dancers swinging too far from their circle. She fought to keep her balance.

Marion was already out of sight. Where was Nicholas!

As she suspected, he was near the prince, at the center of the thickest group of people. It would take an eternity to push her way to him. She had to get his attention, and quickly. There was too much noise with the music, the people laughing and shrieking at each other, for any shout of hers to be detected.

Lucy looked around her and made out a table full of refreshments. Among the cakes and ices and custards, she saw a bowl of fruit. . . . Nicholas and the apples . . . She reached for a plump red apple and selected her target, praying her aim would be as good as the young Nicholas's.

She threw the apple.

For a horrified instant as Prinny raised his arm, gesturing to emphasize some statement, Lucy thought that her missile might hit her future monarch instead. But the fruit sailed on and struck Nicholas squarely in the chest. She could not hear the thump, but she saw his startled expression as the fruit landed at his feet and rolled away into the crowd.

He looked around. Finally, she could catch his eye and signal frantically to him.

She saw him murmur an excuse to the prince, then he shoved his way through the mob of people. As he closed the gap between them, she saw him frown.

"There's blood on your throat," he said into her ear as he grabbed her arm. "What has happened?"

"Marion has a knife—" she began.

"Marion?" He touched her skin, frowning so fiercely that she felt a small throb of joy deep inside her. No matter what he said, or could not bring himself to say, he did care.

"We must get you some water and some plaster to stop the bleeding," he told her, his tone worried. He started to turn, and she grabbed his arm.

"There's no time, she has realized—Nicholas, I know where the ruby is!"

"What?" He paused to stare at her.

"Well, not exactly, but it's somewhere on Bird's Nest Lane. Stanley and Eve apparently had rooms there—I should have realized he would never have frequented a place like the bawdy house on the heath. Stanley was too fastidious, for one thing! Eve must have removed to the heath after his death, when she ran out of money."

"Do you know the exact address?"

She shook her head, then felt more drops fall from her abused throat. Nicholas pulled out his handkerchief, and she pressed it to the small cut, wincing. "No, but we must go at once. Marion realized the import of the street name, and she and her husband are on their way now, I have no doubt. They are the jewel thieves, Nicholas! They lured Stanley into helping them, with his gaming debts and—"

He was already looking about him. "Then I must go—I will call for my carriage. First, I must see that you are cared for—"

"Oh, no, you don't!" Lucy took a deep breath. "I'm

going with you. I have a few scores to settle with Marion, and you may need help."

"Lucy!"

"We have no time to waste on argument, come," she told him. Turning, the bloodstained cloth still pressed to her neck, Lucy ignored the startled looks from other guests around her and pushed her way toward the door.

Downstairs, Nicholas sent a footman running for his carriage, but Lucy did not wait; she headed into the warm night.

"Nicholas, what is the commotion?"

He came out with her and peered into the darkness past the circle of light thrown by the flambeaux. "Someone seems to have tried to turn a carriage and bungled it; it's hit another chaise and blocked the rest of the line of vehicles."

"Marion!" Lucy said grimly. "She has done this, somehow. Nicholas, we cannot wait for your carriage to get here. We'll go on foot if we have to."

She tucked the handkerchief into her waist—the bleeding seemed to have slowed—and he took her hand. They rushed together down the pavement, edging around the jammed carriage and the various coachmen and postilions who argued fiercely over whose fault this had been—and together they ran into the darkness.

It was fortunate that Nicholas knew London so well, Lucy thought. She herself would have been lost within minutes, but Nicholas led them through the streets, crossing alleys when a shortcut was advised.

She ran beside him, panting from the unaccustomed exertion. Then in the third alley Nicholas pulled her to the side, warning, "Look out!"

A shadow detached itself from the blackness of the alley and approached them.

" 'And over your blunt, govs," the coarse voice said. A short man with broad shoulders confronted them; he seemed to have a knife. More blades!

"Not tonight, I think," was Nicholas's calm reply. He stepped closer to the thug, evaded the swinging dagger and punched him neatly in the stomach. Dropping his knife, the would-be thief doubled over, groaning. Nicholas kicked it aside, grabbed her hand, and he and Lucy ran on.

When the pain in her side threatened to steal any breath she had left, and Lucy knew she could not run any further, she found that they had at last gotten past the congestion. The streets were now relatively uncrowded. Nicholas flagged down a hackney, and, slipping the driver a guinea, gave quick directions before they scrambled inside. Lucy sank into the musty interior of the hired vehicle and allowed her labored breathing to slow.

"We must find the ruby first," she told Nicholas, between her gulps. "If Marion and her husband locate it, they will be out of the country, and we shall never find them! They must have an escape route already prepared."

Nicholas's face was hard to read in the dimness inside the cab—but she saw him nod.

When they reached the small narrow lane, they jumped out of the hired vehicle and conferred quickly. "There's an alehouse," Lucy said. "If we asked there?"

Nicholas considered. "This is a rough part of town. We have to be careful how much we reveal." He stopped, his expression contorted for an instant.

"What?"

"I was here the night after the theft. Marion brought me here—I thought it was a strange trysting place! I only wanted to escape my own anxious thoughts until I heard from my agent that the gem was safely in England. What a fool I was!" He swore under his breath.

"They must have had a meeting place set up somewhere nearby, except Stanley tried to slip away and keep the jewel for himself," Lucy added, preferring not to dwell on the image of Nicholas and Marion together.

"But even though he apparently hid the jewel before they caught up with him, he didn't get away," Nicholas finished, his tone as grim as hers. "And, rattled by the attempted blackmail, they killed him before they determined he did not have the gem on him. Here, we'll try the inn over there, first."

Nicholas banged on the door until a man in a nightshirt and dirty cap admitted them, then he made hurried inquiries of the landlord.

But the man claimed to have no knowledge of any apartments kept by a Stanley Contrain. Had Stanley used a different name here? While Nicholas urged him to think, and the man, grumpy from being roused from his bed at such an hour, shook his head, Lucy saw a timid-looking maidservant peering around the corner of the stairwell.

Lucy eased down the hall to whisper to her. "Do you know a woman named Eve, with dark hair and a well-rounded figure, who lived on this lane a year or so ago?"

The servant looked ill at ease. " 'O wants to know?"

"No one who will harm her. I just need to know where she and her—her husband had rooms," Lucy said.

"But she's gone—she moved out months ago," the maid argued, twisting the ends of the shawl she'd flung over her nightgown. "And the bloke was killed, I 'eard, run over by a carriage and smashed all to pieces."

Lucy winced. "Yes, but tell me where they had their rooms."

The servant whispered to her, and then, just as Nicholas frowned down at the protesting landlord, Lucy ran back to him and whispered in his ear. He stopped and nodded, then slipped a coin into her hand so that Lucy could hurry back and reward the startled servant girl, while Nicholas told the inn's grumpy host farewell.

The man slammed the door behind them, but Lucy hardly noticed. They ran half a block east, then Lucy pointed. "There, the house with the crooked gable," she said. . . .

They woke up another landlord, skinny and gray about the temples this time, who seemed even more irascible than the first, and although he hesitated when Nicholas asked the question, it was easy to see, when his eyelids flickered and his mouth dropped open, that he recognized the name of the late Stanley Contrain.

"What's it's worth to you, gov?" the man demanded.

Nicholas took hold of his shoulders, and the man winced. "It's worth keeping your hide in one piece if you tell me the truth!"

The man tried to pull away, but Nicholas held him easily.

"All right, then, just wanted to make a small profit, that's all. Anyhow, the room's empty, now. I've had two tenants in and out since the woman left, owing me ten bob."

Lucy shut her eyes. Were they too late after all?

"We'll see the room anyhow," Nicholas commanded.

Holding a smelly tallow candle, the man led them up a flight of narrow stairs and down the hall to the third door.

He unlocked the door and pushed it open, lifting the candle as she and Nicholas peered inside. The tiny flat held only a bed, a few chairs and a table, a shabby wardrobe.

Nicolas reached for the candlestick as the landlord protested, then silenced the man with a handful of coins. They searched the room and its contents quickly, but found nothing.

There must be more than this! Lucy tried to think.

"What have you taken away?" she demanded, turning to face the landlord. "Since the woman—Eve—left the rooms?"

He blinked, his gaze shifting. "Owed me rent money, they did, when I turned out the woman. I 'ad the right to take a few bits and pieces."

Nicholas put down the candle and took the man by his dirty nightshirt, shaking him as if he weighed nothing at all. "Tell us!"

"A small gold chain the 'ore used to wear, a copper ewer, nothing much," the man said.

Nothing that sounded as if it could hide a large gem, Lucy thought. "What else?"

"T'at were all," he said, but his gaze shifted again.

Nicholas shook him. "What else?"

The man winced. "I got a few pieces of stuff put away in the attic, but like I said, I got a right—they owed me rent, they did."

Nicholas glanced at Lucy, and she knew the anticipation on his face was reflected on her own.

"Show us!"

Smothering curses, the landlord led them up a rickety flight of steps to the top floor of the building. Lucy took the candlestick from him and held it as high as she could. In one corner, dim in the taper's flickering light, Lucy made out a varied collection of small furniture and other effects. There was a tin washbasin, empty, and on a chair with a broken back, a pile of clothes. She held her breath.

Nicholas moved quickly, patted the pockets and ran his hands over the seams, then shook his head.

She heard the landlord's quick steps as he clattered back down the steps. Would he cause them trouble? She wished they had had time to bring more help with them. They should have told the prince—but he would have likely had hysterics, and by the time they had calmed his volatile nature, the ruby could have been long gone.

But where was it?

Nicholas was moving through the attic, checking boxes and baskets, ruffling through a pile of dirty blankets.

Lucy looked around, trying to think. Where would Stanley have hidden the ruby? It could not have been a careless choice—that was not like him.

And then she drew a deep breath. Hearing the sound, Nicholas turned.

"There!" Lucy pointed. In the deepest shadows, she had made out the small cradle, and the tall pediments that crowned its four corners, wooden ovals lovingly carved by a father's hand.

And inside them—was it possible?

As usual, Nicholas followed her thought. He jumped to pull the cradle out from behind the clutter that had half hidden it.

"Try the tops of the posts," she suggested.

He knocked lightly on one, then another. The third wooden oval rang with a different sound.

Lucy held her breath. Nicholas twisted, and the piece of wood moved, slowly, then fell into his hands.

The inside was hollow, and in its center winked a ruby the size of a hen's egg.

Lucy gasped. Good lord, it was beautiful, this lethal gem that had led to so many deaths.

Nicholas gently pried it out, and then held it inside his palm. It glimmered, even in the dim light from the candle.

Stanley had held this in his hand, after the courier's death—which she still hoped he had had no part in planning or committing—then he had somehow evaded his fellow thieves, at least for a time, and perhaps had dreamed of wealth and an easy future.

Sighing, Lucy wondered if it was only Eve and the baby whom Stanley had wished the money for, or if he had planned to continue his double life, with his wife in Cheapside and his mistress in Bird's Nest Lane. She would never know.

But they had the ruby—

"Hand it over," a new voice said. Lucy jumped so violently that she almost dropped the candle.

William Tennett stood at the top of the stairs, a long slim pistol in one hand, with Marion just behind him. Her smile was twisted with victory, and her eyes taunted them.

Lucy stood frozen, and Nicholas, too, did not move.

"Hand it over," William repeated. "And don't expect that cowardly landlord to come to your aid. His head has been bashed, and he will not wake this sennight."

"You have only one bullet," Lucy remarked, some part of her remaining strangely calm as she exhibited her new knowledge of guns. "There are two of us."

"I have a knife," Marion warned.

"Yes, you've tried that already," Lucy agreed. "And I am still here."

"Nicholas will never allow you to be shot!" Marion snapped. "He is too weak, underneath, to see a woman hurt. He never raised his hand to me, while we were . . .

close, and I gave him provocation enough. Step aside, and give us the ruby!"

"You said yourself that Nicholas cares little for me," Lucy countered, willing Nicholas to hold his peace. "What do I matter, next to his returning the ruby safely to the prince? Besides, if you shoot me, Nicholas will overpower you—you must know that."

William Tennett, who stood at least six inches shorter than Nicholas, and had a much wider girth as well as more years, hesitated.

But Marion was more stubborn, or more hard-hearted.

"Shoot Richmond," she directed her husband. "He is stronger and more dangerous. I will dispatch the woman."

Nicholas took a step forward, but Lucy was closer to the murderous pair. As William Tennett lifted the pistol to take aim, Lucy moved her hand and snuffed the candle.

The small flame died, and the attic was plunged into deepest darkness.

An instant of surprise, a muffled curse, then she heard the explosion, deafening in the small space, as the gun fired. Had the bullet gone wide? Or was Nicholas lying on the dusty floor, mortally wounded as his lifeblood seeped away?

She could not tell. There was no way to relight the candle, even if she'd dared.

"Nicholas, are you hurt?" Lucy called, hearing the desperation in her own voice.

There was no answer. She dropped to her knees, trying to feel for him. Then she heard grunts, and bangs, and sounds of a struggle.

The two men were fighting, she guessed, but just where? She followed the noise, then had to draw back as two male bodies twisted and writhed, pounding against the bare boards, grunting and cursing in voices too hoarse to be distinguished.

And where was Marion, with her small but deadly dagger?

Lucy left Nicholas, trusting him to best his opponent, and crept across the black space, trying to make out the other woman. She might be the greater danger here. Marion, with her sharp wits and sharper blade, would realize that her best chance to reclaim the ruby would be by stabbing Nicholas. Then she and her husband, together, could certainly overpower Lucy.

Even as Lucy thought it, she detected a movement, perhaps by the whisper of moving air, though she could not see through the blackness.

A man cried out in pain.

Oh, God, was it Nicholas? Had the curse of the ruby struck again? Lucy rushed forward. Banging painfully into a hard object, she fell to her knees, but continued to crawl toward the sound, sneezing at the dust that rose to tickle her nose.

And rammed into another body, a body wearing lace and long skirts—Marion!

Lucy reached out, grasping at moving fabric, at a leg that kicked at her, grabbing a hand that reached for her face. She pushed the clutching fingers aside.

Where was the knife?

Lucy tried to cling to the hand she had seized, though its fingers curved, the long nails raking at her face and tangling in her hair. But though Lucy winced, she was more concerned with the location of the blade.

Again, she felt the whisper of air, and she flung herself to the side. She heard silk ripping, but she felt no pain, though her whole body seemed to cringe in anticipation of the thrusting knife.

Marion was muttering to herself, and she was moving, ready to strike again. If she continued to flail about with the dagger in her hand, she must eventually hit Lucy in some vital area.

Lucy grabbed hold of the woman, who was somehow on her feet while Lucy still knelt against the bare boards, hampered by her long skirts and her awkward position. She took hold and pushed, as hard as she could, hoping to knock Marion off her feet.

She heard a startled cry that rose into a high-pitched shriek, and then the sound of thumps and thuds.

The narrow stairwell! In the darkness, Lucy had long ago lost track of where it might be, but now, as she patted the bare floor, it seemed that Marion had found it. And still there was no light.

"Lucy!" a familiar voice shouted. "Lucy, are you hurt?"

"I'm all right," she called back. "And you?"

Moving toward his voice, she bumped into several chair legs and sent some unknown china object crashing to the floor. Wincing as a sharp shard nicked her hand, she crawled on, and at last encountered him halfway across the attic. She met his reaching fingers and was pulled into his arms.

They clung together. She patted his chest, which seemed undamaged, and his face, which was damp, whether with sweat or blood she could not tell, though she smelt the sharp tang which warned of blood spilled.

"Are you shot?" she whispered, clinging hard to him.

"I dropped to the floor when the candle went out, and the bullet missed me, thanks to you. Are you hurt, my love?"

The endearment brought a lump to her throat. "No, except for a few scratches. Where is William?"

"Behind us. I had to sit on him, after I pummeled him, and I tied him up with his own cravat. Marion?"

"I think she fell, or slid, down the steps," Lucy answered, still keeping her tone low. "We must hurry. She may have gone for help. With all the thugs in this part of London—"

"Then we shouldn't dally," he agreed. But he held her close for another moment, running his hands lightly over her body as if he, too, needed reassurance that she was whole. "I thought it was you," he said into her ear, and she felt his pain and the sharpness of his fear for her.

Oh, Nicholas, she thought. Would he ever again be able to bear the risk of loving?

But now he moved, cautiously, toward the open stairs. By patting the floor as they went, coughing from the clouds of dust they stirred up, they found the stairwell and made their way gingerly down through the blackness, step by narrow step.

And at the bottom, in a heap of satin skirts and twisted limbs, they found Marion Tennett, who would plot no more intricate crimes. . . . She seemed to have broken her neck when she fell.

∽

*Finding the woman's body made Lucy feel strangely hol-*low. Marion had been a murderess, hardly deserving of mercy, and yet—Lucy shivered.

When Nicholas had flagged down another hackney, and they were on their way back to Carlton House, Lucy tried to explain. "But I pushed her, Nicholas. I killed her."

"Not deliberately," he told her, holding her tightly, one arm about her shoulders. "If she had lived, she would most likely have been hung, as her husband surely will be. This way was quicker and less painful."

"Maybe." Lucy trembled again. He held her even closer, and she lay her cheek against his chest, trying not to think at all . . . until she suddenly sat up straight.

"Nicholas, the ruby! Where is it?"

He grinned at her—she could just make out the movement of his lips in the dimness as they approached the better lit streets. "In my pocket, my dear. I slipped it there before William tackled me. I really didn't want to have to search that confounded attic again, and in the dark, to locate it a second time."

She laughed a little wildly as the cab drew up.

"I think we're as close to Carlton House as we can get, just now," Nicholas said. He got out and helped her down. Tossing the driver a coin, Nicholas offered her his arm and they hurried up the street.

At the entrance the young soldier did not want to admit them.

And glancing at Nicholas, now that they were back in the light, Lucy could hardly blame him. Nicholas was grimy from rolling about the attic floor, his cravat was half untied, and his coat ripped in two places.

And she herself—she glanced down at the once pristine skirts of her ball gown. The netting that overlay the satin had been ripped off, and the satin underskirt was gray with patches of dust. Her hair was in her face, the gold comb sagging over one ear, and a wisp of cobweb hung down across her cheek; she brushed it away. The wound on her throat still stung. How much more disreputable could they appear?

But Nicholas drew himself up to his full six feet and more and stared at the guard, his gaze as arrogant as if he were his usual immaculate self. "I am Viscount Richmond, and I have urgent business with the prince regent. His royal highness will want to see us, so I suggest that you allow us to pass!"

And, of course, when Nicholas spoke in that manner, the man gave way. Nicholas clasped her hand as he strode inside, and she almost ran to keep up with him.

They hurried back into the ball, and Nicholas pushed his way through the guests, pulling her along, straight to the center of the room where the prince still held court.

Buzzing with whispers, the crowd stared wide-eyed at the strange image they made and fell back to give them room.

When the prince caught sight of them, his jaw dropped. "Richmond, here, what's this?"

Nicholas bowed, and Lucy managed a curtsy. "It is the missing jewel, your highness, the Royal Ruby of Mandalay."

Gasps, and a woman shrieked in excitement. Prinny's eyes widened, and he gaped at them. "Are you—are you sure?"

Nicholas drew the incredible gem out from an inner pocket of his jacket and cradled it in his palm, holding it out very carefully.

All the light in the room, the sparkling candelabra, the glittering chandeliers, seemed reflected in the enormous ruby; its crimson depths flashed like a dying star.

The whole room fell silent with awe. The prince drew a deep breath.

"Oh, good show," he muttered. "Richmond, you are a splendid fellow, I knew you would do it."

He accepted the ruby and held it up so that the whole crowd could see it. A sigh ran through the room, and Lucy saw that all the eyes, of men and women, highborn and servants alike, were focused only on the ruby.

And considering her present disordered condition, it was just as well!

"Call my guard," the prince commanded. With the ruby found and the scandal now a thing of the past, he could even sound regal again, she noted, hiding her amusement. "Call the guards! I want a dozen men, no a whole regiment, damn it! See this gem is taken and locked up safely with the other crown jewels. I shall hold it myself until they arrive."

"Yes, highness," one of his entourage said, and hurried away.

Gradually the guests around them began to chatter once more, a buzz of excited speculation and commentary that grew to a small roar.

"You'll have a earldom for this, Richmond!" the prince said jovially. "Or, anyhow, something splendid. And, um, is this—good God. My dear lady, there is blood on your neck, did you know?"

He sounded genuinely concerned.

Lucy glanced down at the once spotless bodice of her ball gown. "I'm afraid so, your highness."

"You must be seen to at once, Miss—I fear I've forgotten your name, my dear." The prince regent looked to Nicholas for help.

Nicholas smiled slightly. "Allow me to introduce you to Lucy Contrain, my future viscountess, your highness. If she will have me."

For a moment, Lucy thought she had not heard correctly. "Nicholas?"

But the prince was shaking his hand and pounding his back, and she could not get Nicholas's undivided attention. At last a whole army, or so it seemed to Lucy, of red-coated soldiers appeared to take charge of the ruby, and Nicholas persuaded the prince to allow them to withdraw.

"I shall send the five thousand pounds around first thing tomorrow," the prince called after them as they departed. "No, ten thousand, at least!"

Lucy gaped at him, but Nicholas did not pause, guiding her back through the crowd until this time they were mercifully able to slip away and be handed uneventfully into Nicholas's carriage.

As the driver inched the chaise along until he could pick up speed, Lucy sat very close to Nicholas. But though she had had more questions to ask, for the moment, she could think of nothing at all to say.

"Are you all right, my love?" Nicholas asked, glancing down at her.

"I feel as if I am dreaming." she said. "Are you sure?"

He understood. "Quite sure."

"But I thought you were afraid—"

"Oh, I am, I shall worry about you every day," he said, sighing. "I shall worry about your health when you cough, and about your security when you so much as take a drive through the park without me. But when I heard Marion fall, when I thought that it was you who had plunged down those steps, I knew that if we made it out of that wretched house alive, I could not waste another moment, another day, without you by my side."

She smiled slowly, relishing the emotion that deepened his voice as much as the touch of his hand as he stroked her cheek.

"Nicholas, you haven't even told me you love me," she pointed out.

He looked taken aback. "I haven't?"

"But you've shown me," she went on, remembering all the thoughtfulness he had demonstrated, in small actions and large, almost from the first day they had met. "Oh my dear, you've shown me. However, you have not asked me to marry you. You're just issuing commands, as usual."

"Oh," he said blankly. His smile faded. "Lucy, dearest love, you won't say no? Tell me you will not refuse me? I could not bear it!"

"No," she said dutifully, but when his eyes widened and his consternation grew, she laughed and added, "Yes, I mean, no, I will not say no. I say yes! You know that I love you, Nicholas, you arrogant, wonderful man!"

And she had meant to explain further, but his lips were meeting hers, and it was much too lovely a kiss to interrupt. . . .

Only later, as they approached their home, did she murmur, "He isn't really going to make you an earl, is he?"

She heard him chuckle, deep in his throat, but he only kissed her harder.

Turn the page for a preview of
Nicole Byrd's new novel,

Beauty in Black

Coming soon from
Berkley Sensation!

1817

The marquess of Gillingham traveled by night.

Everyone agreed that, in his dull black carriage with the faded crest on the door, bumping along a country lane by moonlight, the man whose face made babies cry appeared more comfortable with darkness. Some speculated he might feel uneasy with the stares his marred countenance evoked; others thought him indifferent to such vanity and suggested darker motives. Lurid rumors abounded as to why he preferred such a cloak of obscurity, tittle-tattle of devil worship and toasts made with virgins' blood, all of which had spurred the vicar of the local church to preach endless sermons about the dangers of superstition and idle talk, but such liturgical warnings did little to stem the gossip. If anything, they appeared in a backward way to support it.

Since the marquess never ventured far from his own estate in Kent, the whispers did not seem to bother him, though errant children on the edges of his county were sometimes threatened with his name.

"Crack another egg by swinging your basket like that,

Jimmy, and I'll feed you to the Black Beast of Gillin'am, I will."

And the child in question would gulp and cross himself, or finger a scruffy charm hidden beneath his smock, and pay more mind to his chores.

The marquess himself, his scarred face habitually shrouded by darkness, stayed close to home, ensconced in a large, dim mansion, ill-cared for by the few servants who could be induced to stay with him.

Until that spring, when the chatter around the neighborhood took on a new note, incredulous and eager, whispered with lowered voices and wide eyes.

"The marquess is going to London!"

"The Beast is taking a bride!"

~⚬~

"I hear he is quite hideous," Louisa Crookshank said, her tone complacent. She bit into a plump peach. The juice dripped down her fair skin, and she rubbed it away, shaking back golden curls as she did so.

Any other female would have looked quite unkempt, Marianne Hughes thought as she watched, but Louisa, even with her hair straying into her face and juice stains on her chin, managed to look as beautiful as always. Among Bath society, it had earned her the nickname of "The Comely Miss Crookshank," and it was likely her biggest misfortune.

"So why in the name of heaven are you contemplating his suit?" Louisa's aunt by marriage, Cara Hughes Crookshank, asked, her tone as usual slightly harassed. "Evan, put down that rock, and do not throw it at your sister!"

The small boy tossed the missile anyhow, but his aim was off. The pebble hit the smooth dove-gray skirts of their houseguest, but there was little strength behind the pitch, and it bounced harmlessly away. Marianne smiled and moved her feet away from the path of an even smaller boy, who was pushing a wooden carriage pulled by two wooden horses. As much as Marianne loved her sister-in-law and her children, Cara's brood were a trifle unpredictable. Because the day was so fair, they were sitting outside by the rose garden, having tea on the lawn and letting the children run up and down the gravel walkways.

"Because Lucas Englewood jilted her, of course," Caroline Hughes; who was eleven, observed as she reached for another scone.

"He did not jilt me!" Louisa snapped. "And I shall box your ear if you utter such a falsehood!"

"Only because he never proposed, but you thought he was going to." Caroline plunged ahead, despite frantic signals from her mother to desist. But although she grinned at her older cousin, the child took the precaution of retreating behind her aunt's chair.

"Act your age, Louisa," Marianne murmured as Louisa jumped to her feet, seeming ready to put her threat into words. "You are approaching one and twenty, not twelve."

Louisa sat down again, but her perfect features twisted into a frown.

"I care nothing about Sir Lucas. He's barely more than a child—"

"He's two years older than you," Caroline muttered, but this time, mercifully, her cousin did not hear.

"I should like to meet someone more mature. Anyhow, why should I settle for a mere baronet when I could have someone whose title is inferior only to a duke's? Perhaps I have a fancy to be a marchioness. And I'm told he's ridiculously wealthy."

"You don't need money. And you still have to look at him," the younger child argued.

"Caroline, that is unkind," her mother scolded. "You know what the vicar says about beauty lying inside a person, not out."

But the vicar did not have to contemplate an ugly face over his morning tea, Marianne couldn't help thinking; she had met the vicar's plump wife, who was quite adorable with her round red cheeks and sweet smile. Then she scolded herself for being as shallow as Caroline—besides, because of her tender years, the child had an excuse; Marianne did not—even as Cara finished her lecture to the children.

"Since you have all finished your tea, I think it is time the children went back to the nursery. I shall check on them and the baby before I change for dinner."

Caroline pouted, but she turned toward the house. Her oldest brother was made of sterner stuff.

"But I wanted to play another round of bowls with Auntie Marianne," Evan wailed, waving his handful of pebbles.

"Later, we will have another game," Marianne promised as their mother wavered.

Fortunately, the governess, Miss Sweeney, who had all the firmness their doting mother sometimes lacked, said, "Come along, now. And drop those stones, Master Evan."

She herded the children back toward the nursery suite. Their progress was reasonably peaceful—Evan only once reaching over to pinch his older sister, who shoved him away—until Louisa muttered while the young ones were still in earshot, "Thank heavens, infants make such a noise."

"I am not an infant!" Evan roared.

His younger brother, Thomas, took up the cry, bawling, too. "Not a 'fant!"

Cara winced. "Louisa, please don't aggravate the children."

Still bellowing, the children disappeared into the house, Miss Sweeney's erect form just behind them. There was a moment of silence. A bird sang at the edge of the lawn, and a bee buzzed as it hovered above a nearby rosebush. The impassive footman offered them a selection of cakes from a silver tray.

Louisa looked innocent as she accepted a raisin cake. After "artless," it was her second most practiced expression, Marianne thought, trying not to laugh.

"But seriously, Louisa, why would you consider his suit?" her aunt continued. "You haven't even met the man. Looks aside, because he can hardly be judged on such a consideration, I have heard rumors that he is most unpleasant."

"If you haven't met him, how do you know he is interested in your hand?" Marianne asked, taking a sip of her cooling tea.

Louisa looked blank. "He will be, when I do meet him. When I go to London!" The last was uttered in a rapturous tone, and she turned eagerly to their visitor. "It would be such an amusement for you, Aunt Marianne. I know your official mourning is long past, even if you do still wear such drab colors, and think how diverting it would be to chaperone me to all of the parties and amusements of the Season!"

Marianne glanced at her sister-in-law, who had the grace to blush. "An ambush, is it?" Marianne said dryly. "*Diverting* would hardly begin to describe the role of chaperoning 'the Comely Miss Crookshank.'"

"Please, please, Aunt Marianne. I will be so useful, never a bother to you. And I have been longing to go to London and do a proper Season. You know how many times I've had to put it off! First, because Papa was sure that my little cold would turn into lung fever if I left home, then the next spring Aunt Cara was increasing, and then the next year there was poor Papa's illness. Now that my own mourning is months past, as much as I miss dear Papa—" to her justice, the girl's voice wavered a moment before she finished—"I know he would wish me to go and enjoy myself."

The problem was, she was quite right. If her indulgent father had not pampered her so much, Marianne thought, Louisa might not be quite such a self-centered and naive young beauty. The girl's mother had died years earlier, and her father had felt even more compelled to deny his golden girl nothing. And this was the result.

Marianne wished she was as young as Thomas and

could enjoy a proper tantrum. She glanced again at her sister-in-law, who put down her embroidery.

"Louisa, why don't you go and apologize to your cousins for calling them names while I have a chat with Marianne," Cara suggested.

Louisa's brilliant smile flashed. "So you can plead my case? Oh, I will. I will be so good, you will see. Please, please say yes, dearest aunt. You will never be sorry!" She gave Marianne an impulsive hug that almost upset the teacup on the small table at her elbow, then floated off toward the house.

When the two women were left alone, Cara waved away the servant and turned at last to face her guest.

"You might have warned me." Marianne lifted her brows.

"I know, I did mean to," Cara said. "Please forgive me for thrusting you into this. I have tried to persuade her that coming out here is just as appropriate, but nothing will do Louisa until she is able to taste the delights of London. And you remember that when she turns one and twenty, she will inherit that enormous fortune, so I must entrust her to someone who will keep a sharp eye on her, so that she is not enthralled by the first fortune-hunter she meets. And she has no aunts on her father's side, only a couple of bachelor cousins. . . . And she is, indeed, somewhat vulnerable at the moment because no matter what she says, I think she expected young Lucas to offer for her, and when he pulled away—and then, too, you are really the only person she actually listens to!"

The reasons tumbled out as if they had been often rehearsed. Marianne closed her eyes for a moment. The spring had seemed so peaceful, until now. In this quiet setting she had hoped to escape the vague frustration that had dogged her for months. Yet, the prospect of having to ride herd on a high-spirited and somewhat self-centered young lady enjoying London for the first time made her mood darken.

"Cara, why can't you—" Marianne began, then paused

and asked bluntly, "I know you don't care for London, but—are you unwell?"

Cara bit her lip. "I hated to beg off for such a reason but the fact is, I am increasing again, Marianne. I don't think Louisa has discerned my condition, although with her, you never know—one moment acting so childish and the next, putting on airs like a matron."

"Ah," Marianne said. The baby in the nursery was barely a year old. No wonder Cara was looking a little wan. "My felicitations!" She leaned across to give her sister-in-law a quick hug "How are you feeling?"

"Wretched," the other woman admitted. "I can barely keep anything down. And the thought of trying to negotiate a London Season in this condition—you know I much prefer the quieter pace of Bath."

Marianne sighed. It looked as if she were well and truly shared. How could she say no when she saw that Cara, her late husband's sister as well as her oldest friend, was so pale and had barely touched her food as they had eaten. And in any case, who could blame her sister-in-law for wanting to delegate such a task? Louisa would be a charge to a more resolute woman than the gentle Cara, of whom Marianne was deeply fond. She still felt connected to her husband's family, by affection if no longer by the marital vows. In addition, she and Cara had been intimates since they were girls, growing up in neighboring estates in the West Country.

"Then I'd best be prepared. Tell me about this notorious marquess," she said, giving in to the inevitable. "And why Louisa is so eager to captivate a perfect stranger."

Looking more at ease, Cara leaned back into her chair. "It's all gossip, really, but you know how it is in Bath."

Marianne grinned and sipped her tea. No answer was necessary. Gossip was as common in the watering place as the ill-tasting mineral waters which visitors sipped at the Pump Room.

"The local squire's wife, in the village next to the marquess' estate, wrote to our Mrs. Howard that the marquess was on his way to London to look for an eligible bride. Apparently, after inheriting the title on his father's death, he feels it is time to set up his nursery. A perfectly normal decision."

"And there are no eligible ladies in his neighborhood?" Marianne asked.

"I'm not sure any would have him," her usually mild-spoken sister-in-law said.

Startled, Marianne looked up. "He's that ill-favored?"

"He contracted the smallpox when he was a young man, as I understand it, and was left gravely scarred."

Marianne blinked in surprise. Most people of means, in the progressive years of the early nineteenth century, were inoculated to avoid the killing, maiming, much-feared illness which had once struck down so many. Most saw that their servants and farm laborers were also protected. Her parents had made sure that it was done when Marianne was only little Evan's age. But she had heard that the pricking of the arm did not work for everyone. And the phrase, *when he was young*, was also ominous; the man was old, as well as maimed?

"Oh, dear," she muttered.

"And ill-natured, I hear, which concerns me more," Cara added. "I cannot allow Louisa to throw herself away on some rude boorish person, no matter if he has titles to spare."

Marianne nodded. Even if the girl was a bit vain, none of them wished her to be unhappy in an ill-conceived union, certainly not Marianne, who had had the rare choice of marrying her childhood sweetheart. It looked as if she would be forced, despite her better judgment, into the role of duenna.

She shook her head.

The other woman gave her a questioning look.

"Ironic," Marianne explained. "After Harry died, I always thanked heaven that I was left with enough funds not to be forced to hire myself out as a governess."

Cara laughed. "Oh, come now. It will not be as bad as

all that! You only have to go to parties with her, and keep
an eye on the men she meets."

"And theaters and parks and breakfasts and teas and
balls and who knows what, and the men will gather
around her like bees to a fragrant flower. I shall be beating
them off with a cane," Marianne predicted. "Beauty and
wealth, both? Louisa will be a bigger success than even
she has imagined."

If such a thing were possible.

But at least, it might induce the girl to forget her goal
of conquering the unknown marquess, and it should certainly ease the pain of her rejection by her first suitor.
Marianne sighed. "I must tell my maid to start packing.
I'm sure Louisa will not wait a week before she expects
to get under way. And you should lie down for a time
before you have to change for dinner."

Cara, who had been trying to hide a yawn, did not
argue. They both strolled toward the house, and inside,
Marianne found her new charge lying in wait.

"Well?" Louisa demanded, jumping up from the chair
where she had been sitting, apparently trying to look vir-
tuous by stabbing the linen in her embroidery hoop with
large, untidy stitches. "I have begged pardon of all my
cousins, even Evan. Have you decided? Will you take me
with you back to London, darling aunt?"

Marianne barely had time to nod before the girl grabbed
her in a delighted hug. "Oh, you are the dearest aunt in
the world. You won't regret it! And you shall enjoy the
diversions, too, you know. Aunt Cara always says you
should get out more. Even old people need some merriment."

Cara protested weakly, "Louisa!"

Marianne, who was two years past her thirtieth birthday, blinked. What on earth had she committed herself
to?

She sat with Louisa for a time, listening to the girl
natter on about all the delights of London that she could
not wait to taste, everything from a visit to Vauxhall Gardens to her formal court presentation as she made her bow

before royalty. Finally, Marianne reminded Louisa of the approaching dinner hour, and they both went up to change.

In her guest room, Marianne tried to convince herself that it would indeed be diverting to have a younger companion for several months. " 'Old' people needed such young things around them," she told herself dryly, glancing into the looking glass as she changed into a dinner dress.

"The black with the silver trim?" her maid had inquired when Marianne came into the room.

Marianne shook her head. "Tonight, the lavender, I think. There is a concert after dinner at Sydney Gardens, and I know Louisa is set on going."

Her maid harrumped at the idea of her mistress's actions being directed by the younger woman's wishes, but she took out the other dress.

Louisa's comments had stung more than Marianne cared to admit. So she still owned several gowns of somber shades; gray and even black were perfectly becoming colors, and she was not so wealthy that she could replace her entire wardrobe every Season.

Did she look old? Her dark hair, which curved smoothly past her cheek, was not yet streaked by gray, and her gray-blue eyes had only a few laugh lines about their edges. Her complexion was clear.

If she had had a husband, still, and a family, perhaps she would not have given the passing years a second thought. After her husband's death, when she had been only a few years older than Louisa was now, Marianne had had the awful image of her life as a rosebud destined never to fully open, a bud not allowed to bloom. Sometimes in the middle of the night when she lay alone in her bed, the picture still recurred, to be pushed away along with the self-pity that followed it like a doleful ghost. All these dreams she had had . . . not just the happy marriage, the children never to be born, but the other ambitions she had dreamed of . . . yet she knew ladies of quality did not have such thoughts.

After all, she was luckier than many widows. She had a modest but adequate income, a small house in London, and the quiet pleasures of her books and her female friends, as well as frequent visits to see Cara and her family, and Marianne's brother and his brood, who with Marianne's widowed mother lived further west in Devon.

Old.

Sighing, Marianne told her lady's maid about their new charge.

"She'll lead you on a merry dance, that one will," Hackett warned, her tone dire. But then, her abigail, who had been with Marianne's family even before Marianne herself had let down her skirts, was always a pessimist. "She hasn't the wits God gave a gnat, I sometimes think."

"Please don't make unpleasant comments about Miss Louisa, Hackett," Marianne responded, her tone firm. All she needed was to see a feud set off between the girl and Marianne's small household staff.

Her abigail sniffed, her long face twisted into a frown, and brushed her mistress's dark hair back into a smooth French knot at the base of her neck.

When Marianne went down to dinner, she found her brother-in-law already apprised of the plan.

"And we shall start for town at once," Louisa volunteered, her voice eager.

"That depends on your uncle," Marianne warned. "It is his carriage we shall have to beg the use of, you know, unless you plan to take the common coach." Marianne did not have the funds to keep her own carriage, so her visits were always planned to accommodate someone else's comings and goings from London to the west. Fortunately, Charles Crookshank was a noted Bath barrister who occasionally had business in the larger city, so it was usually easily enough done.

Louisa made a face and looked appealingly toward her uncle, who had become her guardian after her father's death. The amiable Charles laughed.

"I think we can manage that, on Friday or Saturday, if not tomorrow."

Louisa pouted at having to wait three whole days, but then she returned to her plans for her coming out, which seemed to become more ambitious with every hour.

"I shall need a whole new wardrobe, of course," she assured Caroline, who looked sympathetic.

"I hope I can have a coming out in London when I am of age," the child declared, throwing a glance toward her aunt.

Marianne bit back a rueful laugh, but the comment reminded her of more practical matters. A coming out would require a considerable expenditure. Apparently, her brother-in-law had already considered the problem. After dinner, when Charles rejoined them in the drawing room, and the children, emitting their usual clamor, were brought down from the nursery to say good night, he drew Marianne aside.

"I shall have funds made available to you to cover the cost of Louisa's Season, of course," he told her. "She has a comfortable allowance, and you must make use of any sums you need, for your own wardrobe as well as hers, and for the cost of extra entertaining."

Marianne gazed at him with affection. "I do not wish to make a profit from this temporary guardianship," she protested.

He waved her qualms away. "Of course not; I trust you implicitly, you know that. But I do understand that such an upswing in social activity must increase your sartorial needs as well as Louisa's."

"Such wisdom, from a mere man," she teased him gently.

"I have not been married for so many years for nothing," he assured her, and Marianne laughed.

Then the two boys barreled into their papa, begging for a ride on his knee before the governess took them up to bed, and Charles allowed himself to be led away.

It seemed that her in-laws would give her no excuse to change her mind about this plan, Marianne thought, just a wee bit cynically. Apparently, she might as well put her mind at ease and enjoy the new charge.

It also appeared her chaperonage would begin at once, as Louisa was determined to attend the concert, and Cara, yawning again, just as obviously wanted only her bed. So it was Marianne and Louisa who donned light cloaks and set off, in the Hughes' carriage, for the musical evening. Charles had volunteered to accompany them, but since Marianne knew perfectly well that he had a tin ear and did not care for opera tunes, she waved away his polite offer.

So he saw them off with obvious relief, and Louisa chatted about her wardrobe plans all the way through the short drive into Bath, until Marianne thought that if she heard any more discussion of pleated sleeves and lace trim, she might scream. And she enjoyed fashion as much as anyone, anyone except perhaps a young lady on the brink of her long-delayed coming out.

By the time they had crossed the bridge and the horses were straining to climb another of Bath's famous seven hills, Marianne was more than ready to be handed down in front of Sydney Gardens, the location of the night's concert.

Louisa, who had been explaining exactly how much Bath's popularity, and thus its fashionableness, had declined over the years, seemed eager to step down, too, despite the "sad lack of the presence of people of real importance," which she had just explained to her aunt made Bath inferior to London.

They walked past the white columns and into the garden, where they found seats. Louisa sat for only a moment until she saw a friend, a younger lady with which she was eager to share the exciting news about her imminent visit to London.

"Oh, Aunt Marianne, do you mind if I go over and chat with Amelia until the concert begins?"

"Not at all," Marianne concurred.

So Louisa moved away, and Marianne fanned herself

and looked about her. The musicians were tuning their instruments, the famed soprano had not yet appeared, and the seats gradually filled with men and women. Many of them—she had to admit, in deference to Louisa's references to invalids and the elderly—were indeed somewhat inclined to graying heads and paunchy silhouettes. Of course, Louisa would consign Marianne into the same category, she told herself, trying to laugh about it. Perhaps chaperonage was all she had left to enjoy, since her own girlhood was well behind her.

This thought was so melancholy that she gave herself a mental shake and turned to see who sat on her other side. She found two older women, one short and stout and gray, the other a tall, still erect lady with lovely silver hair and a lorgnette.

Marianne smiled. "Good evening," she said to the shorter woman. "I believe my sister-in-law, Mrs. Charles Crookshank, introduced us at the Pump Room the other morning?"

"Yes, indeed, I remember." The other woman beamed at her. "I noticed the two of you when you sat down, and I thought I recognized your companion, the comely Miss Crookshank."

Marianne managed not to laugh. Louisa would have been gratified to hear herself praised, but she was on the other side of the assembly at the moment, giggling and bending her head toward a shorter girl with reddish hair.

"I am Mrs. Knox, as you no doubt remember. This lady is Miss Sophie Hill, who has lately removed from London to Bath."

The silver-haired matron gave a slight inclination of her head. "How do you do?"

Marianne returned the greeting. "I reside in London, myself," she admitted. "But I enjoy Bath's quieter pace."

"Do you plan to stay long, then?"

"I had meant to," Marianne explained. "But I have been given the task of playing chaperone to my niece by marriage, so I find that I will be going back to London sooner than I had planned. She is eager to be presented in London."

Miss Hill gave a ladylike snort. "I have sustained that fate, myself," she said. "With a pretty girl, and one of means, you will find your time never your own, and too many simpletons aspiring for her hand. Of course, my niece was well worth the inconvenience, but I am happy enough to have her safely married at last."

Marianne nodded. "I am sure that Louisa will not want for suitors," she agreed.

"Many of them a bunch of vain poppycocks." The older lady frowned. "One hopes she will not be disappointed in what she finds."

Obviously a lady of strong opinions. Marianne couldn't completely suppress her smile even as she gave a discreet signal with her fan in Louisa's direction. The concert was about to start; it was time to take a seat.

With some reluctance, Louisa whispered one last comment into her friend's ear, then made her way back to the seat beside Marianne.

"I have told Amelia all about my wonderful adventure," the girl said, her clear voice easily heard even above the first notes from the orchestra. "And about the marquess of Gillingham, and his plans to take a bride, a design that I intend to aid."

"Hush," Marianne told her, and the girl subsided at last into her chair, with an expression of respectful attention on her lovely face as she gazed toward the musicians, although Marianne had no doubt that her charge's expression simply concealed more daydreams of titled suitors and splendid new wardrobes.

"The marquess of Gillingham, you say?" The silver-haired lady on her other side inquired, for some reason frowning at the mention of the name.

"Yes," Marianne said in surprise. "Do you know the gentleman? I understood he comes seldom to London."

A pause as a violin trilled, then the other woman pursed her lips. "For good reason. You have undertaken a greater responsibility than you know, Mrs. Hughes."

Marianne blinked. "I don't understand."

"Your charge had best take care," Miss Hill murmured, so low that Marianne was not sure she caught the words. "The marquess is not a man to be taken lightly."

Berkley Books proudly introduces

Berkley Sensation

a **brand-new** romance line
featuring today's **best-loved** authors—
and tomorrow's **hottest** up-and-comers!

Every month...
Four sensational writers

Every month...
Four sensational new romances from
historical to contemporary,
suspense to cozy.

Now that Berkley Sensation is around...

**This summer is going to
be a scorcher!**